In the background on the cover of this book is the image of Jaroslav Hašek's letter of resignation from the Czechoslovak Corps in Russia:

To the Branch of the Czechoslovak National Council

I hereby let it be known, that I do not agree with the policy of the Branch of the Czechoslovak National Council and with the departure of our Corps to France.

Therefore I declare, that I am leaving the Czechoslovak Corps until such time, that both within it and the whole leadership of the National Council, a new direction prevails.

I request, that this decision of mine be noted. I will even now continue to work for a revolution in Austria and the liberation of our nation.

*Jaroslav Hašek, in own hand*

The Fateful Adventures of
**THE GOOD SOLDIER**
ŠVEJK [sh-vake]
During the World War

Book(s) Three & Four

**presents**
still as a samizdat

**The Centennial Edition**
of The "Chicago Version" English rendition of

# Jaroslav Hašek's

# The Fateful Adventures of The Good Soldier

# During the World War

# Book(s) Three & Four

Visit our websites
zenny.com
SvejkCentral.com
for additional information and enjoyment of the
Good Soldier Švejk

Copyright© 2026
Zdeněk "Zenny" K. Sadloň
All rights reserved.
ISBN: 979-8-9943084-3-1

v. 1/10/2026

**Dedication**

To **Antonín Bukovjan**, *1890 - †1964
  Farmhand
  Infantry man, 25th Reserve Regiment, Austro-Hungarian Army
    Wounded
    Captured: September 17, 1915, Rovno, Volhynian Governorate, Russian Empire (currently Rivne, Ukraine), imprisoned in a POW camp
  Private, 8. Rifle Regiment, Czechoslovak Legions in Russia,
    Enlisted: September 1, 1917
    End of service: March 30, 1918

This translation is based on *Osudy dobrého vojáka Švejka za světové války*, edited by Jaroslava Myslivečková (**Praha: Odeon, 1968**).

The final paragraph of the unfinished and last Book Four, which does not appear in any published edition of the novel, is presented here as dictated by Jaroslav Hašek.

Recent research at the Památník národního písemnictví (*Museum of National Literature*) in Prague has brought to light the relevant manuscript page, clarifying the paragraph's authorship (see Česká televize, 2025 and Radiožurnál, 2025).

I gratefully acknowledge independent researcher Jomar Hønsi, who, with the permission of *the Museum* archivist, provided me with a photograph of the manuscript page on October 21, 2025. This photographic evidence confirmed that the closing lines—previously unknown to readers and translators—are authentically Hašek's. This edition restores the paragraph in English on the basis of this documentation.

# Table of Contents

Dedication................................................................................................v
Introduction to Book(s) Three & Four of the Centennial English Edition................................................................................................1

### Book Three
### THE ILLUSTRIOUS THRASHING[1]

1 ACROSS MAGYARIA.................................................................7
2 IN BUDAPEST.............................................................................61
3 FROM HATVAN TO THE BORDERS OF GALICIA..............110
4 FORWARD MARCH!................................................................157

### Book Four
### THE ILLUSTRIOUS THRASHING CONTINUED

1 ŠVEJK IN THE TRANSPORT OF RUSSIAN
  PRISONERS OF WAR................................................................206
2 SPIRITUAL CONSOLATION...................................................230
3 ŠVEJK AGAIN WITH HIS *MARCH COMPANY*......................239

Endnotes.......................................................................................278
Translator's Postscript..................................................................339
Note on Editorial Assistance........................................................341
Švejk on Trial...............................................................................348
Read Švejk First, Then Ask Me Again........................................357

# Introduction to Book(s) Three & Four of the Centennial English Edition

After 399 pages of the translated text of Books One and Two, with 41% of Jaroslav Hašek's novel remaining, the second half starts with a sentence that signals a pivot on several levels:

"At last all of them lived to see the moment, when they stuffed them into the railroad cars in the ratio of 42 men to 8 horses."

This sentence completes a trajectory first marked in Book Two, when the fat one-year volunteer, lying on the straw of the regimental brig, spoke the sardonic verse: "By human limbs we'll make fertile the field. Eight horses or forty-eight men."

That earlier mention on page 69 in this edition, 66% into the first half of the novel, planted the ratio as a part of an ironic prophecy. There it is spoken in mock-epic tones by a malingerer, whose life is a tangle of failed evasions, scams, and "medical" improvisations. By the time we reach the opening of Book Three, the prophecy has hardened into military fact. The number of men has slipped from 48 to 42, but the frame is the same: human lives stacked against horses in the ledgers of transport. Thus the second part of the prophecy becomes the instrument of fulfilling its first part, one limb at a time.

The ratio becomes a hinge between the novel's first and second halves. What is voiced first as verse in the brig re-emerges as bureaucratic reality on the transport. The grotesque couplet is split by the war machine: the ratio is absorbed into military machinery, while the image is realized as fact.

Hašek's structural irony lies in this doubling. The volunteer's sardonic rhyme, half defiant resignation, half lament, finds its echo not in poetic exaggeration, but in the ledger-precision of the train manifest. The novel's humor pivots into something heavier, as the prophecy is fulfilled.

Placing this ratio at one-third into Book Two and then again at the very opening of Book Three, when just less than half of the novel remains to reveal itself, organizes the novel's massive sprawl around a precise recurrence. The reader is carried from a prophetic verse to fulfillment, from the comic voice of a shirker to the faceless mechanism of transport.

That grotesque couplet was not imagined out of thin air. Its second line echoes the stenciled transport ratios on wartime railroad cars; its first belongs to the rhetoric of war poetry, already present earlier in the novel's imagery of accumulated, smoldering human flesh remains.

In Germany, military rail cars bore the marking "M.T. 48M. 6Pf.", i.e. Militärisch Tracht 48 Mann 6 Pferde (*Military Transport Gear, 48 men, 6 horses*). French "quarante-huit" cars carried the chalked "40–8", 40 men or 8 horses. A photo reproduced on the Czech website svejkmuseum.cz shows such a German rail car, and the site's curator, Jaroslav Šerák, notes that Austro-Hungarian rail cars were described in the same format, confirmed by a photo of the regulations sheet provided to him by Czech Railways, showing "0" and "00" as placeholders for standardized horse and personnel counts.

Hašek would have known these markings firsthand. Though he never performed the compulsory service (likely for health reasons), he was conscripted in 1915 and joined Infantry Regiment No. 91, the same regiment Švejk serves in. Many of the geographical details and military conditions in Švejk reflect those he encountered while serving with IR 91. That July he was transported to the Galician front, and the experience of regimental life and wartime logistics fed directly into the fabric of the novel. This journey, the steps of which he would later fictionalize in *The Good Soldier Švejk*, included the same military boxcars marked for horses and men. The numbers were no abstraction. Hašek had seen them printed on the wood.

So the transport ratio, voiced as verse — 'Eight horses or forty-eight men' — is not just mockery. It is reportage, refracted through satire. And when the novel reintroduces the same ratio at the opening of Book Three, the grotesque is completed. What was once a soldier's cynical jingle becomes the army's official metric.

Many observers report that Book One and Book Two of Hašek's novel are more polished and accessible. They are appealing to unliterary readers, because sharper, more vibrant, popular episodic humor anecdotes shine and are dominating them in the civilian and early military settings of the early parts.

The text, which you are about to immerse yourself in, is said to lack the polished wit of the earlier parts, and deepen existential, nihilistic critique. Books Three and Four are described as darker, exhibiting chaotic and despairing tone, while growing crude and monotonous in a decline from the first half of the novel. They are said to be repetitive and more fragmented, demanding greater reader engagement. Some say it's due to Hašek's incomplete vision, which he struggled to complete, while writing under declining health.

Yet, it is said that the two parts of the novel you are about to embark on, are profound and carry tragic weight that elevates the novel's significance. In them, according to one writer, "Švejk becomes the tragic bard of European nihilism." In a book I chose to analyze in college, a Marxist philosopher exclaimed: "Švejk is an expression of the absurdity of the alienated world…"

For Jaroslav Hašek, Švejk was a result of unusually rich, varied and uncommon life experiences. His book is about life and truth, especially as they are experienced by working class people, rather than members of the elites.

The vision that the author reportedly lacked or struggled with, is not what he needed to have or even to search for. His text is an attempt to share a literary rendition of a lived experience, driven by the torments of a sensitive soul seeking peace. The missing, or rather by some undetected vision is that lived experience of a prolific peacetime author of over 1,200 short stories, feuilletons, articles, numerous poems, and co-author of some cabaret plays, war veteran of three armies involved in the slaughter of millions, and a survivor of the cataclysm of a passing world.

As for readability and appeal of the novel, Jaroslav Hašek did not write to become a darling of the *New York Times Literary Supplement* readers, to get an offer for a block-buster movie version, having an agent ready to make the deal, a lawyer to make it fool-proof, and an accountant who would add it all up. (Not that he would not welcome success. After all, he was not likely to have sent back the dollars that must have accompanied the serial publication of Švejk in Chicago.) Švejk also is not a hermetically closed literary text written to satisfy the needs of scientific research. As Don DeGrazia put it: "Švejk is no dainty classic meant to fade quietly into obscurity on the dusty shelves of academia, but a bellowing barroom brawl of a book that will forever have everyday people doubled-up with the painful laughter of recognition."

Book Three

**THE ILLUSTRIOUS THRASHING**

# 1

## ACROSS MAGYARIA[2]

At last all of them lived to see the moment, when they stuffed them into the railroad cars in the ratio of 42 men to 8 horses. The horses however were having a more comfortable ride than the troops, because they could sleep standing up, but it didn't matter. The military train was hauling to Galicia again a new group of humans being driven to slaughter.

On the whole however all of those creatures became after all a little relieved; it was something finally concrete, when the train moved, but before that it had been only an embarrassing uncertainty, panic, whether the haul would begin today already, or tomorrow, or the day after tomorrow. Some felt like the ones sentenced to death, who are awaiting with fear, when will the executioner come for them. And then the calm starts setting in, that it will already be done with.

That's why one soldier was screaming from the railroad car as if he'd lost his mind: "We're going, we're going!"

Accounting Master Sergeant Vaněk was absolutely right, when he was telling Švejk, that there was no hurry.

Before there was reached the moment to be crawling into the railroad cars, several days had floated by, and all the while there was talk of food cans and the experienced Vaněk proclaimed, that it was only a fantasy. What food cans! Well, a field mass maybe yet, because even with the previous marchy that's the way it was. When there are food cans, then the field mass is dropped. Otherwise the field mass is a substitute for the food cans.

And so there showed up instead of goulash cans Chief Field Chaplain Ibl[3], who killed three flies with one blow. He managed to serve up a field mass at the same time for three march battalions, two of which he blessed off to Serbia and one off to Russia.

While at it he was giving a very enthusiastic speech and it was obvious, that he would get his material from military calendars[4]. It was such a moving speech that when they were speeding away to Moson[5], Švejk, who was together in the railroad car with Vaněk in an improvised office, remembered that speech and told the Accounting Master Sergeant: "It will be very fine, as the Field Chaplain was saying, when the day tips over toward the evening and the sun with its golden rays sets behind the mountains and on the battlefield one will hear, as he was saying, the last breath of the dying, the braying of the fallen horses and moaning of the wounded men and the wailing of the populace, when their cottages are burning above their heads. I like it very much, when people are thus acting stupid to the squared power."

Vaněk nodded in agreement: "It was a damn touching case."

"It was very nice and instructive," said Švejk, "I remember it very well, and when I return from the war, then I'll be telling it at The Chalice. He assumed, the mister Field Chaplain, when he was telling us about it, such a nice straddling stance, that I was afraid, lest one of his dumb legs would slip and he'd fall into the field altar and bust his coconut against the monstrance. He was giving us such a nice example from the history of our military, the time when there was still serving good old Radetzky and blending with the red evening sky was fire, as the barns were burning on the battlefield, as if he had seen it."

And the same day Chief Field Chaplain Ibl was already in Vienna and there again he was telling some other march battalion the touching story, which Švejk had been mentioning and which he liked so much, that he called it stupidity to the squared power.

"Dear soldiers," is how was exercising his rhetorical skills Chief Field Chaplain Ibl, "so think then that the year is 'forty-eight and in a victory ended the battle at Custozza[6], where after a ten-hour long strenuous fighting the Italian King Albert[7] had to yield the bloody battlefield to our father of enlisted men, Marshal Radetzky, who in the 84th year of his life won such a splendid victory.

"And behold, soldiers dear! On a height outside the conquered Custozza there stopped the venerable old military leader. Round about him his loyal military leaders. The solemnity of the moment had gripped the whole little circle, because, soldiers, at an insignificant distance from the Marshal one could observe a private, who wrestling with death was. With smashed limbs on the field of honor was the wounded Ensign Hrt[8] perceiving Marshal Radetzky gazing at him. The worthy wounded Ensign was still squeezing in his stiffening right hand a gold medal in spasmodic enthusiasm. Casting a look at the exalted Marshal livened up once again the pulsation of his heart and through the paralyzed body permeated the last remnant of strength and the one dying was trying with a superhuman effort to crawl forth towards his marshal. 'Allow yourself the peace of resting, my worthy soldier,' cried out toward him the Marshal, dismounted the horse and wanted to offer his hand. 'It won't go, Marshal, Sir,' said the dying private, 'I've had both my arms blown off, but one thing I beg of you.

Relay to me the full truth: Has the battle ended entirely in a conquest?' 'Completely, dear old boy,' proclaimed kindly the Field Marshal, 'it's a pity that your joy is clouded by your wound.' 'Of course, noble Sir, I'm finished,' said the soldier in a dark voice, pleasantly smiling. 'Are you thirsty?' asked Radetzky. 'The day was steaming hot Marshal, Sir, we had ninety-degree heat.' Then Radetzky, having grabbed the field flask of his adjutant, was handing it to the dying man. And that one took a drink, having downed a powerful gulp. 'May God repay you a thousand fold,' he cried out, straining to kiss the hand of his commander. 'How long have you been serving?' asked him the latter. 'Over forty years, Marshal, Sir! At Aspern[9] I earned a gold medal. Also at Leipzig I was, and a Cannon Cross[10] I have as well, five times I was fatally wounded, but now I've met the clear end of me. But what happiness and bliss, that I have lived to see this day. What do I care about death, when we attained a glorious victory and to the Emperor is restored his land!"

"At that moment, dear soldiers, out of the camp rose the reverent sounds of our anthem Preserve For Us, Lord, and carried mightily and nobly down the battlefield. The fallen private, parting with his life, one more time tried to pull himself together. 'Glory to Austria,' he cried out enthusiastically, 'glory to Austria! Let be continued the brilliant song! Glory to our military leader! Long live the army!'

"The dying one leaned one more time toward the Marshal's right hand, to which he affixed a kiss, he then wilted, and the quiet last breath was wrested out of his noble soul. The military leader was standing here with his head uncovered in front of the carcass of one of the worthiest soldiers. 'This beautiful end is, I trust indeed, worthy of envy,' proclaimed the Marshal, having been moved, lowering his face into his clasped hands.

"Dear soldiers, I too wish for you all to live to have such a beautiful end."

Remembering this speech of the Chief Field Chaplain Ibl, Švejk could really call him, without doing him an injustice in the least, an imbecile to the squared power.

After that, Švejk started talking about the known orders, which had been read before entering the train. One was an Army order signed by Franz Josef and the second was an order by Archduke Josef Ferdinand[11], the Supreme Commander of the Eastern Army and Corps, both of which had to do with the events in the Dukla pass on the 3rd day of April 1915, when two battalions of the 28th Regiment, including their officers, crossed over to the Russians to the sounds of the Regimental Band.

Both orders were read to them by a quivering voice and in Czech translation they read:

### Army order of the 17th day of April 1915:

Overfull of pain I am ordering, that I&R Infantry Regiment No. 28 be for cowardice and high treason expunged from my military. Let the Regimental Colors be taken away from the shamed Regiment and turned over to the Military Museum. As of this day ceases to exist the Regiment, which, having been morally poisoned at home, drew into the field to commit high treason.

Franz Josef I

### An order by Archduke Josef Ferdinand:

Czech troops disappointed and failed during the field campaign, especially in the latest field campaign. They failed especially in the defense of the positions at which they were finding themselves for a rather long time in trenches, which fact the enemy had used often to establish contacts and links with the perfidious elements of these troops.

Usually the attacks by the enemy, supported by these traitors, were then always directed against those detachments at the front, which had been taken over by such troops.

Often the enemy managed to surprise our military components and practically without resistance penetrate our positions and capture a significant, large number of defenders.

Thousand times shame, dishonor and contempt for these scoundrels without honor, who committed treason against the Emperor and the Realm and who are staining not only the honor of the glorious regiments of our glorious and courageous Army, but also the honor of that nationality, which they claim as their own.

Sooner or later there will catch up with them the bullet or the rope of the executioner.

The duty of each individual Czech soldier, who has any honor in his body, is to point out to his commanding officer such a scoundrel, instigator and traitor.

Whoever won't do so, is himself such a traitor and scoundrel.

Let this order be read to all the troops of the Czech regiments.

I&R Regiment No. 28 by an order of our ruler has already been struck from our Army list and all the captured deserters will repay with their blood their heavy guilt.

Archduke Josef Ferdinand

"They read that to us a little late," said Švejk to Vaněk, "I am very amazed, that they were reading it to us only now, since the lord Emperor issued the order already on April 17<sup>th</sup>. It could appear so, as if for some reasons they didn't have it read to us right away. If I were the lord Emperor, then I would not put up with such being pushed aside. If I issue an *order* on April 17<sup>th</sup>, then it also must be on the seventeenth read to the troops of all the regiments, even if awls were raining from the sky."

On the other side of the railroad car sitting opposite Vaněk was the cook-occultist from the officers' mess and was writing something. Behind him were sitting the servant of Senior Lieutenant Lukáš, the bearded giant Baloun, and the telephone operator assigned to the 11th march-gang, Chodounský. Baloun kept chewing on a piece of commissary ration bread and, sounding horrified, was telling the telephone operator Chodounský, that it's not his fault, when in the crowd of pressing people boarding the train he was not able to get in the Staff railroad car to join his Senior Lieutenant.

Chodounský was trying to scare him, that all the fun was over now, and that for that he would get a bullet.

"If only the trouble and anguish were come to an end for once," was lamenting Baloun, "I was once already close to being done for during the maneuvers at Votice[12]. There we were walking hungry and thirsty and when the *Battalion Adjutant* arrived where we were, I hollered: 'Give us water and bread.' He turned his horse to face me and said, that if it were during a war, I would have to step out of the rank and he'd have me shot, and that now he'd have me locked in the garrison prison, but I had great luck, because when he went to report it to the staff, then on the way his horse spooked, he fell and broke, glory be to God, his neck."

Baloun let out a heavy sigh and choked on a morsel of bread and coughed for a second, and when he recovered, he covetously glanced at the two sacks of Senior Lieutenant Lukáš's, which he had in his care.

"They were getting issued, the gentlemen officers," he said in a melancholy state of mind, "canned liver pâté and Hungarian salami. What about just a little piece."

He was looking all the while so desirously at the two sacks of his Lieutenant's like an abandoned-by-all little dog, who is as hungry as a wolf and is sitting, inhaling the vapors coming out of the cooking smoked meat, by the door of a smoked meat shop.

"It wouldn't do any harm," said Chodounský, "if they were somewhere waiting for us with a good lunch. You see, when we were at the beginning of the war riding to Serbia, then we overfed ourselves at every station, that's how well they were hosting us everywhere. From the goose thighs we were carving out little wedges of the best meat and played sheep-pen checkers with them on tablets of chocolate. At Osijek[13] in Croatia[14] two gentlemen from the veterans outfit brought into the railroad car for us a big cauldron of baked hare, and right there we couldn't hold back anymore and poured it all on their heads. Along all the tracks we were doing nothing else but puking out of the railroad cars. Corporal Matějka[15] in our railroad car overstuffed himself so much, that we had to put a plank across his belly and be jumping on it, like when cabbage is stomped, and only that made him feel a little relieved, and it was coming out of him top and bottom. When we were riding across Magyaria, they were throwing into the railroad cars for us at every station baked chickens. Off those we would eat nothing else but the little brains. In Kaposfalva[16] the Hungarians were pitching into the railroad cars whole large pieces of roasted pigs and one pal got hit with a whole roasted head of a porker in the skull so hard, that he was then chasing the benefactor with the *belt* in his hand across three tracks. On the other hand once we were in Bosnia we didn't even get water. But for Bosnia, although it was forbidden, we had as much assorted booze, as the gullet would please, and of wine creeks-full. I remember that in one station some pampered women and young ladies were honoring us with beer and into their can of beer we urinated, and did they beat it away from the railroad car!

We all were like in a sort of daze along the whole trip, I couldn't even see the ace of acorns while looking at it, and before we knew what hit us, all of a sudden there was an order, we didn't even finish the card game, and the whole lot was to be out of the railroad cars. Some corporal, I don't know anymore what his name was, he was screaming at his people to sing: '*And the Serbs must know that we Austrians are winners, winners.*' But somebody kicked him from behind and he rolled over and splayed across the tracks. Then he hollered for the rifles to be stacked in pyramids, and the train turned around and went back empty, except, wouldn't you know it, as it usually is in such a panic, it hauled away two days' worth of our *provisions*. And as far as from here to the trees over there, there already started cracking the shrapnel. There arrived coming from the other end the *Battalion Commander* and called on all to gather for a consultation, and then came our *Senior Lieutenant* Macek, a Czech through and through, but would speak only in German, and he says, pale as chalk, that nobody could ride further, that the track was blown up in the air at night, that the Serbs had made it across the river and were now on the left flank. But it was still far away. We would get reinforcements, he said, and then we'd cut them to pieces. Let nobody give up if something were to happen, the Serbs, it is said, cut off the prisoners' ears, noses and prick out their eyes. That not far from us shrapnels were cracking, but about that we shouldn't worry. They say it's our artillery zeroing in. All of a sudden came from somewhere behind the mountain the sound of ta-ta-ta-ta-ta-ta-ta-ta. That, he said, were ours zeroing in the *machine guns*. Then one could hear from the left the cannon fire, we heard it first and were lying on the belly, over us there flew several shells and set ablaze the railroad station and from the right side above us began whistling bullets and in the distance one could hear the salvos and rattling of the rifles. *Senior Lieutenant* Macek ordered us to take apart the pyramids and load the guns. The *Watch Commander* went to him and said, that it was not at all possible, because we didn't have any ammunition with us, that he after all knew well, that we were supposed to be issued ammunition only at the next stage before the frontline position. That the train with ammunition had gone ahead of us and that it apparently fell into the Serbs' hands. *Senior Lieutenant* Macek stood a while as if made of wood and then gave the order '*Fix bayonet*', although not knowing why, just like that out of desperation, so that something was being done. Then we were again standing on the alert a pretty while, then again we were crawling down to the railroad ties, because there emerged some airplane and the officers were screaming: '*Everybody take cover, take cover!*' Then it was discovered, that it was ours, and was also mistakenly by our artillery shot from below. So we got up again, and there was no 'at ease!' command. From one side there was rushing toward us some cavalryman. Still far away, he was screaming: '*Where is the Battalion Command?*' The Battalion Commander rode out to meet him, he handed him some letter and again was already riding away off to the right. The Battalion Commander was reading it along the way, and then all of a sudden as if he'd gone mad. He unsheathed his saber and flew toward us. '*Everybody back, everybody back!*' he was hollering at the officers. '*In the direction of the hollow, single file!*' And here it began. From all sides, as if they were waiting for it, they started firing at us. To the left side there was a corn field and it was all one demon from hell. We were crawling on all fours into the valley, the rucksacks left on those damned railroad ties. *Senior Lieutenan*t Macek got it in the head from the side and didn't as much as peep. By the time we ran away into the valley, there had been a lot killed and wounded. Those we left there and kept running until the evening and the countryside ahead of us was already as if swept clean of our men. All we saw was a ransacked *supply train*. Until at last we got to a station, where new orders were obtained after all to board the train, sit down and ride back to the Staff, which we could not carry out, because the whole Staff had fallen the day before into captivity, which we learned of only in the morning. Then we were like orphans, nobody wanted to hear or know anything about us and they attached us to the 73rd Regiment, in order for us to be retreating with it, which we with the greatest joy did, but first we had to march forward about a day, before we came to the 73rd Regiment. Then we…"

Nobody was listening to him anymore, because Švejk and Vaněk were playing pull-style mariáš, the cook-occultist from the officers' mess kept on writing a long letter to his wife, who in his absence started publishing a new theosophical magazine, Baloun was dozing on the bench, and so there was nothing left for the telephone operator Chodounský but to repeat: "Yes, I won't forget that…"

He got up and went to kibitz at the pull-style mariáš game.

"If at least you'd light up the pipe for me," said Švejk in a friendly manner to Chodounský, "since you're coming to kibitz. Pull-style mariáš is a more serious thing than the whole war and that damn adventure of yours at the Serbian border. — What a stupid thing I just did, I should be slapping my face. Why didn't I wait a while with that king, just now an overknave[17] came my way. What a dumb beast I am."

The cook-occultist in the meantime finished writing his letter and was reading it to himself apparently satisfied, how nicely he composed it on account of the military censorship.

Dear wife!

> When you receive these lines, I will have been situated for several days already on a train, because we are riding off to the front. It does not please me much, because on the train I have to be idle and cannot be useful, since there's no cooking going on in our officers' mess and the food is obtained at staging railroad stations. I would have liked to cook for our gentlemen officers during the ride through Hungary the Szeged goulash, but no dice. Perhaps when we arrive in Galicia, I will have an opportunity to cook Šoule[18], a genuine Galician one, goose meat stewed in barley or rice. Believe me, dear Helenka, that I am really trying to the utmost to make a little more pleasant for our gentlemen officers their cares and exertions. I was transferred from the regiment to the march battalion, which was my most fervent wish, so that I could, although with humble means, set the officers' field kitchen up at the front on the best tracks. Do you remember, dear Helenka, that when drafted I was mustering with the regiment you wished for me, that I get nice superiors. Your wish came true, and not only can I not complain in the least, on the contrary all the gentlemen officers are our genuine friends and especially toward me they behave like a father. As soon as possible I will inform you of our field post office number...

This letter was necessitated by circumstances, when the cook-occultist got for good on the wrong side of Colonel Schröder, who up to now kept his fingers crossed for him, but for whom during the parting dinner for the officers of the march battalion, again through an unfortunate coincidence, no portion of rolled veal kidney was left to be gotten, and Colonel Schröder sent him with the march-gang into the field, having entrusted the officers' kitchen in the care of some hapless teacher from the Institute of the Blind[19] in Klárov[20].

The cook-occultist glanced one more time over what he had written and what seemed to him to be very diplomatic, in order to manage to hang on at least a bit farther from the battlefield, because let anybody say what he wants, it is still a do-nothing job after all even at the front.

It's true though, he had written, when he was still a civilian and was an editor and owner of an occultist magazine devoted to the sciences of the beyond-the-grave, a great essay, that nobody should fear death, and an essay about migrating of souls.

He also stepped near Švejk and Vaněk to be a kibitzer. Between the two game players there were at the moment no differences of military rank. They weren't playing a two anymore, but a three-hand mariáš with Chodounský.

*Messenger* Švejk was coarsely berating Account Master Sergeant Vaněk: "I'm amazed, that you can play so idiotically. You can see, can't you, that he's playing betl[21]. I have no rounds and you won't turn over an eight, and like the biggest numskull beast you are pitching the acorn underknave and he, the bumbler, wins it."

"That's some hollering on account of one lost betl," came the sound of a polite answer by the Accounting Master Sergeant, "you yourself are playing like an idiot. I'm supposed to suck the eight of rounds out of my pinkie, when I don't have any rounds at all either, I had only high greens and acorns, you whorehouse fly."

"So you should have played, you smart-ass, a *nonstop*[22]," said with a smile Švejk. "It is just like once at Valeš's, downstairs in the restaurant, there also some slowpoke had a *nonstop*, but he wasn't playing it and always laid off the lowest cards into the talon[23] and let everybody to betl. But the cards he had! Of all the suits the highest. Just like now I'd gain nothing from it, if you were playing a nonstop, so neither would I have back then, but none of us would have gained anything, the way it went, we would have been paying all the time. I said at last: 'Mister Herold, be so kind, do *they* play a *nonstop* and don't *they* act idiotically.' But he ripped into me, that he can play what he wants, to keep our traps shut, that he's got a college degree. But that came to cost him dearly. The pubkeeper was an acquaintance, the waitress was far too familiar with us, so to the police patrol we explained it all, that everything was in order. First of all, that it was vulgar of him to be disturbing the peace of the night by calling the patrol, when somewhere in front of a pub he slipped on an icy sidewalk and rode it with his nose until it was all broken. That we did not even touch him, when he had cheated at mariáš, and that when he was exposed, he ran out so fast, that he took a spill. The pubkeeper and the waitress confirmed for us, that we behaved toward him really too much gentlemanly. He didn't deserve anything else anyway. He sat from seven in the evening till midnight by one beer and a soda and was acting like a God-knows-what kind of a big shot, because he was a university professor, and as for mariáš, he understood it like a billy-goat understands parsley. So who's to deal now?"

"Let's play kaufcvik[24],' suggested the cook-occultist, "sixpence and two."

"Then you better be telling us about the migrating of souls," said the Accounting Master Sergeant Vaněk, "like you were telling it to the miss in the mess hall, when you broke your nose."

"I have also heard about that migrating of souls already," sounded up Švejk. "I too set my mind years ago, that I would, as it is called, if you pardon me, be self-educating myself, so I don't stay lagging behind, and I used to go to the reading room of the Industrial Union[25] in Prague, but for I was in tatters and I had shining holes on my behind I could not be educating myself, for they did not let me in and escorted me out, for they thought, that I set out to be stealing winter coats. So I put on holiday clothes and went to the museum library once and I borrowed some book about this migrating of souls with my pal, and I ended up having read in there, that an Indian[26] emperor changed after death into a pig, and when they stuck the pig, that it changed into a monkey, and from the monkey he turned into a badger and from the badger a government minister. Afterwards, in the military, I became convinced, that there had to be some truth to it, because anybody anywhere, who had a little star or two, would name soldiers sea pigs, or any animal name at all, and based on that one could conclude, that thousand years ago these crude common soldiers were some famous military leaders. But since there's the war, then such migrating of souls is a tremendously silly thing. The demon knows how many transformations a man goes through, before he becomes, let's say, a telephone operator, a cook, or an infantryman, and all of a sudden a grenade tears him apart and his soul enters into some horse with the artillery, and into the whole battery, when it's rolling on the way to some elevation point, slams a new grenade and it kills that horse now, into which the deceased had incarnated, and right away that soul moves perhaps into some cow in a supply convoy, from which they'll make goulash for the troops, and from the cow perhaps it moves right away into the telephone operator, from the telephone operator..."

"I'm amazed," said the telephone operator Chodounský, evidently offended, "that of all people I'm to be the butt of numskull jokes."

"Isn't that Chodounský, who has the private detective agency[27] with the eye like the Trinity of God[28], your relative?", asked innocently Švejk. "I very much like private detectives. I also once served years ago in the military with a private detective, with some Stendler. He had such a cone head, that our *quartermaster* would always say that he had already seen many military cone-heads in twelve years, but that such a cone he had not ever even imagined in his mind. 'Listen, Stendler,' he'd always be telling him, 'if there were no maneuvers this year, then that cone head of yours would not be of any use even in the army service, but this way at least the artillery will be using your cone zeroing in, when we arrive in a terrain, where there is no better reference point for orientation.' The things he suffered from him. Sometimes, on march, he'd send him five hundred steps ahead and then ordered: '*Direction* cone head.' He had overall, this Mister Stendler, even as a private detective nothing but unusually bad luck sticking to him like sap. Quite a few times he would be in the mess telling us about it, what trouble he often had. He used to get such tasks, as for example to search out, whether a wife of some client, who came to the agency all beside himself, hadn't nuzzled up with another, and if she had already nuzzled up, then with whom had she nuzzled up, where and how she had nuzzled up. Or again the other way around. Some such jealous broad wanted to search out, with which one her husband was loafing, so that she could make an even greater hub-bub for him at home. He was an educated man, spoke only in a refined manner about breaching marital fidelity and it was always a wonder he didn't weep, when he was telling us, that they all wanted him to catch her or him in flagranti. Someone else would perhaps derive pleasure from finding such a pair in flagranti, and could gawk his eyes clean out, but this Mister Stendler, as he was telling us, was all beside himself from it. He was saying very intelligently, that he could not even stand watching those obscene licentious acts anymore. We had quite a few times saliva drooling from our beastly mouths, like when a dog he is pooping, when past him they're carrying a boiled ham, when he was telling us about all those various positions, as he came across the pairs. When we were given confinement to the barracks, he always drew it for us. 'This is the way,' he says, 'I saw such-and-such lady with such-and-such gentleman…' Even the addresses he told us. And he was kind of sad. 'The number of slaps,' he would always say, 'that I got from both parties; and I didn't regret that so much as the fact, that I was taking bribes. One such bribe I won't forget until I die. He's naked, she's naked. In a hotel, and they didn't lock themselves in, the idiots! They couldn't fit onto the divan, because they were both fat, so they were frolicking on the carpet, like kittens. And the carpet all worn out, dusty and lying around on it were cigarette butts. And when I walked in, they both jumped up, he stood facing me and held his hand like a fig leaf. And she turned her back toward me and one could see that she had the whole lattice pattern of the carpet embossed on her skin and on her spine she had a cigarette paper tube stuck to it. 'Forgive me,' I say, 'Mister Zemek, I am the private detective Stendler, from Chodounský's, and I have the official duty to find you in flagranti on the basis of a report by your wife. This lady, with whom you are engaged in a forbidden relation here, is Mrs. Grotová.' Never in my life have I seen such a calm citizen. 'Excuse me,' he said, as if it was naturally understood, 'I will dress myself. The only one at fault is my wife, who is by baseless jealousy seducing me into a forbidden relationship, and who, driven by a mere suspicion, is offending her husband by reproaches tossed in his face and by base mistrust. When there's no doubt left, however, that the shame can no longer be concealed... Where are my long johns?' he asked calmly at the same time. 'On the bed.' While he was pulling his long johns on, he was telling me further: 'If the shame cannot be kept secret, then the word is divorce. But the stain of the reproach won't be kept secret thereby. But thereby will the stain of disgrace not be concealed. Divorce is an altogether precarious matter,' he kept talking, while dressing himself, 'the best is when the wife arms herself with patience and does not provide a cause for a public scandal. Anyhow do as you want, I will leave you here with the gracious lady alone.' Mrs. Grotová in the meantime crawled in the bed, Mister Zemek offered me his hand and left.' I don't remember that well anymore, as Mister Stendler kept on telling us, what it all was, that he was saying, because he was engaging the lady in bed so intelligently, that, like, marriage is not established to lead each completely to happiness, and that the duty of each in marriage is to vanquish lust and one's carnal part to refine and imbue it with spirit. 'And at the same time,' was relaying Mister Stendler, 'I started slowly to undress myself, and when I was undressed and all stupefied and wild as a deer in rutting season, there walked into the bedroom but my good acquaintance Stach, also a private detective, from our competitor's agency of Mister Stern, where Grot turned to for help as it pertains to his wife, who, it is said, has some liaison, and said no more than: 'Aha, Mister Stendler is in flagranti with Mrs. Grotová, congratulations!' He closed the door again quietly and left.

'Now it makes no difference whatsoever,' said Mrs. Grotová, 'you don't have to be dressing so quickly, you have enough room for a position next to me.' 'For me, gracious lady, right now the position with my employer is at stake,' I said and already I didn't even know what I was saying, I remember only that I was saying something about, that when contentions reign between a husband and his wife, even the upbringing of the little children will suffer.' Then he was still telling us, how quickly he was dressing and how he split out of there and how he made up his mind, that he would immediately tell it to his boss Chodounský, but that he went to fortify himself for it, and that before he arrived, it was already like coming with a crucifix after the funeral is over. He said that in the meantime Stach had been there already on the order of his boss, Mister Stern, to punch Mister Chodounský, on account of the sort of employees he had working at his private detective agency, and he in turn knew of nothing better than to send quickly for the wife of Mister Stendler, for her to fix it with him herself, since he was sent somewhere on official duty and they, from the competing agency, found him in flagranti. 'From that time on,' used to say Mister Stendler, when the conversation came to this subject, 'my cobhead is even more coney.'"

"Then we're playing five — ten?" They played.

The train stopped at the Moson station. It was already evening and they were not letting anybody out of the railroad cars.

When they moved, there came the sound from one of the railroad cars of a loud voice, as if trying to drown out the rumble of the train. Some soldier from Kašperské Hory in a pious mood of the evening was singing praises by horrible hollering to the quiet night, which was approaching the Magyar flatlands:

*Good night! Good night!*
*To all tired ones be it brought.*
*Bows the day quietly to end,*
*Rest all diligent hands,*
*Until the morning is awakened.*
*Good night! Good night!*

"*Shut your trap, you shameless rube,*" interrupted somebody the sentimental singer, who fell silent.

They pulled him away from the window.

But the diligent hands were not resting until the morning. Just as everywhere on the train, under the light of candles, so even here, in the light of a small kerosene lamp, hung on the wall, they kept playing čapáry and Švejk, whenever someone bit the dust during the looting, was proclaiming, that it is the most fair game, because everybody can swap as many cards, as he wants.

"In kaufcvik," was claiming Švejk, "only an ace and a seven must be looted, but then you can give up. The other cards you don't have to loot. That you do then always at your own risk."

"Let's play zdravíčko," was suggesting to general acclamation Vaněk.

"Red seven," was Švejk reporting, cutting the deck. "Everybody's in for a nickel each and cards are dealt four at a time. Hurry up so we get some playing done."

And on the faces of all one could see such contentment, as though there was no war and they were not located on the train, which was hauling them into position for great bloody battles and massacres, but in some Prague coffeehouse, sitting at the game tables.

"I did not think," said Švejk after one game, "that when I went for nothing and was changing all four cards, that I'd get the catface (ace). Where did you think y'all were crawling trying to catch up to me with a king? I'll trump a king before he could say cracker-jack."

And while here they were trumping a king with the catface, far away at the front the kings were trumping one another with their subjects.

*

In the Staff car, where there sat NCOs of the march battalion, there was reigning a queer silence at the beginning of the ride. Most of the officers were buried in a small book in canvas binding with the title "*The Sins of the Fathers. A novel by Ludwig Ganghofer*[29]" and all were at the same time busy reading page 161. Captain Ságner, the Battalion Commander, was standing by the window, holding in his hand the same book, having it also opened on page 161.

He was looking at the landscape and was thinking, how to actually explain to them all in the most understandable way, what they were to be doing with the book. It was actually most strictly confidential.

Meanwhile, the officers were pondering whether Colonel Schröder had gone utterly mad for good. He was, that is to say, goofy long since, but still one could not expect, that it would grip him so suddenly. Before the departure of the train he had them called to the last *conference*, during which he informed them, that each had coming a book *The Sins of the Fathers* by Ludwig Ganghofer, which books he had ordered to be taken to the Battalion Office.

"Gentlemen," he said with a horribly mysterious countenance, "never forget page 161!" Immersed in this page, they could not make anything out of it. That some Martha[30] on that page stepped up to the desk and pulled out of there some script of a role and was thinking aloud, that the audience must feel empathy for the hero of the role. Then in addition there emerged on that page some Albert[31], who was incessantly trying to speak jokingly, which having been ripped out of the unknown plot, that preceded it, seemed to be such beastly crud, that the enraged Senior Lieutenant Lukáš bit in half the cigarette tip.

"He's gone mad, the old geezer," were thinking all of them, "it's the end of him already. Now they'll transfer him to the Ministry of Military Affairs."

Captain Ságner at the window got up once he had composed it all well in his head. He did not have too much pedagogical talent, that is why it took him so long before he put together in his head the whole plan of a lecture on the significance of the page one-hundred-and-sixty-one.

Before he started laying it out, he addressed them "*Gentlemen*", as used to do it the old geezer Colonel, although earlier, before they crawled in the train, he called them "*Comrades*".

"*Well, gentlemen...*" And he proceeded to lecture, that last night he got from the Colonel instructions pertaining to the page 161 in *The Sins of the Fathers* by Ludwig Ganghofer.

"*Well, gentlemen,*" he continued ceremonially, "altogether confidential information pertaining to a new system of ciphering of dispatches in the field." Cadet Biegler pulled out a notebook and a pencil and said in an unusually diligent tone: 'I am ready, *Captain, Sir*."

They all took a look at the moron, whose diligence in the one-year volunteer school bordered on idiocy. He voluntarily joined the army and at the first opportunity was telling the commander of the one-year volunteer school, when he was familiarizing himself with the home circumstances of the pupils, that his forefathers originally went by the Büglers of Leuthold and that in their crest they had a stork wing with a fish tail.

From that time on they named him after his crest and "the stork wing with a fish tail" was mercilessly persecuted and became at once unlikable, because it in no way went together with his father's honest commerce in hare and rabbit skins, although the romantic enthusiast was honestly trying hard to lap up the whole of military science, he made his mark by outstanding diligence and knowledge of not only all, that would be put in front of him to learn, but rather in addition he himself was boxing his head in ever the more so by studying writings about martial arts and the history of warfare, about which he would always strike up a conversation, until he was put in his place and destroyed. In the officers' circles he viewed himself as of equal worth in comparison with those of higher ranks.

"*You, Cadet,*" said *Captain* Ságner, "until I permit you to speak, keep quiet, because nobody has asked you anything. After all, you are a damn smart soldier. Now I am putting altogether confidential information in front of you, and you are writing it down in your notebook. In case of a loss of the notepad a field court martial awaits you."

Cadet Biegler had in addition to all also the bad habit of always trying to convince everybody with some excuse, that his intentions are good.

"I dutifully report, *Captain*, Sir," he answered, "that even in the eventual case of a loss of the notebook nobody will decipher what I have written, because I record it by stenography, and nobody will be able to read my abbreviations after me. I use the English system of stenography."

They all looked at him with disdain, *Captain* Ságner waved his hand and continued in his lecture.

"I've mentioned already the new manner of ciphering dispatches in the field, and if for you it was perhaps incomprehensible, why was commend to you from among the novels by Ludwig Ganghofer *The Sins of the Fathers* the very page 161, it is, gentlemen, the key to the new ciphering method, current on the basis of the new direction from the Staff of the Army Corps, to which we are assigned. As is known to you, there are many methods of ciphering important messages in the field. The newest one, which we use, is an additive numeric method. Thereby are also being discarded the ciphers delivered to you last week from the Staff of the Regiment and the advisory regarding their deciphering."

"*The Archduke Albrecht's*[32] *system,*" mumbled to himself the eager Cadet Biegler, "8922 = R, borrowed from the method of Gronfeld[33]."

"The new system is very simple," carried through the railroad car the *Captain's* voice. "I personally received from mister Colonel the second book and information.

Should we for example get the order: '*Top elevation 228, direct machine-gun fire to the left,*' we obtain, gentlemen, this dispatch: '*thing — with — us — it — we — look up — in — the — been promised — the — Martha — you — it — anxious — then — we — Martha — we — him — we — thanks — well — board of directors — end — we — been promised — we — improved — been promised — really — think — idea — whole — reigns — voice — last.*' So there, tremendously simple, free of all unnecessary combinations. From the Staff down the phone-line to the battalion, the battalion on the phone to the *companies.* Having obtained this encoded dispatch, the commander will decipher it in this manner. He will take *The Sins of the Fathers*, open it up on p. 161 and start looking from the top on the opposite page 160 for the word *thing*. There, gentlemen. The first instance of *thing* on page 160 is the 52nd word in the sentence order, thus on the opposite page 161 one looks up the fifty-second letter from the top. Take notice that it is 'T'. The next word in the dispatch is *with*. It is the 7th word in the sentence order on page 160, corresponding to the 7th phoneme on page 161, the letter 'o'. Then comes *us*, that is, watch me carefully please, the 88th word, corresponding to the 88th letter on the opposite page, which is 'p', and we have deciphered '*Top*'. And thus we continue, until we detect the order: 'Top elevation 228, direct machine-gun fire to the left.' Very ingenious, gentlemen, simple and impossible to decipher without the key: p. 161, Ludvík Ganghofer: *The Sins of the Fathers.*"

All were silently examining the hapless pages and were somehow precariously mulling it over. Silence was reigning for a while, until suddenly Cadet Biegler hollered anxiously: "*Captain, Sir, I dutifully report: Jesus and Mary! It doesn't add up!*"

And it was truly very enigmatic.

No matter how they exerted themselves, nobody aside from *Captain* Ságner found on the page 160 those words or on the opposite page 161, with which the key began, the letters corresponding to it.

"Gentlemen," stuttered *Captain* Ságner, when he verified for himself, that the desperate scream of Cadet Biegler corresponded to the truth, "what is it that happened? In my Ganghofer's *The Sins of the Fathers* it is there, and in yours it isn't?"

"Allow me, *Captain*, Sir," sounded up again Cadet Biegler. "I take the liberty to bring to attention, that the novel by Ludvík Ganghofer has two parts. Please, condescend to verify for yourself on the first title page: '*A novel in two volumes*'. We have **Volume I** and you have **Volume II**," continued the thorough Cadet Biegler, "it is therefore as clear as the light of the day, that our 160th or 161st page doesn't correspond to yours. We have there something altogether different. The first word of the dispatch deciphered by you should be '*Top*' and for us it came out as '*hay*'!"

It was now clear to all, that Biegler was perhaps not after all such an idiot.

"I have Volume II from the Brigade Staff," said *Captain* Ságner, "and apparently there has been a mistake. Mister Colonel had ordered Volume I for you. According to all that is known," he continued in such a way, as though it were exact and clear and he had known it long before he held his lecture about a very simple manner of ciphering, "they mixed it up at the Brigade Staff. They did not inform the Regiment, that it was Volume II, and that's how it happened."

Cadet Biegler was in the meantime looking victoriously at all of them and Lieutenant Dub whispered to Senior Lieutenant Lukáš, that the "stork wing with a fish tail" cut Ságner down as was proper.

"A queer case, gentlemen," sounded up again *Captain* Ságner, as if he wanted to strike up a conversation, as the silence was very embarrassing. "They at the Brigade Office are ignorant nitwits."

"I take the liberty to remark," sounded up again the tireless Cadet Biegler, who again wanted to show off his harebrained ideas, "that similar things of confidential, strictly confidential nature should not be going from the Division to the Brigade Office. A subject pertaining to a most confidential matter of the Army Corps could be announced only through a strictly confidential circular to the commanders of division components, even brigades, regiments. I know the ciphering systems, which were used in the wars for Sardinia[34] and Savoy[35], by the Anglo-French company at Sevastopol[36], during the boxers' rebellion in China[37] and during the last Russo-Japanese[38] war. These systems were being handed off..."

"We care an old goat's worth about that, Cadet Biegler," said with a countenance of contempt and displeasure *Captain* Ságner; "it is certain that the system, which was the subject of the talk and which I was explaining to you, is not only one of the best, but we can say unequaled. All counterintelligence departments of our enemy's Staffs can go sit on the pot. Even if they slice themselves to pieces, they won't manage to read our ciphers. It is something altogether new.

These ciphers have no predecessor."

Eager Cadet Biegler coughed meaningfully.

"I take the liberty," he said, "*Captain*, Sir, to bring attention to a book by Kerickhoff[39] on military ciphering. Everybody can order this book from the publishers of the Explicatory Military Dictionary. In there is thoroughly described, *Captain*, Sir, the method, about which you were telling us. The inventor of it is Colonel Kircher, serving during the reign of Napoleon I in the Saxon[40] military. Kircher's[41] ciphering by words, *Captain*, Sir: each word of the dispatch is explicated on the opposite page of the key. That method was perfected by Senior Lieutenant Fleissner[42] in the Handbook of Military Cryptography which everybody can buy at the publishing house of the Military Academy in Wiener Neustadt[43]. Here, *Captain*, Sir." Cadet Biegler reached into a small suitcase and pulled out the book, of which he was speaking, and continued: "Fleissner gives the same example, please condescend all of you and verify it for yourselves. The same example, as we heard:

Dispatch: *Top elevation 228, direct machine-gun fire to the left.*

Key: Ludwig Ganghofer: *The Sins of the Fathers. Second Volume.*

And look further, please: The cipher '*Sache mit uns das wir aufsehen in die versprachen die Martha...*' and so forth. Just like we heard a while ago."

Against that could be raised no objection. That snot-nosed "stork wing with a fish tail" was right.

At the Army Staff one of the lord generals made his work a little easier for himself. He discovered Fleissner's book on military ciphering, and it was done already.

All during that time one could see, that Senior Lieutenant Lukáš was overcoming some strange mental upset. He was biting his lip, wanted to say something, but in the end started talking about something different from what was his first intention.

"It shouldn't be taken so tragically," he said with peculiar hesitation, "during our stay in the camp at Bruck on the Leitha there had come and gone several systems of dispatch deciphering. Before we arrive at the front, there'll be again new systems, but I think, that in the field there's no time for solving such cryptograms. Before any of us solved a similar encoded example, the company, the battalion, and even the brigade would long since be goners. Practical value is has none!"

*Captain* Ságner very unwillingly nodded. "In practice," he

proclaimed, "at least as far as my experiences from the Serbian battlefield are concerned, nobody had time for solving ciphers. I'm not saying that ciphers would not have utility during a longer stay in the trenches, when we dig ourselves in and wait. That ciphers change, is also true."

*Captain* Ságner was retreating along the whole line: "A great part of the reason, why nowadays from the Staffs to the field positions ciphers are used less and less, is the fact, that our field telephones are not precise and don't reproduce, especially during artillery fire, clearly the individual syllables. You simply don't hear anything and it causes unnecessary chaos." He fell silent.

"Confusion is the worst thing you can have in the field, gentlemen," he added prophetically and fell silent.

"In a while," he said looking through the window, "we'll be in Győr[44]. *Gentlemen*! There the troops will be issued fifteen decagrams of Magyar salami each. Half an hour *rest break*."

He took a look at the *march route*: "At 4:12 we're leaving. At 3:58 all in the railroad cars. That is, boarding by the companies. The eleventh and so on. *By the platoon in the direction of the supply store No.6*. Oversight during issuing: Cadet Biegler."

Everybody looked at Cadet Biegler with the look of: you'll have some tough army service, you fuzzless chin.

But the eager Cadet Biegler had already pulled out of the small briefcase a sheet of paper and a ruler, he ruled the sheet, divided it according to *march* companies and was asking the commanders of the individual companies for the number of men, which none of them knew by heart and they could give Biegler the requested numerals only according to unclear notes in their notepads.

*Captain* Ságner in the meantime started out of desperation to read the hapless book The Sins of the Fathers, and when the train stopped at the railroad station in Győr, he shut the pages he'd read and remarked: "This Ludwig Ganghofer doesn't write badly."

Senior Lieutenant Lukáš was the first to have rushed from the Staff railroad car and he went toward the railroad car wherein was located Švejk.

*

Švejk and the others had long since already stopped playing cards and the servant of Senior Lieutenant Lukáš, Baloun, was already so hungry, that he started to rebel against the military overlords and tell everybody, that he knew very well, how the gentlemen officers stuffed their faces. It's worse, than when there was indentured servitude. That in earlier times in the military it had not been like that. That the officers even, as his grandpa says at his retirement homestead, during the 'sixty-six war were sharing their chicken and bread with the soldiers. His lamentation had no end, until at last Švejk judged it good to praise the military estate during the current war.

"You have some young grandpa," he said affably, when they arrived in Győr, "who is only able to remember the war in the 66th year. Well, I know this guy Ronovský and he had a grandpa, who was in Italy back during the indentured servitude times and there he served his twelve years and came home as a corporal. And he had no work, so his father took him, the grandpa, to work in his service. And back then at one time they went to do indentured labor hauling tree stumps and one such stump, as was telling us the grandpa, who was serving his daddy, was like a big brute, and so they couldn't even make it budge. And he, like, said: 'Let's leave it here, the miscreant, who's supposed to be exerting himself with it.' And the gamekeeper, who heard it, started screaming and raised his cane, that he must load the stump. And the grandpa of that Ronovský of ours said nothing else but: 'You beater, I'm an old veteran.' But in a week he received a summons and having been drafted again he had to go to Italy, and he was there again for ten years and wrote home, that as for the gamekeeper, when he returns, he'd whack him across the head with an ax. It was only luck, that the gamekeeper died."

In the door of the railroad car appeared right then Senior Lieutenant Lukáš.

"Švejk, come here," he said, "leave your numskull expositions be and better come and explain something to me."

"Right away, I dutifully report, *Senior Lieutenant*, Sir."

Senior Lieutenant Lukáš was leading Švejk away and the look, with which he was watching him, was very suspecting.

During the whole lecture by *Captain* Ságner, which ended in such a fiasco, Senior Lieutenant Lukáš attained a certain detective ability, for which accomplishment were not needed too many very special thought combinations, as the day before the departure Švejk was reporting to Senior Lieutenant Lukáš: "Senior Lieutenant, Sir, at the Battalion there are some books for the gentlemen *lieutenants*. I brought them from the Regimental Office."

That is why when they had crossed the second railroad track, Senior Lieutenant Lukáš directly asked, as they stepped behind an extinguished locomotive, which had been waiting a week already for some train with munitions: "Švejk, what was it that happened back then with those books?"

"I dutifully report, Senior Lieutenant, Sir, that it is a very long story, and you always deign to get upset, when I'm telling you everything in great detail. Like at that time, when you wanted to give me the head slap, as you tore up that official letter pertaining to the war loan and I was telling you, that I read once in some book that earlier, when there was a war, then people had to pay a tax on windows, for each window a twenty-cent coin, for geese also as much..."

"This way we'd never be done, Švejk," said the Senior Lieutenant Lukáš, continuing the interrogation, while he resolved, that what's the most strictly confidential must naturally remain totally hidden, so that the churl Švejk would not be putting it to some use again.

"Do you know Ganghofer?"

"What's he supposed to be?", asked Švejk with interest.

"He is a German writer, you numskull of a guy," answered Senior Lieutenant Lukáš.

"On my soul, *Senior Lieutenant*, Sir," said Švejk with the countenance of a martyr, "I don't know any German writer personally. I only knew one Czech writer personally, some Hájek, Ladislav by first name, from Domažlice. He was an editor of the Animal World and I sold him once such a mutt as a pure-blooded spitz. That one was a very merry gentleman and kind. He used to go to a pub and there he would always read his stories, such sad ones, until they were all roaring with laughter, and he would then be weeping and paying for everyone in the pub and we had to sing for him: The Domažlice town gate, nicely painted, the one who painted that gate used to love the maidens... he's not here anymore, he's already buried..."

"Com'on, you're not at a theater, you're hollering like an opera singer, Švejk,' sounded up the spooked Senior Lieutenant Lukáš, when Švejk sang the last sentence 'he's not here anymore, he's already buried'. "I was not asking you about that. I only wanted to know, whether you noticed, that the books, which you yourself mentioned to me, were by Ganghofer. — What's with the books then?" he erupted angrily.

"The ones I had brought from the Regimental Office to the Battalion?" asked Švejk. "Those were indeed written by the one, about whom you were asking me, whether I didn't know him, *Senior*

*Lieutenant*, Sir. I had received a telephonegram directly from the *Regimental Office*. The thing is they wanted to send those books to the Battalion *Office*, but they all were gone from there, including the *Duty Officer*, because they had to be at the mess, since we're hauling to the front, and because nobody knew, whether he'd be ever again sitting in the mess. They were there then, Senior Lieutenant, Sir, they were and drinking, nowhere over the telephone or from the other marchgangs could they find anybody, but because you had ordered me to be for the time being as the *messenger* by the telephone, until they transfer to us telephone operator Chodounský, then I was sitting there, waiting, until my turn came up too. From the *Regimental Office* they were complaining bitterly that they can't get through ringing anyone, that there was a telephonegram, to have the *March Battalion Office* pick up in the *Regimental Office* some books for the gentlemen officers from the whole marchbatty. Because I know, *Senior Lieutenant*, Sir, that in the military one must act quickly, I telephoned the *Regimental Office*, that I myself would pick up those books and that I would carry them over to the Battalion *Office*. There I received such a sack, that I barely dragged it over to us at the *Company Office*, and I examined the books. But I had my own thoughts about that. You know, the *Regimental Accounting Master Sergeant* at the *Regimental Office* was telling me, that according to the telephonegram to the Regiment they already knew at the Battalion, what they were to pick from among the books, **which volume**. Those books, that is to say, came in **two volumes**. The first volume separate, the second volume separate. Never in my life have I laughed so hard at something, because I have in my life read already many books, but never have I started reading something beginning with the second volume. And he's telling me there one more time: 'Here you have the first volumes and here you have the second volumes. *Which volume* the gentlemen officers are to read, they already know.' So I thought to myself, that they all were drunk, because when a book is to be read from the beginning, such a novel, as the one which I brought, about those *Sins of the Fathers*, because I also know German, that one had to start **with the first** volume, because we're not Jews and won't read it backwards. That is also why I was asking you, *Senior Lieutenant*, Sir, on the telephone, when you returned from the officers' club, and was reporting to you about those books, whether perhaps nowadays in the military it's turned upside down and whether books weren't read in the reversed order, first **the second** and only then **the first volume**. And you told me, that I was a drunk dumb beast, since I didn't even know, that in the Lord's Prayer there was first the 'Our Father' and only then the 'amen'. — Are you feeling ill, *Senior Lieutenant*, Sir?" asked with interest Švejk, when the pale Senior Lieutenant Lukáš grabbed the footboard on the water tank of the extinguished locomotive.

In his pale face wasn't apparent any expression of anger. It was something desperately hopeless.

"Go on, go on, Švejk, it doesn't matter, it's alright now…"

"I was, as I've been saying," one could hear on the abandoned track the soft voice of Švejk's, "also of the same mind. Once I bought a blood-and-guts book about Róža Šavaňů[45] from the Bakony[46] forest and there the first volume was missing, so I had to be guessing about the beginning, and even in such a robber's story one cannot do without the first volume. So it was totally clear to me, that it would be actually pointless, if the gentlemen officers started reading first the second volume and then the first, and how silly it would look, if at the Battalion I were to pass on, what they were saying at the *Regimental Office*, that the gentlemen officers already knew, **which volume** they were to read. The whole thing with the books, *Senior Lieutenant*, Sir, struck me as altogether terribly suspicious and mysterious. I knew, that the gentlemen officers read altogether little, and when there's the tumult of the battle…"

"Keep the idiocies to yourself, Švejk," let out a moan Senior Lieutenant Lukáš.

"But I was, *Senior Lieutenant*, Sir, asking you therefore right away on the telephone, whether you wanted right away both of the volumes together, and you told me, just like now, to keep the idiocies to myself, as if on top of all, you said, anybody needed to be dragging some books along. And here I thought, that since that was your view, then the rest of the gentlemen had to be seeing it that way too. I also asked our Vaněk about that, he has after all already had experiences at the front. He was saying, that at first each of the gentlemen officers thought, that the whole war was some little shitty joke, and was hauling into the field a whole library as if to a summer home. They were even getting from archduchesses as a gift whole collected works by various poets into the field, so that the spotshines were bowing under them and were cursing the day of their birth. Vaněk was saying, that the books didn't use to be at all of any use, as far as smoking was concerned, because they were printed on very nice paper, thick, and that in the latrine a man would with such poems scrape, if you excuse me, *Senior Lieutenant*, Sir, his whole behind. For reading there wasn't left any time, because it was constantly necessary to be fleeing, so the whole lot was being dumped, and then there was already such a custom, that as soon as there was heard the first artillery fire, the spotshine would throw out all the light entertainment books. After what I had heard, I wanted to hear one more time, *Senior Lieutenant*, Sir, your view, and when I asked you on the telephone, what was to be done with those books, then you said, that when something gets inside my stupid cob head, that then I won't let up a bit, until I get one across the yap. So I then, *Senior Lieutenant*, Sir, carried to the *Battalion Office* only those **first volumes** of that novel and the second volume I left for the time being in our *Company Office*. I had the good intention, that once the gentlemen officers would have read the first volume, then they would be issued the second volume, like from a library, but all of a sudden there came the word, that we were hauling, and a telephonegram across the whole battalion, that all which was unnecessary was to be put into the *Regimental stores*. So I still managed to ask Mr. Vaněk, whether he considered the second volume of the novel as something unnecessary, and he told me, that since the time of those sad experiences in Serbia, in Galicia, and in Magyaria no light entertainment books were hauled to the front, and those boxes in the cities, to collect old newspapers for the soldiers, that only those were good, because in the newsprint one can roll well tobacco or hay, which the soldiers smoke in the *dugouts*. At the Battalion they had already distributed those first volumes of the novel and the second volumes we carried off to the stores."

Švejk fell silent and immediately added: "There you've got all kinds of things, in that *storehouse*, *Senior Lieutenant*, Sir, even the top hat of the Budějovice *choir-leader*, in which he mustered at the regiment after having been drafted..."

"I'll tell you something, Švejk," sounded up with a heavy sigh Senior Lieutenant Lukáš, "you are not at all aware of the reach of your actions. Even for me it is already repulsive to keep calling you an imbecile. For your kind of idiocy there's not even a word. When I tell you 'you imbecile', then I am labeling you still with a kind word. You have done something so horrible, that the most dreadful crimes of yours, which you have committed over the time, that I have known you, are in comparison genuine angelic music. If you, Švejk, knew, what you did... But you will never find out... And should perhaps the talk ever come to those books, then don't you dare to blabber, that I was telling you something over the telephone, for you to have the second volume... If ever the talk came to, what happened with the first and second volume, don't pay any attention to it. You don't know anything, you are familiar with nothing, remember nothing. It better not be that you'd want to implicate me in something, you singular..."

Senior Lieutenant Lukáš was speaking with such a voice, as though a fever was trying to take hold of him, and the moment, when he fell silent, Švejk used for an innocent question: "I dutifully report, *Senior Lieutenant,* Sir, to be excused, why will I never find out, what a horrible thing I carried out. I, *Senior Lieutenant*, Sir, dared to ask about it only so that the next time, I could be making sure to avoid such a thing, since the general talk is, that by a mistake a human learns, like that metal caster Adamec from the Daňkovka[47], when by mistake he had a drink of muriatic acid..."

He didn't finish, because Senior Lieutenant Lukáš interrupted his example from life by the words: "You singular nitwit! I'll be explaining nothing to you. Crawl again back into the railroad car and tell Baloun, that when Budapest comes up, he is to bring for me to the Staff railroad car some braided bun and then the liver paté, which I have at the bottom of the small suitcase in aluminum foil. Then tell Vaněk, that he's a piece of a mule. Three times I've asked him to give me the exact headcount of the troops. And when today I needed it, I had the old *status* from last week."

"*As ordered, Lieutenant, Sir*," barked out Švejk and was slowly increasing the distance moving toward his railroad car.

Senior Lieutenant Lukáš took a walk down the track, while he beheld a thought: "I clearly should have slapped his face a few times, and instead I'm gabbing with him like with some pal."

Švejk was crawling solemnly into his car. He respected himself. It didn't happen every day, that he would commit something so horrible, that he must never find out, what it was.

*

"*Accounting Master Sergeant*, Sir," said Švejk, when he was sitting in his spot, "mister *Senior Lieutenant* Lukáš seems to me today to be in a very good mood. He's having me bring you a message, that you are a mule on account of the fact, that three times already he has asked you to give him the correct head count of the troops."

"*Lord God*," Vaněk got burning hot, "I'll get my pound of flesh from those *squad leaders*. Really now, is it my fault, that every such layabout squad leader does whatever he wants, and doesn't send me the *head count*? Am I perhaps to suck the *head count* out of my little finger? Well, what a situation that is at our gang. That can happen only at the eleventh marchgang. But I suspected it, I knew it. I didn't even for a minute doubt, that here among us there was disorder. One day there are missing four portions at the kitchen, the next day for a change there are three extra ones. If the crooks would at least notify me, if somebody is at the hospital. Just last month I had some Nikodém on the roster and only at *pay-day* I found out that that Nikodém had died in the Budějovice hospital of quick consumption. And without stopping stuff was being issued against his name. We got a uniform issued on his account, but God knows, where it all ended up. Then on top of it mister *Senior Lieutenant* will tell me, that I'm a mule, when he himself cannot see to it that there's order in his own C*ompany*."

The Accounting Master Sergeant Vaněk walked about the railroad car agitated: "If I were the *Company Commander*! Then everything would have to be clicking like clockwork. I would know the moves of each guy. The NCOs would have to report to me the *head count* twice a day. But since the NCOs are good for nothing. And the worst here with us is that *squad leader* Zyka. Nothing but jokes, nothing but anecdotes, but when I'm informing him that Kolařík has been *transferred* from his *squad* to the *Supply Company*, he's reporting to me the next day the very same *head count*, as if Kolařík kept lying around in the *Company* and in his *squad*. And when it is to be repeated daily and then in addition said about me, that I am a mule... This is not the way mister *Senior Lieutenant* will gain friends. The *Accounting Master Sergeant* of a *company* is no *Lance Corporal* with whom everybody can wipe his..."

Baloun, who was listening with his mouth opened, now proclaimed in Vaněk's stead the nice word, which Vaněk did not finish saying, whereby he wanted perhaps to also get himself mixed into the conversation.

"You over there, shut up," said the agitated Accounting Master Sergeant.

"Listen up, Baloun," sounded up Švejk, "I'm supposed to relay to you, that you are to, for mister *Senior Lieutenant*, once we arrive in Pest, bring to the railroad car some braided bun and that liver paté, which mister *Senior Lieutenant* has at the bottom of the small suitcase in aluminum foil."

Giant Baloun hung in desperation his long chimpanzee arms low, bowed his back and remained in that position a pretty while.

"I don't have it," he said softly, sounding desperate, looking at the dirty floor of the railroad car.

"I don't have," he was repeating in fragments, "I thought... before the departure I unwrapped it... I put my nose to it and took a whiff... to see whether it wasn't spoiled... — I tasted it," he cried out with such sincere desperation, that they all totally saw the light.

"You gobbled it up along with the aluminum foil," stopped in front of Baloun Accounting Master Sergeant Vaněk, being grateful, that he didn't have to keep defending his view, that he himself was not a mule, as the Senior Lieutenant had it relayed to him, but that the cause of the unknown fluctuating *head count* X had a deeper basis in other mules, and that now the conversation had shifted and was revolving around the insatiable Baloun, around a new tragic event. Vaněk got such a taste for telling Baloun something unpleasantly morally instructive, when at that moment beat him to it the cook-occultist Jurajda, who put aside his beloved book, a translation of the ancient Indian sutras Pragnâ-Paramitâ, and turned to the crushed Baloun, who hunched over even more under the weight of fate: "You, Baloun, are to be vigilant over your own self, so that you don't lose confidence in yourself and confidence in fate. You are not to take credit for that, which is the doing of others. Whenever you end up facing a similar problem, that you gobbled up, always ask yourself: In what relation to me is liver paté?"

Švejk judged it appropriate to augment this considered reflection by a practical example: "You yourself, Baloun, were previously telling me, that back home they will be slaughtering and smoking, and as soon as you know, once we're on the spot, the field post office number, that they'll send you a slab of ham right away. Now imagine, that they would send the ham from the *field post office* to us at the *marchgang* and we along with mister *Accounting Master Sergeant*, would each cut off a little piece, and it turned out to taste good to us, then another little piece, until the ham would end up like one mailman I know, some Kozel. He had the bone-eater, so first they cut off his foot up to the ankle, then the leg up to the knee, then the thigh, and if he didn't die in time, they would have whittled him down like sharpening a snapped pencil. "Imagine then, Baloun, that we'd have gobbled up that ham of yours, just like you wolfed down Mister Senior Lieutenant's liver paté."

Giant Baloun looked at everyone sadly.

"Only through my effort and to my credit," said the Accounting

Master Sergeant to Baloun, "have you remained an orderly with mister *Senior Lieutenant*. You were to be transferred to the Ambulance Corps and carry the wounded out from *combat*. Under the Dukla pass the corpsmen from our outfit went three times in a row for one wounded *Ensign*, who got a *bellyshot* in front of the *barbed wire obstacles* and none of them came back, nothing but *headshots*. Only the fourth pair brought him, but before they carried him to the *aid station*, the *Ensign* was now the poor departed one.

Baloun could not hold himself back anymore and gave a loud sob.

"You should be ashamed," said Švejk with disdain, "and you call yourself a soldier…?"

"But I'm not made for the military," began to wail Baloun, "I am, it's true, insatiable, never filled, because I've been torn out of proper life. It's in our clan line. My poor departed daddy, he was betting in a pub in Protivín that he would eat in a sitting fifty fat smoked sausages and two loaves of bread, and he won it. I once, on a bet, ate four geese and two mixing bowls of dumplings with sauerkraut. At home I'll have the idea after lunch, that I'd still like something to bite into. I go into the pantry, cut a piece of meat, send for a pitcher of beer and gobble up as fast as you can spit two kilos of smoked butt. I had at home an old stable hand, Vomel, and he would always remind me not to be getting so easily prideful, not to be stuffing myself, that he remembered, how his grandpa was telling him long ago about one such bottomless glutton. And then when there was some war, the fields bore nothing to harvest for eight whole years and that they would bake bread from straw and from that, which was left of the flax seed; and it was a holiday, when they could sprinkle a little farmer's cheese into milk, when there was no bread. And that farmer, as soon as that hardship started, died in a week, because his stomach was not used to such farmer's want…"

Baloun lifted his mournful face: "But I think, that Lord God punishes people, and yet will not abandon them."

"The Lord God has brought the perpetual eaters into the world, and the Lord God will take care of them," remarked Švejk, "once already you were tied up and now you'd deserve to be sent onto the front line; when I was the orderly of mister *Senior Lieutenant*, he could rely on me for everything and it never even crossed his mind then, that I would gobble up something of his. When there was being issued something special, then he would always say: 'Keep it, Švejk,' or: 'Oh well, I'm not that interested in it, pass a bit over here and with the rest do what you want.' And when we were in Prague and he would sometimes send me to a restaurant for a lunch, so that he wouldn't think perhaps I was bringing him a small portion, because I gobbled up half of it on the way, on my own, with my last money, when the portion seemed to me too small, I would buy an additional one, so that mister *Senior Lieutenant* would eat his fill and think nothing bad of me. Until this one time he found out about it. I always had to bring him the menu from the restaurant and he would choose. So he chose that day stuffed young pigeon. I thought, when they gave me a half, that perhaps mister *Senior Lieutenant* could think that I gobbled up the other half of his, so I bought another portion with my own money and brought him such a beautiful portion, that mister *Senior Lieutenant* Šeba, who was that day chasing down a lunch and came just before noon for a visit at **my** *Senior Lieutenant's*, also ate his fill. But when he finished eating, he says: 'Now don't be telling me, that this is one portion. Nowhere in the whole world will you get on the menu the whole stuffed young pigeon. If I chase down some money today, I'll send to that restaurant of yours for a lunch. Admit it sincerely, that it is a double portion.' Mister *Senior Lieutenant* asked me in front of him for me to testify, that he gave me money only for one single portion, because he didn't know, that he would come. I answered, that he had given me money for an ordinary lunch. 'So you see,' said my *Senior Lieutenant*, 'this is still nothing. The last time Švejk brought me two goose thighs for lunch. Imagine then: soup with noodles, beef with anchovy sauce, two goose thighs, dumplings and sauerkraut up to the ceiling, and crepes!"

"Tsk, tsk, tah-tah, damn!" smacked Baloun.

Švejk continued: "That was the stumbling block. Mister *Senior Lieutenant* Šeba really sent the next day his *spotshine* for a lunch to that restaurant of ours, and he brought as a side dish this tiny little pile of pilaf of hen, like when a six-week old baby poops into the down feather blanket, just about two teaspoons worth. And mister *Senior Lieutenant* Šeba laid into him, that he gobbled up a half. And he, that he was innocent. And mister *Senior Lieutenant* Šeba gave him a few across the yap and was putting me up as an example. That I bring portions to mister *Senior Lieutenant* Lukáš. And so the innocent slapped-around soldier, the next day at the restaurant, when he had gone to fetch a lunch, asked about it all, told his master, he in turn to my *Senior Lieutenant*. I'm sitting in the evening with my face behind a newspaper, and I'm reading the news of the enemy Staffs from the battlefield, when my mister *Senior Lieutenant* enters, all pale, and right away goes directly after me, to tell him, how many of those double portions I have paid for at the restaurant, that he knows everything, that absolutely no denying will help me, that he's known long since, that I am an imbecile, but that I would be crazy, that did not occur to him. I have supposedly embarrassed him so much, that he has the greatest hankering to shoot me dead first and then himself. '*Senior Lieutenant*, Sir,' I told him, 'when you were mustering me in, that first day you were talking about it, that each *spotshine* is a thief and a morally degenerate guy. And since at that restaurant they would actually give such tiny side dish portions, then you could have thought, that I was actually also one such degenerate guy, that I gobbled up your…"

"My God in heaven," whispered Baloun and bent over to get the small suitcase of Senior Lieutenant Lukáš' and was walking away with it to the back.

"Then Senior Lieutenant Lukáš," continued Švejk, "started frisking himself one pocket after another, and when it proved futile, he reached into his vest and gave me his silver watch. He was so kind of moved. 'When I get paid, Švejk,' he said, 'add it up for me then and write down, how much I owe you… Keep this watch separate from that. And next time don't be crazy.' Then once, such poverty struck us both, that I had to take the watch to a pawn shop…"

"What are you doing in the back, Baloun?" posed the question at that moment Accounting Master Sergeant Vaněk.

Instead of answering, the hapless Baloun choked coughing for a second. That is to say, he had opened the small suitcase of Senior Lieutenant Lukáš' and was stuffing himself with his last braided bun…

\*

Through the railroad station rolled another military train without stopping, packed from top to bottom by Deutschmeisters, whom they were sending to the Serbian front. They had not yet recovered from their excitement of saying goodbyes to Vienna and were hollering without taking a breath from Vienna all the way here:

> *Prince Eugen, the noble knight*
> *wanted for the Emperor again to conquer*
> *the city and fortress Belgrade.*
> *He had a bridge thrown down,*

> *so one could cross over*
> *with the army right up before the city.*

Some *corporal* with a menacingly curled up mustache, leaning out, being propped on his elbows against the troops, who were dangling their legs stuck out of the car, was keeping time and hollering to the round about:

> *As the bridge was built*
> *so one could with cannon and wagons*
> *freely cross the Danube stream,*
> *near Semlin*[48] *they pitched the camp,*
> *to chase all the Serbs away...*

At that moment however he lost his balance and flew out of the railroad car and with full force hit his belly in flight against the lever of the rail switch, on which impaled he remained hanging, while the train kept on going and in the rear cars they were singing another one:

> *Count Radetzky, noble blade,*
> *swore to sweep the Emperor's foe*
> *out of the unfaithful Lombardy.*
> *in Verona*[49], *long he waited,*
> *but as more troops arrived*
> *the hero felt and stirred himself free...*

Impaled on the stupid switch, the *corporal* spoiling for a fight was already dead and it didn't take long, there was already standing guard by him with a bayonet some young little soldier from the railroad station command contingent, who was taking his role very seriously. He was standing erect by the switch and had quite a victorious countenance, as if it were his handiwork, the impaling of the corporal on the rail switch.

Because he was a Hungarian, he was screaming up and down the track, when they were coming here from the *Battalion military transport* of the 91st Regiment to look: "*Not allowed! Not allowed!* Komision militär *not allowed!*"

"He's done with it all now," said the good soldier Švejk, who also was among the curious onlookers, "and it has the advantage, that since he already has a piece of iron in the belly, at least everybody knows, where he was buried. It is right on the railroad, and they don't have to be chasing down his grave from one battlefield to another. — He pronged himself up just right," said in addition Švejk expertly, walking around the corporal from the other side, "he's got the guts in his pants."

"*Not allowed! Not allowed!*" the very young little Hungarian soldier was screaming, "*Railroad station military commission, not allowed!*"

Behind Švejk there sounded up a stern voice: "What are you doing here?"

In front of him was Standing Cadet Biegler. Švejk saluted.

"I dutifully report, we're looking over the poor departed, Cadet, Sir."

"And what agitation have you been conducting in here? What business do you have being here?"

"I dutifully report, Cadet, Sir," with dignified calm answered Švejk, "that I have never conducted any whatagitation."

Back behind the Cadet several soldiers broke into laughter and forward in front of the Cadet stepped Accounting Master Sergeant Vaněk.

"Mister Cadet," he said, "Mister *Senior Lieutenant* sent the *messenger* Švejk here, so that he would tell him what happened. I was just by the Staff railroad car and the *Battalion Messenger* Matušič is looking for you on the order of mister *Battalion Commander*. You are to go right away to mister *Captain* Ságner."

One and all were dispersing to their railroad cars, when in a little while sounded the signal to board the railroad cars.

Vaněk, walking with Švejk, said: "When there are other people around, then keep, Švejk, your harebrained ideas to yourself. You could regret it. It could happen, since the Corporal was with the Deutschmeisters, that it could be interpreted as you deriving pleasure from it. That Biegler is a terrible Czech-devourer."

"But I haven't said anything," answered Švejk in a tone, which excluded any reason for a doubt, "other than, that the corporal pronged himself up just right, he had his guts in his pants... He could have..."

"So then, Švejk, let's stop talking about it already." And the Accounting Master Sergeant Vaněk spat.

"It makes no difference," still remarked Švejk, "should the guts be coming out his belly for the lord Emperor here or there. He's done his duty either way... He could have..."

"Take a look, Švejk," interrupted him Vaněk, "how again there is strutting *Battalion Messenger* Matušič toward the Staff car. I am surprised, that he hasn't tripped yet and stretched himself across the tracks."

Shortly before that there was taking place between *Captain* Ságner and the eager Cadet Biegler a very sharp exchange.

"I am amazed by you, Cadet Biegler," was saying *Captain* Ságner, "Why didn't you immediately come to inform me, that there were not being issued the fifteen decagrams of Magyar salami. So now I'm the one who has to go out there and see for myself why the troops were returning from the storehouse. And the gentlemen officers too, as if an order were not an order. I did say: 'Into the storehouse *by the platoon* one company at a time.' That meant, when at the storehouse we hadn't gotten anything, that everybody was to be going also *by the platoon* one company at a time into the railroad cars. I commanded you, Cadet Biegler, that you see to keeping order, but you let it all float down the stream. You were glad, that you didn't have to be taking care of counting the portions of salami, and you went without a second thought to take a look, as I saw from the window, at the pronged up corporal of the Deutschmeisters. And when I had you afterwards called, then you didn't have anything else to do than in your cadet fantasy babble, that you went to ascertain for yourself, whether there wasn't around the pronged up corporal being conducted some agitation…"

"I dutifully report that the *Messenger* of the 11th Company Švejk…"

"Leave me alone about Švejk," screamed *Captain* Ságner, "don't think, Cadet Biegler, that you'll be conducting some intrigue against Senior Lieutenant Lukáš. We sent Švejk there… You're looking at me so, as if you were thinking, that I have decided to pick on you… Yes, I have decided to pick on you, Cadet Biegler… Since you don't know to respect your superior, you're trying to fool him, then I'll give you such a rough army service time, that you, Cadet Biegler, will always remember the Győr station… Ever boasting with your theoretical knowledge… Wait, until we are at the front… Until I order you to go on an *officer patrol* across *barbed wire obstacles*… Your report? You didn't even give me the report, when you came… Not even theoretically, Cadet Biegler…"

"I dutifully report, *Captain* Sir,* that instead of fifteen decagrams of Magyar salami have the troops received two postcards apiece. If you please, *Captain*, Sir…"

Cadet Biegler handed the Battalion Commander two of those postcards, which were published by the headquarters of the Military War Archive in Vienna, where the chief was infantry General Wojnowich[50]. On one side there was a caricature of a Russian soldier, a Russian muzhik with an overgrown beard, who was being hugged by a skeleton. Under the caricature there was the text:

*The day on which perfidious Russia croaks will be a day of redemption for our monarchy.*

The second postcard originated in The German Empire. It was a gift from Germans to Austro-Hungarian soldiers.

On the top there was "*By united forces*" and under it was a picture of Sir Edward Grey[51] hanging from the gallows and down under him merrily saluting an Austrian and a German soldier.

The little poem down below was taken from the book of Greinz's[52] The Iron Fist. Little funny barbs aimed at our enemies, of which the imperial newspapers wrote, that the verses of Greinz's were lashes of the cat-o'-nine-tails, while they contained genuine untamed humor and unsurpassable wit.

The text under the gallows, in a translation:

GREY

*From the gallows at a pleasant height
should swing Edward Grey,
for that, it's already high time,
however, it's needed that you be notified
that no oak has lent its lumber
for the execution of that Judas[53].
Hanging on the lumber of aspens
from the French Republic.*

*Captain* Ságner was not even finished reading these verses "of untamed humor and unsurpassable wit" yet, when there barged into the Staff railroad car *Battalion Messenger* Matušič.

He was sent by *Captain* Ságner to the telegraph center of the

---

* All conversations of officers with officers are naturally taking place in the German language.

railroad station military command to see whether there weren't perhaps other instructions there, and he brought a telegram from the Brigade. It wasn't necessary, however, to be reaching for any cipher key. The telegram read simply, unciphered: "*Quickly cook up, then get marching to Sokal*[54]." *Captain* Ságner alarmingly shook his head.

"I dutifully report," said Matušič, "the station commander begs you for a consultation. There's one more telegram there."

Afterward there was between the station commander and Captain Ságner a consultation of a very confidential nature.

The first telegram had to be handed over, even though its content was very surprising, since the Battalion was at the station in Győr: "Quickly cook up, then get marching to Sokal." It was addressed unciphered to the March Battalion of the 91st Regiment with a copy to the March Battalion of the 75th Regiment, which was still in the back. The signature was correct: Brigade Commander Ritter von Herbert.

"Very confidential, *Captain*, Sir," said secretively the military commander of the railroad station. "*Secret* telegram from your Division. The Commanding Officer of your Brigade has gone crazy. He was hauled to Vienna, after he had sent from the Brigade several dozen similar telegrams in all directions. In Budapest you will see certainly a new telegram. All his telegrams should be naturally annulled, but so far we have gotten no instruction in this regard. I have, as I've been saying, only an instruction from the Division, for unciphered telegrams not to be taken into consideration. To deliver them I have to, because in this regard I haven't received from **my** higher authorities an answer. Through the agency of **my** higher authorities I have inquired at the Army Corps Command and found there had been started an interrogation of me... — I am an active duty officer of the old corps of engineers service," he added, "I was present at the construction of our strategic rail in Galicia... — *Captain*, Sir," he said after a while, "with us old hands it's straight to the front! Nowadays the civilian railroad engineers with a one-year volunteer exam certification are as plentiful as dogs at the Ministry of Military Affairs... Besides, in a quarter of an hour you're again riding on... I remember only one thing, that once in the Cadet School in Prague, I was helping you up onto the horizontal bar, as one from a more senior class. Back then we both were confined to quarters. You brawled with the Germans in the class?* There was also Lukáš there with you. You used to be the best of pals. When we received the telegram here with the list of the officers of the marchbattalion, who were passing through the station, then I clearly remembered... It's already been a pretty long couple of years... Cadet Lukáš used to strike me as very likable back then..."

The whole conversation left *Captain* Ságner with a very embarrassing impression. He recognized very well the one, who was talking to him and who at the caddy conducted opposition against Austrianism, an idea later knocked out of their heads by their effort at a career. The most unpleasant for him was the mention of Senior Lieutenant Lukáš, who for any reason found against him was **everywhere** shoved aside.

"Senior Lieutenant Lukáš," he said with emphasis, "is a very good officer. When is the train leaving?"

The commander of the railroad station looked at the watch. "In six minutes."

"I'm going," said Ságner.

"I thought that you'd tell me something, Ságner."

"Then nazdar!" answered Ságner** and walked out to the front of the railroad station command building.

*

When Captain Ságner returned before the departure of the train to the Staff car, he found all the officers in their places. They were playing čapáry (frische viere) in groups, only Cadet Biegler wasn't playing.

He was paging through a whole lot of manuscripts he had begun about war scenes, because he wanted to make his mark not only on the field of war, but also as a literary phenomenon, describing war events. The man of the queer wings "with a fish tail" wanted to be an outstanding war writer. His literary attempts would begin with titles promising much, in which the militarism of that time was being mirrored, but had not been worked out yet, so that on the quarto sheets there remained only the titles of works that, were to come into being..

"The Characters of the Soldiers of the Great War — Who Started the War? — The Policy of Austria-Hungary and the Origin of the

---

\* In the **German** conversation, which the two conducted between themselves: "Sie haben sich damals auch mit den deutschen Mitschülern gerauft."

\*\* In the conversation: "Also: Nazdar!"

World War — The War Notes — Austria-Hungary and the World War — Lessons from the War — Popular Lecture on the Outbreak of the War — Military Political Essays — Glorious Day of Austria-Hungary — Slavic Imperialism and the World War — War Documents — Documents on the History of the World War —Diary of the World War— Daily Digest of the World War — The First World War — Our Dynasty in the World War — The Nations of the Austro-Hungarian Monarchy at Arms — World Struggle for Power — My Experiences in the World War — The Chronicle of My Military Campaign — How Fight the Enemies of Austria-Hungary — Whose Is the Victory? — Our Officers and Our Soldiers — Memorable Acts of My Soldiers — From the Times of the Great War — Of the Battle's Tumult — The Book of Austro-Hungarian Heroes — The Iron Brigade — Collection of My Letters from the Front — Heroes of Our Marchbattalion — The Handbook for Soldiers in the Field — Days of Combat and Days of Victory — What I Saw and Lived Through in the Field — In the Trenches — An Officer Relays... — With the Sons of Austria-Hungary Forward! — Enemy Aeroplanes and Our Infantry — After the Battle — Our Artillery, Loyal Sons of the Homeland — Even If All the Demons Were Going Against Us... — War, Defensive and Offensive — Blood and Iron — Victory or Death — Our Heroes in Captivity."

When *Captain* Ságner stepped up to Cadet Biegler and looked through everything, he asked why he did it and what he meant by it.

Cadet Biegler answered with genuine enthusiasm, that each title signified a book, which he would compile. As many titles, that many books.

"I'd wish for myself, that when I fall in in battle, for there to be left of me a memento, *Captain*, Sir. My model has been the German professor Udo Kraft[55]. He was born in the year 1870, now in the world war he signed up as a volunteer and fell on August 22nd, 1914 in Anloy[57]. Before his death he published the book Raising Oneself to Die for the Emperor.'"

*Captain* Ságner led Cadet Biegler to the window.

"Show what else you have, Cadet Biegler, I am terribly interested in your activity," said with irony *Captain* Ságner, "what little notebook did you stuff under your blouse?"

---

[*] Udo Kraft: Selbsterziehung zum Tod Für Kaiser. C.F. Amelang's Verlag[56], Leipzig.

"That's nothing, *Captain*, Sir," with child-like blush answered Cadet Biegler, "condescend to verify it for yourself."

The little notebook was titled:

>Schemas of outstanding and glorious battles
>of the troops of the Austro-Hungarian Army,
>compiled according to historical studies
>by I&R officer Adolf Biegler.
>Notes and explanations provided
>by I&R officer Adolf Biegler.

The schemas were terribly simple.

From the battle at Nördlingen[58] on September 6, 1634, on to the battle at Zentaa[59] on September 11, 1697, at Caldiero[60] on October 31, 1805, on to the battle at Aspern on May 22, 1809 and the battle of the nations at Leipzig in 1813, on to St. Lucia[61] in May 1848 and the battle at Trutnov[62] on June 27, 1866, all the way to the conquest of Sarajevo on August 19, 1878. In the schemas and sketches of the plans for those battles nothing ever changed. Everywhere drew Cadet Biegler empty little rectangles on one side, whereas the enemy was represented by hatched ones. On both sides there was the left flank, the center, and the right flank. Then in the back the reserves and arrows pointing here and there. The battle at Nördlingen just as the battle at Sarajevo looked like the players' position layout at any soccer match at the opening of the game and the arrows pointing to where whichever side is to kick out the ball.

That also immediately occurred to *Captain* Ságner who posed the question: "Cadet Biegler, you play soccer?"

Biegler blushed even more and batted his eyes nervously, so that he created an impression, as if he was getting ready to bawl.

*Captain* Ságner kept with a smile paging on through the little notebook and stopped at the note to the schema of the battle at Trutnov during the Prusso-Austrian war.

Cadet Biegler wrote: "The battle at Trutnov was not to take place, because the mountainous terrain made impossible the fanning out of the division of General Mazzuchelli[63], menaced by strong Prussian convoys, situated in the highlands surrounding the left flank of our division."

"According to you the battle at Trutnov," said with a smile *Captain* Ságner, returning the little notebook to Cadet Biegler, "could take place only in the case, if Trutnov were in a flat land, you Benedek[64] of Budějovice.

"Cadet Biegler, it is very nice of you that in such a short time of your stay in the ranks of the military you have been striving to gain an understanding of strategy; however the way it ended in your case is, like when boys play soldiers and take the titles of generals. You've advanced yourself so quickly, that it's nothing but all joy. I&R officer Adolf Biegler! Before we reach Pest, you'll be a field marshal then. The day before yesterday you were still somewhere at home by your daddy weighing cow hides. I&R *Lieutenant* Adolf Biegler!... Human one, but you aren't even any kind of officer. You are a cadet. You're hanging mid-air between an *ensign* and NCOs. You are far from being called an officer, like when somewhere in a pub a *lance corporal* has everybody address him 'staff quartermaster, Sir'. — Listen up, Lukáš," he turned to the Senior Lieutenant, "you have Cadet Biegler in your Company, so flail the boy into shape. He signs his name with the title of an officer, let him earn it in combat. When there's *drum-roll fire* and we're attacking, let him, *the good youth* and his platoon, be cutting the *barbed wire obstacles*. À propos, Zykán says hello, he's the railroad station commander in Győr."

Cadet Biegler saw that the conversation with him was over, so he saluted and all red in his face walked through the railroad car, until he found himself at the very end, in the crosswise passageway.

Like a sleep-walker he opened the door of the bathroom, and looking at the German-Hungarian sign "Use of the bathroom allowed only while underway", he whimpered, made a sobbing gulp and broke into a silent weep. Then he dropped his pants... Then, wiping his tears, he was pushing. Then he used the little notebook with the title "Schemas of outstanding and glorious battles of the troops of the Austro-Hungarian Army, compiled by I&R officer Adolf Biegler", which disappeared dishonored in the hole, and having landed on the tracks, it was floating between the rails under the rolling away military train.

Cadet Biegler washed in the sink in the bathroom his reddened eyes and walked out into the passageway making up his mind, that he had to be strong, damn strong. He'd had a headache and bellyache since the morning already.

He was walking past the rear compartment, where the *Battalion Messenger* Matušič was with the military servant of the Battalion Commander Batzer playing the Viennese game Schnapsen (sixty six).

Looking into the open doorway of the compartment, he coughed. They turned and kept playing.

"Don't you know what you're supposed to do?" Cadet Biegler asked.

"I couldn't," answered the servant of Captain Ságner, Batzer, in his terrible German from around Kašperské Hory, *"I'v' run 'ut of trumps.* — I should have played drums, Mister Cadet," he continued, "high drums, and right after that I should have pulled out and played the green king of leaves... I should have done that..."

Cadet Biegler didn't say even a single word and crawled into his corner. When later there came to him Ensign Pleschner, in order to let him have a gulp from the bottle of cognac, which he had won in cards, he was amazed, how Cadet Biegler was diligently reading in the book by professor Udo Kraft, Raising Oneself to Die for the Emperor.

Before they arrived in Pest, Cadet Biegler was so drunk, that leaning out of the window of the railroad car, he was screaming into the desolate landscape ceaselessly: *"Charge at it! In God's name, charge at it!"*

Then, on the order of *Captain* Ságner, the *Battalion Messenger* Matušič dragged him into the compartment, where he and the *Captain's* servant Batzer laid him down on the bench, and Cadet Biegler had this dream:

Cadet Biegler's Dream Before Budapest

He had the Signum Laudis, the Iron Cross and was a major and was going on an inspection of a detachment of the brigade, that was assigned to him. Yet he didn't know how to explain to himself, when he had an entire brigade under him, why he was still only a major. He had a suspicion, that he was to be appointed a major general and that the 'general' got somewhere in the rush at the field post office lost.

He had to laugh inwardly, about how on the train, when they were riding to the front, *Captain* Ságner was threatening him, that he would have to be cutting through *barbed wire obstacles*. As it happened *Captain* Ságner was long since, on his recommendation at the Division, transferred to another regiment with Senior Lieutenant Lukáš included. To another Division, to another Army Corps.

Somebody was also telling him, that both perished wretchedly somewhere in a marsh while running away.

As he was riding in an automobile to a field position to inspect the detachment of his brigade, everything was clear to him. He was actually dispatched from the General Staff of the Army.

Marching by there were soldiers and they were singing a song, which he had read in a collection of Austrian military songs *Now's the time*:

*Hold yourselves brave, ye valiant brothers,*
*throw the enemy down right heartily,*
*let the Kaiser's flag wave...*

The landscape had the same character as in the pictures of the *Viennese Illustrated Newspaper*[65].

On the right side one could see by a barn the artillery, as it was shooting into the enemy trenches next to the road, on which he was riding by in the automobile. On the left stood a house, from which they were shooting, while the enemy using the butts of rifles was attempting to pry the door open. Next to the road there was burning an enemy aeroplane. On the horizon one could see the cavalry and a burning village. Then trenches of a march battalion with a little rise, where shooting into the enemy there were machine guns. Further on there were enemy trenches winding along the road. And the chauffeur keeps driving him on toward the enemy down the road.

He's screaming through the hearing piece at the chauffeur: "Don't you know, where we're going? There is the enemy."

But the chauffeur is calmly answering:

"General, Sir, this is the only good enough road. The roadway is in good condition. On those side roads the tires would not hold up."

The closer they're getting to the enemy, the fire is becoming more intense. The grenades are all around throwing up over the trenches on both sides an alley of plum trees.

But the chauffeur is calmly answering into the hearing piece:

"This is an excellent road, General, Sir, riding on it is as smooth as butter. If we turned onto the fields, we'd blow a tire. — Take a look, General, Sir," is hollering into the hearing piece the chauffeur, "this road is so well built, that even thirty-and-a-half-centimeter mortars will do nothing to us. The road is like a threshing floor, but down those stony roads in the fields we'd blow the tires. We can't return anyhow, General, Sir!"

"Bzz — dzum!" is what Biegler is hearing, and the automobile made a huge jump.

"Didn't I tell you, General, Sir," is screaming the chauffeur into the hearing piece, "that it's a demon's grade of a well-built road? Just now really close ahead of us there exploded one thirty-eighter. But no hole, the road is like a threshing floor. But take a ride into the fields, and the tires are goners. Now they're shooting at us from the distance of 4 kilometers."

"Where is it though we're going?"

"That remains to be seen," answered the chauffeur, "as long as the road is like this, I vouch for everything."

A flight, a tremendous flight, and the automobile is coming to a stop.

"General, Sir," is screaming the chauffeur, "don't you have the Staff map?"

General Biegler is turning on a little electric lamp. He can see, that he has the Staff map on his knees. But it is a nautical map of the Helgoland[66] coast from the year 1864, during the Austro-Prussian war against Denmark[67] for Schleswig[68].

"There's a crossroad here," says the chauffeur, "both crossroads lead to enemy positions. I'm interested in a good enough road, so the tires won't suffer, General, Sir... I am responsible for the Staff car..."

Then a bang, a deafening detonation, and stars as big as wheels. The Milky Way is as thick as cream.

He's floating through the universe on the seat next to the chauffeur. The whole automobile is just ahead of the seat snipped off as if by scissors. Of the automobile there is left only the aggressive, offensive front.

"A lucky thing," says the chauffeur, "that you were showing me the map over my back. You flew over to join me and the rest was gone with a scream. It was a two-and-forty piece... I had a feeling right away, that as soon as there's a crossroad, the road would be worth an old nothing-hag then. After the thirty-eighter it could have been only a forty-twoer. Nothing else is being manufactured so far, General, Sir."

"Where are you driving to?"

"We're flying into heaven, General, Sir, and we have to avoid the comets. Those are worse than a forty-twoer. — Now below us there's Mars," said the chauffeur after a long pause.

Biegler was feeling already calm again.

"Do you know the history of the battle of the nations at Leipzig?" he asked, "when Field Marshall Duke Schwarzenberg[69] went against

Libertkovice[70] on October 14th of the year 1813 and when on October 16th there was the struggle over Lindenau[71], the battles of General Merweldt[72], and when the Austrian troops were in Wachava[73] and when on October 19th Leipzig fell?"

"General, Sir," said at that moment seriously the chauffeur, "we've just arrived at the heaven's gate, crawl out, General, Sir! We cannot drive through the heaven's gate, there's a press of people here. Nothing but troops."

"Just run over one of them," he's hollering at the chauffeur, "they'll dodge after all."

And leaning out of the automobile he is screaming: "*Attention, you pack of swine!* They're all cattle beasts, they see a general, and they can't do an eyes right."

The chauffeur responds by calmly soothing him: "'Tia a hard thing, General, Sir, most have had their head whacked off."

General Biegler only now noticed, that those, who are pressing at heaven's gate, are the most varied invalids, who have lost during the war parts of their bodies, which they had however with them in a rucksack. Heads, arms, legs. Some righteous artilleryman, pressing at heaven's gate in a tattered overcoat, had in the backpack stacked his whole belly even with the lower limbs. From another backpack of some righteous *home army soldier* was looking at General Biegler a half of a butt, which he lost at Lwów[74].

"That is on account of order," sounded up the chauffeur again, driving through a thick throng, "it is apparently on account of heavenly doctors' grand rounds."

At heaven's gate they were letting people through only with a password, which immediately occurred to General Biegler: "*For God and Emperor.*"

The automobile rode into Paradise.

"General, Sir," said some officer angel with wings, when they were riding past the barracks with recruit angels, "you have to report at the Command Headquarters."

They drove on past some training ground, which was just swarming with recruit angels, whom they were teaching to holler "Alleluia".

They were driving past a group, where a rust-haired corporal angel was just then riding one clumsy recruit hard, was punching the fist into his belly and screaming at him: "Open up your trap better, you swine of Bethlehem[75]. Is this how one calls 'Alleluia'? As if you had a dumpling in your yap. I would love to know, which ox here, you cattle beast, let you into Paradise. Try it one more time… Hlahlehluyaah? What, you bestial creature, on top of it you're mumbling here in our Paradise… Try it one more time, you cedar of Lebanon[76]."

They kept driving away and behind them for a long time one could still hear the anxious hollering of the mumbling recruit angel "Hla-hle-hlu-yaah" and the screaming of the angel corporal "A-le-lu-ia, al-le-lu-ia, you Jordanian[77] cow!"

Then enormous glow over a big building like the Marian barracks in České Budějovice and above it two aeroplanes, one on the left, the other on the right side, and in the middle between them strung a huge canvas with the enormous inscription *I&R Headquarters of God*.

Two angels in uniforms of the field military police unseated General Biegler from the automobile, took him by the collar and escorted him into the building, up to the second floor.

"Behave yourself politely in front of the Lord God," they told him in addition upstairs in front of a door and shoved him inside.

In the middle of the room, in which on the walls there were hanging portraits of Franz Josef and Wilhelm, the successor to the Austrian throne of Karl Franz Josef, General Viktor Dankl[78], Archduke Friedrich[79] and the Chief of the General Staff Konrad von Hötzendorf, stood the Lord God.

"Cadet Biegler," said the Lord God with emphasis, "you don't recognize me? I am your former *Captain* Ságner of the 11th March Company."

Biegler turned to wood.

"Cadet Biegler," sounded up again the Lord God, "by what right have you appropriated for yourself the title of major general? By what right have you, Cadet Biegler, been joy-riding in a Staff automobile down the road among enemy positions?"

"I dutifully report…"

"Shut your trap, Cadet Biegler when talking to you is the Lord God."

"I dutifully report," chattered Biegler once more.

"So you then won't keep your trap shut?" started screaming at him the Lord God, opened the door and hollered: "Two angels in here!"

There entered two angels with rifles hung over the left wing. Biegler recognized in them Matušič and Batzer.

And from the mouth of the Lord God sounded the voice: "Throw him into the latrine!"

Cadet Biegler was falling somewhere into horrible stench...

\*

Opposite the sleeping Cadet Biegler was sitting Matušič with the servant of *Captain* Ságner, Batzer and they were still playing six-and-sixty.

"*But da guy do stink 'ike a codfish,*" suggested in passing Batzer, who was watching with interest, how the sleeping Cadet Biegler was fidgeting considerably, "*must've da pants full.*"

"That can happen to anybody," said philosophically Matušič, "let him be, you won't be changing him anyhow. Better deal the cards."

Over Budapest one could already see the glow of lights and above the Danube a searchlight kept jumping over.

Cadet Biegler was already dreaming about something else, because he was talking in his sleep: "*Tell my brave army that it has erected for itself in my heart an imperishable monument of love and gratitude.*"

Because with those words again he started turning over, an intense fragrance flashed under Batzer's nose, so that he remarked, spitting: "*Stinks like a shithouse cleaning woman, like a shit-smeared shithouse cleaning woman.*"

And Cadet Biegler was wriggling, the longer the more restlessly, and his new dream was very fantastic. He was defending Linz[80] in the war of inheritance and succession to the Austrian throne.

He saw redoubts, entrenchments and palisades round the city. His General Headquarters was turned into an enormous hospital. All around were wallowing the sick and they were clutching their bellies. Under the palisades of the city of Linz there were riding about French dragoons of Napoleon I.

And he, the commander of the city, was standing over that desolation and was also clutching his belly and was hollering at some French negotiator: "Relay to your Emperor that, I will not surrender..."

Then it was as if the bellyache had suddenly left him, and he was hurtling with the battalion over the palisades out of the city onto the road of glory and victory and saw, how Senior Lieutenant Lukáš was intercepting with his breast the swinging blow of the broadsword of a French dragoon, which was meant for him, Biegler, the defender of the besieged Linz.

Senior Lieutenant Lukáš is dying at his feet with the scream: "*A man like you, Colonel, is more important than a useless lieutenant!"*

The defender of Linz is turning full of deep emotion away from the one dying, when just then flies in a grape-shot and hits Biegler in the sitting muscles.

Biegler mechanically reaches to the back of his pants and feels dampness, something sticky is smearing onto his hand. He's screaming: *"Ambulance! Ambulance!"* and he's falling off the horse..."

Cadet Biegler was picked up by Batzer and Matušič off the floor, whereto he rolled off from the bench, and they deposited him again in his spot.

Then Matušič had gone to *Captain* Ságner and announced, that very queer things were happening with Cadet Biegler.

"It's probably not on account of the cognac," he said, "it could rather be cholera. Cadet Biegler would at all the railroad stations drink the water. In Moson I saw him, as he..."

"It doesn't go that fast with cholera, Matušič, tell the doctor in the next compartment to go and take a look at him."

Assigned to the Battalion was a 'war doctor', an old medical student and a real Kraut college boy, Welfer. He knew how to drink, brawl and at the same time he'd had all the medical arts crammed inside his pinkie. He'd been through the medical schools in various university towns in Austria-Hungary, even internships in most varied hospitals, but he was not passing the boards for his doctorate for the simple reason, that in the will, which his uncle left for his inheritors, there was written, that there should be paid out to the medicine studying Friedrich Welfer annually a stipend until the time, when Friedrich Welfer obtains his physician's diploma.

This stipend was about four times bigger than the salary of an assistant in hospitals, and MUC[81], Bedřich Welfer earnestly strove to postpone his being appointed Doctor of Universal Medicine until a time in a future as distant as possible.

The heirs were so mad they could turn rabid. They kept pronouncing him an imbecile, they were making attempts forcing him to accept wealthy brides, in order to get rid of him. And to get them to seethe even more, MUC Bedřich Welfer, member of about twelve German university fraternities, published several collections of very decent poems in Vienna, in Leipzig, in Berlin. He wrote for the Simplicissimus[82] and studied on, as if nothing out of the ordinary was happening.

Until the war came, that fell upon MUC Bedřich Welfer disgracefully from behind.

The poet of the books *Laughing Songs*, *Jug and Science*, *Fairy Tales and Parables*, they absolutely rudely conscripted into army service and one heir at the Ministry of Military Affairs added his effort, so that the jovial Bedřich Welfer made the grade and got his "wartime doctorate". He got it through a written exam. He received a number of questions to fill out, all of which he answered stereotypically: *"Lick my ass!"* In three days the Colonel informed him, that he got the diploma of a doctor of universal medicine, that he had long since been ripe for the doctorate, that the chief Staff physician was assigning him to a hospital expansion unit and only on his behavior depended his quick advance, and that, true enough, he had had in various university towns duels with officers, all of that was known about him, but that nowadays during the war everything was being forgotten.

The author of the poems Jug and Science bit his lips and went to serve.

After the discovery of several cases, in which he behaved unusually leniently toward soldier patients, extending their stay at the hospital, as long as it was possible, when the watchword was "Are they all to roll around at the hospital or preferably croak in the trenches — are they all to croak at the hospital or in an *assault line*", they sent doctor Welfer to the front with the 11th March Battalion.

Active duty officers of the Battalion viewed him as something of an inferior value. Reserve officers would also ignore him and not establish any friendship with him, lest the abyss between them and the active duty officers widened.

*Captain* Ságner felt himself naturally terribly exalted above the former MUC, who cut up in his time of long years of studies who knows how many officers. When doctor Welfer, the "wartime doctor", passed him by, he would not even look at him and would keep on speaking with Senior Lieutenant Lukáš about something absolutely insignificant, that in Budapest they grow gourds, to which Senior Lieutenant Lukáš would retort, that when he was in the third year of the caddy, he and several pals "as civilians" were in Slovakia and came to an evangelical minister, a Slovak. That he served them cabbage made of gourd to go with the pork roast and that he then poured for them wine and said:

> Gourd the swine,
> has a hankering for wine,

and that he took horrible offense.*

"Of Budapest we won't see much," said *Captain* Ságner, "they're hauling us around it. According to the *march route* we are to stand here for two hours."

"I think they're *shunting* the railroad cars," answered Senior Lieutenant Lukáš, "we'll come to the transshipment yard. *Military transport railroad station*."

The 'wartime doctor' Welfer passed by.

"That's nothing," he said with a smile, "The gentlemen, who aspire to become in the course of time officers of the army and in Bruck were still bragging about their strategic history knowledge at the officers' club, should have been advised, that it is dangerous to eat up at once the whole shipment of sweets, which his mommy has sent for him into the field. Cadet Biegler, who since that time, when we hauled out of Bruck, has eaten thirty cream rolls, as he confessed to me, and would drink everywhere at the railroad stations only boiled water, *Captain*, Sir, brings to mind a verse of Schiller's: '*Who speaks of...*"

"Listen, doc," interrupted him *Captain* Ságner, "it's not about Schiller. What's with Cadet Biegler actually?"

The 'wartime doctor' Welfer gave a smile. "The one aspiring to officer's rank **your** Cadet Biegler shat himself... It's not cholera, it's not dysentery, but plain and simple shitting oneself. He drank a bit much cognac, **your aspirant to an officer's rank**, and dumped in his pants... He would have apparently dumped in his pants even without your cognac. He gobbled up so many cream rolls, that they had sent him from home... He's a child... At the officer's club, as far as I know, he'd always drink only a quarter. A teetotaler."

Doctor Welfer spat. "He used to buy Linzer slices for himself."

"Then it is nothing serious?" sounded up *Captain* Ságner, "but clearly such a thing... if it were to spread."

Senior Lieutenant Lukáš got up and said to Ságner: "Thanks for such a *squad commander*..."

"I helped him a bit to his feet," said Welfer, whose smile wasn't

---

\* The conversation of *Captain* Ságner with Senior Lieutenant Lukáš was carried on in the Czech language.

leaving him, "mister *Battalion Commander* will provide for further... That is I will turn this here Cadet Biegler over to the hospital... I will issue a certificate, that it is dysentery. A hard case of dysentery. Isolation... Cadet Biegler will end up in the disinfection barrack... — It is decidedly better," continued Welfer with the very same irritating smile, "either a shitted up cadet, or a cadet beset by dysentery..."

*Captain* Ságner turned to his Lukáš using a strictly official tone: "Mister Senior Lieutenant, Cadet Biegler of your company has become ill with dysentery and will remain under care in Budapest..."

*Captain* Ságner had the impression, that Welfer was smiling terribly aggressively, but when he took a look at the 'wartime doctor', he saw, that the same had a terribly disinterested countenance.

"Then everything is alright, *Captain*, Sir," answered calmly Welfer, "The ones aspiring to officer's..." He waved his hand: "With dysentery everybody dumps in his pants."

So it happened, that the valiant Cadet Biegler was hauled away to the military isolation hospital in Uj Buda[83].

His dumped-in-pants got lost in the whirlwind of the world war.

Dreams of Cadet Biegler's great victories were enclosed in one hospital room of the isolation barracks.

When he learned, that he had dysentery, Cadet Biegler was thereby ecstatic.

Was it better to be wounded, or fall ill for the lord Emperor, carrying out one's duty?

Then a little accident happened to him. Because all the places for the ones having come down with dysentery were overcrowded, they carried Cadet Biegler over to the choleric barrack.

Some Hungarian Staff physician, when they had bathed Cadet Biegler and put a thermometer under his arm, shook his head: "98.6 degrees!" With cholera the worst symptom is a considerable drop in temperature. The sick becomes apathetic.

Cadet Biegler really was not showing any signs of upset. He was uncommonly calm, repeating in his mind, that either way he was suffering for the lord Emperor.

The Staff physician ordered them to insert the thermometer into Cadet Biegler's rectum.

"The final stage of cholera," thought to himself the Staff phyian, "a symptom of the end, the utmost weakness, as the sick loses his sense of his surroundings and his consciousness is veiled. He is smiling in pre-mortal convulsions."

Cadet Biegler was during that manipulation indeed smiling in a martyr fashion, acting the hero, when they were shoving the thermometer into his rectum. But he did not make a move.

"The symptoms," thought to himself the Staff physician, "which in cholera lead slowly to death, passive state…"

He then asked a Hungarian ambulance NCO, whether Cadet Biegler vomited and had diarrheal runs in the bathtub.

Having received a negative answer, he fixed his eyes on Biegler. When in cholera cases the diarrheal runs and gagging cease, it is again, as with the previous symptoms, a picture of that, which happens with cholera in the last hours of death.

Cadet Biegler, totally naked, carried out of the warm bathtub onto the bed, felt the cold and chattered his teeth. Also goose bumps popped up all over his body.

"You see," said the Staff physician in Hungarian, "great chattery, the extremities are cold. It is the end."

Leaning over toward Cadet Biegler, he asked him in German: "*So, how's it going?*"

"*V-v-ve-r-r-yy-goo-goo-dd*," chattered up his teeth Cadet Biegler, "*…A-a bl-blank-et —*"

"Consciousness partly veiled, partly retained," said in Hungarian the Staff physician, "the body very skinny, the lips and nails are to be black… This is the third case, when they died on me of cholera without black nails and lips…"

He leaned over Cadet Biegler again and continued in Hungarian: "The second murmur above the heart stopped…"

"*A-a-a bla-bla-bla-blank-et-et*," chattered up Cadet Biegler.

"That, which he's saying, are his last words," said the Staff physician to the ambulance NCO in Hungarian, "tomorrow we'll bury him with Major Koch. Now he'll fall into unconsciousness. The papers about him are at the office?"

"They'll be there," answered calmly the ambulance NCO.

"*A-a-a bla-bla-bla-blank-et-et*," Cadet Biegler was chattering after those who were leaving.

In the whole room there were on sixteen beds five people. One of them was a late deceased. He died two hours ago, was covered with a bed sheet and had the same name as the discoverer of cholera germs. It was *Captain* Koch, of whom the Staff physician mentioned, that he'd have a funeral tomorrow with Cadet Biegler.

Cadet Biegler raised himself up on the bed and saw for the first time, how one dies for the lord Emperor of cholera, because of the four remaining two were dying, they were choking and turning blue, while they were ejaculating something, but it was impossible to say what, and in which language they were speaking, it was rather a rattling of a suppressed voice.

The other two in their conspicuously stormy reaction to healing, were reminiscent of people beset by typhoid delirium. They were screaming unintelligibly and were throwing from under the blanket skinny legs. Standing over them was a bearded ambulance corps soldier, speaking in Styrian dialect (as Cadet Biegler realized), and was calming them down: "I too have already had cholera, my lordships of gold, but I was not kicking into the covers. Now it's alright with you. You'll get leave, when... — Don't toss around so much," he screamed at one, who kicked the blanket so, that it rolled back up over his head, "that's not done here. Be glad that you have a fever, at least they won't be hauling you out of here with a funeral music band. You both have already gotten over it."

He looked around.

"Over there two more died already. We expected that," he said good-naturedly, "be glad that you both have already gotten over it. I have to fetch bed sheets."

He returned in a while. With the bed sheets he covered the deceased with totally black lips, pulled out their hands with black nails, which they were, in the last agony of suffocating, holding on their erected genitals, he was attempting to push their tongues into their mouths and then he kneeled by the beds and let them have it: "*Holy Mary, Mother of God...*" And the old ambulance corps soldier from Styria was at the same time looking at his recuperating patients, whose delirium meant a reaction to a new life.

"*Holy Mary, Mother of God,*" he was repeating, when at that moment some naked man tapped him on the shoulder.

It was Cadet Biegler.

"Listen," he said, "I was... bathing... That is, they were giving me a bath... I nee-d a blanket... I'm cold."

"That's a strange case," a half hour later the very same Staff physician said to Cadet Biegler, who was resting under the blanket, "You are, mister Cadet, a convalescent; tomorrow we'll send you to the reserve hospital in Tarnov[84]. You are a carrier of cholera germs... We have advanced so far, that we know all that. You are from the 91st Regiment..."

"The 13th March Battalion," answered the ambulance NCO in behalf of Cadet Biegler, "the 11th Company of a Hundred."

"Write," said the Staff physician: "Cadet Biegler, 13th March Battalion, 11th March Company of a Hundred, 91st Regiment, for observation to the cholera barracks in Tarnov. Carrier of cholera germs..."

And so that's how Cadet Biegler, ecstatic warrior, became a carrier of cholera germs.

2

## IN BUDAPEST

Matušič brought at the military train station in Budapest to Captain Ságner a telegram from headquarters, which was sent by the hapless brigade commander who had been transported to the sanatorium. It was of the same content, unciphered, as at the last station: "Quickly cook up mess, then get marching to Sokal." Attached to that was: "The transport unit is to muster with the Eastern group. The intelligence group is being abolished. The 13th March Battalion is building a bridge over the river Bug. Details in the newspaper."

Captain Ságner took off immediately to the railroad station command. He was greeted by a small fat officer with a friendly smile.

"He sure was acting up, that brigade general of yours," he said, laughing with a wide grin, "but we had to deliver that idiocy to you, because there hasn't come yet from the Division an order, that his telegrams are not to be delivered to the addressees. Yesterday there rolled through here the 14th March Battalion of the 75th Regiment, and the Battalion Commander had here a telegram, that all the troops be issued six crowns a piece as a special award for Przemyśl[85], and at the same time a directive, that of the six crowns each man put down here at the office two crowns toward the war loan... According to reliable news your Brigade General has paralysis."

"Major, Sir," asked *Captain* Ságner a question of the commander of the military railroad station, "according to the Regimental orders, according to the *march route* we're hauling to Gödöllö[86]. The troops are to get fifteen decagrams of Swiss cheese there. At the last stop the troops were to get fifteen decagrams of Magyar salami. And nothing was gotten."

"Apparently here too the plan will fall through," answered the Major, still pleasantly smiling, "I don't know of any similar order **for regiments from Bohemia**. After all it is not my business, take it up with the Supply Command."

"When are we rolling out, Major, Sir?"

"There's standing ahead of you a train of heavy artillery to Galicia. We'll let it go in an hour, *Captain*, Sir. On the third track there's standing an ambulance train. It is leaving 25 minutes after the artillery. On the twelfth track we have a train with ammunition. It is leaving ten minutes after the ambulance train and twenty minutes after it rolls your train. — If, that is to say, there aren't any changes," he added again with a smile, so that he became totally irritating to *Captain* Ságner.

"Allow me, Major, Sir," asked Ságner, "can you give me an explanation of the statement, that you don't know of any similar order having to do with issuing fifteen decagrams of Swiss **cheese for the regiments from Bohemia**?"

"That is a secret circular," responded to *Captain* Ságner, while constantly smiling, the commander of the military railroad station in Budapest.

"I sure did it to myself," thought to himself *Captain* Ságner, walking out of the building of the Command, "why for all demons did I tell Senior Lieutenant Lukáš, that he round up all the squad commanders and go with them to the supply detachment with the troops for fifteen decagrams of Swiss cheese per person."

Before the Commander of the 11th Company Senior Lieutenant Lukáš in accordance with the order by *Captain* Ságner issued orders having to do with the march of the troops of the Battalion to the storehouse for fifteen decagrams of Swiss cheese for each man, there emerged in front of him Švejk with the hapless Baloun.

Baloun was trembling all over.

"I dutifully report, Senior Lieutenant, Sir," said with customary flexibility Švejk, "the matter, which this is about, is immensely important. I'd like to beg, Senior Lieutenant, Sir, for us to be able regarding the whole matter **to settle it somewhere aside**, as was saying a pal of mine, Špatina from Zhoř, when he was acting as a witness at a wedding and he had to suddenly in the church…"

"So what's going on, Švejk?" interrupted him Senior Lieutenant Lukáš, who had already felt himself missing Švejk a bit, just as Švejk missed Senior Lieutenant Lukáš, "let's go then a bit farther out."

Baloun followed behind them, having not stopped trembling. This giant totally lost his mental balance and was dangling his arms in horrible, hopeless desperation.

"So what's going on, Švejk?" asked Senior Lieutenant Lukáš, when they'd walked to the side.

"I dutifully report, *Senior Lieutenant*, Sir," said Švejk, "that it is always better to admit something earlier, rather than only when it breaks out. You have issued a certain order, *Senior Lieutenant*, Sir, to have Baloun, when we arrive in Budapest, bring that liver paté and braided buns of yours. — Did you get that order or not?" Švejk turned to Baloun.

Baloun started dangling his arms even more, as if he wanted to defend against repeating attacks of an enemy.

"This order," said Švejk, "could not be, to God's grief, *Senior Lieutenant*, Sir, carried out. I have gobbled up that liver paté of yours... — I gobbled it up," said Švejk, nudging the horrified Baloun, "because I thought, that liver paté can go bad. I have read several times in the newspaper, that a whole family got poisoned by liver paté. Once in Na Zderaze, once in Beroun[87], once in Tábor, once in Mladá Boleslav[88], once in Příbram[89]. All succumbed to that poisoning. Liver paté, that's the worst plague..."

Baloun, trembling all over, stood himself to the side and stuck a finger in his throat and vomited in short bursts.

"What's with you, Baloun?"

"I'm h-h-heav-ing, ur-hee *Sen*...urh-ehee *Sen-ior Lieu-ten-ant*, Sir, ur-hee," was calling the hapless Baloun, employing the pauses, "I-I ate-ur-hee, ate-ur-hee-te-te-te, ur-hee, I-ate-ur-hee, it my-ur-hee, self-ur-hee, ur-hee."

Out of the hapless Baloun were coming through his trap even little pieces of aluminum foil wrapping of the liver paté.

"As you can see, *Senior Lieutenant*, Sir," said Švejk, not having lost any of his mental balance, "each such gobbled-up liver paté will come out just as oil to the surface of water. I wanted to take the blame up on myself, and he the stupid idiot gives himself away like this. He is quite a nice man, but he'll gobble up everything, that is put under his care. I knew also one such man. He was a servant in a bank. They could entrust thousands to him; so once he picked up money at another bank and they gave him one thousand crowns over and he returned it immediately on the spot, but send him for fifteen pennies' worth of neck meat, then half of it he'd gobble up on the way. He was so eager when it came to grub, that when the office workers would send him for jitrnice, he was ripping them open on the way with a pocket knife and the holes he was gluing shut with *English patch*[90], which cost him in case of five jitrnice more than one whole jitrnice."

Senior Lieutenant Lukáš gave a sigh and was walking away.

"Would you condescend to have some orders, *Senior Lieutenant*, Sir?" was hollering after him Švejk, while the hapless Baloun kept on sticking a finger into his throat.

Senior Lieutenant Lukáš waved his hand and was walking away to the supply warehouse, in the course of which entered his mind a queer thought, that since the soldiers do gobble up their officers' liver paté, then Austria cannot win.

In the meantime Švejk was leading Baloun to the other side of the military track. At the same time he was consoling him, that together they would go to town to have a look and bring from there for the mister Senior Lieutenant Debrecen sausage, the concept of which as a sausage-making specialty was blending in the case of Švejk's mind with the concept of the capital of the Magyar Kingdom.

"It could happen we'll miss the train," lamented Baloun, who was linking up his insatiable gobbling gluttony also with tremendous stinginess.

"When hauling to the front," pronounced Švejk, "then nothing is ever missed, because each train, which is going to the front, is going to think really hard, before bringing to the destination station only half the *military transport trainful*. After all, I understand you well, Baloun. You have your pocket sewn shut."

They didn't go anywhere though, because there sounded the signal to board the train. The troops of the individual squads were returning from the supply warehouse to their railroad cars again empty-handed. Instead of fifteen decagrams of Swiss cheese, which was supposed to be distributed here, each received a matchbox and one postcard, which was issued by the Committee for War Graves in Austria (Vienna XIX/4, Canisiusgasse[91]). Instead of fifteen decagrams of Swiss cheese everybody had in his hand a west Galician cemetery of soldiers in Siedliska[92] with a memorial to the unlucky Home Army soldiers, made by a shirking sculptor, one-year volunteer Quartermaster Scholz[93].

Over by the Staff railroad car there also reigned uncommon excitement. Officers of the March Battalion gathered round *Captain* Ságner, who was sounding upset telling them something. He had just returned from the railroad station Command and had in his hand a very confidential, actual telegram from the Brigade Staff, of much-too-long content, with the instructions and advice, how to carry on in this new situation, in which Austria found itself on the 23rd day of May, 1915.

The Brigade was telegraphing, that Italy declared war on Austria-Hungary.

Back in Bruck on the Leitha, at the officers' club they often talked during lunches and dinners with mouths full about the queer acting and behaving of Italy, but all in all, nobody expected, that fulfilled would be the prophetic words of that idiot Cadet Biegler, who once at a dinner pushed away a plate of macaroni and proclaimed: "Of these

I'll eat only at the gates of Verona."

*Captain* Ságner having studied through the instruction obtained just then from the Brigade, had them blow the alarm.

When all the troops of the march battalion gathered, they were made to stand in a square formation and *Captain* Ságner read to the troops in an unusually exalted voice the, by the telegraph delivered to him, Brigade-wide order:

"Out of unprecedented treason and greed has the Italian king forgotten his fraternal obligations, to which he was bound by duty as an ally of our Monarchy. Since the outbreak of the war, in which he was to stand by the side of our valiant troops, has the treacherous Italian king played the role of a masked backstabber, behaving duplicitously, maintaining at the same time secret negotiations with our enemies, which treason culminated at night of the $22^{nd}$ to $23^{rd}$ of May by declaring war on our Monarchy. Our Supreme Commander is convinced, that our always valiant and glorious troops will answer the scoundrelly betrayal of the unfaithful enemy with such a blow, that the traitor will come to the realization of how, having started shamefully and treacherously the war, he destroyed himself. In this we hope firmly, that with God's help soon the day will dawn, when the Italian plains will again behold the victor of Santa Lucia, Vicenza[94], Novara[95], Custozza. We want to win, we have to win, and certainly will win!"

Then there was the usual "*Three cheers!*" and the troops took their seats on the train again, somewhat stunned. Instead of fifteen decagrams of Swiss cheese, they have hanging around their necks a war with Italy.

\*

In the railroad car, where Švejk was sitting with Accounting Master Sergeant Vaněk, telephone operator Chodounský, Baloun and the cook Jurajda, there started being woven an interesting conversation about the intervention of Italy in the war.

"In Táborská Street in Prague there was also such a case," started Švejk. "There was some merchant Hořejší, a bit of a way down from him on the other side had his store the merchant Pošmourný and between the two of them was the grocer Havlasa. So the merchant Hořejší once got this idea, to like join up with the grocer Havlasa against the merchant Pošmourný, and he started negotiating with him over whether they could combine the two shops under the single firm 'Hořejší and Havlasa'. But the grocer Havlasa went immediately to the merchant Pošmourný and is telling him, that Hořejší is giving him twelve hundred for that grocery shop of his and that he wants him to go into a *business pact* with him. But if he, Pošmourný, gives him eighteen hundred-crown bills, then he would rather make a *business pact* with him against Hořejší. So they made a deal, and that Havlasa guy for some time kept hanging around this Hořejší, whom he betrayed, and kept acting, as if he were his best friend, and when the talk came around to, when they would, like, put it together, he would say: Yea, that'll be already soon. I'm only waiting, until the renters come back from their summer apartments.' And when the renters did arrive, then it was really a done deal, as he kept promising to this Hořejší guy, that it would be put together. And he, when he had gone to open the shop one morning, he saw a big sign over the shop of his competitor, a huge marquee 'Pošmourný and Havlasa'."

"In our parts," remarked the stupid Baloun, "there also was once such a case: I wanted to buy in the next village a heifer, I had a deal made on her and the Votice butcher snatched her away on me right under my nose."

"Since already once again we have a new war," continued Švejk, "since we have one extra enemy, since we have again a new front, then one will have to conserve ammunition. 'The more children there are in the family, that many more switches are used up,' used to say grandpa Chovanec in Motol, who used to mete out switch-whippings to the kids for the parents in the neighborhood for a flat fee."

"I'm only afraid," said Baloun shaking all over, "that on account of that Italy there will be smaller portions."

Accounting Master Sergeant Vaněk pondered for a moment and said seriously: "All that could be, because now that victory of ours is going to somewhat drag out."

"Now we'd need a new Radetzky," threw in Švejk, "he was already familiar with the landscape over there, he already knew where the weakness of the Italians was and what was to be taken by storm and from which side. It is not so easy to crawl in somewhere. Anybody can do that, but to get out of there, that is a genuine military skill. When a human has already crawled in somewhere, then he must know about everything, that is going on around him, so that he would not find himself facing some *sticky situation*, which is called a catastrophe. Well, in our building once, when we were still in the old apartment, they caught a thief in the attic, and he, the guy, happened to notice, when he crawled in there, that the bricklayers were just then repairing the light shaft, so he yanked himself free of them, felled the female custodian and slid down the scaffolding into the light shaft and from there he couldn't get out at all. But our daddy Radetzky knew of each road, they could not get him anywhere. In one book about the General it was all described in there, how he fled from Santa Lucia and the Italians fled too, and how only the next day he discovered, that he had actually won it, since he didn't find the Italians there and didn't see them with the binoculars, so he returned and occupied the abandoned Santa Lucia. Since that time he was appointed and called marshal."

"As far as Italy, that's a nice land," threw in the cook Jurajda, "I was once in Venice[96] and I know, that an Italian will call everybody a pig. When he gets angry, everybody is for him porco maladetto. Even the pope is for him porco, even 'madonna mia e porco', 'papa e porco'."

Accounting Master Sergeant Vaněk on the other hand expressed himself very sympathetically about Italy. He runs in Kralupy as a part of his drugstore a production line of lemon juice, which he makes from rotten lemons, and the cheapest and the most rotten lemons he always used to buy from Italy. Now it'll be the end of the transportation of lemons from Italy to Kralupy. There's no doubt, that the war with Italy will bring various surprises, because Austria will want to have revenge.

"It's easy to say," gave a smile Švejk, "to have revenge. Someone thinks, that he'll have revenge, and in the end the one who gets it, is the one whom such a man had chosen as an instrument of his revenge. When I lived years ago in Vinohrady, then there lived on the ground floor a custodian and in his apartment there was subletting this petty official from some bank, and he used to go to a taproom on Krameriova street[97] and he once got into a squabble there with a gentleman, who had some sort of institute in Vinohrady for analyzing urine. That gentleman thought of altogether nothing else and also talked of nothing else and used to carry nothing but little bottles filled with urine, shoving the stuff under everybody's nose, to relieve themselves of urine too and have his urine examined, because on such an examination depended the happiness of a human, of the family and it was also cheap, it cost six crowns. All who used to go to the taproom, even the pubkeeper and his wife, had their urine analyzed, only the petty banking official was still holding out, although the gentleman kept crawling after him into the bathroom, as he was leaving, and would always tell him with concern: 'I don't know, mister

Skorkovský, to me that urine of yours somehow doesn't look good, relieve yourself of some urine into this little bottle, before it's too late!' At last he talked him into changing his mind. It cost the petty official six crowns and that gentleman sweetened up the analysis for him properly, as he had already done so for all those in the taproom, not excluding even the pubkeeper, whose business he was spoiling, because such an analysis would always be accompanied by the talk, that it was a very serious case, that all mustn't drink anything besides water, that he mustn't smoke, that he mustn't marry, and that he was to eat nothing but vegetables. So that petty official was like all of them terribly angry with him and chose the building custodian for the instrument of his revenge, because he knew the custodian to be a brute. So one time he's telling the gentleman, who used to do the urine analysis, that the custodian had already not been feeling healthy for some time and that he begs him to come to him tomorrow morning toward the seventh hour for the urine, that he'd let it be examined. And he went there. The custodian was still sleeping, when that gentleman woke him up and was telling him in a friendly manner: 'My respects, Mr. Málek, I'm wishing you good daybreak. Here, if you please, is a little bottle, condescend to relieve yourself of some urine and I'll get six crowns.' But you should have seen the calamity God permitted, as the custodian in his drawers jumped out of the bed, how he grabbed that gentleman by the neck, how he slammed him against a wardrobe, until he stuffed him into it! When he pulled him out of the wardrobe, he grabbed a blackjack and already was chasing him in his drawers down Čelakovského street[98], and he was squealing, like when you step on a dog's tail, and on Havlíčkova boulevard he jumped into a streetcar, and the custodian got caught by a patrolman, brawled with him, and because the custodian was in his drawers and everything of his was coming out and showing, then on account of such an outrage that they threw him into a košatinka and hauled him to the police station, and he, still in the košatinka, was screaming from it like a wounded hoofed animal: 'You henchmen, I'll show you what you get analyzing my urine.' He sat doing time for six months for public violence and for insulting a patrolman, and still after the verdict was announced he committed an insult to the Ruling House, so he's perhaps still sitting today, and that's why I say, wanting to have revenge on somebody, that means some innocent human gets it."

Baloun in the meantime was with great effort thinking something over, until in the end he fearfully asked Vaněk: "I beg you, Accounting

Master Sergeant, Sir, you then think, that on account of the war with Italy we'll be getting issued smaller rations?"

"That's as clear as the light of the day," answered Vaněk.

"Jesusmaria," cried out Baloun, lowered his head into his hands and was sitting quietly in a little corner.

With that definitely ended in this railroad car the debate about Italy.

\*

In the Staff railroad car the conversation about the new wartime situation created by Italy having intervened in the war would have been certainly very mundane, since there wasn't present anymore the famous military theoretician Cadet Biegler, if there weren't sort of standing in for him Lieutenant Dub of the Third *Company*.

Lieutenant Dub was in his civilian life a professor of Czech and was already at that time exhibiting an unusual tendency everywhere, just wherever it was possible, to express his loyalty. In writing assignments he would present to his pupils subject themes from the history of the Habsburg[99] dynasty. Scaring the pupils in the lower grades were Emperor Maximilian[100], who climbed atop a rock and could not get down, Josef II[101] as a tiller, and Ferdinand the Benign[102]. In the higher grades were the subject themes of course more concocted, as for example the assignment for the twelfth-graders: "Emperor Franz Josef I, supporter of sciences and art", which working assignment resulted in the case of one twelfth-grader in his being expelled from all the high schools of the Austro-Hungarian Empire, because he had written, that the most beautiful act of this monarch was the erecting of the Franz Josef I. bridge[103] in Prague."

He always very much saw to it, that on the occasion of the Imperial Birthday and other similar Imperial celebrations all his pupils would sing with enthusiasm the Austrian anthem. In social settings he was disliked, because it was certainly known about him, that he was also an informer among his colleagues. In the town, where he taught, he was one of the members of the trio of the biggest idiots and mules, which consisted of him, the District Administrator, and the Principal of the Gymnasium. In this narrow circle he had learnt to talk politics within the framework of the Austro-Hungarian monarchy. Even now he started unloading his harebrained ideas with the voice and diction of a calcified professor:

"All in all I was absolutely not surprised by the intervention of Italy. I was expecting it already three months ago. It is certain, that

Italy's vain pride had grown significantly lately, as a consequence of the victorious war with Turkey over Tripoli[104]. Besides that it is counting too much on its navy and also on the mood of the population in our seaside lands and in southern Tyrol[105]. Back before the war I was talking about it with our District Administrator, warning for our government not to underestimate the irredentist[106] movement in the south. He also totally agreed with me, because every human with foresight, who cares about the preservation of this Empire, had already long ago have to assume, where we would end up being excessively lenient toward such elements. I remember well, that about two years ago I declared in a conversation with mister District Administrator, that Italy, this was during the time of the Balkan war on the occasion of the affair of our consul Prochaska, was waiting for the earliest opportunity to fall upon us insidiously. — And now we have it!" he yelled in such a voice, as though they all were arguing with him, although all the present active duty officers were during his speech wishing for that civilian motor mouth to crawl up their backsides.

"It is true," he continued in an already milder tone, "that in most cases even in school assignments used to be overlooked our former relation to Italy, those great days of glorious victorious armies both in the year one-thousand-eight-hundred-forty-eight, and in the year one-thousand-sixty-six, of which nowadays speak the Brigade-wide orders of the day. But I have always done my duty and before the school-year end, at just about the beginning of the war, I gave my pupils a composition assignment: *'Our Heroes in Italy from Vicenza up to Custozza, or...*"

And the little idiot Lieutenant Dub ceremonially added: "..., *Blood and life for the Habsburg*[107]*! For one Austria, whole, united, great!'*"...

— — — — —

He fell silent and was waiting apparently and expecting, that the others in the Staff railroad car also would talk about the newly created situation and that he would prove to them at some time, that he had already known five years ago, how one day Italy would act toward its ally. He ended up being totally disappointed, because Captain Ságner, for whom *Battalion Messenger* Matušič brought from the railroad station the evening edition of the Pester Lloyd, said, while looking in the newspaper: 'So there you see, this Weiner[108] woman, whom we saw in Bruck in a guest appearance, performed here yesterday on the stage of the Small Theater."

Thereby was concluded in the Staff railroad car the debate about Italy.

*

Except for those, who were sitting in the back, Battalion *Messenger* Matušič and Captain Ságner's servant Batzer were looking at the war with Italy from a strictly practical point of view, because once, long years ago, while still on active duty, they both participated in some maneuvers in southern Tyrol.

"We'll be having a hard time dragging ourselves up the hills," said Batzer, "Captain Ságner has a pile of those suitcases. I am from the mountains, you know, but it is something altogether different, when a man puts a rifle under his coat and goes to stake out some hare on the estate of Duke Schwarzenberg."

"That is if they throw us down there against Italy. That wouldn't be striking a chord with me either, to be flying up and down the hills and icecaps with orders. Then the grub down there, nothing but polenta and oil," sadly said Matušič.

"And why wouldn't they stick us of all people into those mountains," was working himself up Batzer, "Our Regiment has already been to Serbia, the Carpathians, I have already been dragging mister *Captain's* suitcases up and down the mountains, twice already I've lost them; once in Serbia, the second time in the Carpathians, in a sort of trouble, and it may be, that it's awaiting me for the third time at the Italian border, — and as for the grub down there..." He spat. He sat himself confidentially closer to Matušič: "You know, back home in Kašperské Hory we make these tiny kind of dumplings from raw potato dough, they get boiled, then coated in egg, they get sprinkled nicely with braided bun bread crumbs and then they are fried with bacon." The last word he proclaimed with a sort of mysteriously solemn voice.

"And they're the best with sauerkraut," he added in a melancholic manner, "so the macaroni must go into the shitcan."

Thereby even here ended a conversation about Italy...

———

In the rest of the railroad cars, because the train had been standing already for more than two hours at the railroad station, only one word was making the rounds, that they'd probably turn the train around and send it on against Italy.

That would be indicated also by the fact, that so far there had been happening with the military transport train strange things. Once again all the troops were chased out of the railroad cars, there came the sanitation inspection detail with the disinfection corps and sprinkled thoroughly the insides of all the railroad cars with Lysol, which was received, especially in the railroad cars, in which they carried supplies of the commissary ration bread, with great displeasure.

An order is however an order, the sanitation commission issued an order to disinfect all the railroad cars of the *military transport train* 728, and that is why absolutely calmly they sprayed the piles of commissary ration bread and bags of rice with Lysol. At this point it was apparent after all, that something special was happening.

Then again they chased the whole lot into the railroad cars and a half an hour later again they chased the whole lot out, because there came to have a good look at the military transport train some frail old little general, so that Švejk was immediately struck with an altogether natural label for the old man. Standing in the back of the line he remarked toward the Accountant Quarter Master: "He is a little croaking stiff."

And the old general kept on strolling along the line, being accompanied by *Captain* Ságner, and he stopped in front of a young soldier, in order to sort of elate all the troops, and asked him, where he was from, how old he was and did he have a watch. It's true the soldier had one, but because he thought, that he'd get from the old gentleman another one, he said, that he had none, to which the frail old croaking stiff of a general, with such a touch-of-a-numskull smile like the Emperor Franz Josef used to do, when addressing the mayors somewhere in their towns, said: "That is good, that is good," after which he bestowed the honor of being addressed on the corporal standing next to him, whom he asked, whether his wife was in good health.

"I dutifully report," screamed the Sergeant, "that I am not married," to which the General said again with his condescending smile his customary: "That is good, that is good."

Then the General in his elderly infantility requested of *Captain* Ságner, that he demonstrate for him, how the soldiers count themselves out into a double file, and in a little while there was already the sound of: "One – two, one – two, one – two."

That did the little croaking stiff of a general like very much. He even had at home two *military servants*, whom he'd have stand in front of him at the house, and they had to count by themselves: "One – two, one – two…"

Of such generals had Austria a heap.

When the parade review was then happily over with, at which time the General was not miserly with praise in front of *Captain* Ságner, the troops were allowed to move within the perimeter of the railroad station, because there arrived the news, that they would be going only in three hours. The troops were then strolling around and gawking things over, and because there usually is at railroad stations plenty of audience, here and there after all a soldier managed to bum a cigarette.

One could see, that somehow the initial enthusiasm, expressing itself in the glorious welcoming of *military transport trains* at the railroad stations, had already deeply declined and fell all the way to begging.

Coming to see *Captain* Ságner arrived a deputation of the Association for Welcoming Heroes, consisting of two terribly worn out dames, who turned over a gift belonging to the *military transport train*, that is twenty little boxes of aromatic oral pastilles, those being advertisements of a Pest candy factory. The boxes of the aromatic oral pastilles were nicely executed of sheet metal, on the lid there was painted a *Magyar Hungarian Land Defense soldier*, who was squeezing the hand of an *Austrian Home Defense soldier,* and above them was the radiant crown of Saint Stephen. Encircling them was a German and Hungarian inscription: "*For Emperor, God and Homeland.*"

The candy factory was so loyal, that it gave precedence to the Emperor before the Lord God.

Each little box contained eighty pastilles, so that altogether roughly five pastilles came out to three men. Besides that did the careworn, burnt-out dames bring a large package of printed copies of two prayers composed by the Budapest archbishop Géza of Szatmár[109]-Budafal[110]. They were in German and Hungarian and contained the most frightful curses for all enemies. Written were these little prayers so passionately, that the only thing missing at the end was the snappy Hungarian "Bazsom a Krisztusmárját!"

According to the honorable archbishop should the benevolent God chop up the Russians, Englishmen, Serbians, Frenchmen, Japanese to noodles and paprika goulash. The benevolent God was to bathe in the blood of enemies and kill them all off, as did that brute Herod with the little ones.

The reverend archbishop of Budapest used in his little prayers for example these nice sentences: "God bless your bayonets, so that deep would they penetrate into the belly of your enemies. Let the supremely just Lord direct the artillery fire over the heads of the enemy Staff Headquarters. May the merciful God make it so, that all enemies choke on their own blood, from the wounds, with which you will cover them!"

That's why it's necessary one more time to repeat, that these little prayers were in the end missing nothing else than the "Baszom a Krisztusmárját!"

When both of the dames turned all of it over, they expressed to *Captain* Ságner a desperate wish, asking whether they couldn't be present during the distribution of the gifts. One even had such nerve as to mention, that on that occasion she could say a few words to the troops, whom she did not call anything but *"our brave field grays"*.

Both were putting on terribly insulted faces, when *Captain* Ságner rejected their request. For the time being were these charitable gifts on a journey to the railroad car, where the supplies were stored. The honorable dames passed through a file of soldiers and one of them did not forget on that occasion to pat one unshaven soldier on the cheek. He was some guy Šimek from Budějovice, who knowing nothing about the exalted mission of those dames, threw out a remark to his comrades after the departure of the dames: "But aren't the whores here cheeky. If a monkey like that at least looked presentable to the world, but the thing is like a stork, a man sees nothing at all but those dumb long legs and the thing looks like the torture death of the Lord God, and yet such an old rasp still wants to be starting something with soldiers."

At the railroad station it was very lively. The event with the Italians has caused here a certain panic, because there were intercepted two *military transport trains* with artillery and sent to Styria. There was here also a *military transport train* of Bosnians, which had been waiting here already two days due to some unknown causes and it was totally forgotten and lost. The Bosnians had for two days already not been issued any rations and were going begging for bread up and down New Pest[111]. Also nothing else was being heard but the upset talk of the lost Bosnians, animatedly gesticulating, who were ejaculating constantly out of their mouths: *"I fuck your god—I fuck your soul, I fuck your mother."*

Then was the March Battalion of the ninety-firsters again rounded up and boarded, taking their places in their railroad cars. In a little while, however, the Battalion *Messenger* Matušič returned from the railroad station Command Headquarters with the news, that they'd be going only after three hours. Therefore the once again gathered troops were released from the railroad cars. Just before the departure of the train there entered the Staff railroad car a very upset Lieutenant Dub and was requesting of *Captain* Ságner, that he have without delay Švejk locked up. Lieutenant Dub, the long since well-known informer at his place of operation as a Gymnasium professor, enjoyed getting into conversation with the soldiers, whereby he was searching for their convictions, and at the same time, so that he could teach them a lesson and explain, why they were fighting, what they were fighting for.

During his rounds he saw in the back, behind the railroad station building, Švejk standing by a lantern, looking with interest over a poster of some charitable military lottery. That poster was depicting, how an Austrian soldier was pinning a bug-eyed bearded Cossack to a wall.

Lieutenant Dub tapped Švejk on the shoulder and asked, how he liked it.

"I dutifully report, Lieutenant, Sir," answered Švejk, "that it is idiocy. I have already seen many stupid posters, but such bullshit I haven't seen yet."

"What about it you don't like?" asked Lieutenant Dub.

"The thing, *Lieutenant*, Sir, about the poster I don't like is how that soldier handles weapons entrusted to him, why, he might even break that bayonet against the wall, and besides it is altogether pointless, he would be punished for it, because that Russian has his hands up and is surrendering. He is a prisoner of war, and prisoners of war have to be treated decently, because disputing it is in vain, they are people too."

Lieutenant Dub then kept on searching for Švejk's views and asked him: "You then feel sorry for that Russian, isn't that so?"

"I feel sorry, *Lieutenant*, Sir, for both, the Russian on one hand, because he's pierced through, and the soldier on the other hand, because he'd be locked up for it. Look, *Lieutenant*, Sir, he must have broken the bayonet doing it, disputing it is in vain, it sure looks like a stone wall, where he's ramming it into, and steel is brittle. This one time, let me tell you, *Lieutenant*, Sir, still before the war, on active duty, we had this one mister *Lieutenant* in the *Company*. Even an old souper couldn't so express himself as that mister *Lieutenant* did. On the training ground he used to tell us: 'When there is *attention*, then you must be bugging your eyes out, like when a tomcat is shitting into chopped straw.' But otherwise he was a very nice man. Once on Baby Jesus' birthday he'd gone crazy, bought for the *Company* a whole wagon of coconuts, and since that time I've known, how brittle bayonets are. Half the *Company* broke their bayonets over the nuts and our *Lieutenant Colonel* had the whole *Company* locked up, for three months we were not allowed out of the barracks, mister *lieutenant* was under house arrest…"

Lieutenant Dub directed an angry look into the carefree face of the good soldier Švejk and asked him maliciously:

"Do you know me?"

"I do know you, *Lieutenant*, Sir."

Lieutenant Dub rolled his eyes and quickly stomped several times: "I'm telling you, that you don't know me yet."

Švejk replied again with that carefree calm, as if giving a report: "I do know you, *Lieutenant*, Sir, you are, I dutifully report, from our *March Battalion*."

"You don't know me yet," was screaming once again Lieutenant Dub, "you might know me from the good side, but once you get to know me from the bad side. I am mean, don't think to yourself otherwise, I'll drive everyone to tears. So do you know me or you don't know me?"

"I do, *Lieutenant*, Sir."

"I'm for the last time telling you, that you don't know me, you ass, Mister. Do you have any brothers?"

"I dutifully report, *Lieutenant*, Sir, that I have one."

Lieutenant Dub got jolted with anger at the sight of Švejk's calm, carefree face, and not being in control of himself anymore, he cried out: "Then he too, that brother of yours, must be as dumb a beast as you are. What was he by trade?"

"A professor, *Lieutenant*, Sir. He too was in the military and passed the officer exam."

Lieutenant Dub looked at Švejk, as if he wanted to pierce him through. Švejk withstood with dignified balance the mean look of Lieutenant Dub, so that for the time being the whole discourse between him and the Lieutenant ended with the words '*Fall out!*"

Each went his own way and each thought his own thoughts.

What Lieutenant Dub thought of Švejk was, that he'd tell mister *Captain*, to have him locked up, and Švejk in his turn thought to himself, that he'd already seen a lot of stupid officers, but such, as is Lieutenant Dub, was after all at the Regiment a rarity.

Lieutenant Dub, who especially today put in his head, that he had to be raising up soldiers, found for himself beyond the railroad station a new victim. They were two soldiers of the Regiment, but from another company, who were negotiating in the dark in broken German with two street-walking tramps, of whom there were hanging whole dozens around the railroad station.

Increasing the distance Švejk still heard absolutely clearly the sharp voice of Lieutenant Dub: "Do you know me?!... But I am telling you, that you don't know me!... But once you get to know me!... You might know me from the good side!... I am telling you, once you get to know me from the bad side!... I'll drive you all the way to tears, you asses!... Do you have any brothers?... Then they too must be such dumb beasts, as you are!... What were they by trade?... With the *supply train*?... Well, alright... Remember, that you are soldiers... Are you Czechs?... Do you know, that Palacký[112] said, that if there weren't Austria, we'd have to create it... *Fall out...*!"

The rounds of Lieutenant Dub did not have however on the whole any positive result. He stopped about three more groups of soldiers and his educating effort "to drive all the way to tears" totally shipwrecked. The material, which was being hauled into the field, was such, that from the eyes of each individual was Lieutenant Dub getting a feeling, that everyone thought of him something certainly very unpleasant. He was offended in his pride and the result of it was, that before the departure of the train he was requesting in the Staff railroad car of *Captain* Ságner, that Švejk be locked up. While doing it, justifying the necessity of isolating the good soldier Švejk, he was talking about the most curious, insolent behavior, while he characterized the sincere answers of Švejk's to his own last question as snide remarks. If it were to go on like this, the officer corps would be losing all respect in the eyes of the rank-and-file, of which certainly none of the gentlemen officers have any doubts. He himself, back before the war, spoke about it with mister District Administrator, that every superior must take care to preserve a certain authority toward his subordinates. Mister District Administrator was also of the same opinion. Especially now in the army service, the closer one is getting toward the enemy, it is necessary to maintain a sort of terror hanging over the soldiers. That is why then he was requesting that Švejk be subjected to disciplinary punishment.

*Captain* Ságner, who as an active duty officer hated all those reserve officers from various sectors of civilian life, alerted Lieutenant

Dub, that such denouncements can only be taking place in the form of a report, and not in such a strange shopkeeper manner, like when haggling over the price of potatoes. As pertains to Švejk himself, the first official authority, under whose jurisdiction Švejk falls, he says, is mister Senior Lieutenant Lukáš. That such a thing is done strictly by the report. That from the *Company* such a thing goes to the Battalion and that perhaps mister Lieutenant is aware of that. If Švejk did anything wrong, then he'll come to face the *Company Report*, and if he appeals, the *Battalion Report*. Should however mister Senior Lieutenant Lukáš desire and should he consider the telling of mister Lieutenant Dub to be an official report for the purpose of punishment, that then he'd have nothing against Švejk to be brought and interrogated.

Senior Lieutenant Lukáš raised no objections against it, only remarked, that from Švejk telling him he himself knew very well, that Švejk's brother was really a professor and a reserve officer.

Lieutenant Dub wavered and said, that he was requesting punishment only in the wider sense and that it may be, that the said Švejk isn't able to express himself, and so his answers effect the impression of impudence, biting sarcasm and disrespect toward superiors. Aside from that, that from the whole appearance of the said Švejk it was apparent, that he was of a feeble mind.

Thereby in fact passed the whole storm over the head of Švejk, and the thunder didn't even strike.

In the railroad car, where the office and the storehouse of the Battalion were, the Accounting Master Sergeant of the March Battalion Bautanzel very condescendingly distributed to the two scribes of the Battalion each a handful of the oral pastilles from those boxes, which were to be distributed among the men of the Battalion. It was a customary phenomenon, that everything, which was intended for the rank-and-file, had to be subjected to the same handling in the Battalion Office as the hapless pastilles.

It was everywhere something so customary in the war, that when it was found out somewhere during an inspection, that no stealing was going on, each of those Accounting Master Sergeants in every conceivable office was still under the suspicion, that he's been exceeding the budget and is engaged again in other shady activities, so that it all clicks.

That is why here, when all were stuffing themselves with these pastilles, so that they would at least enjoy this swine filth, since there was after all nothing else that could be ripped off from the rank-and-file, Bautanzel spoke up about the sad conditions on this trip: "I have gone through two march battalions already, but such a miserable journey as now we did not have. Lordy, by the time we arrived back then at Prešov[113], we had piles of everything a man could think of. I had stashed away ten thousand Memphis cigarettes, two wheels of Swiss cheese, three hundred food cans, and then, when the drive onto Bardejov[114] into the trenches was already under way, Russians from around Muszyna[115] cut off the communications to Prešov, then were being made nice little deals. I turned over from it all just for show the tenth part to the Battalion, that I had, like, saved it, and I sold off the rest at the *supply train*. We had there with us Major Sojka, and he was a pretty big swine. He, truth be told, was no hero and most liked loafing around among us at the *supply train*, because up above were whistling rounds and crackling shrapnel. And he always came to us under the pretext, that he had to check, whether the troops of the Battalion were being cooked for properly. Usually he'd come down to us, when the news had arrived, that the Russians were again getting something ready; he was trembling all over, had to, at the kitchen, drink up some rum and only then he was conducting the inspection in all the field kitchens, that were all around the *supply train*, because to go up to the battle positions was impossible and rations were being brought up there at night. We were in such a situation back then, that of some officers' rations there could not even be any talk. One road, which was still open to the rear, had been taken over for themselves by Germans from the Reich, who were intercepting everything of the better sort, which was being sent to us from the rear, and they gobbled it up themselves, so none came our way; all of us at the *supply train* were left without any officers' rations. During all that time I didn't manage to save anything for us at the office but one piglet, which we had smoked, and so that this Major Sojka wouldn't find out about it, we had it stashed away an hour's journey away at the artillery, where I had an acquaintance *Master Gunnery Sergeant*. So this Major, when he'd come our way, always started in the kitchen tasting the soup. True, there wasn't much meat we could be cooking, only what pigs or skinny cows could be chased down in the vicinity. And on top of it the Prussians were a big competition for us and they were paying out twice as much during requisitions for the cattle. During all that time, when we were encamped at Bardejov, while buying cattle I had not saved for myself any more than a little over twelve hundred crowns, even though we would mostly instead of money be giving them vouchers with the stamp of the Battalion, especially of late, when we knew that the Russians east of us were in Radvaň[116] and to the west in Podolín[117]. The worst is trying to work with such a people, as found there, who can't read or write and for a signature uses only three little crosses, of which our Quartermasters knew well, so that when we would send for money to the Quartermaster Administration, I couldn't include forged receipts in the addendum, showing that I paid out money to them; that can be done only where a people is more educated and knows to write its signature. And then, as I've been already saying, the Prussians were outdoing us by paying more and they were paying cash, and when we'd come somewhere, they regarded us then as robbers, and on top of it the Quartermaster Administration issued an order, that receipts signed with little crosses were being turned over to the Field Accounting Audit Command. And the place was swarming with these guys. There came such a guy, gorged himself at our place and drank, and the next day he went to turn us in. This Major Sojka kept going making rounds of those kitchens, upon my soul, believe me, he pulled out once from the cauldron the meat for the whole fourth company gang. He started with the porker's head, of which he said, that it wasn't done cooking, so he had them cook it still a while; true, back then there wasn't much meat cooked, for the whole *Company* there came about twelve old, honest portions of meat, but he ate it all, then tasted the soup and raised a thunderous racket, that it's like water, what sort of order was this, meaty soup without meat, so he had it browned and threw into it my last macaroni, which I had saved over all that time. But I didn't regret that as much as that for the browning were blown two kilos of tea-time butter, which I had scrimped and saved back at the time, when there was still officers' mess. I had it on a sort of a *simple shelf* over the bunk, and he ripped into me, hollering, who that supposedly belonged to. So I told him, that according to the budget for feeding the soldiers, by the latest Division order, there comes to an individual soldier for the betterment of his lot fifteen grams of butter or twenty-one grams of lard, and because that's not enough, all supplies of butter remain suspended so long, until the condition of the rank-and-file could be improved by butter at full weight. Major Sojka got very angry, started screaming, that perhaps I was apparently waiting, until the Russians came and took away the last two kilos of our butter, that right away it had to go into the soup, since the soup was meatless. That's how I came to lose the whole supply, and believe me, that this Major used to bring me, as soon as he showed up, nothing but bad luck as thick as sap. He had his sense of smell almost so developed, that he immediately knew all I had in stock. Once I saved beef liver by scrimping on the men and we wanted to stew it for ourselves, when just then he went under the bunk and pulled it out. I told him responding to his screaming, that the liver was earmarked to be buried, that in forenoon a blacksmith from the artillery, who had taken a veterinary course, determined that. The Major grabbed a warm body from the *supply train* and then he and the guy were cooking the liver for themselves up there under the rocks in kettles, and that was also his fate, that the Russians saw the fire, slammed into the Major, into the kettle, with an eighteen caliber round. Afterward we went there to take a look, and one couldn't tell, whether on the rocks was scattered the liver of beef or the liver of mister Major."

*

Then the news arrived, that we'd be hauling out still only after four hours. The track up above to Hatvan[118], they said, was blocked by trains with the wounded. Also being spread around the railroad station was, that at Jágr there collided an ambulance train transporting the sick and wounded with a train carrying artillery. That from Pest assistance trains were rolling in there.

After a while was at work already the imagination of the whole Battalion. The talk was of 200 dead and wounded, of the fact, that the collision happened intentionally, so that the scams in supplying the sick would not be found out.

That sparked sharp criticism of the insufficient supplying of the Battalion and of the thieves at the office and the storehouse.

The majority was of the opinion, that the Accounting Master Sergeant of the Battalion, Bautanzel, was splitting everything in half with the officers.

In the Staff railroad car *Captain* Ságner announced, that according to the *march route* they were to be already in fact at the Galician border. That in Jágr they were to have been already issued bread and food cans for the troops for three days. That to Jágr they still had ten hours of riding. That in Jágr there were really so many trains with the wounded from the offensive on the other side of Lwów, that according to the telegram there wasn't in Jágr either a loaf of commissary ration bread or a single food can. He received an order to pay out in place of bread and food cans 6 crowns and 72 pennies per man, which was to be paid out at distribution of the military pay in nine days, if, that is to say, he gets by that time the money from the Brigade. In the cashbox there was only something over twelve-thousand crowns.

"Now that's a swine filth deed by the Regiment," said Senior Lieutenant Lukáš, "to let us loose so miserably into the world."

There arose mutual whispering between *Ensign* Wolf and Senior Lieutenant Kolář, that Colonel Schröder had over the last three weeks sent to his account at a Viennese bank sixteen-thousand crowns.

Senior Lieutenant Kolář was then telling, how saving was done. One steals at the Regiment Headquarters Office six thousand crowns and shoves them into one's own pocket and with consistent logic an order is issued to all the kitchens, that daily in the kitchen three grams of peas per man are to be deducted from the rations.

In a month that comes up to ninety grams per man, and in a kitchen at each *company* there has to be at minimum saved the stock of 16 kilograms of peas and the cook must account for that and show it.

Senior Lieutenant Kolář was chatting with Wolf only in a general vein about certain cases which he had noticed.

It was however certain, that with such cases was filled to overflowing the whole military administration. It started with the Accounting Master Sergeant at some hapless *company* and it ended with a hamster with general's epaulets, who was stockpiling for himself for the postwar winter.

The war demanded valor even in theft.

The *army supply administrators* were looking with a gaze full of love at one another, as if they wanted to say: We are one body and one soul, we steal, buddy, we scam, brother, but you can't help yourself, to swim against the stream is hard. If you don't take, then another will take and to boot he'll say about you, that the reason you're not stealing anymore is, because you have already raked for yourself enough.

Into the railroad car stepped a gentleman with red and golden trouser stripes. It was again one of the generals taking rides along all the tracks on an inspection.

"Sit down, gentlemen," he motioned kindly, being glad, that he surprised again some *military transport train*, of which he didn't know, that it would be standing there.

When *Captain* Ságner wanted to give him the report, he only waved his hand: "Your *military transport train* is not in order. Your *military transport train* isn't asleep. Your *military transport train* is supposed to be already sleeping. In the *military transport trains* they are to be sleeping, when they are standing at a railroad station, like at the garrison — at nine o'clock."

He spoke choppily: "Before the ninth hour are the troops led to the latrines behind the railroad station — and then everyone goes to sleep. Otherwise the troops will during the night soil the track. Do you understand, mister *Captain*? Repeat it to me. Or don't repeat it to me but do for me, as I wish. Trumpet the alarm, drive it to the latrines, trumpet *taps* and off to sleep, checking who isn't sleeping. Punish infractions! Yes! Is that all? The supper to be issued at six o'clock."

He was talking now about something in the past, about that, which did not happen, which was somehow around some other corner. He was standing here like an apparition from a realm of the fourth dimension.

"The supper to be issued at six o'clock," he continued, looking at the watch, which was showing ten minutes past the eleventh hour of the night. "*At half past eight, alarm, latrine shitting, then off to sleep.* For supper here at six o'clock goulash with potatoes instead of fifteen decagrams of Swiss cheese."

Then there followed the order to show battle readiness. Once again had them then *Captain* Ságner trumpet the alarm and the inspecting General, watching the Battalion falling into formation, was strolling with the officers and was constantly talking to them, as if they were some idiots and couldn't get it right away, while at the same time he was pointing to the hands of the watch: "*So, look. At half past eight shit and half an hour later sleep. That is perfectly sufficient.* During this transitional time, the troops have runny stools anyhow. Above all I put stress on sleep. That is a boost for further marches. As long as the men are on the train, they have to have a rest. If there is not enough room in the railroad cars, the men sleep in shifts. One third of the men in the railroad car will lie down comfortably and sleep from nine to midnight, and the rest are standing and watching them. Then the first ones having slept make room for the second third, which sleeps from midnight until the third hour of the morning. The third shift sleeps from three until six, then there's reveille and the men are washing themselves. No-jump-ing-off while the train is moving! Place patrols in front of the *military transport train*, so that the troops are not-jumping-off during the ride! When the enemy breaks a soldier's leg…," the General while saying that tapped his leg, "it is something commendable, but to cripple oneself by unnecessary jumping off the train at full speed is worthy of punishment. — So this is then your Battalion?" he was asking of *Captain* Ságner, while observing the sleepy figures of the men, of whom many couldn't restrain themselves, and having been roused out of sleep, were yawning in the fresh night air. "It is, mister *Captain*, a yawning battalion. The men must go to sleep at nine o'clock."

The General stood himself in front of the 11th *Company*, where there was standing on the left flank Švejk, who was yawning at full stretch and, while doing that, he was holding his hand in good-mannered fashion in front of his mouth, but from under the hand was coming out the sound of such lowing, that Senior Lieutenant Lukáš was trembling, lest the General pay to it any closer attention. It occurred to him that Švejk was yawning deliberately.

And the General, as if he was familiar with it, turned toward Švejk and stepped up to him: "*Czech or German?*"

"*Czech, I dutifully report, Major General, Sir.*"

"Koot," said the General, who was a Pole and new a bit of Czech, "Yoo skreem onza hey like za kau. Curl your lip closed, keep your maut shut, don't low! Have yoo bin already to za lahtreen?"

"I haven't, I dutifully report, Major General, Sir."

"Why did you not go sheet wid za rest of za mensches?"

"I dutifully report, Major General, Sir, during maneuvers near Písek, there used to tell us mister Colonel Wachtl, when during a *rest break* the troops were scattering in the rye patches, that a soldier must not constantly think only of shitting, that a soldier is to think of fighting. Needless to say, I dutifully report, what would we be doing on the latrine? There is nothing to push out. According to the *march route* we should have already gotten supper at several stations and we got nothing. You don't crawl up on a latrine with an empty stomach!"

Švejk, having clarified in simple words for the Mister General the overall situation, directed a sort of intimate look at him, so that the General perceived a request, that he help them all. When there is already an order to go to the latrine in an organized march formation, then that order must also be backed up internally by something.

"Send the whole lot back into the railroad cars," said the General to *Captain* Ságner; "How come, that there was no supper issued? All *military transport trains* rolling through this station must get supper. This here is a supply station. There's no other way. There is a definite plan."

The General said it with such certainty, which meant, that it was, to be sure, close to the eleventh hour of the night, and the supper should have taken place at six o'clock, as he had already earlier remarked, so nothing else was left but to hold the train overnight and through the day until six o'clock in the evening, in order for them to get the goulash with potatoes.

"Nothing is worse," he said with tremendous seriousness, "than in war to forget during transport of the troops about supplying them. My duty is to find the truth, what it really looks like in the office of the railroad station Command Headquarters. Because, gentlemen, sometimes at fault are the commanders of *military transport trains* themselves. During an inspection of the station Subotiště[119] on the Southern Bosnian Railroad I had determined, that six *military transport trains* did not get supper, because the commanders of the *military transport trains* forgot to request it. Six times there was at the station being cooked goulash with potatoes, and nobody would request it. They were pouring it out onto piles. It was, gentlemen, a veritable potato *storage pit*, and three stations farther on were the soldiers from *military transport trains*, which had passed by the piles and hills of goulash in Subotiště, begging at the railroad station for a piece of bread. Here, as you see, the military administration was not at fault."

He waved abruptly his hand: "The commanders of *military transport trains* had not fulfilled their duties. Let's go into the office."

They followed him, thinking about why all generals had gone mad.

At the Command Headquarters it was discovered, that there was indeed nothing known about the goulash. True enough, it was to be cooked here today for all the *military transport trains*, which would pass through, but then the order came to subtract in the internal accounting of supplying the troops 72 pennies per man, so that each detachment rolling through had 72 pennies per man coming, which they would obtain from their army supply administrator to be paid out with the next closest military pay distribution. As for the bread, the troops would obtain in Watian[120] at the station half a loaf each.

The commander of the supply node was not afraid. He told the General straight in his face, that orders change every hour. Sometimes he has mess for the *military transport trains* ready. In rolls however an ambulance train, presents a higher order, and that's the end, the *military transport train* faces the problem of empty cauldrons.

The General was nodding in agreement and remarked, that the situation was decidedly getting better, at the beginning of the war it was much worse. Nothing can go right all at once, for that is decidedly needed experience and practical knowledge. Theory actually puts the brakes on practice. The longer the war lasts, the more will everything be put in order.

"I can give you a practical example," he said with great pleasure, because he came across something significant. "Two days ago the *military transport trains* rolling through the Hatvan station didn't get bread, and you will be tomorrow getting it issued there. Let's go now to the railroad station restaurant."

At the railroad station restaurant the mister General started again talking about the latrine and how it's not a good look, when everywhere on the tracks there are piles. All the while he was eating a steak and it seemed to all that a pile was rolling back and forth in his yap.

He was putting such emphasis on the latrines, as if on them depended the victory of the Monarchy.

In view of the newly forming situation with Italy he declared, that it was exactly in the very latrines of our military where our indisputable advantage in the Italian campaign rested.

The victory of Austria was crawling out of the latrine.

For the mister General everything was so simple. The road to martial glory was unfolding according to the recipe: at six o'clock in the evening soldiers get goulash with potatoes, half past eight the troops drop a load in the latrine and at nine go to sleep. Facing such a military the enemy flees in horror.

The Major General paused in thought, lit up an operas[121] for himself and was looking at the ceiling a long, long time. He was mulling, what else he would say, since he was already here, and with what he would enlighten the officers of the *military transport train*.

"The core of your Battalion is healthy," he said abruptly, as all were expecting that he'd keep on looking at the ceiling and remain quiet, "your post is in absolute order. The man, with whom I spoke, presents by his directness and military bearing the best hope on behalf of the whole Battalion, that it will strive to the last drop of blood."

He paused and was looking again at the ceiling, propped up against the back of a chair, and then continued in the same position, while only Lieutenant Dub driven by the instinct of his slavish soul was looking at the ceiling along with him: "Your Battalion needs, however, that its deeds not pass into oblivion. The battalions of your Brigade already have their history, which your Battalion must continue. And what you are missing is the very man, who would keep exact records and compose the history of the Battalion. To him must lead all the threads of what whichever *company* of the Battalion did. He must be an intelligent man, no dumb beast, no cow. Mister *Captain*, you must designate within the Battalion a *Battalion Chronicler*."

Then he was looking at the clock on the wall, the hands of which were reminding the whole sleepy social gathering, that it was time to disperse.

The General had on the railroad track his inspection train and requested of the gentlemen, that they accompany him off to his sleeping car.

The commander of the railroad station gave a sigh. The General did not remember, that he was to pay for the steak and bottle of wine. He again had to pay for it himself. Of such visits there were every day several. On those, two cars worth of hay, which he had pulled to a dead-end siding and which he sold to the firm Löwenstein, military suppliers of hay, just like standing rye is sold, had already been blown. Army in turn again bought the two railroad cars from them, but he left them standing there, to make sure. Perhaps at some time he would have to sell them off to the firm Löwenstein again.

But at least all the military inspections rolling through this main station in Pest were saying, that there at the station commander's, one drank and ate well.

*

In the morning was the *military transport train* still standing at the railroad station, there was reveille, the soldiers were washing themselves by the pumps from the mess kits, the General with his train had not taken off yet and went to inspect personally the latrines, where they went according to the order of the day that was making rounds of *Captain* Ságner's Battalion, "*By platoon under the command of the platoon commanders*," in order that the Major General have joy. And so that Lieutenant Dub would also have joy, *Captain* Ságner informed him, that today he had inspection duty.

Lieutenant Dub was then looking after the latrines.

The expansive long two row latrine would hold two *squads* of a company.

And now the soldiers were nicely next to each other squatting over the dug-out trenches, like swallows on telegraph line wires, when they're getting ready in fall for the journey to Africa.

Each had knees sticking out of the dropped down pants, each had the belt hanging around the neck, as if at any moment he wanted to

Jaroslav Hašek

hang himself and was waiting for some command.

One could see in all of it the military iron-willed discipline, organized character.

On the left flank was sitting Švejk, who somehow ended up here, and was with interest reading a fragment of paper, ripped out from God-knows which novel by Růžena Jesenská[122]:

...re boarding school unfortunately the ladies
em indefinite, real, perhaps more
re mostly introverted loss
h menu into their chambers, or are
to the unique entertainment. And
in case they have uttered t
gone just man and only longing for c
getting better, since she didn't want so successfully
ie, as they themselves would wish.
was nothing for the young Křička

When he tore his eyes away from the fragment, he looked unawares toward the latrine exit and he marveled. There stood in full glory mister Major General of last night with his adjutant and next to them Lieutenant Dub, eagerly telling them something.

Švejk took a good look round him. All kept on squatting calmly over the latrine and only the NCOs were somewhat rigid and motionless.

Švejk sensed the seriousness of the situation.

He jumped up as he was, with the dropped down pants, with the belt around his neck, having still made use of the fragment of paper, and hollered: "*Interrupt! Stand up! Attention! Eyes right!*" And he was saluting. Two *squads* with their dropped down pants and belts around their necks rose above the latrine.

The Major General gave an amiable smile and said: "*At ease, carry on!*" Sergeant Málek gave the first example to his *squad*, showing them they had to assume their original position. Only Švejk was standing and saluting, because from one side was approaching him ominously Lieutenant Dub and from the other the Major General, with a smile.

"You I shaw at night," said toward the strange posture of Švejk the Major General; after which the upset Lieutenant Dub turned to the Major General: "*I dutifully report, Major General, Sir, the man is feeble-minded and known as an idiot, a fabled dumbbell."*

*"What are you saying, mister Lieutenant?"* hollered all of a sudden the Major General at Lieutenant Dub and let him have it, that it was just the other way around. A man, who knows, what is proper, when he sees a superior, and the NCOs who don't see him and are ignoring him. It is like on the battle field. An ordinary soldier in time of danger takes over the command. And it is exactly mister Lieutenant Dub who himself should have given the command, which this soldier gave: '*Interrupt!! — Stand up! — Attention! Eyes right!*'"

"Haf you viped your arsh?" the Major General asked of Švejk.

"I dutifully report, Major General, Sir, that everything is in order."

"You von't sheet any more?"

"I dutifully report, Major General, Sir, that I'm *done*."

"So pull your hohses back up and then stand up again *at attention!*" Because the Major General said the *'at attention'* a bit louder, the closest ones began to rise up over the latrine.

The Major General in a friendly manner, however, waived his hand to them and in a soft fatherly tone said: "*But no, at ease, at ease, at ease, just carry on.*"

Švejk was already standing in front of the Major General fully squared away and the Major General presented a short speech to him in German: "Respect for the superiors, knowledge of *service regulations* and presence of mind mean everything in the military. And when in addition there is intertwined with it bravery, there isn't an enemy, whom we would have to fear."

Turning to Lieutenant Dub he said, poking his finger into Švejk's belly: "Make a note: this man is to be immediately upon arrival at the front *promoted*, and at the earliest opportunity nominated for the bronze medal for exact execution of duties and for knowledge... *You know, I'm sure, what I mean... Fall out!*"

The Major General was putting distance between himself and the latrine, where in the meantime Lieutenant Dub, so that the Major General would hear it, was giving loud orders: "*The first squad stand up! Double file... The second squad...*"

Švejk in the meantime walked out and when walking past Lieutenant Dub, he snapped for him, true enough, a proper military salute, but Lieutenant Dub still said: "*Hold it and stand over here*", and Švejk had to salute again, while he had to hear again: "Do you know me? You don't know me! You know me from the good side, but once you get to know me from the bad side, I'll drive you all the way to tears!"

Švejk was walking away at last to his own railroad car and as he was he entertained the thought: Once there was, when we were still in Karlín at the garrison, Lieutenant Chudavý and he used to say it differently, when he got upset: "Lads, remember, when you see me, that I'm a tough swine for you to deal with and that the tough swine I will remain, as long as you are with the *Company*."

As Švejk was walking past the Staff railroad car, Senior Lieutenant Lukáš called after him, to relay to Baloun, that he was to hurry it up with that coffee and as for the can of condensed milk, to close it nicely again, so it wouldn't spoil. Baloun, that is to say, was cooking on a little self-contained spirit-stove in the railroad car by Accounting Master Sergeant Vaněk coffee for Senior Lieutenant Lukáš. When Švejk went to relay it, he realized, that in the meantime during his absence had been drinking coffee the whole railroad car.

The coffee and milk cans of Lieutenant Lukáš' were already half empty and Baloun, sipping coffee from his cup, was poking with a teaspoon inside the milk can, in order to still improve his coffee.

The cook-occultist Jurajda and Accounting Master Sergeant Vaněk were promising one another, that when coffee and milk cans arrive, they would make it up to mister Senior Lieutenant Lukáš.

Švejk was also offered coffee, but Švejk declined and said to Baloun: "There just came an order from the Army Staff, that each *spotshine*, who embezzles his officer's milk and coffee can, is to be without ado hanged within 24 hours. That's what I am supposed to relay to you from mister *Senior Lieutenant*, who desires to see you immediately with the coffee."

The spooked Baloun ripped from telegraph operator Chodounský the portion, which he just a moment ago poured for him, he set it back on the stove to warm up, added the canned milk and ran with it, burning up the trail, to the Staff railroad car.

With eyes bulging out he handed the coffee to Senior Lieutenant Lukáš, at which time the thought flashed through his mind, that Senior Lieutenant Lukáš must see in his eyes, how he was managing his cans.

"I was delayed," he stammered, "because I couldn't open them."

"That suggests you lost the milk spilling, right?" asked Senior Lieutenant Lukáš, sipping the coffee, "or you were gobbling it by the spoonful like soup. Do you know, what awaits you?!"

Baloun gave a sigh and lamented: "I have three children, I dutifully report, *Senior Lieutenant*, Sir."

"Watch out, Baloun, I'm warning you one more time, mind your gluttony. Hasn't Švejk told you anything?"

"Within 24 hours I might be hanged," sadly answered Baloun, swaying his whole body.

"Don't be swaying here on me, you idiot," said with a smile Senior Lieutenant Lukáš, "and improve. Let already that voracity out of your head and tell Švejk, to take a look somewhere around the railroad station or the vicinity for something good to eat. Give him this tenner here. You I won't send. You'll be going only at such time, when you're stuffed to bursting. Haven't you gobbled up that little box of sardines on me? You're saying that you haven't. Bring it and show it to me!"

Baloun relayed to Švejk, that mister *Senior Lieutenant* is sending a tenner to him, in order for him to chase down somewhere around the railroad station something good to eat, with a sigh he pulled out of the Senior Lieutenant's small suitcase a little box of sardines and with a depressed feeling was carrying it for an inspection to the Senior Lieutenant.

The poor guy was looking forward, that perhaps Senior Lieutenant Lukáš had already forgotten those sardines, and now all had come to an end. The Senior Lieutenant will probably keep them in the railroad car and do him out of them. He felt robbed.

"Here are, I dutifully report, *Senior Lieutenant*, Sir, your sardines," he said with bitterness, turning them over to the owner. "Should I open them?"

"Alright, Baloun, don't be opening anything and take them back again to their place. I just wanted to see for myself, whether you hadn't taken a peek at them on the inside. It sort of seemed to me, when you brought the coffee, that your yap was somewhat greasy as if with oil. Has Švejk gone already?"

"I dutifully report, *Senior Lieutenant*, Sir, that he's set out already," the brightened up Baloun was reporting. "He said, that mister Senior Lieutenant would be satisfied and that all would be jealous of mister Senior Lieutenant. He went somewhere from the railroad station and was saying, that he knew his way around here all the way past Rákospalota[123]. If perhaps the train were to take off without him, that he'd join the automobile convoy and catch up with us at the nearest station in an automobile. We're not to have any concern for him, he knows, what his duty is, even if he were to at his expense take a fiacre and ride it following the *military transport train* all the way to Galicia. He would then let them deduct it from his *soldier's pay*. You are definitely not to have any concern for him, *Senior Lieutenant*, Sir."

"Go away," said sadly Senior Lieutenant Lukáš.

They brought the news from the office of the Command Headquarters, that they would be hauling only at two hours after noon toward Gödöllö-Aszód[124] and that they will be issuing to the officers at the railroad stations each two liters of red wine and a bottle of cognac. It was being said, that it was some lost shipment for the Red Cross. Let things have been as they have been, it dropped straight from heaven and in the Staff car they were making merry. The cognac had been rated with three little stars and the wine brand was Gumpoldskirchen[125].

Only Senior Lieutenant Lukáš was still somewhat withdrawn. There had already passed an hour, and Švejk still wasn't coming. Then again a half an hour, and there was approaching the Staff car an odd procession, which walked out of the office of the railroad station Command Headquarters.

At the head of it was walking Švejk, in a serious and exalted manner, like the first Christian martyrs, when they were being dragged into the arena.

On either side a *Hungarian Land Defense soldier* with the bayonet attached. On the left flank a Corporal from the railroad station Command Headquarters and behind them some woman in a red skirt with accordion pleats and a man in boots with a round little hat and a bashed-in eye, who was carrying a live, screaming, terrified hen.

The whole lot was crawling into the Staff car, but the Corporal hollered in Hungarian at the man with the hen and the woman, for them to stay below.

Having beheld Senior Lieutenant Lukáš, Švejk began winking super-significantly.

The Staff Sergeant wanted to speak to the commander of the 11th March Company. Senior Lieutenant Lukáš took over the file from the station Command Headquarters from him, wherein he read, turning pale:

To the commander of the 11th *March Company*, March Battalion N of the 91st Infantry Regiment for further processing.

Being presented is the infantryman Švejk, Josef, according to the statement by the *messenger* of the same March Company N of the 91st Infantry Regiment, for the crime of robbery, committed against Mr. and Mrs. István in Isatarcsa[126] in the precinct of the railroad station Command Headquarters.

**Reasons**: Infantryman Švejk, Josef, having usurped the hen running about behind the house of Mr. and Mrs. István's in Isatarcsa in the precinct of the railroad station Command Headquarters and belonging to Mr. and Mrs. István (in the original a famously crafted new German word "*Istvanspouses*") and having been apprehended by the owner, who the hen to take away from him wanted, prevented that, having struck the owner István with the hen across the right eye, and having been apprehended by the summoned patrol, was transported to his detachment, while the hen was returned to the owner.
Signature of the officer on duty

When Senior Lieutenant Lukáš was signing the receipt for having received Švejk, the knees under him were trembling.

Švejk was standing so close, that he saw, how Senior Lieutenant Lukáš forgot to wri*te in the* date."I dutifully report, Senior Lieutenant, Sir," sounded up Švejk, "that today is the twenty fourth. Yesterday was the 23rd of May, when Italy declared war on us. As I was now out there, there is nothing else being talked about."

The *Hungarian Land Defense soldier* and the Corporal departed and down below remained only Mr. and Mrs. István, who kept wanting to crawl into the railroad car.

"Should you have, *Senior Lieutenant*, Sir, another fiver on you, then we could buy the hen. The hoodlum wants fifteen golden pieces for it, but he's included in it a tenner for the black and blue eye of his," said Švejk in narrator's style, "but I think, *Senior Lieutenant*, Sir, that ten gold pieces for such a stupid eye is too much. Get this, they dislocated At the Old Lady's[127] pub the lathe operator Matějů's whole jaw with a brick for twenty gold coins, including six teeth, and back then money was worth more than today. The Prague executioner Wohlschäger[128] himself does hangings for four gold pieces. — Come here," Švejk motioned to the man with the bashed-in eye and the hen, "and you, hag, you stay there!"

The man stepped into the railroad car. "He knows a bit of German," remarked Švejk, "and understands all the cusses and can himself also cuss in German fairly well. — *So ten guilders*," he turned to the man, *"five guilders hen, five eye. Five forints, see, cock-a-doodle-doo, lookey here, yeah*? This is the Staff railroad car here, you thief. Hand over the hen!"

He shoved into the surprised man's hand a tenner, took his hen away, wrung its neck and then shoved him out of the railroad car, having extended his hand to him in a friendly way, which he shook vigorously: Jó napot, barátom, adieu, go, crawl to your hag. Or I'll knock you down off here. — So you see, *Senior Lieutenant*, Sir, that everything can be settled smooth," said Švejk to Senior Lieutenant Lukáš, "The best thing is, when everything can take place without a scandal, without great ceremonies. Now Baloun and I will cook for you such a chicken soup, that one will be able to smell it all the way to Transylvania[129]."

Senior Lieutenant Lukáš couldn't hold himself back anymore and knocked the hapless hen out of Švejk's hand and then started screaming: "Do you know, Švejk, what deserves a soldier, who in wartime robs the peaceable populace?"

"Honorable death by powder and lead," ceremonially replied Švejk.

"You of course deserve the rope, Švejk, because you were the first to begin robbing. You are, you sonofagun, I don't know really what to call you, you have forgotten your oath. My head could just start spinning."

Švejk cast at Senior Lieutenant Lukáš an inquisitive look and quickly sounded up: "I dutifully report, that I have not forgotten the oath, which our war-folk is to fulfill. I dutifully report, *Senior Lieutenant*, Sir, that I swore solemnly to my most luminous Duke and lord Franz Josef I, that I would be loyal and dutifully obedient also to the generals of His Highness, and altogether all of my superiors and higher-ups obey, honor and defend, their orders and commands in all service fulfill, against every enemy, whomever he may be and wherever the will of His Imperial and Royal Highness demands it, on the water, under the water, on the land, in the air, during the day and at night, in battles, attacks, struggles and whatever other undertakings, all in all in every place..."

Švejk picked up the hen off the ground and continued standing straight and looking into Lieutenant Lukáš's eyes: "...at any time and every opportunity to fight valiantly and in a manly way, that I will never abandon our military troops, flags, pennants and cannons, with the enemy I will never enter into the least collusion, always will behave as the military laws demand it and as for good and worthy soldiers is proper, that in this manner I want with honor to live and die, so help me God. Amen. And as for the hen, I have, I dutifully report, not stolen it, I have not been robbing and I have been behaving properly, being aware of my oath.

"Will you let go of that hen, you cattle beast," hollered at him Senior Lieutenant Lukáš, having struck Švejk with a file folder across the hand wherein he was holding the poor deceased, "Take a look at these files. See, here you have it black on white: 'Being presented is infantryman Švejk, Josef, according to the statement by the *messenger* of the same march company... for the crime of robbery'...' And now tell me, you marauder, you hyena — no, I will after all one day kill you, **kill**, you understand — tell me, you robbing idiot, how did you stoop so low."

"I dutifully report," said in a friendly manner Švejk, "that it definitely cannot be anything else but a mistake. When I received that order of yours to secure somewhere and buy something good to eat, then I began to ponder, what would perhaps be the best. Behind the railroad station there was altogether nothing, only horsemeat sausage and some dried donkey meat. I have, I dutifully report, *Senior Lieutenant*, Sir, deliberated everything thoroughly. In the field one needs something very nutritious, so that one can better bear the war hardships. And so I wanted, *Senior Lieutenant*, Sir, to cook for you a soup from hen."

"A soup from hen," repeated after him the Senior Lieutenant, grabbing his head.

"Yes, I dutifully report, *Senior Lieutenant*, Sir, a soup from a hen, I bought onion and five decagrams of noodles. Here is if you please all of it. Here in the pocket is the onion and in this one the noodles. Salt we have at the office and black pepper too. Nothing was left to do other than to buy a hen. I went then on the other side of the railroad station to Isatarcsa. It is actually a village, not quite a town, although a sign in the first street there reads Isatarcsa varosz. I went through the length of one street with front yard gardens, the second, the third, the fourth, the fifth, the sixth, the seventh, the eighth, the ninth, the tenth, the eleventh, and only in the thirteenth street at the very end, where behind one little house the lawns already began, there was grazing and strutting a herd of hens. I went toward them and chose the largest, heaviest, condescend to look at it, *Senior Lieutenant,* Sir, it is nothing but lard, one doesn't even have to feel it and he realizes at first sight, that they must had been scattering a lot of grain for it. I took it then, absolutely publicly, in the presence of the populace, which was screaming at me something in Hungarian, I'm holding it by the legs and I asking several people, both in Czech and German, to whom does belong the hen, so that I could buy it from him, when just then there runs out of the little house at the end a man with a woman and starts first cursing me in Hungarian and then in German, that I stole from him in broad daylight a hen. I told him to stop screaming at me, that I'd been dispatched to buy it for you, and I was telling him, how things are. And the hen, as I was holding it by the legs, all of a sudden started waving its wings and wanted to take off flying, and as I was holding it only lightly in my hand, it raised my arm and wanted to land on its master's nose. And right away he started hollering, that I supposedly slammed him with the hen across his trap. And the broad was squealing something and kept screaming at the hen 'puta, puta, puta, puta.' At that very moment some idiots, who didn't understand it, were bringing over the patrol, *Hungarian Land Defense soldiers*, and I myself challenged them to come with me to the railroad station Command Headquarters, in order for my innocence to come up like oil rises to the top of water. But there was no talking to that mister *Lieutenant*, who was on duty there, not even when I was begging him to ask you, whether it was true, that you'd sent me to buy something good for you. On top of it he screamed at me, to keep my trap shut, that regardless, gazing into my eyes he could see coming out of them a thick branch with a good rope. He was apparently in some very bad mood, when he was telling me, that someone so well-grazed and fattened-up could only be a soldier who robs and steals. There are supposedly already other complaints registered at the station, the day before yesterday supposedly there disappeared somewhere next door somebody's turkey, and when I told him, that at that time we were still in Győr, then he said, that such an excuse had no currency with him. So they sent me to you and on top of it, there still started screaming at me, when I didn't see him, a *corporal*, whether it could be that I didn't know whom I had in front of me. I told him, that he's a *corporal*, that if he were with the rangers, he'd be a *patrol leader* and with the artillery the *chief gunner*."

"Švejk," said after a while Senior Lieutenant Lukáš, "you have already had so many strange coincidences and accidents, so many, as you say misunderstandings and mistakes, that perhaps after all one day you will be helped out of your troubles of yours by a strong rope around your neck with the whole military honors in a square formation. Do you understand?"

"Yes, I dutifully report, *Senior Lieutenant*, Sir, that the square of the so-called *Battalion locked in the square formation* consists of four, exceptionally also of three or five companies. Is it your command, *Senior Lieutenant*, Sir, to put into the soup from this hen more noodles, so that it would be thicker?"

"Švejk, I command you to disappear already with the hen included, or I'll knock it around against your head, you idiot…"

"As commanded, *Senior Lieutenant*, Sir, but as for celery, I dutifully report, I haven't found any, carrots neither! I'll put pota…"

Švejk did not finish saying the "toe" and he flew even with the hen outside of the Staff railroad car. Senior Lieutenant Lukáš downed a wine tumbler of cognac.

Švejk saluted in front of the windows of the railroad car and was walking away.

\*

Baloun was just getting himself ready after a happily ended mental struggle, that he'll open after all the little box of sardines of his Senior Lieutenant, when there emerged Švejk with the hen, which gave rise to natural commotion among all those present in the railroad car, and all gave him such a look, as if they wanted to definitely say: Where did you steal it?

"I bought it for mister *Senior Lieutenant*," answered Švejk pulling out of his pockets onion and noodles. "I wanted to cook soup from it for him, but he doesn't want it anymore so he gifted it to me."

"Didn't it croak on its own?" asked the Accounting Master Sergeant Vaněk suspiciously.

"I myself wrung its neck," answered Švejk pulling out of his pocket a knife.

Baloun gratefully and at the same time with an expression of respect looked at Švejk and started without a word preparing the self-contained spirit-stove of the Senior Lieutenant's. Then he took coffee pots and ran with them to get water.

The telegraph operator Chodounský approached Švejk and offered, that he will help him pluck it, while he whispered into his ear an intimate question: "Is it far from here? Must one be climbing over into the yard, or is it free range?"

"I bought it."

"Do be quiet, and you call yourself a friend, we saw, as they were escorting you."

He was participating however enthusiastically in the plucking of the hen. The grand, glorious preparations were joined even by the cook-occultist Jurajda, who sliced the potatoes and onion for the soup.

The feathers thrown out of the railroad car drew the attention of Lieutenant Dub, who was making rounds of the cars.

He called inside, for the one, who was plucking the hen, to show himself, and in the doorway emerged the contented face of Švejk's.

"What is this?" hollered Lieutenant Dub, picking up off the ground the hen's cut-off head.

"That is, I dutifully report," retorted Švejk, "the head of a hen of the Black Leghorn breed. They are, *Lieutenant*, Sir, very good egg layers. They lay as many as 260 eggs a year. Condescend please to look, what fruitful ovaries it had." Švejk was holding in front of Lieutenant Dub's nose the intestines and other innards from the hen.

Dub spat, walked away and in a while returned:

"Who will the hen be for?"

"For us, I dutifully report, *Lieutenant*, Sir. Take a look, see how much lard it has."

Lieutenant Dub was leaving murmuring: "At Philippi[130] we will meet."

"What is it that he was telling you?" turned to Švejk Jurajda.

"Oh, we've made an appointment to meet somewhere at Filipa's. You know these noble gentlemen are usually fags."

The cook-occultist proclaimed, that only esthetes are homosexual, which he said already follows from the very essence of estheticism.

Accounting Master Sergeant Vaněk was then telling about the indecent misusing of children by pedagogues in the Spanish monasteries.

And while the water in the kettle on the spirit-stove began to boil, Švejk mentioned, how at one time they charged a guardian with looking after a whole colony of abandoned Viennese children and that guardian molested the whole colony.

"No two ways about it, that's a passion, but the worst thing is, when it grabs the broads. In Prague II[131] there were years ago two abandoned pampered ladies, divorced, because they were hussies, some Mourková and Šousková, and they at one time, when the cherries were blossoming in an alley of trees by Roztoky[132], caught an old impotent hundred-years-old barrel organ-grinder there and dragged him in the evening away into the Roztoky grove for themselves and there they raped him. What they were doing with him! There is in Žižkov mister professor Axamit[133] and he used to dig there looking for the graves of crouchers[134], and several of them he emptied, and they dragged him, the hurdy-gurdy man, into one such dug out barrow for themselves and there they kept grinding him and indecently violating him. And professor Axamit came there next day and he sees that something is lying in the barrow. He rejoiced, but it was the organ-grinder done for by the cruelty and torture of those divorced pampered ladies. Round about him were nothing but some pieces of wood. Then the organ-grinder on the fifth day died, and the bitches were so insolent on top of it that they came to his funeral. Now that amounts to a perversion. — Have you salted it?" Švejk turned to Baloun, who had made use of the general interest over Švejk's narrative and was hiding something into his backpack, "show me, what are you doing there? — Baloun," said Švejk seriously, "what do you want with the hen thigh? So take a look everyone. He stole a hen thigh from us, so he'd then secretly cook it for himself. Do you know, Baloun, what you've done? You know, how it is punished in the army, when somebody robs his buddy in the field. He's tied to the barrel of a cannon and the sonofagun is shot with a grape-shot. Now it's late to be sighing. When we come across artillery somewhere at the front, then you'll muster with the nearest *Chief Gunny Sergeant*. For the time being though you'll be exercising for punishment. Start crawling out of the railroad car."

Hapless Baloun got out and Švejk, sitting in the doorway of the railroad car, was giving out commands: *"Attention! At ease! Eyes right!* Look straight again! *At ease!* — Now you'll be doing body movements in place. *Right face!* Man! *They* are a cow. *Their* horns are supposed to end up there, where *they* had the right shoulder before. *Hold it and stand over here! Right face! Left face! Half-right!* Not like that, you ox! *Hold it and stand over here! Half-right!*, there you see, you mule, that it can be done! *Half-left! Left face! Left! Front face! Front face*, you imbecile! Don't you know, what front face is? *Forward march! About face! Kneel! Down! Sit! Up! At ease!* — So you see, Baloun, it is healthy, at least you'll work up an appetite!"

All around they started gathering in large clumps and breaking out in cheers.

"Kindly make room," was hollering Švejk, "he'll be marching. Then, Baloun, watch out, so that I won't have to make you *stop and come over*. I don't like to harass the *troops* unnecessarily. So then: *In the direction of the railroad station!* Look where I'm pointing. *Forward march! Section — stop!* Stop, damn it, or I'll lock you up! *Section — stop!* It's about time that you the idiot stopped. *Shorten step!* Don't you know what the *shorten step* is? I'll show it to you and drill you until you turn blue! *Extend the step! Change step! Mark time!* You singular buffalo! When I say *mark time*, then you're laying the dumb legs over and back in place."

All around were already at least two *companies*.

Baloun was sweating and was not aware of himself and Švejk kept on ordering:

"*In the same step! Section to the rear march! Section stop! On the double! Section march! In step! Section stop! At ease! Attention! In the direction of the railroad station! On the double march! Stop! About face! In the direction of the car! On the double march! Shorten step! Section stop! At ease!* Now you'll rest a little while! And then we start from scratch. With good will, all will be accomplished!"

"What is it that's going on here?" sounded up the voice of Lieutenant Dub, who came running disturbed.

"I dutifully report, *Lieutenant*, Sir," said Švejk, "that we're sort of practicing a bit, so that we wouldn't forget the *drill practice* and unnecessarily wallow through and waste precious time."

"Crawl down off the railroad car," was ordering Lieutenant Dub, "I have really had enough of it. I'm taking you to face your *Battalion Commander*."

When Švejk found himself in the Staff railroad car, Senior Lieutenant Lukáš left the railroad car through the other exit and went to the platform.

*Captain* Ságner, when Lieutenant Dub was reporting to him the odd mischiefs, as he expressed himself, of the good soldier Švejk, was just then in a very good mood, because the Gumpoldskirchen was truly remarkable.

"Then you don't want to unnecessarily wallow through and waste precious time," he gave a meaningful smile. "Matušič, come here!"

The Battalion *Messenger* received an order to call the Quartermaster of the 12th *Company*, Nasáklo, who was known as the greatest tyrant, and to immediately provide for Švejk a rifle.

"This man here," said *Captain* Ságner to Quartermaster Nasáklo, "does not want to unnecessarily wallow through and waste precious time. Take him behind the railroad car and practice rifle positions with him for an hour. But without any mercy, without catching a breath.

Above all in a nice succession, *order arms, shoulder arms, order arms!* — You will see, Švejk, that you won't be bored," he said in his direction as he was departing. And in a while there was already heard behind the railroad car the sound of the rough order, which ceremonially carried between the rails. Quartermaster Nasáklo, who was just then playing the one-and-twenty and was holding the bank, was hollering into God's expanse: "*Order arms! — Shoulder arms! Order arms! — Shoulder arms!*"

Then it quieted down for a while and there could be heard Švejk's voice, contented and deliberate: "I was learning all that on active duty years ago. When there's *Order arms!*, then the rifle is standing propped on the right side. The toe of the rifle butt is directly in line with the foot tips. The right arm is naturally stretched and its hand is holding the rifle so, that the thumb is hugging the *barrel*, the rest of the fingers must be gripping the front of the butt, and when there's *Shoulder arms!*, then the rifle is loosely slung over the right shoulder and the *mouth of the barrel* pointing upward and the barrel to the back..."

"So enough of the babbling already," was coming again the sound of the command from Quartermaster Nasáklo. "*Attention! Eyes right! Lord Go*d, how are you doing it..."

"I'm *shouldered* and at *Eyes right!* my right hand slides down the sling, I hug the small of the stock and throw my head to the right, in response to the *Attention!* I grab the sling again with the right hand and my head is gazing forward at you."

And again rang out the voice of the Quartermaster: "*Carry arm! Order arms! Carry arm! Shoulder arms! Fix bayonet! Unfix bayonet! Sheath the bayonet! To prayer! End prayer! Kneel down for prayer! Load! Shoot! Shoot half to the right! Target the Staff car! Distance 200 paces Ready! Aim! Fire! Ease up! Aim! Fire! Aim! Fire! Ease up! Sights normal! Stow away cartridges! At ease!*" The Quartermaster was rolling a cigarette for himself.

Švejk was in the meantime looking over the number on the rifle and sounded up: "4268! That was the number on a locomotive at the railroad in Pečky[135], on the 16th track. They were to haul it away to the depot in Lysá nad Labem[136], for repairs, but it couldn't be done so easily, because, Quartermaster, Sir, the engineer, who was to haul it away, had very bad memory for numbers. So the track master called him into his office and is telling him: 'On the 16$^{th}$ track there is a locomotive number 4268. I know, that you have bad memory for

101

numerals, and when one writes some number down on paper for you, you will lose that paper. But pay good attention, since you're so bad with numerals, and I will show you, that it is very easy to remember any number. Take a look: The locomotive, which you're supposed to haul away to the depot in Lysá nad Labem, bears the number 4268. So pay attention: The first numeral is a four, the second a two. Then remember already 42, that is two times 2, which is in the order starting from the front 4, divided by 2=2, and there again you have 4 and 2 next to each other. Don't spook now. How many times is two times 4, eight, isn't that true? So engrave into your memory, that the eight is in the number 4268 the last one in the row. Still left to do, since you remember already, that the first is 4, the second 2, and the fourth eight, is somehow to cleverly remember the six, which comes before the eight. And this is terribly simple. The first numeral is a 4, the second a two, four and two is six. So you're already sure, the second one from the back is a six, and now already the sequence of the numbers will never disappear from our memory. You have imbedded in your head the number 4268. Or you can also arrive at the same result in an even more simple...'"

The Quartermaster stopped smoking and popped out his eyes and only mumbled: "*Cover off*!"

Švejk seriously continued: "So he then started telling him the simpler way, of how he would remember the number of the locomotive 4268. Eight, take away two, is six. So he already knows 68. 6, take away 2, is 4, so then he already knows 4-68, and the two into it makes 4-2-6-8. It is also not very exerting, when it's done still differently, with the help of multiplication and division. One also arrives at that result. 'Remember', the track master was saying, 'that two times 42 is 84. There are 12 months in a year. Then 12 is subtracted from 84, and we are left with 72, take from that another twelve months, that is 60, so we have then the six secured already and we cross out the zero. So we know 42 68 4. Since we crossed out the zero, we'll cross out the four at the back as well, and maintaining a calm disposition we have again 4268, the number of the locomotive, which belongs to the depot in Lysá nad Labem. It is also easy, as I've been saying, using division. We compute the coefficient according to the customs tariff.' You're not getting sick *Quartermaster*, Sir, I hope. Should you wish, I will start then with, let's say, *Get ready for a salvo! Ready! High aim! Fire!* Thunder on high! Mister *Captain* should not have sent us into the sun! I must go to fetch the stretcher."

When the doctor came, he stated then, that it was either sun stroke or acute inflammation of the brain lining.

When the Quartermaster came to, standing next to him was Švejk who said: "So that I would finish telling it to you. Do you think, Quartermaster, Sir, that the engineer did commit it to memory? He mixed it up and multiplied it all by three, because he remembered the Divine Trinity, and he did not find the locomotive, it is still standing there on the track number 16."

The Quartermaster closed his eyes again.

And when Švejk had returned to his railroad car, the question, where he had been so long, he answered: "He who is teaching another one *On the double*, ends up doing a hundred times *Shoulder arms!*" In the back of the railroad car there was trembling Baloun. He devoured in Švejk's absence, when a part of the hen got done cooking, half of Švejk's portion.

\*

Before the departure of the *military transport train* there caught up with it a combined military train with various detachments They were stragglers or soldiers from *hospitals*, catching up with their detachments, and other suspicious individuals, returning from official trips or detention.

From that train stepped out also one-year volunteer Marek, who had been charged with mutiny, when he didn't want to be cleaning the latrines, but the Divisional Court let him go free, the investigation of him was stopped, and one-year volunteer Marek therefore now appeared in the Staff railroad car, in order to report to the *Battalion Commander*. That is, the one-year volunteer still did not belong anywhere, because they kept escorting him from one detention to another.

*Captain* Ságner, when he saw the one-year volunteer and received from him the papers pertaining to his arrival with the very secret note "*Politically suspect! Caution!*", he was not overjoyed and luckily remembered the latrine-general, who so interestingly recommended they augment the Battalion with a *Battalion Chronicler*.

You are very lackadaisical, you one-year volunteer," he said to him, "in the one-year-timer school you were a genuine scourge, instead of looking to it, that you would make your mark and earn a rank, which you are due according to your intelligence, you were floating from detention to detention. The Regiment must be ashamed for you, you one-year volunteer. But you can correct your error, when through proper discharging of your duties you emerge again in the line of the good privates. Devote your strengths to the Battalion with love. I will give it a try with you. You are an intelligent young man and surely have even the ability to write, stylize. I'll tell you something. Each battalion in the field needs a man, who would keep a chronological summary of all the events of the war touching directly upon the battalion's performance on the battlefield. It is necessary to describe all victorious campaigns, all significant glorious moments, in which the Battalion takes part, in which it plays a leading and outstanding role, to slowly assemble a contribution to the history of the army. Do you understand me?"

"I dutifully report, yes, *Captain*, Sir, it's a question of episodes from the life of all the detachments. The Battalion has its history. The Regiment is assembling on the basis of the history of its Battalions the history of the Regiment. The regiments comprise the history of the Brigade, the history of the brigades make up the history of the Division, and so forth. I will try with all my strength, *Captain*, Sir.

"I will be recording with real love the glorious days of our Battalion, especially nowadays, when the offensive is in full swing and when it gets tough, when our Battalion will cover the battlefield with its heroic sons. I will conscientiously record all events, that must occur, in order that the pages of the history of our Battalion are filled with laurels."

"You will be stationed at the Staff of the Battalion, one-year volunteer, you will be taking notice of who was recommended for decoration, recording — albeit according to our notes — the marches, which especially would draw attention to the outstanding zeal for fighting and steely discipline of the Battalion. It is not so easy, one-year volunteer, but I hope, that you have so much observation talent, that you, receiving from me certain directives, would lift up our Battalion above the other groups. I am sending a telegram to the Regiment, that I have named you the *Battalion Chronicler*. Muster with Accounting Master Sergeant Vaněk of the 11th *Company*, in order for him to place you there in the railroad car. There is still about the most room there, and tell him to come to me over here. However, you'll be carried on the roster of the Battalion Staff. That will be done by an order distributed throughout the Battalion.

\*

The cook-occultist was sleeping. Baloun was still trembling, because he had already opened even the Senior Lieutenant's sardines,

Accounting Master Sergeant had gone to *Captain* Ságner and the telegraph operator Chodounský had rustled somewhere at the railroad station a little bottle of borovička, drank it up, and was now in a sentimental mood and singing:

> As long as in sweet days I was wandering,
> Faithful everything seemed to me to be,
> Here breathed my chest faith
> And my eye with love was aflame.
>
> However when I beheld, that the whole Earth
> is treacherous like a jackal,
> wilted the faith, wilted the love
> And I for the first time wept.

Then he got up, walked to the desk of Accounting Master Sergeant Vaněk and wrote on a piece of paper in large letters:

*I hereby respectfully request to be named and promoted to Regimental bugler.*

*Chodounský, telegraph operator*

\*

*Captain* Ságner didn't have an excessively long conversation with Accounting Master Sergeant Vaněk. He alerted him only to the fact, that for the time being the *Battalion Chronicler*, one-year volunteer Marek, would be stationed in the railroad car with Švejk.

"I can tell you only this much, that the man Marek is, so to speak, suspect. *Politically suspect.* My God! That is nowadays nothing so outlandishly strange. Who isn't that said about. There are certain various speculations. You, I'm sure, understand me. Then I'm only putting you on notice, for you to, if he were perhaps to be saying something, which would, well you know, immediately stop him dead in his tracks, lest I too would be having some unpleasant difficulties. Tell him simply to stop all the talk, and that will already fix it. But I don't mean, that you should then be running to me right away. Take care of him in a friendly manner, such talking to is always better than some silly denunciation. In short, I don't wish to hear anything, because… You understand. Such a thing here reflects always on the whole Battalion."

When Vaněk then returned, he took aside one-year volunteer

Marek and told him: "Human one, you are suspect, but that doesn't matter at all. Just don't say much of anything unnecessary here in front of that Chodounský, the telegraph operator."

As he barely finished saying that, Chodounský teetered over and fell into the arms of the Accounting Master Sergeant, and was sobbing in a drunken voice, which perhaps was supposed to pass for singing.

> When all had forsaken me,
> I to your breasts my head lowered,
> Onto your ardent, pure heart
> painfully tears was shedding.
>
> And in your eye flared up a flame
> like a star with a glitter bright,
> coral mouth whispered:
> I will never forsake you.

"We'll never forsake one another," was bellowing Chodounský, "whatever I hear on the phone, I'll immediately tell you. I'll shit on the oath."

In the corner Baloun crossed himself from the horror of it and started to loudly pray: "Birth mother of God, do not reject my pleading cry, but hear me out mercifully, cheer me up kindly, help me, the miserable one, who is calling upon You with living faith, firm hope and fervent love in this valley of tears. Ah, Queen of Heaven, make your intercession, so that I would also in the mercy of God and under Your protection all the way until the end of my life remain…"

Blessed Virgin Mary really interceded on his behalf, because out of his poor backpack pulled in a while the one-year volunteer several little boxes of sardines and distributed one to each.

Baloun dauntlessly opened the small suitcase of Senior Lieutenant Lukáš and returned there the sardines fallen from heaven.

When all of them then opened their fish canned in oil and were savoring them, Baloun met a temptation and opened the small suitcase and the sardines and he gobbled them up, gulping.

And here the most blessed and sweetest Virgin Mary turned her face away from him, because just as he was finishing drinking the oil from the tin can, there emerged in the front of the railroad car Battalion *Messenger* Matušič calling up above: "Baloun, you're to bring to your *Senior Lieutenant* those sardines."

"Those slaps you'll be getting," said Accounting Master Sergeant Vaněk.

"With barren hands you better not go there," was advising Švejk, "Take with you at least five empty tin cans."

"What, I wonder, have you done, that God is punishing you so," remarked the one-year volunteer, "there must be in your past some big sin. Didn't you commit perhaps a sacrilegious theft and eat your priest's ham in the chimney? Didn't you drink up in the cellar all his sacramental wine? Didn't you use to perhaps as a boy sneak after the pears into the rectory garden?"

Baloun walked away swaying with a desperate expression on his face, full of hopelessness. Now his run-down expression of a hunted-down animal was speaking tearing at the heart: When will there already be an end to the anguish?

"The thing is," said the one-year volunteer, who overheard the words of the hapless Baloun, "that you, my friend, have lost the connection to the Lord God. You don't know how to say a prayer well, so that the Lord God would as soon as possible escort you out of this world."

To that Švejk added: "It's just that Baloun constantly cannot bring himself to do it, and will his military life, his military thinking, words, deeds, even his military death to the goodness of the mother's heart of the most high Lord God, as used to put it that *Field Chaplain* of mine Katz, when he had started taking in too much already and going over the top and by mistake bumped on the street into some soldier."

Baloun released a moan, that he has already lost confidence in the Lord God, because who knows how many times he had been praying, that He give him so much strength and somehow shrink that stomach of his.

"It doesn't date from the start of this war," he lamented, "that's already an old disease, this voracity of mine. On account of it my wife and the kids used to go on the pilgrimage to Klokoty[137]."

The cook-occultist began quarreling with the telegraph operator Chodounský, whether it was a to-heaven-crying divulgence of the confessional secret or whether it was even worth talking about, since the brilliants were fake. In the end, however, he proved to Chodounský, that it was karma, that is a predetermined fate from a distant unknown past, when perhaps the hapless church custodian from Slovakia was still a cephalopod on some other foreign planet, and at any rate that the fate was already predetermined long ago, when the father from Klokoty was perhaps still an echidna, some pouched, nowadays already extinct mammal, that he had to violate the sanctity of the confessional secret, although from the legal point of view according to the canon law an absolution is given in such cases, even though at stake is a cloister property.

To that Švejk attached this simple remark: "Yeah well, no man knows, what silly things he is going to be doing in a couple of million years, and can be swearing off nothing. *Senior Lieutenant* Kvasnička, when we used to serve still in Karlín with the *expansion reserve unit*, he would always say, when he was teaching school: 'Don't think, you shitboilers, you lazy cows and Hungarian hogs, that this wartime service will already end for you in this world. We'll even after death get a glimpse of one another, and I'll prepare for you such a purgatory, that you'll be from it like deer in the headlights, you pack of swine.'"

In the meantime Baloun, who having been in total desperation kept thinking, that now anything being said was only about him, that everything had to do with him, continued his public confession: "Not even Klokoty was helping to rid me of voracity. There comes the wife with the children from the pilgrimage and already she begins to count the hens. Missing are one or two. But I couldn't help myself, I knew, that in the household they're needed on account of eggs, but I walk out, end up staring at them, all of a sudden I'm feeling in my stomach a bottomless pit, and in an hour I am already fine, already has the hen been picked clean. Once when they were in Klokoty, to pray for me, so that daddy at home in the meantime wouldn't devour anything and do again new damage, I'm walking in the yard, and all of a sudden my sight fell on a turkey. Back then I could have paid for it with my life. There got stuck from it in my throat a thigh bone, and if it weren't for my powder boy, miller's apprentice, such a little lad, who pulled the bone out for me, then today I wouldn't be sitting here with you anymore and wouldn't even have lived to see the world war. — Aye, aye. That powder boy of mine, he was a sharp cookie. Such a little, plump, rotund, lardy one —"

Švejk stepped up to Baloun: "Show your tongue!"

Baloun stuck his tongue out at Švejk, after which Švejk turned to all, who were in the railroad car: "I knew it, he devoured even that powder boy of his. — Confess, when did you devour him! When yours were in Klokoty again — right?"

Baloun desperately clasped his hands and cried out: "Leave me be, pals! And this on top of it from my own pals."

"We are not condemning you on account of it," said the one-year volunteer, "on the contrary it shows, that you will be a good soldier. When the French were during the Napoleonic wars besieging Madrid[138], here the Spanish commander of the Madrid fortress, rather than give up the fortress due to hunger, ate his adjutant without any salt."

"That's indeed a genuine sacrifice, because a salted adjutant would have certainly been more edible — What again is the name, *Mister Accounting Master Sergeant*, of that adjutant of our Battalion? — Ziegler? He's some kind of a little sneak, from him one couldn't make enough portions for even one *marchgang*."

"Look here," said Accounting Master Sergeant Vaněk, "Baloun has a rosary in his hand."

And really, Baloun in his greatest sorrow was seeking salvation in the little balls of bladder-nuts from the firm Moritz-Löwenstein in Vienna.

"That too is from Klokoty," said sadly Baloun. "Before they brought it for me, two goslings were laid waste, but that's no meat, that's mush."

A short while after that an order came up and down the whole train, that in a quarter of an hour they'd be hauling. Because nobody wanted or could believe that, what happened was, that in spite of all the vigilance, here and there somebody wandered off wherever. When the train moved, eighteen guys were missing, among them Quartermaster Nasáklo of the 12th *March Company*, who, when the train had long ago disappeared on the other side of Isatarcsa, was still quarreling in a little acacia grove behind the railroad station in a dale with some fast streetwalker, who wanted from him five crowns, whereas he was proposing as a reward for the service already performed a crown or a couple of slaps, the latter being the settlement to which it actually came in the end with such vehemence, that responding to her roar people began by running there from the railroad station and gathering in a crowd.

3

# FROM HATVAN TO THE BORDERS OF GALICIA

During the whole time of the railroad transport of the Battalion, which was to be harvesting martial glory, once it will have walked on foot from Laborec[139] through east Galicia to the front, there was carried on in the railroad car, where the one-year volunteer and Švejk were, again queer talk of more or less high-treasonous content, on a smaller scale, but we can say generally, it was happening even in other railroad cars, aye, even in the Staff railroad car there was prevailing some sort of dissatisfaction, because in Füzesabony[140] there came an army-wide order from the Regiment, in which the portion of wine was being lowered for the officers by one eighth of a liter. Of course at that time were not forgotten the rank-and-file, for whom the portion of sago[141] was being decreased by one decagram per man, which was that much more mysterious, because nobody in the army service had ever seen any sago.

Nevertheless it was necessary to inform Accounting Master Sergeant Bautanzel, who felt thereby terribly slighted and robbed, which he also expressed by stating, that sago is nowadays a rare thing and that for a kilo he'd get at least eight crowns.

In Füzesabony it was also discovered, that one *company* had lost its field kitchen, because at last at this station there was to be cooked goulash with potatoes, on which was placing great emphasis the latrine-general. Through a probing inquiry it emerged as apparent, that the hapless field kitchen was not riding along at all from Bruck and that perhaps it is till this day standing there somewhere behind the barrack 186, abandoned and turned cold.

The kitchen personnel belonging to that field kitchen was in fact the day before departure locked up at the *main guard-house* for boisterous behavior in town and was able to fix things for itself so, that it was still sitting doing time, when its *marchgang* was already riding through Magyaria.

The *company* without a kitchen was then assigned to another field kitchen, which however did not pass without a quarrel, because between the men of both companies assigned to peel the potatoes there arose such controversies, that the ones were telling the others, that they were not such dumb beasts, as to be toiling for others. In the end it actually turned out, that as for the goulash and potatoes it was actually

## The Fateful Adventures of the Good Soldier Švejk

a maneuver, so that the soldiers would get used to the fact, that when in the field, facing the enemy, goulash is being cooked, all of a sudden there will come the order "*Everybody back!*", the goulash is poured out of the cauldrons and nobody gets as much as a lick.

This was then some sort of training, in its consequences not so tragic, but nevertheless instructive. That is to say, when the goulash was to be distributed at last, the order came "Into the railroad cars!" and we were already hauling off to Miskolc[142]. Not even there was the goulash distributed, because on the track there stood a train with Russian railroad cars, therefore the troops were not let out of the railroad cars and left to the troops for their imagination was an open field to fantasize, that the goulash would be distributed, when they will have crawled off the train once in Galicia, where the goulash would be deemed spoiled sour, unsuitable for ingestion, and that then it would be poured out.

Then they had the goulash riding along, farther on to Tiszalök[143], Zombor[144] and, when nobody was expecting, that the goulash would be distributed, the train stopped in the New Town under the Šiator[145], where again the fire was kindled under the cauldrons, the goulash was warmed up and was at last distributed.

The station was crammed, first to be dispatched were two trains with munitions, after them two *military transport trains* of artillery and a train with pontoon sections. All in all it's possible to say, that here were gathered trains with the troops from all the possible components of the military.

Behind the railroad station *Hungarian Land Defense cavalry soldiers* were working over two Polish Jews, whose large basket with booze they plundered clean, and now instead of paying up, being in a good mood, they were beating them up across their mugs, which they apparently were allowed to do, because standing quite near was their *captain* and he was pleasantly smiling at the whole scene, while behind the storehouse several other *Hungarian Land Defense cavalry soldiers* were feeling under the skirts of black-eyed dear daughters of the Jews being beaten up.

There was here also a train with a section of airplanes. On other tracks were standing on the railroad cars the same sort of objects, such as airplanes and cannons, except in a broken down state. They were shot-down-from-under flying machines, torn-apart barrels of howitzers. While all that was fresh and new was going over up there, these remnants of glory were rolling to the land's interior for repairs and reconstructions.

Lieutenant Dub however was telling the soldiers, who had gathered around the broken cannons and airplanes, that it was war booty, and he also noticed, that a bit farther was standing again in a group Švejk, who was talking about something. Therefore he went nearer to that spot and heard the prudent voice of Švejk: "Any way you take it, it is after all war booty. It is truly enough precarious at first sight, when somebody here reads on the gun-carriage *I&R Artillery Division*. But what it perhaps will turn out to be is, that the cannon had fallen into the hands of the Russians and we had to capture it back again fighting, and such booty is much more valuable, because... — Because," he said festively, when he caught the sight of Lieutenant Dub, "nothing must be left in the enemy's hands. It is like with the case of Przemyśl, or with the soldier, when in combat the enemy tore away from him his *field flask*. That was back during the Napoleonic wars, and the soldier at night set out for the enemy encampment and brought his field flask back again and he made out after all, because the enemy had gotten issued booze for the night."

Lieutenant Dub said only: "See to it, that you disappear already, Švejk, don't let me see you here a second time!"

"As ordered, *Lieutenant*, Sir." And Švejk was walking away toward the second group of railroad cars, and had Lieutenant Dub heard, what he yet added, he would have certainly jumped out of his uniform, although it was an entirely innocent biblical statement: "A little while, and ye shall see me, and again a little while, and ye shall not see me."

Lieutenant Dub was after Švejk's departure on top of all so stupid, that he was calling the soldier's attention to one shot-down Austrian airplane on the metal rim of which there was clearly marked Wiener Neustadt.

"We shot that down for the Russians by Lwów," said Lieutenant Dub. These words overheard Senior Lieutenant Lukáš, who approached and loudly added: "On which occasion both the Russian fliers burnt to death."

Then he was walking away without a word, having thought, that Lieutenant Dub was a real piece of cattle beast.

Behind the other railroad cars he ran into Švejk and was intending to avoid him, because in the face of Švejk glancing at Senior Lieutenant Lukáš one could see, that this man has a lot on his heart, which he wants to tell him.

Švejk went straight to him: "*I dutifully report Company Messenger* Švejk is respectfully requesting further orders. I dutifully report, *Senior Lieutenant*, Sir, that I've already looked for you in the Staff car."

"Listen, Švejk," said Senior Lieutenant Lukáš in a tone absolutely repulsing and hostile. "Do you know what your name is? Have you already forgotten the name I gave you?"

"I dutifully report, *Senior Lieutenant*, Sir, that such a thing I have not forgotten about, because I am not some one-year volunteer Železný. We were back then, still a long time before the war, in the Karlín garrison and there was some *Colonel* Fliedler von Boomerang or something like that there."

Senior Lieutenant Lukáš involuntarily smiled at the 'something like that' and Švejk kept on relating: "I dutifully report, *Senior Lieutenant*, Sir, that the *Colonel* of ours was half your height, wore a full beard like the duke Lobkovic[146], so that he looked like a monkey, and when he'd get upset, he was jumping twice as high, as he himself was tall, so that we used to call him the India rubber geezer. Back then there was some May Day and we were *on alert*, and he was treating us the night before in the court-yard to a big speech, that the reason why tomorrow we all have to stay in the garrison and not even make a move to go outside, is for us to be able in response to the highest level order, in case of need, to shoot and mow down the whole socialist pack. That is also why, any soldier that has an overtime pass today and doesn't return to the garrison and stretches it over to the next day, that he would have committed treason against the homeland, because such a drunk guy wouldn't hit even one man, when the salvos are being fired, and what's more, he'd be shooting in the air. Then the one-year volunteer Železný returned to the room and says, that after all, the India rubber geezer did have a good idea. Why, it is largely true, tomorrow they clearly won't let anybody into the garrison, so the best is not to come at all, and he also, I dutifully report, *Senior Lieutenant*, Sir, carried that out as smoothly as downing a glass of wine. But that *Colonel* Fliedler, let me tell you, was such a miserable miscreant, give him Lord God heaven, that he was walking the next day around Prague and was looking for anybody, who from our Regiment had dared to crawl out of the garrison, and somewhere by the Powder Tower luckily also he ran into Železný[147] and immediately let him have it: 'I gif it to yoo, I yoo teach, I sveeten it for yoo tvice!' He told him much more, bagged him and brought him to the garrison and along the whole journey was telling him many an ugly, threatening thing and constantly kept asking him, what his name was. Ihrony, Ihronlike, you to get shitslammed for it, I glat, zat I to catch, I you schow *that May Day*. Ihronlike, Ihronlike, yoo to be maayn, lohck up, fine lohck up!' To Železný it didn't make any difference anymore. So, as they walked down Poříč[148], past the Rozvařilů[149], Železný jumped into the courtyard passageway and shook him off via a walk-through and spoiled the India rubber geezer's great joy he'd have, when throwing him in the brig. The *Colonel* got so upset, because he gave him the slip, that on account of his anger he forgot, what his delinquent's name was, mixed it up, and when he arrived at the garrison, he started jumping up to the ceiling, the ceiling was low, and the one, who had the Battalion duty officer's watch, was wondering, why the geezer is speaking all of a sudden broken Czech and is screaming: 'Kopperlike, lohck up, Kopperlike, nah lohck up, Lehdlike, lohck up, Teehnlike lohck up!' And in this way the geezer was tormenting them one day after another and kept asking, whether they had yet caught Copperlike, Ledlike, and Tinlike, and also had them bring out the whole Regiment, but they had put Železný, of whom it was already universally known, into sickbay, because he was a dental technician. Until this one time a guy from our Regiment managed to pierce a dragoon in the pub U Bucků[150], who was going after his girl, and here they had us stand in the square formation, all had to come out, even the sickbay, whoever was too sick, him were holding two guys. So then it was to no avail, Železný had to come out into the yard and there they were reading us the Regiment-wide order in the approximate vein, that dragoons are also soldiers and that it is forbidden to be piercing them, because they are our *war comrades*. A one one-year volunteer was translating it and our *Colonel* was gawking like a tiger. First he strolled past the front, then again he went to the rear, he was walking around the square, and all of a sudden he discovered Železný, who was a mountain of a man, so that, *Senior Lieutenant*, Sir, it was very comical, when he dragged him inside the square formation. The one-year-timer stopped translating, and our *Colonel* started jumping up in front of Železný, like when a dog is pestering a mare, and he was hollering while doing it: 'Zoh you me not slip, you me nah go novehr eeskape, now again be zaying, dat yoo're Ihronlike, and me all time zay Kopperlike, Teehnlike, Lehdlike, he Ihronlike, and he, dat urchin, is Ihronlike, I teech yoo Lehdlike, Teehnlike, Kopperlike, you *hunk of barnyard crap, you pig, you* Ihronlike!' Then he slammed him with a month for it, but then again in about two weeks somehow his teeth started aching, and he remembered that Železný was a dental technician, so he had them bring him from the brig to the sickbay and wanted to have him pull a tooth, and Železný was pulling it out for him for about a half an hour, so that they had to be sponging the geezer down about three times to have him come to, but the geezer got somehow subdued and forgave Železný the second two weeks. So that's the way it is, *Senior Lieutenant*, Sir, when a superior forgets the name of his subordinate, but the subordinate must never forget the name of his superior, as was telling us the very *Colonel*, that even years later we wouldn't forget, that once upon a time we used to have *Colonel* Fliedler. — Wasn't it perhaps too long, *Senior Lieutenan*t, Sir?"

"You know, Švejk," answered Senior Lieutenant Lukáš, "the longer I listen to you, the more I'm coming to the conviction, that you don't respect your superiors at all. A soldier is even years later to speak of his superiors only well."

One could see, that Senior Lieutenant Lukáš was beginning to be entertained.

"I dutifully report, *Senior Lieutenant*, Sir," jumped in Švejk in an apologetic tone, "why, the mister *Colonel* Fliedler has been dead long since, but since you, *Senior Lieutenant*, Sir, wish, I will speak of him nothing but praises. He was, let me tell you, *Senior Lieutenant*, Sir, practically an angel toward the soldiers. He was, let me tell you, so nice like Saint Martin[151], who used to give out Martin's geese to the poor and hungry. He would share his lunch from *the officers' mess rations* with the nearest soldier, whom he'd meet in the yard, and when we had all gotten sick of eating *dumbers*[152] all the time, he had them then make us for mess the *grenade throwers' march* with pork meat, and at maneuvers, he really made a mark with his goodness. When we came to Dolní Královice[153], then he gave an order to drink the whole Dolnokrálovice brewery dry on his account, and when it was his name's day or birthday, he had them cook up for the whole Regiment a hare in cream gravy and braided bun dumplings. He was so nice to the *troops*, that once, *Senior Lieutenant*, Sir…"

Senior Lieutenant Lukáš gently tapped Švejk across the ear and said in a friendly tone: "So go already, you creature, leave him be already."

"*As ordered Lieutenant, Sir!*" Švejk was walking away to his railroad car, while outside the *military transport train* of the Battalion, there, where in the railroad car there were locked the telephone apparatuses and wire, was unfolding this scene: There was standing a posted guard there, because by the order of *Captain* Ságner everything had to be *battlefield ready*. The posted sentries then positioned themselves at intervals alongside the valuables of the *military transport train* on both sides and obtained *field challenge call* and *response passwords* from the Battalion Office.

That day the *field challenge call* was "Kappe", and the *response password* "Hatvan". The sentry posted by the phone apparatuses, who was supposed to remember them, was some Pole from Kolomyje[154], who through some strange chance ended up with the 91st Regiment.

No way could he know, what Kappe was, but because he had in him some embryonic stage of mnemonics, he then did commit to memory after all, that it started with 'k', and proudly answered Lieutenant Dub, who had *battalion duty officer's watch* and was challenging him, getting closer, and asked for the password of the day: "Kafe." It was, however, very natural, because the Pole from Kolomyje still kept remembering the morning and the evening coffee at the camp in Bruck.

And when he hollered one more time "Kafe", and Lieutenant Dub kept coming closer, at this point he, remembering his oath and the fact, that he is standing guard, called out threateningly: '*Stop!*', and when Lieutenant Dub made two more steps toward him and kept demanding a response to the *field challenge call* from him, he aimed his rifle at him and not having perfect knowledge of the German language, he used a queer mixture of Polish and German, screaming: "*I vill schit, I v ill schit.*"

Lieutenant Dub got it and began shuffling back, screaming: "*Watch commander, Watch commander!*"

There appeared Corporal Jelínek, who had posted the Pole for sentry duty, and himself asked him for the password, then Lieutenant Dub, to which questions the desperate Pole from around Kolomyje kept answering by a scream, which was resounding through the railroad station: "*Coffee, coffee.*" From as many *military transport trains* as there were, there started jumping out soldiers with mess kits and there was a horrible panic, the end of which was, when they led the disarmed, dutiful soldier away to the arrestee railroad car.

But Lieutenant Dub was harboring a certain suspicion of Švejk, whom he saw as the first one crawling out of the railroad car with a mess kit, and he would have bet his neck, that had heard him calling out: "Out, with the mess kits, out, with the mess kits."

After midnight the train got moving toward Ladovce[155] and Trebišov[156], where in the morning it was welcomed at the station by a veterans association, because it mistook this marchbattalion for the marchbattalion of the 14$^{th}$ *Hungarian Land Defense Regiment*, which had rolled right through the station in the night. The sure thing was, that the veterans were loaded, and with their screaming of "Isten áld meg a királyt[157]" they woke out of sleep the whole *military transport train*. Several more conscientious ones leaned out of the railroad cars and answered them: "Kiss for us our ass. Éljen! [158]"

After which the veterans gave such a holler, that the windows of the railroad station building rattled: "Éljen! Éljen a tizennegyedik regiment (fourteenth regiment)!"

In five minutes the train kept on rolling toward Humenné[159]. Here already there were visible clear and distinct traces of the fighting, when the Russians were hauling through the valley of the Tisa[160]. Across the hillsides there were stretching primitive trenches, here and there one could see a burnt down homestead, in the vicinity of which a hastily built shack signified, that the owners had again returned.

Then, when toward noon they reached the Humenné station, where the railroad yard was also showing remnants of fighting, preparations for the lunch were executed and the troops of the *military transport train* in the meantime could take a peek at the public secret, how the authorities after the departure of the Russians deal with the local populace, which was by language and religion related to the Russian soldiers.

On the platform, surrounded by Hungarian State policeman, there was standing a group of arrested Magyar Russians. There were several Russian Orthodox priests, teachers and farmers from far and wide around. All had their hands tied up in the back with ropes and in pairs tied one to another. Mostly they had busted noses and lumps on their heads, as they got immediately after the arrest a thrashing from the State Police cops.

A bit farther a Hungarian State policeman was toying with a Russian Orthodox priest. He tied around his left leg a rope, which he held in his hand, and was forcing him with the rifle butt to dance czardas, while he was yanking the rope, so that the priest fell on his nose, and having his hands tied in the back, could not get up and was making desperate attempts to turn over on his back, in order to be able perhaps thus to pick himself up off the ground. The State policeman was laughing at it so sincerely, that tears were running from his eyes, and when at last the priest was getting up, he yanked the rope and the priest was again on his nose.

At last, there put a stop to it a State policeman, who ordered, that the arrestees be led away, for the time being until the train comes, to an empty wood shed behind the railroad station and there they were beating and thrashing them, in order that nobody see it.

Those in the Staff railroad car started discussing this episode and on the whole one can say, that the majority was condemning it.

*Ensign* Kraus was of the opinion, that since they were after all high traitors, they were to be immediately hanged on the spot without any tormenting, while Lieutenant Dub totally agreed with the whole scene as it had taken place, and shifted it right away to the Sarajevo assassination and explained it so, that the Hungarian State policemen at the station in Humenné were avenging the death of Archduke Franz Ferdinand and his wife. To give weight to his words, he said, that he used to get a magazine (*Šimáček's Four-Leafed Clover*[161]) and that in there, still before the war, in the July issue there was written about the assassination, that the unprecedented crime of Sarajevo has left in human hearts a wound incapable of healing for a long time, and that much more painful, because through this crime was annihilated not only the life of the representative of the executive power of the State, but even the life of his loyal and beloved companion, and that by the destruction of these two lives the happy, exemplary family life was torn asunder and children loved by all made orphans.

Senior Lieutenant Lukáš only murmured to himself, that the State policemen here in Humenné were probably getting *Šimáček's Four-Leafed Clover* with that moving article in it. All in all everything began all of a sudden to repulse him and he felt only the need to get drunk, so that the world-grief[162] would leave him. He then got out of the railroad car and went to search out Švejk.

"Listen up, Švejk," he said to him, "don't you know of some bottle of cognac? I don't feel somehow that good."

"The thing that does that, I dutifully report, *Senior Lieutenant,* Sir, is the change of weather. Could be, that when we're on the battlefield, you'll feel even worse. The greater distance a man is putting between himself and the original military base, the fainter he gets. A gardener in Strašnice[163], some Josef Kalenda, he too got a distance away from home once, went from Strašnice to Vinohrady, dropped by At the Stop[164], but nothing was wrong with him yet, but as soon as he entered the Crown boulevard[165] at the water tower[166], he was bagging one pub after another on the Crown boulevard all the way to the other side of the Church of St. Ludmila[167] and was already feeling listlessness. He didn't let that scare him off however, because beforehand that evening in Strašnice in the Streetcar Depot[168] pub he bet a streetcar driver, that he would make a trip around the world on foot in three weeks. He began then putting greater and greater distance between himself and his home, until he rolled into the Black Brewery[169] at Karlovo square, and from there he went to Lesser Quarter, the brewery At St. Tomas'[170] there, and from there he continued via the restaurant At the Montags'[171] and even farther up the hill via the King of Brabant[172] pub, then to At the Beautiful View, from here to the Strahov Monastery[173] into the brewery[174] there. But then already the change of climate stopped agreeing with him. He managed to get all the way to the Loretánské square[175] and there he got suddenly so homesick, that he slammed himself on the ground, started writhing on the sidewalk and was screaming: 'Folks, I won't go any farther. I will,' excuse me *Senior Lieutenant*, Sir, 'blow off that trip around the world.' Should you though wish, *Senior Lieutenant*, Sir, then for *them* some cognac I will chase down, I'm only afraid, that you all could take off on me before that."

Senior Lieutenant Lukáš assured him, that they wouldn't be hauling out of here in less than two hours and that as for the cognac they sell it just behind the railroad station on the sly in bottles, that *Captain* Ságner had already sent Matušič there and that he brought him for fifteen crowns a bottle of quite passable cognac. Here he has fifteen crowns, and for him to go already, and just don't tell anybody, that it is for Senior Lieutenant Lukáš or that he is the one sending him, because it is after all a forbidden thing.

"Rest assured, *Senior Lieutenant*, Sir," said Švejk, "that it will all be alright, because I very much like forbidden things, because I have always found myself in something forbidden, without me even having known about it. Once, in the Karlín garrison they forbade us..."

"*About face — Forward march!*" interrupted him Senior Lieutenant Lukáš.

And so Švejk went to the back of the railroad station, repeating to himself along the way all the components of his mission: that the cognac must be good, therefore he must taste it beforehand, that it is forbidden, therefore he must be careful.

Just when he was turning to behind the platform, he ran again into Lieutenant Dub. "What are you loafing here for?" he asked Švejk. "Do

Jaroslav Hašek

you know me?"

"I dutifully report," answered Švejk saluting, "that I do not wish to get to know you from that bad side of yours."

The startled Lieutenant Dub froze, but Švejk was standing calmly, keeping his hand to the bill of his cap, and continued: "I dutifully report, *Lieutenant*, Sir, that I want to get to know you only from the good side, so that you would not drive me all the way to tears, as you were telling me the last time."

Lieutenant Dub's head spun over such insolence and he managed only an angry scream: "Scram, you miserable oaf, you and I will yet talk!"

Švejk walked away to behind the platform and Lieutenant Dub, having come to, set out after him. Behind the railroad station, right by the road, there was standing a row of burden baskets put down with their bottoms up, upon which there were shallow bread baskets and on the bread baskets various tasty treats looking wholly innocent as if all those goodies were intended for the school youth somewhere on a field trip. Lying there were pieces of extruded hard candy, wafer rolls, a pile of sour candy twists, here and there in addition in one of the bread baskets little slices of black bread with a piece of salami, absolutely for sure of horse origin. Inside, however the burden baskets contained varieties of alcohol, flasks with cognac, rum, rowan brandy and other liqueurs and other kinds of booze.

Right on the other side of the road ditch there was a hut and it was there where all these trades in the illicit drinks were actually being made.

The soldiers first made a deal by the burden baskets and a Jew with temple locks pulled from under the burden basket such an innocently looking booze and brought it under his caftan into the wooden hut, where already the soldier inconspicuously hid it somewhere in his pants or under his blouse.

Here then is where Švejk was aiming, while from the direction of the railroad station was observing him Lieutenant Dub with his detective talent.

Švejk walked directly to the first burden basket. First he picked the hard candy, which he paid for and put in his pocket, while the gentleman with the temple locks whispered to him: "*I have schnapps too, merciful mister soldier.*"

The negotiations were quickly made an end of, Švejk walked away into the hut, and didn't turn the money over, until the gentleman with the temple locks opened the bottle and Švejk had a taste. He was however satisfied with the cognac and was returning to the railroad station, having tucked the bottle under his blouse.

"Where have you been, you miserable oaf?" stood himself in the path leading to the platform Lieutenant Dub.

"I dutifully report, *Lieutenant*, Sir, that I went to buy hard candy." Švejk reached into his pocket and pulled out a handful of dirty, dusty hard candy: "If mister *Lieutenant* were not to find it revolting — I have already tried them, they're not bad. They have a sort of pleasant, unusual taste, like that of prune butter, *Lieutenant*, Sir."

Under his blouse were appearing outlines of the round contours of a bottle.

Lieutenant Dub patted Švejk on the blouse: "What is it you're carrying here, you singular miserable oaf. Pull it out!"

Švejk pulled the bottle of yellowish content, with a totally clear and discernible label Cognac.

"I dutifully report, *Lieutenant*, Sir," answered Švejk fearlessly, "that I went with an empty cognac bottle to pump into it a little water to drink. I still have after the goulash, that we had yesterday, a horrible thirst. But the water there at the pump, as you see, *Lieutenant*, Sir, is somehow yellow, it must be perhaps some water rich in iron. Such waters are very healthy and useful."

"Since you have such a thirst, Švejk," said Lieutenant Dub, devilishly smiling and wanting to prolong for as long as possible the scene, in which Švejk would lose for good, "then take a drink, but as is proper. Drink it all up at once!"

Lieutenant Dub figured it already beforehand, how Švejk would take several gulps and wouldn't be able to go on and how he, Lieutenant Dub, would gloriously prevail over him in a victory and say: "Hand me too the bottle, so that I may have a little drink, I am also thirsty." How that hoodlum Švejk would probably be making faces for him in that horrible moment, and then at the report time, and so on.

Švejk uncorked the bottle, applied it to his mouth and a gulp after gulp was disappearing in his gullet. Lieutenant Dub turned to stone. In the plain view of his eyes Švejk drank the whole bottle empty, not even having batted an eyelash, and he threw the empty bottle across the road into the pond, spat, and said, as if he had drunk a glass of mineral water: "I dutifully report *Lieutenant*, Sir, that the water really had an iron flavor. In Kamýk nad Vltavou[176] one pubkeeper used to make for his summer guests iron-rich water in such a way, that he'd be throwing old horseshoes into the well."

"I'll give you old horseshoes! Come to show me the well from where you got the water!"

"It's a bit away from here, *Lieutenant*, Sir, right here behind the wooden hut."

"Go first, you miserable oaf, so I can see, how you keep in step!"

"That is really strange," thought to himself Lieutenant Dub. One can see no signs of anything about that wretched man that would give him away. On that miserable guy one can see absolutely nothing to give him away."

Švejk then went first, having given himself unto the will of God, but something kept telling him, that the well had to be there, and it also did not surprise him in any way, that it was there. Even the pump was there, and when they came to it, here Švejk pumped it several times, there was running out of it yellowish water so that he could gloriously proclaim: "Here is that iron-rich water, *Lieutenant*, Sir."

The terrified man with the temple locks came nearer and Švejk told him in German to bring some glass, that mister Lieutenant wanted to have a drink.

Lieutenant Dub was so totally stupefied from it, that he drank the whole glass of water, after which he had rolling around in his mouth the taste of horse urine and dung water, and having turned a total numskull, from what he just lived through, he gave the Jew with the temple locks for the glass a five crown bill, and turning toward Švejk, he told him: "What are you gawking here for, scram and go home."

In five minutes Švejk appeared in the Staff railroad car by Senior Lieutenant Lukáš and with a mysterious gesture lured him out of the railroad car, and outside he informed him: "I dutifully report, *Senior Lieutenant*, Sir, that in five, at most ten minutes I will be totally drunk, but I will be lying in my railroad car, and would like to beg of you, that for at least three hours, *Senior Lieutenant*, Sir, you not be calling me and giving me any commands, until I will have slept it off. Everything is alright, but I got caught by mister Lieutenant Dub, I told him that it was water, so I had to drink the whole bottle of cognac empty in front of him, in order to prove to him, that it was water. Everything is alright, I gave away nothing, as you wished, and I was careful too, but now already, I dutifully report *Senior Lieutenant*, Sir, I'm feeling it, my legs are somehow beginning to have pins and needles in them. However, I dutifully report *Senior Lieutenant*, Sir, that I'm used to soaking up booze, because with mister Field Chaplain Katz…"

"Depart, beast!" called out Senior Lieutenant Lukáš, but without any anger, although Lieutenant Dub became fifty percent more unlikable to him than before.

Švejk crawled carefully into his railroad car, and laying himself down on his overcoat and backpack, he said toward the Accounting Master Sergeant and the others: "Once, I tell you, a man got drunk and was asking, that they kindly not be waking him up…"

After those words he turned over to lie on his side and started snoring.

The gases, which he was expelling by burping, soon filled the whole room, so that the cook-occultist Jurajda, sucking the atmosphere through the nostrils, declared: "Damn, this place is fragrant with cognac."

At the collapsible desk was sitting one-year volunteer Marek who at last after all those hardships had made it all the way to *battalion chronicler*.

Now he was composing for the stockpile heroic deeds of the Battalion and one could see, that it brought him a great pleasure, this look into the future.

Accounting Master Sergeant Vaněk was observing with interest how the one-year volunteer was diligently writing and laughing with a wide grin while doing it. That is also why he stood up and leaned over the one-year volunteer, who began to explain to him: "Here's the thing, it is terribly funny to be writing up the history of the Battalion in advance to keep in stock. The main thing is to proceed systematically. In everything there has to be a system."

"Systematic system," remarked Accounting Master Sergeant Vaněk with a more or less disdaining smile.

"Yes," said the one-year volunteer offhandedly, "systematized, systematic system in writing up the history of the Battalion. We can't roll out a great victory up front right away. It all has to go slowly, according to a certain plan. Our Battalion cannot win this world war at once. Nihil nisi bene[177]. The main thing for a thorough chronicler of history, like I am, is to make first a plan of our victories. For example, I'm describing here how our Battalion, this will perhaps be two months from now, almost crosses the Russian border, very heavily manned, by, let us say, the enemy's Don[178] regiments, while several enemy divisions are getting around our positions. At the first sight it seems, that our Battalion is doomed, that they will chop us up into noodles, when at that moment *Captain* Ságner gives this Battalion-wide order: 'God does not want for us to perish here, let's flee!' Our Battalion then takes off running away, but the enemy division, which had already gone around us, sees, that we are actually rushing it, starts fleeing in horror, and falls without a shot into the hands of our army reserves. Thereby then actually the whole history of our Battalion will begin. From an insignificant event, I'm speaking prophetically, mister Vaněk, will evolve much farther- reaching things. Our Battalion goes from victory to victory. The interesting thing will be, how our Battalion ambushes the sleeping enemy, for which however the composition style needed is that of the Illustrated War Bulletin, which used to be published by Vilímek[179] during the Russo-Japanese war. Our Battalion will set upon the camp of the sleeping enemy. Each of our soldiers looks up one of the enemies, with all the might rams the bayonet into his bosom. The excellently sharpened bayonet rides in like into butter and only now and then a rib will crack, the sleeping enemies' whole bodies jerk, for a moment bugging out their amazed, but no longer seeing eyes, give a death rattling sound and come down flat. On the sleeping enemies' lips are emerging bloody spittle, thereby the matter is finished and the victory is on the side of our Battalion. Or it will be better yet about three months from now, when our Battalion captures the Russian Czar. About that we'll talk, mister Vaněk, only later, in the meantime I have to prepare little episodes for the stockpile, testifying to unprecedented heroism. I will need to think up wholly new martial terms. I have invented one already, I will write of the self-sacrificing determination of our troops, interlarded with the fragments of grenades. By the explosion of an enemy mine will one of our corporals, let's say of the Twelfth or Thirteenth *Company*, lose his head. — À propos[180]," said the one-year volunteer, having hit himself on his head, "I would have almost forgotten, *Accounting Master Sergeant*, Sir, or as spoken among citizens, Mister Vaněk, you must get a list of the NCOs for me. Name a quartermaster of the Twelfth Company. — Houska? Good, so then Houska will lose his head to that mine, the head will fly off, the body however will still make several steps, it will aim and still shoot down an enemy airplane. It goes without saying, that the echoes of these victories must be in the future celebrated in the family circle at Schönbrunn. Austria has very many battalions, but only one battalion, ours, which will distinguish itself, so that only on its account there will be organized a small intimate family celebration of the Imperial House. The way I imagine it is, as you can see in my notes, that the archduchy family of Marie Valérie[181] will relocate on account of it from the Wallsee[182] to Schönbrunn. The celebration is purely intimate and is taking place in the hall next to the monarch's bedroom, which is illuminated with white wax candles, because as is known, at the court they do not love electrical bulbs on account of short circuits, against which is the frail old monarch prejudiced. At the sixth hour of the evening commences the party to honor and praise our Battalion. At that time the grandsons of His Majesty are escorted into the hall, which actually belongs to the chambers of the immortalized Empress. Now the question is, who will be present besides the Imperial family. There must be and there will be the General Adjutant of the monarch, Count Paar[183]. Because at such family and intimate banquets now and then somebody gets faint, by which however I don't mean, that Count Paar will perhaps puke, there is required the presence of the personal physician, Court Counselor Dr. Kerzl[184]. On account of order, so that the court footmen would not dare to afford themselves some intimacies toward the court ladies present at the banquet, there emerges the *Chief Court Steward*, Baron Lederer[185], the *Chief Chamberlain*, Count Bellegarde[186] and the *Chief Court Lady-in-waiting*, Countess Bombelles[187], who plays the same role among the court ladies-in-waiting as the madam in the Šuhas' brothel. When their exalted lordships had gathered, they apprised of it the Emperor, who then appeared escorted by his grandsons, sat down at a table and proclaimed a toast to honor our *marchbattalion*. After him taking her turn spoke Archduchess Marie Valérie, who mentions in an especially laudatory manner you, *Accounting Master Sergeant*, Sir. Of course according to my notes our Battalion will suffer heavy and severely felt losses, because a battalion without any dead is no battalion. It will be necessary still to fashion a new article about our dead. The history of the Battalion must not consist only of dry facts about victories, of which I have already in advance marked down about forty-two. You for example, Mister Vaněk, will fall by a little creek and this one here Baloun, who is gawking at us so amazed, he will perish by quite a different death rather than by a bullet, shrapnel or grenade. He will be strangled with a lasso ejected from an enemy airplane just at the moment, when he is devouring the lunch of his *Senior Lieutenant* Lukáš."

Baloun stepped back, desperately waved his hands and uttered dejectedly: "But I cannot help my nature. Back when I was still serving on active duty, sometimes I would appear at the kitchen as many as three times for rations, until they locked me up. Once I had a rib for lunch three times, for which I was sitting for a month doing time. The Lord's will be done."

"Don't worry, Baloun," was consoling him the one-year volunteer, "in the history of the Battalion there won't be any mention of you, that you had perished feeding on the way from the officers' mess to the trenches. You will be named together with all the men of our Battalion, who fell for the glory of our Empire, like for example Accounting Master Sergeant Vaněk."

"What death have you determined for me, Marek?"

"Just don't be rushing so, *Accounting Master Sergeant*, Sir, it can't go so fast."

The one-year volunteer paused in thought for a moment: "You're from Kralupy, isn't it true; then write home, to Kralupy, that you'll disappear without a trace, but write rather carefully. Or do you wish to be heavily wounded, remain lying behind the barbed wire obstacles? You're just lying there nicely with a leg busted into pieces the whole day. At night the enemy is lighting up your position with a searchlight and notices you; he thinks, that you are on reconnaissance duty, starts slamming you with grenades and shrapnel. You have performed a tremendous service for the military, because the enemy military has used as much ammunition on you as on a battalion, and your component parts floating freely through the air after all those explosions above you, boring the air by rotating, are singing the song of grand victory. In short and well, everyone gets his turn and everyone from our Battalion will distinguish himself, so that the glorious pages of our history will be overflowing with victories — although I would not like at all to be filling it over the limit, but I cannot help it, everything must be executed thoroughly, so that some memento of us will be left by the time, let's say in the month of September, nothing at all is left of our Battalion, except those glorious pages of history, which will be finding their way into the hearts of all Austrians, telling them that it is certain, that all of those, who won't set their eyes on their home, were fighting equally vigorously and bravely. The end of it I have already composed, you know, Mister Vaněk, for the obituary. Honor to the memory of the fallen! Their love for the Imperial realm is a love most sacred, because it peaked ending in death. Let their names be uttered with respect, as for example Vaněk. Those then, whom the loss of the bread-winners touched most severely, let them proudly wipe off their tears, because the fallen — they were the heroes of our Battalion."

Telephone operator Chodounský and cook Jurajda were listening with great interest to the exposition by the one-year volunteer of the Battalion history being readied.

"Come closer, gentlemen," said the one-year volunteer, paging in his notes, "Page 15: 'Telephone operator Chodounský fell September 3$^{rd}$ at the same time as the Battalion cook Jurajda.' Hear further my notes: 'Unprecedented valor. The first, risking his life, is saving the telephone wire in his shelter, having not been relieved at the telephone for three whole days. — The second one, seeing the looming danger of the enemy's sweeping around the flank, is with a cauldron of boiling soup throwing himself at the enemy, sowing horror and scalds among the enemy. — A beautiful death for both. The first torn apart by a mine, the other asphyxiated by toxic gases, which they stuck under his nose, when he had nothing anymore with which to defend himself. — Both are perishing with the cry: *Long live our Battalion Commander!*" The High Command cannot but be bringing us daily thanksgivings in the manner of an order, so that even other components of our Army may acknowledge the bravery of our Battalion and have us for an example. I can read an excerpt from an Army order for you, which will be read to all the army units, which is very akin to that order which Archduke Karel[188] gave when he was standing with his army before Padua[189] in the year 1805 and the day after the order he had a pretty good paint-over job done on him. Listen up then to what will be read about our Battalion as an exemplary heroic body for all the troops: 'I hope that the whole Army takes the above-mentioned Battalion as an example, especially that it will make its own the spirit of self-assurance and self-courage, firm indomitability in danger, that exemplary valiance, love and trust in one's superiors, these virtues, which the Battalion excels in, lead it to admirable acts, to well-being and victory of our Empire. Let all follow its example!"

From the spot, where Švejk was lying, came the sound of a yawn and one could hear, as Švejk was talking in his sleep: "*They* are right, Mrs. Müller, that people resemble one another. In Kralupy there used to build pumps some mister Jaroš[190] and he resembled the watchmaker Lejhanz from Pardubice so much, you'd think he had fallen out of his eye, and he in turn so conspicuously resembled Piskora from Jičín[191] and all four together resembled an unidentified suicide victim, whom they found hanged and totally decomposed in a pond near Jindřichův Hradec[192], right under the railroad, where he probably hurled himself under the train." — There came the sound of a new yawn and then still an addendum: "Then they sentenced all the rest to a big fine, and tomorrow *they* make me, Mrs. Müller, strained noodles —" Švejk rolled over onto his other side and kept on snoring, while between the cook-occultist Jurajda and the one-year volunteer there commenced a debate having to do with the things of the future.

The occultist Jurajda was of the mind, that it may seem at first sight to be nonsense, when a man writes for fun about something, that will be in the future, but it is certain, that even such fun very often contains prophetic facts, when the spiritual sight of a man penetrates, under the influence of mysterious forces, the curtain veiling the unknown future. From that moment on was Jurajda's speech nothing but curtains. Every other sentence there appeared his curtain veiling the future, until at last he switched even to regeneration, that is the renewal of the human body, he thrust into it the ability of the infusorians to renew their body, ended by the statement, that every man could tear the tail off a common lizard and that it would grow back.

Telephone operator Chodounský added the remark, that people would have a honey-sweet time, if it worked in their case as with the tail among the common lizards. As for example let's say in the military, somebody gets his head or other body parts torn off, and for the military administration would such a thing be terribly welcome, because there would be no invalids. One such Austrian soldier, who would constantly grow legs, hands, heads, would be certainly more valuable than a whole brigade.

The one-year volunteer declared, that nowadays, thanks to advanced war technology, it was possible to successfully cut the enemy asunder perhaps even into three crosswise pieces. There is a law of regeneration of the body among stentors of the infusorian family; each half of the torn part regenerates itself, gains new organs and grows independently as a stentor. In an analogous case after each battle would the Austrian troops having participated in this battle increase threefold, tenfold, each leg would develop a new fresh infantryman.

"If only Švejk heard you," remarked Accounting Master Sergeant Vaněk, "he would present to us at least some example."

Švejk reacted to his name and murmured: "*Present*," and kept on snoring, having emitted this expression of military discipline.

In the slightly opened door of the railroad car there appeared the head of Lieutenant Dub.

"Is Švejk here?" he asked.

"He's sleeping, I dutifully report, *Lieutenant*, Sir," answered the one-year volunteer.

"When I am asking for his whereabouts, you one-year volunteer are to immediately jump and call him."

"It won't work *Lieutenant*, Sir, he's sleeping."

"Then wake him up! I am amazed that to you, one-year volunteer, it didn't occur right away? You are clearly to express more willingness toward your superiors! You don't know me yet. — But once you get to know me —"

The one-year volunteer started waking Švejk up.

"Švejk, there's a fire, get up!"

"When way back when the Odkolek's[193] mills were on fire," mutter Švejk, turning over again to his other side, "there came firemen all the way from Vysočany…"

"Condescend to see," said the one-year volunteer kindly to Lieutenant Dub, "that I'm waking him up, but that it won't work.

Lieutenant Dub got angry. "What is your name, one-year volunteer? — Marek? — Aha, so you are the one-year volunteer Marek, who's been sitting doing time in the brig all the time, isn't that right?"

"Yes, *Lieutenant*, Sir. I've gone through the one-year course so to speak in the pen, and I was undemoted, that is after my release from the Divisional Court, where my innocence was revealed, appointed the *Battalion Chronicler* retaining the rank of one-year volunteer."

"You won't remain that long," screamed Lieutenant Dub, all red in the face, which transition from a color to another was making the impression, that his cheeks were swelling after getting slapped, "I'll personally make sure that happens!"

"I beg, *Lieutenant*, Sir, that I be brought to the Report," said seriously the one-year volunteer.

"Don't you play with me," said Lieutenant Dub. "I'll give you some Report. We will yet meet again, but you'll feel a damn colossal remorse over it then, because you will get to know me, since now you still don't know me!"

Lieutenant Dub was walking away angrily from the railroad car, having in the upset forgotten Švejk, even though he had a moment ago the best intention to call Švejk and to tell him: "Exhale at me!" in a reach for the last means of detecting Švejk's unlawful alcoholism. Now it was however late, because when in half an hour he again returned to the railroad car, they had distributed in the meantime to the troops black coffee and rum, Švejk was already up and to the calling by Lieutenant Dub he jumped out of the railroad car like a roe deer.

"Exhale at me!" hollered at him Lieutenant Dub.

Švejk exhaled at him the whole store of his lungs, like when a hot wind carries into the fields the fragrance of a distillery.

"What's that I smell on you, man?"

"I dutifully report, *Lieutenant*, Sir, that the odor coming out of me is rum."

"So you see, sonny," victoriously exclaimed Lieutenant Dub. "At last I got you."

"Yes, *Lieutenant*, Sir," said Švejk without any expression of unease. "We have just been issued rum to put in the coffee but I first drank up the rum. If however, *Lieutenant*, Sir, there's some new regulation, that one is to drink first coffee and only then rum, I beg for forgiveness, next time it won't happen."

"And why were you snoring when I was by this railroad car about a half hour ago? Look, they could not wake you up."

"I have, I dutifully report, *Lieutenant*, Sir, not slept all night, because I was thinking back on those times, when we were still having maneuvers near Veszprém[194]. Back then the *supposed* First and Second Army Corps went through Styria and by the way of western Magyaria encircled our Fourth Corps, which was at the camp in Vienna and in the vicinity, where we had *fortifications* everywhere, but they went around us and got all the way to the bridge, which our pioneers were building from the right bank of the Danube. We were supposed to be doing the offensive and, to help us, there were to arrive troops from the north and then also from the south from around Vosek. That is what they read to us in the order of the day, that the Third Army Corps was on the move to help us, so that they wouldn't bust us up between the Lake Balaton[195] and Prešpurk[196], when we were *advancing* against the Second Army Corps. But it was all for nothing; when we were supposed to win it, they blew the end and it was won by the ones with the white armbands."

Lieutenant Dub did not say even a word and perplexed walked away, shaking his head, but immediately he again returned from the Staff railroad car and said to Švejk: "Remember all of you, that the time will come, when you are whining before me!" He did not manage any more and again walked away to the Staff railroad car, where *Captain* Ságner was just then interrogating one unfortunate from the 12th Company, whom brought in Quartermaster Strnad, because the soldier had already started to take care of his safety in the trenches now and from somewhere at the station had dragged with him over here a wicket from a pigsty, covered with sheet metal nailed onto it. He was standing there now dumbstruck, bug-eyed, excusing himself, that he wanted to take it along with him to the *dugouts* against the shrapnel, that he wanted to *make sure he was safe*.

Lieutenant Dub used this for a great sermon, on how a soldier was to behave, what were his duties and obligations to his homeland and monarch, who was the supreme commander and the supreme military lord. If however there were such elements in the Battalion, that those needed to be uprooted, punished and locked up. The babbling was in such bad taste, that *Captain* Ságner tapped the offender on the shoulder and said to him: "As long as you meant it well, next time don't do it, that was a silly thing of you, put the wicket back again, where you took it, and blow to hell with all the demons!"

Lieutenant Dub bit into his lips and set his mind on the idea, that on him actually depended the complete rescue of the disintegrating discipline in the Battalion. That is why he took one more stroll around the open space of the whole railroad station and by one warehouse, where there was a large Hungarian and German sign, that smoking there was not allowed, he found some soldier, who was sitting there and was reading a newspaper, with which he was covered to the point, that one could not see his shoulder boards. He barked out at him "*Attention!*", because it was some man from the Hungarian regiment, which was standing in Humenné in reserve.

Lieutenant Dub shook him, the Hungarian soldier stood up, didn't even think it good to salute, only shoved the newspaper into his pocket and was leaving in the direction of the road. Lieutenant Dub followed him like in a daze, but the Hungarian soldier quickened his pace, and then having turned around, mockingly put his hands up, so that Lieutenant Dub would not for even a moment be in doubt, that he immediately recognized he belonged to one of the Czech regiments. Then right away the Hungarian disappeared trotting among the nearby cottages on the other side of the road.

Lieutenant Dub, so as to show somehow, that he had nothing to do with this scene, majestically entered a little shop by the road, confusedly pointed to a large spool of black thread, and, having shoved it in his pocket, he paid and returned to the Staff railroad car, where he had the *Battalion Messenger* call his servant Kunert, whom while giving him the thread he told: "So it's for me to look after everything, I know, that you forgot the thread."

"I dutifully report, *Lieutenant*, Sir, that we have a whole dozen."

"Then show them to me right away, and see to it that you're right away here with them. Do you think, that I trust you?"

When Kunert returned with a whole box of spools, white and black, Lieutenant Dub said: "See, man, take a good notice of the thread, that you have brought, and this big spool of mine! See, how thin your thread is, how easily it'll snap, and now take a look at mine, what labor it requires, before you manage to snap it. In the field we don't need any rags, in the field everything must be solid. So take all the thread with you again and wait for my orders and remember, next time don't do anything on your own, relying on your own head, and come and ask me, when you're buying something! Don't wish to get to know me, you don't know me yet from my bad side."

When Kunert left, Lieutenant Dub turned to Senior Lieutenant Lukáš: "My *orderly* is a very intelligent man. Here and there he'll make a mistake, but otherwise he comprehends very well. His main thing is his total honesty. I had received In Bruck a shipment from my brother-in-law in the country, several baked young geese, and do you believe, that he did not even touch them, and because I could not consume them quickly, he preferred to let them go rank? That of course is what discipline does. An officer must raise his soldiers."

Senior Lieutenant Lukáš, in order to make it apparent, that he was not listening to the babbling of the idiot, turned away to the window and said: "Yes, today is Wednesday."

Lieutenant Dub then turned, feeling the need to be saying anything, to *Captain* Ságner, to whom he in a wholly intimate, pal-to-pal tone said: "Listen, *Captain* Ságner, what do you think..."

"Pardon me, just a moment," said *Captain* Ságner and walked out of the railroad car.

\*

In the meantime Švejk was talking to Kunert about his master.

"Where have you been all the time, since one could not even get a glimpse of you?" asked Švejk.

"But you know how it is," said Kunert. "With that old lunatic of mine it's always hard time. He's always calling you to him every little while and asking about things, which are none of your business. He was also asking me, whether I was your pal, and I said, that we saw one another very little."

"That is very nice of him, that he's asking about me. I like him very much, that mister *Lieutenant* of yours. He's so kind, good-hearted and treats his soldiers like a genuine father," said Švejk seriously.

"Yeah, that's what you think," contradicted Kunert, "he's a pretty big swine, and stupid as shit. I've had it up to here with him, he's just constantly busting my chops."

"Get out," Švejk was amazed, "here I thought, that he was such a really nice man, that's some strange way you're talking about your *Lieutenant*, but that's already congenital to all *spotshines*. Just take the orderly of Major Wenzel, he won't say about his master anything other than, that he's a piece of a damned, idiotic moron, and the *spotshine* of Colonel Schröder, when he was talking about his master, would not call him anything but a piss-wetted miscreant and a stinking stench. You get that from the fact, that each *orderly* learns that from his master. If the master himself weren't swearing and calling people names, then the *spotshine* wouldn't repeat it after him. In Budějovice there was on active duty *Lieutenant* Procházka, he on the other hand didn't call people names much, he only used to call his *spotshine* 'you sublime cow'. That *spotshine*, some Hibman, never heard any other insult from him. He, this Hibman, got so used to it, that when he came back to the civilian life, he'd call his daddy, mommy and sisters 'you sublime cow', and he said it also to his bride, who left him and sued him for defamation of honor, because he said it to her, her daddy and mommy at some dance party entirely in public. And she did not forgive him for it and in court she also stated, that were he to have called her a cow somewhere out of the way, that perhaps she would go for reconciliation, but that this way it was a European scandal. Speaking between you and me, Kunert, I would have never thought that about your *Lieutenant*. He made such a nice impression on me already back then, when I spoke to him the first time, like fresh fat smoked sausage just taken out of the smokehouse, and when I talked to him the second time, then he seemed to me very well-read and somehow such-like endowed by spirit. — Where from actually are you? From Budějovice proper? This I praise, when somebody is actually from somewhere and not just from around there. — And where do you live there? — Under the arcades? That is good, there is at least in the summer shade there. Have a family? — A wife and three children? — Then you're lucky, pal, at least there will be somebody to wail over you in mourning, as used to always say in the sermon my Field Chaplain Katz, and it is also true, because I once heard this talk by a *colonel* to the reservists in Bruck, who were riding from there to Serbia, that the soldier who leaves a family at home and falls on the battlefield, that he, it's true, severs all family contacts — that is he said it like this: 'When there's kohrps, kohrps from za fahmily, fahmily tayz brohken, mohr be a hero beekohz sacrificed heez leif for beeger fahmily, for *Fatherland*.' Do you live on the fourth floor? — On the ground floor? — You're right there, now I remembered, that there, in the Budějovice square, there isn't even one four story house. — Then you're already leaving? — Ah, that mister officer of yours is standing in front of the Staff railroad car and is looking this way. When then he perhaps asks you, whether I perhaps too have spoken about him, tell him without any regard at all, that I was speaking about him, and don't forget to tell him, how nicely I spoke of him, that have I seldom met such an officer, who would in such a friendly and fatherly manner behave as he. Don't forget to tell him, that he seems to me very well-read, and tell him also, that he is very intelikent[197]. Tell him also, that I was admonishing you, to be nice and to do for him everything, that you see in his eyes. Will you remember it all?"

Švejk crawled into the railroad car and Kunert with the thread went again to his den.

A quarter of an hour later they were riding on further to Nová Čabyna[198] through the burnt-out villages Brestov[199] and Veliký Radvaň. One could see, that here things were already getting tough.

The Carpathian hillsides and slopes were furrowed by trenches going from valley to valley along the tracks with new railroad ties, on both sides big grenade craters. In some places, going across the brooks flowing into the Laborec river, the upper reaches of which the track followed, one could see new bridges and the charred beams of the old bridge crossings.

The whole valley leading to Medzilaborce[200] was furrowed and tossed into disarray, as if there had been working here armies of giant moles. The road on the other side of the creek was furrowed, busted and one could see trampled expanses alongside, as the armies were rolling through.

Downpours and rains were uncovering on the edges of the pits created by grenades torn tatters of Austrian uniforms.

Past Nová Čabyna on an old scorched pine in the tangle of

branches there was hanging a shoe of some Austrian infantryman with a piece of his shin.

One could see forests without leaves, without needles, as there had raged here artillery fire, trees without crowns and lone shot-to-pieces homesteads.

The train was rolling slowly on the freshly built railroad embankments, so that the whole Battalion could thoroughly perceive and taste the joys of war and at the sight of the military cemeteries with white crosses, which were shining white in the little flat clearings and on the slopes of devastated hillside meadows, to be preparing slowly, but surely for the fields of glory, which end in a muddy Austrian cap fluttering on a white cross.

The Germans from around Kašperské Hory, who were sitting in the rear railroad cars and when still back in Milovice[201] at the station were hollering on arrival *"When me comes, when ag'in me comes..."*, had since Humenné considerably quieted down, because they were looking on and realized, that many of those, whose caps were on the graves, had been singing the same, about how nice it could be, when he again returns and will always remain home with his beloved.

In Medzilaborce there was a stop past the busted, burnt out railroad station, from the sooted up walls of which were sticking out twisted steel girders.

A new long building of wood, quickly built in the place of the burnt out station, was covered with posters plastered on in all languages: "Keep underwriting the Austrian war loan!"

In another long building there was a Red Cross station, from which walked out with a fat military physician two nurses and they were laughing with a wide grin at the fat physician, who was for their amusement imitating various animal sounds and was in a bad imitation oinking.

Under the railroad embankment, in the valley of the brook, there lay a broken field kitchen. Pointing to it, Švejk said to Baloun: "Take a look, Baloun, at what awaits us in the near future. They were about to be dishing out the rations, just then a grenade flew in and finished it off this way."

"That is horrible," sighed Baloun, "it had never occurred to me, that awaiting me was something like this, but at fault was that pride of mine, after all, I, the miscreant, bought for myself in Budějovice last winter gloves of leather. Already it was not enough for me to wear knitted old mittens on my farmer's claws, like used to wear my poor deceased father, and I just kept ailing for those leather, city-style ones. — Dad was feeding on *soaked and baked peas*, and I couldn't as much as look at peas, nothing but poultry. Ordinary roast pork also couldn't pass under my nose; the lady-mother of the house had to always make it, God don't punish me, stewed in beer."

Baloun in absolute desperation started making a general confession: "I have, I'll tell you, blasphemed the saints of God, both men and women, in the Malše pub and in Dolní Zahájí[202], I thrashed the chaplain. I still believed in God, I'm not denying that, but I had doubts about Saint Joseph. I tolerated all the saints in the house, only the picture of Saint Joseph, that one had to go, and so now the Lord God has punished me for all those sins of mine and for my immorality. The number of those immoralities I had committed at the mill, how I was often badmouthing the *dadmaster of the house* and was making his *retirement* bitter and was busting my own wife's chops."

Švejk pondered for a moment: "You are a miller, isn't that right? — So you could have known that God's mills grind slowly, but surely, when on account of you broke out that world war."

The one-year volunteer mixed himself into the conversation: "With the blaspheming, Baloun, and not acknowledging all the saints, men and women, you have decidedly served yourself badly, because you must know, that our Austrian army has for years been a strictly Catholic army, having the most brilliant example in our supreme military lord. How can you even dare to go to battle with the poison of hate toward some saints of God, men and women, when there have been instituted for garrison commands by the Ministry of Military Affairs Jesuit exhortations for the officer gentlemen and since we had seen the ceremony of military resurrection. Do you understand me well, Baloun? Do you comprehend, that you are actually carrying out something against the glorious spirit of our glorious Army? Like with that Saint Joseph, whom you mentioned, that his picture was not allowed to be hanging at your place in a living room. C'mon Baloun, he is actually the patron of all those, who want to get out of army service at war. He was a carpenter, and you know the password 'Let's see, where the carpenter's left a hole.' How many people have already gone into captivity with this password — seeing the inevitability, when surrounded on all sides, they were looking to save themselves not perhaps from an egoistic point of view, but themselves as members of the army, so that afterwards, when they come back from captivity, they could tell the lord Emperor: We are here and we are waiting for the next order! Do you then understand that, Baloun?"

"I don't understand," sighed Baloun, "I have an altogether dull club for a head. For me everything better be repeated ten times."

"You won't let up?" asked Švejk, "so I am going to explain it to you one more time. Here you've heard, that you have to stick with what spirit is dominating in the Army, that you will believe in Saint Joseph, and that when you are surrounded by enemies, you'll be looking to see, where the carpenter has left a hole, so that you would save yourself for the lord Emperor, for new wars. Now perhaps you understand it and will do well, if you confess to us a little more thoroughly, what immoralities you used to commit at the mill, but better not be telling us something similar to that joke about the farm girl, who went to confess to Father the priest and then, when she had already told the various sins, she started being embarrassed and said, that she was committing immoralities every night. You know it, when the priest heard it, immediately drool started oozing out of his pie-hole and he said: 'Well, don't feel embarrassed, dear daughter, I am here after all in God's place, and recount for me nicely in great detail about your immoralities.' And she started crying there on him, that she is embarrassed, that it was such horrible immorality, and he in turn was putting her on notice, that he is the spiritual father. At last after a long time of unwillingness she began with that she would always undress and crawl into bed. And again he could not get a word out of her and she only started bawling more. He then again, for her not to feel embarrassed, that man was a sinful vessel by his nature, but that divine mercy was without ceasing. She then found the resolve and weeping was saying: 'When I then laid myself naked in the bed, I started picking the dirt from between my toes then and I was sniffing it.' That was then that whole immorality of hers. But I hope, Baloun, that you did not used to do this at the mill and that you'll tell us something more genuine, some real immorality."

It came out, that Baloun, according to his own statement, used to commit immoralities at the mill with the farmers' wives, which immorality consisted in his commingling their flour, which in his simplemindedness he called immorality. The most disappointed was the telegraph operator Chodounský and he was asking, whether he really didn't have anything going on with the farmers' wives in the mill, on the flour bags, to which Baloun kept answering, swaying his arms: "For that I was too dumb."

The troops were informed, that lunch would be had past Palota[203] in the Łupków pass[204], and indeed there went out into the town of Medzilaborce the Battalion Accounting Master Sergeant with the cooks from the *companies* and Lieutenant Cajthaml, who was in charge of the economic administration of the Battalion. Four men were assigned to them as a patrol.

They returned in less than half an hour with three pigs tied by a hind leg, a screaming family of a Magyar Russian, from whom the pigs were being requisitioned, and the fat military physician from the barrack of the Red Cross, who was zealously telling something to Lieutenant Cajthaml, who was shrugging his shoulders.

In front of the Staff railroad car the whole feud reached its climax, when the military physician began to insist in *Captain* Ságner's face, that the pigs were designated for the hospital of the Red Cross, of which the farmer did not want to know anything, and was demanding, for the pigs to be returned to him, that it was his last possession and that he definitely couldn't give them for the price, which they had paid out to him.

At the same time he was shoving the money, which he had in his hand for his pigs, to *Captain* Ságner, whom the farmer's wife was holding by his other hand, was kissing it for him with such servility, by which this region has always distinguished itself.

*Captain* Ságner was all spooked from it and it took a while, before he managed to push away the old farmer's wife. It was to no avail however, young reinforcements came in her place which proceeded again to suck his hands.

Lieutenant Cajthaml reported however in an entirely business-like tone: "That guy still has twelve pigs and got paid entirely properly, according to the last Division-wide order number 12420, economic section. By this order, §16, are hogs to be bought in places not afflicted by the war at a price of no more than 2 crowns 16 pennies for one kilogram of live weight; in places afflicted by the war are to be added for one kilogram of live weight 36 pennies, thus paying for one kilogram 2 crowns 52 pennies. A note added to that: Should there be such cases discovered, that in places afflicted by the war the farms remained intact with a full complement of hogs, which could be sent for the purposes of supplying the detachments passing through, pay the for the requisitioned pork meat as in places not afflicted by the war, with a special extra payment of 12 pennies for one kilogram of live weight. Should this situation not be completely clear, set up a commission immediately on the spot consisting of the interested party,

## The Fateful Adventures of the Good Soldier Švejk

the commander of the detachment passing through and that officer or accountant sergeant major (in case of a smaller unit), who is entrusted with the economic component."

All this had read Lieutenant Cajthaml from the copy of the Division-wide order, which he always carried on him and almost knew by heart, that in the battle front area the reward for one kilogram of carrots was being raised to 15.30 pennies and for the *officers' mess kitchen department* for cauliflower in the area adjacent to the battlefront to 1 crown 75 pennies for one kilogram.

Those, who were working on things in Vienna, imagined the front area as a land awash in carrot and cauliflower.

Lieutenant Cajthaml read it however to the upset farmer in German and was asking in the same way, whether he understood it; when that one shook his head, he screamed at him: "Do you want the commission then?"

He understood the word commission, therefore he nodded, and while his pigs had already a while ago been dragged to the field kitchens for execution, there surrounded him soldiers with bayonets detailed to requisition duty and the commission set out to his farm, in order to be determined, whether he should receive 2 crowns 52 pennies for one kilogram or only 2 crowns 28 pennies.

They had not yet even stepped out onto the road leading to the village, when right then came from the field kitchens the sound of the triple death squeals of the pigs.

The farmer realized, that everything was over, and he desperately cried out: *"Gimme for each swine two Rhine florins!"*

The four soldiers surrounded him more tightly and the whole family blocked the way for *Captain* Ságner and Lieutenant Cajthaml, having kneeled into the dust of the road.

The mother with two daughters were hugging the knees of both, calling them benefactors, until the farmer stopped them with a scream in the Ukrainian dialect of the Magyar Russians, for them to stand up, have the soldiers gobble the pigs and croak from them.

So the idea of the commission was abandoned, and because the farmer all of a sudden rebelled, was threatening with his fist, he got it once from one soldier with the butt of the rifle, so that it thumped against his fur coat, and the whole family of his crossed itself and took to flight, the father included.

Ten minutes later the Battalion Accounting Master Sergeant was already along with *Battalion Messenger* Matušič savoring the pork brain in his railroad car, stuffing himself valiantly, in a snide way every now and then telling the scribes: "You'd love to feed, wouldn't you? Yeah, lads, that is only for the officers. To the cooks go kidneys and liver, brain and boiled head and feet to the gentlemen Accounting Master Sergeants and to the scribes only double portions of meat for the rank-and-file."

*Captain* Ságner already gave also an order having to do with the officers' kitchen: "Pork with caraway seed; choose the best meat, so that it won't be too fatty!"

And so it happened, that when in the Łupków pass there were being distributed to the rank-and-file the *mess portions*, in each military mess kit in his portion of soup found the individual two tiny pieces of meat, and he who was born on even a worse planet, found only a piece of skin.

There prevailed at the kitchens the usual military nepotism, distributing to all who were close to the ruling clique. The *spotshine*s emerged in the Łupków Pass with greasy mugs. Each *messenger* had a belly like a little boulder. There were things taking place calling up unto heaven.

One-year volunteer Marek caused in the kitchen a scandal, because he wanted to be just, and when the cook was putting along with the remark "That is for our *Chronicler*" into his mess kit with the soup a proper slice of boiled haunch, here he proclaimed, that in the military they were all equal among the troops, which caused a general agreement and gave rise to name-calling and cursing the cooks.

The one-year volunteer threw the chunk of meat back, emphasizing, that he did not want any preferential treatment. At the kitchen, however, they didn't get it and were under the impression, that the *Battalion Chronicler* was not satisfied, and the cook told him on the side to come only after all the rations would be distributed, that he'd give him a piece of a leg.

The scribes' yaps were also glistening, the ambulance corpsmen were breathing heavily due to such prosperity and surrounding this God's blessing all around the still not cleared away mementos of the latest battles. Everywhere there were lying around cartridge cases, empty tin boxes of canned food, tatters of Russian, Austrian, and German uniforms, parts of broken up wagons, bloodied long strips of gauze bandages and cotton.

Into an old pine tree by what used to be a railroad station, of which remained only a pile of rubble, there was lodged a grenade, which had not exploded. Everywhere could be seen fragments of grenades and somewhere in the immediate vicinity they must have apparently buried the corpses of the soldiers, because it reeked here terribly with rot.

And as the armies had been going through here and camp around here, everywhere could be seen little mounds of human excrement of international origin, of all the peoples of Austria, Germany and Russia. Excrements of soldiers of all nationalities and all religious confessions were lying side by side or were layering themselves on top of one another, without getting into a brawl among themselves.

A half-razed water reservoir, a wooden shed of the railroad watchman, and actually everything that had any wall, was riddled with rifle rounds like a sieve.

To provide a more complete impression of military joys, behind a not-too-distant peak there were rising mountains of smoke, as if there was a whole village burning and the center of big military operations. What it was is they were burning up choleric and dysenteric barracks there to the great joy of those gentlemen, who had anything to do with setting up that hospital under the protectorate of Archduchess Marie and who were stealing and loading their pockets by presenting invoices for nonexistent choleric and dysentery barracks.

Paying for it now was one grouping of barracks on behalf of all the other ones and in the stench of the burning straw mattresses was floating up to the sky the whole scam of the archduchy protectorate.

Behind the railroad station on a rock had already hurried up Germans from the Reich to erect a memorial to the fallen Brandenburgers[205] with the inscription *"To the heroes of the Łupków Pass"*, with a large German Imperial eagle cast of bronze, while on the pedestal it was explicitly noted, that the symbol was made of the Russian cannons, booty captured during the liberation of the Carpathians by German Imperial regiments.

In this strange and up to now unusual atmosphere was the Battalion resting after lunch in the railroad cars, and *Captain* Ságner and the Battalion adjutant still kept on not being able to come to an understanding through encoded telegrams with the divisional base regarding a further course of action for the Battalion. The messages were so unclear, that it looked approximately, as if they were not even to arrive at the Łupków pass and were to ride in an altogether different direction from New Town under the Šiator, because in the telegrams there was some talk of such places as Csap[206] — Ungvár[207], Kis-

Berezna[208] — Uszok[209].

In ten minutes it becomes apparent, that the Staff officer sitting over there at the Brigade base is some numskull, because a ciphered telegram is coming, asking whether it is the 8th March Battalion of the 75th Regiment (military code G3) speaking. The numskull at the Brigade base is amazed by the answer, that it is the 7th March Battalion of the 91st Regiment, so then he's asking, who gave the order to ride onto Munkačevo[210], down the military track to Stryj[211], when the *march route* runs through the Łupków pass onto Sanok[212] and into Galicia. The numskull is terribly amazed, that the telegraph is coming from the Łupków pass, and sends a coded message: *March route* unchanged, onto Łupków pass — Sanok, where further orders.

After the return of *Captain* Ságner there is unfolding in the Staff railroad car a debate about certain headlessness and some hints are made that if it weren't for the Germans from the Reich, that the whole eastern military group would be totally headless.

Lieutenant Dub is attempting to defend the headlessness of the Austrian general staff and is blabbering something about that the landscape here had been considerably devastated by the recent battles and the track could not yet have been put in proper order.

All the officers are looking at him with an expression of extending condolences, as if they wanted to say this gentleman isn't responsible for his idiocy. Having encountered no resistance, Lieutenant Dub expanded his blabbering to the magnificent impression, which this busted landscape is exerting on him, giving testimony to how capable of hitting is the iron fist of our military. Again nobody answers him, whereupon he repeats: "Yes, indeed, of course, the Russians were retreating here in absolute panic."

*Captain* Ságner sets his mind, that he will send Lieutenant Dub at the nearest opportunity, when the situation in the trenches is dangerous to the utmost, as a *patrol officer* beyond the barbed wire obstacles for reconnoitering of the enemy positions, and is whispering to Senior Lieutenant Lukáš, with whom he's leaning out of a window of the railroad car: "These civilians, the devil must have owed them to us too. The more intellectual, the more the dumb beast."

It seems that Lieutenant Dub will not at all stop talking. He keeps on telling all the officers, what he had read in the newspaper about the Carpathian fighting and also of the struggle for the Carpathian passes during the Austro-German offensive against San.

He's narrating it in such a way, as though he not only participated in the fighting, but as if he even directed all the operations himself.

Unusually annoying are especially his sentences of this sort: "Then we went in the direction of Bukovsko[213], so that we would have the line Bukovsko — Dynov[214] secured, having connection with the Bardejov group at Velká Polanka[215], where we smashed the Samara[216] Division of the enemy."

Senior Lieutenant Lukáš could not hold back anymore and remarked to Lieutenant Dub: "Of which you apparently spoke already before the war with your District Administrator."

Lieutenant Dub looked at Senior Lieutenant Lukáš with hostility and walked out of the railroad car.

The military train was standing on top of the railroad embankment and several meters down under the slope there were lying various objects thrown away by the retreating Russian soldiers, who apparently were retreating through this ditch. One could see here rusted teapots, some cooking pots, cartridge pouches. Also lying around here alongside the most varied objects there were rolls of barbed wire and again those bloodied strips of gauze bandages and cotton. Above this ditch at one spot there was standing a group of soldiers and Lieutenant Dub immediately found out, that among them was standing Švejk and was telling them something.

So he went there.

"What happened here?" sounded up the stern voice of Lieutenant Dub, while he stood himself directly in front of Švejk.

"I dutifully report, *Lieutenant*, Sir," answered Švejk for all of them, "that we are looking."

"And what are you looking at?" burst out shouting Lieutenant Dub.

"I dutifully report, *Lieutenant*, Sir, that we are looking down into the ditch."

"And who gave you permission to do that?"

"I dutifully report, *Lieutenant*, Sir, that it is the wish of our *Colonel* Schröder from Bruck. When he was saying his good-byes to us, when we were taking off now for the battlefield, then in his speech he said, that all of us should, when we're strolling through abandoned battlefields, be taking good notice of everything, how the fighting had gone and anything that could be of benefit to us. And we are now seeing here, *Lieutenant*, Sir, in this hollow, all of that which a soldier must throw away in his flight. We are seeing here, I dutifully report, *Lieutenant*, Sir, how silly it is, when a soldier drags along with him all kinds of unnecessary things. He is unnecessarily weighed down by them. He unnecessarily tires by it, and when he's dragging such weight with him, he cannot easily fight."

For Lieutenant Dub a ray of hope suddenly flashed, that at last he'd get Švejk to face a field court-martial for anti-militaristic grand-treasonous propaganda, and there-fore he quickly asked:

"So then you think, that a soldier is to be throwing away cartridges, which are lying around here in the hollow, or bayonets, as I see over there?"

"Oh, not at all, no, I dutifully report, *Lieutenant*, Sir," answered Švejk, smiling pleasantly, "condescend to look here down below at the cast off sheet-metal chamber pot."

And indeed, under the railroad embankment there was lying about provocatively and defiantly a chamber pot, with the enamel banged up, eaten through by rust, among shards of pots, all of which objects, unsuitable for a household anymore, used to deposit here the station master, apparently as material for discussions among archaeologists of future ages, who, once they have discovered this settlement, would on account of it become phantasmagoric nuts, and in schools children would be learning about the age of the enameled chamber pots.

Lieutenant Dub began peering at this object, yet couldn't but simply realize, that it was indeed one of those invalids, who used to spend their fresh youth under a bed.

It was exerting on all of them a huge impression, and when Lieutenant Dub kept silent, there sounded up Švejk: "I dutifully report, *Lieutenant*, Sir, that with such a night pot there was once pretty good fun had in the spa Poděbrady[217]. About that they used to talk at our pub in Vinohrady. Back then, that is to say, they began to publish a little magazine *Independence*[218] and the Poděbrady pharmacist was the heady head[219] of it, and as the editor they named some Ladislav Hájek of Domažlice. And that mister pharmacist, he was, I tell you, such an odd man, that he collected old pots and other such trifles, until he was nothing but all a museum. And he once, this Hájek of Domažlice, invited for a visit to Poděbrady spa a pal, who also used to write for a newspaper, and got plastered there together, because for over a week already they hadn't seen one another, and he promised him, that in return for the treat he'd write a feuilleton[220] in that *Independence*, that independent magazine, in which he was dependant[221]. And he, that pal of his, wrote for him this feuilleton about one such collector, how he found in the sand on the bank of the Labe river an old sheet-metal night pot and thought, that it was the helmet of Saint Wenceslaus, and created such a commotion with it, that there came to take a look at it bishop Brynych[222] from Hradec with a procession with banners and pennants. That pharmacist from Poděbrady thought, that it was falling on him, and so they were both, he and that Mister Hájek, at odds."

Lieutenant Dub would have liked the best to smite Švejk down there, below, but composed himself and burst out yelling at them all: "I am telling you, not to be uselessly gawking here! You all don't know me yet, but once you get to know me! — You will stay here, Švejk," he said in a horrifying voice, when Švejk and the rest wanted to leave toward the railroad cars.

They remained standing alone facing one another and Lieutenant Dub was figuring, what terrible thing he should say.

Švejk however beat him to it: "I dutifully report, *Lieutenant*, Sir, if only this weather would last for us. During the day it's not too hot and nights are also quite pleasant, so that it is the most opportune time for warring."

Lieutenant Dub drew the revolver and asked: "Do you know this?"

"I dutifully report, *Lieutenant*, Sir, I do. Mister Senior Lieutenant Lukáš has an *exactly* such a one."

"Then make sure, you shameless rube, to remember it!" said gravely and in a dignified tone Lieutenant Dub while, tucking the revolver back again, "so that you'd know that something very unpleasant could happen to you, if you were to continue in those propagandas of yours."

Lieutenant Dub was walking away, repeating to himself: "Now I said it to him the best: in propagandas, yes, in propagandas!"

Before Švejk enters his railroad car again, he's strolling still a while and muttering to himself: "Just how am I to classify him?" And with every step the classification of this species coming to Švejk is clearer: a half-fart geezer.

In the military jargon the term old fart has been used since times immemorial with great love, and mainly has this honorary title belonged to colonels or older captains and majors and it was a certain gradation of the words in common use, the "old geezer sonofabitch". Without these modifiers the term old geezer was an expression of a kind appreciation of the old colonel or major, who screamed a lot, but at the same time liked his soldiers and protected them against other regiments, when at stake were mainly somebody else's patrols, which would pick up his soldiers from beer joints, when they didn't have overtime passes. Old geezer was looking after his soldiers, the rations had to be in order, but he'd always latch onto something and ride it hard, and therefore was "an old geezer".

But when the old geezer was unnecessarily busting the chops of the rank-and-file and the NCOs, was thinking up nighttime exercises and similar things, he was "an old geezer sonofabitch".

From the "old geezer sonofabitch", as the next higher degree in evolution of nastiness, chop-bustery and idiocy, he became "an old fart". This term meant everything, and huge was the difference between an old fart in civilian life, and an old fart in the military.

The former, the civilian one, is also a superior and that's also the name given him universally in the offices by the servants and subordinate office workers. He is a stale, narrow-minded bureaucrat, who holds against one, for example, that the draft has not been properly dried by a blotter and the like. It is an altogether stupid beastly phenomenon in human society, because at the same time is such a mule acting the honest, judicious part, wants to understand everything, knows how to expound on everything and takes offense at everything.

He who has been in army service, understands however the difference between this apparition and an old fart in uniform. Here the word meant an old geezer, who was a "sonofabitch", a real sonofabitch, approached everything ready to cut, but even so stopped in front of every obstacle; he didn't like soldiers and wrestled with them in vain, he was unable to earn any authority, which was enjoyed by "the old geezer" and even "the old geezer sonofabitch".

In some garrisons, as for example in Trident[223], instead of old fart they would say "our old shithead". In all cases the person in question was older, and if Švejk called in his mind Lieutenant Dub a half-fart geezer, he captured absolutely logically, that both in age and in rank, and actually in everything, Lieutenant Dub was still short fifty percent of making an old fart.

Returning with those thoughts to his railroad car, he met *spotshine* Kunert, whose cheek was swollen and who was blabbering something unintelligible, that he just ran into his master, Lieutenant Dub, who out of the clean-and-clear slapped him a fill, because supposedly he as in possession of ascertained facts, that he hobnobs with Švejk.

"In this case," said calmly Švejk, "we'll go to the Report. An Austrian soldier must let himself be slapped only in certain cases. Bu he, that master of yours, stepped over all limits, as used to put it old

Eugene of Savoy: 'No more and that's it.' Now you yourself have to go to the Report, and if you don't, I'll slap you a fill myself, so that you would know, what discipline is in the Army. In the Karlín garrison there used to be some *Lieutenant* Hausner and he also had an *orderly*, and he also slapped him and kicked him. Once that *orderly* had been so slapped up, that he was stupefied from it and mustered himself at the Report and at the Report he announced, that he had been brutally kicked, because he was confusing it all up, and that master of his also really proved, that he was lying, that he on that day was not kicking him, but only slapping, so that dear *orderly* they locked up on account of a false accusation for three weeks. — But regarding the whole matter that doesn't change anything," continued Švejk, "it happens to be exactly the same, as what the medical student Houbička used to be always telling us about, that it didn't matter, to slice to pieces at the pathological institute some man, who hanged himself or poisoned himself. And I'm going with you. A couple of slaps go a long way in the Army."

Kunert turned totally stupefied and let Švejk lead him toward the Staff railroad car.

Lieutenant Dub shouted, leaning out of a window: "What do you want here, shameless rubes?"

"Behave in a dignified manner," was Švejk admonishing Kunert and pushing him ahead into the railroad car.

In the passageway there emerged Senior Lieutenant Lukáš and behind him *Captain* Ságner.

Senior Lieutenant Lukáš, who had already had so much with Švejk, was terribly surprised, because his face did not have the familiar good-natured expression, rather a sign of new unpleasant events.

"I dutifully report, *Senior Lieutenant*, Sir," said Švejk, "a thing is going to the Report."

"Just don't again start any foolishness, Švejk, I have also had enough already."

"Condescend to allow me," said Švejk, "I am the *Messenger* of your *Company*, you, condescend to allow me, you are condescending to be the *Company Commander* of the Eleven. I know that it looks frightfully strange, but I also know that mister *Lieutenant* Dub is situated in a position under you."

"You have, Švejk, gone altogether mad," interrupted him Senior Lieutenant Lukáš, "You are drunk and will do best when you leave!

Do you understand, you imbecile, you dumb beast."

"I dutifully report *Senior Lieutenant*, Sir," said Švejk pushing Kunert ahead of him, "it happens to look just like when once in Prague there was an experiment being conducted with a safety frame for protection against getting run over by a streetcar. That very mister inventor sacrificed himself for that experiment and then the city had to pay damages to his widow."

*Captain* Ságner, not knowing what to say, was nodding along to it, while Senior Lieutenant Lukáš had on his face an expression of desperation.

"Everything must go by the Report, I dutifully report *Senior Lieutenant*, Sir," Švejk continued inexorably, "when still in Bruck you were telling me, *Senior Lieutenant*, Sir, that since I was the Messenger at the *Company*, that I also had other duties aside from some orders. That I was to be, about all that happens at the company, informed. On the basis of that ordinance I take the liberty to inform you, *Senior Lieutenant*, Sir, that mister *Lieutenant* Dub slapped to a fill *just like that* his *orderly*. I would, I dutifully report, *Senior Lieutenant*, Sir, perhaps not even be saying this. But since I see, that mister *Lieutenant* Dub is assigned under your command, then I set my mind to it, that it had to go to the Report."

"This is a strange matter," said *Captain* Ságner, "why you are shoving, Švejk, that Kunert in here."

"I dutifully report *Battalion Commander*, Sir, that everything must go by the Report. He's a numskull, he got slapped a fill by mister Lieutenant Dub and he cannot dare to go to the Report alone. I dutifully report, *Captain*, Sir, if you were to take a look at him, how his knees are shaking, he's all unalive, because he must go to the Report. And if not for me, then to the Report he would perhaps never make it at all, like that Kudela from Bytouchov[224], who on active duty kept on going to the Report so long, until he was transferred to the Navy, where he became an Ensign, and was on some island, in the Pacific Ocean, declared to be a deserteer. He then got married there and also spoke with the explorer Havlasa[225], who did not even realize, that he was not a native. — It is at all very sad, when somebody is to go on account of a couple of stupid slaps to the Report. But he didn't want at all to come here, because he was saying, that he wouldn't go. He is at all such a slapped-up-and-down *orderly*, that he doesn't even know, which slap is being dealt with here. He would not have come here at all, he didn't want at all to go to the Report, he will let himself be beaten up sometimes even more. I dutifully report *Captain*, Sir, *they* take a look at him, he's already on account of it scared all shitless. But on the other hand again, he should have right away complained, that he received that couple of slaps, but he didn't dare, because he knew that it was better, as had written this one poet, to be a humble violet. The thing is he serves with Lieutenant Dub."

Pushing Kunert to the front of himself, Švejk said to him: "Don't be constantly trembling like an oak in an aspen grove!"

*Captain* Ságner asked Kunert, how it actually did happen.

Kunert however declared, trembling all over his body, that they could ask mister *Lieutenant* Dub, that that one did not slap him at all.

Judas Kunert, still trembling with his whole body, even declared, that Švejk made it all up.

This embarrassing event was brought to an end by Lieutenant Dub, who suddenly appeared and began screaming at Kunert: "Do you want to get a couple of **new** slaps?"

The thing was then totally clear and *Captain* Ságner simply declared to Lieutenant Dub: "Starting today, Kunert is assigned to the Battalion kitchen, and as far as getting a new *orderly*, turn to Accounting Master Sergeant Vaněk."

Lieutenant Dub saluted and only when exiting he told Švejk: "I bet, that one day you will hang."

When he left, Švejk turned to Senior Lieutenant Lukáš in a gentle, friendly tone: "In Mnichovo Hradiště[226] there was also one such gentleman and he also talked that way to the other one, and he answered him: 'In the execution yard we'll meet.'"

"Švejk," said Senior Lieutenant Lukáš, "you are so stupid, and don't dare to tell me, as is your custom: I dutifully report, that I'm stupid."

"*Surprise*," sounded up *Captain* Ságner leaning out in the window and he would have liked so much to step away from the window, but he didn't have time anymore, because there appeared the disaster: *Lieutenant* Dub under the window.

Lieutenant Dub started by saying, that he very much regretted, how *Captain* Ságner had left, not having heard out his reasons for the offensive at the eastern front.

"If we are to understand the huge offensive," was calling Lieutenant Dub up to the window, "we must realize, how the offensive evolved toward the end of April. We had to break through the Russian front and we found the most advantageous place for this breach to be the front between the Carpathians and the Visla river."

"I'm not arguing over it with you," answered dryly *Captain* Ságner and walked away from the window.

When half an hour later the ride to Sanok continued, *Captain* Ságner stretched out on the bench and pretended, that he was sleeping, so that Lieutenant Dub would in the meantime forget his hackneyed conjectures about the offensive.

From the railroad car with Švejk was missing Baloun. That is to say, he begged for and got the permission to sop the empty goulash cauldron clean with bread. He was now located atop a flatbed railroad car with the field kitchens in an unpleasant situation, because as the train made the first move, he flew head first into the cauldron and his legs were sticking out past the cauldron's rim. He'd however become accustomed to this situation and out of the cauldron were coming lip smacking sounds, like when a hedgehog chases after cockroaches, and later Baloun's pleading voice: "I beg you, pals, For God's sake, throw a piece of bread in here for me, there's still here a lot of gravy." This idyll lasted until the nearest station, where they arrived with the cauldron of the 11th *Company* already cleaned out, that the tin-plating was just gleaming.

"God repay you for it, pals," was thanking them Baloun from his heart. "The whole time, since I got in the army service, for the first time Lady Luck flashed her smile at me."

And indeed there was something to talk about. In the Łupków Pass did Baloun manage to come upon two portions of goulash, Senior Lieutenant Lukáš also exhibited his contentment over the fact, that Baloun had brought him from the officers' kitchen an untouched ration, and left for him a good half. Baloun was completely happy, swinging his legs, which he stuck out of the railroad car, and all of a sudden the whole Army seemed to be something warm, familial.

The company cook began to make fun of him, that when they arrive in Sanok, they will be cooking supper and yet another lunch, because they have the supper and lunch coming for the whole trip, since they didn't get it. Baloun was in agreement just nodding and whispering: "You'll see, pals, that the Lord God won't abandon us."

All were sincerely laughing about it and the cook sitting on the field kitchen broke into a song:

> Zhoopaidyah, zhoopaidah,
> After all Lord God won't shove us away.

Should He shove us into the mud,
After all He'll claw us out again...
Should He shove us into a thicket,
After all He'll bite us out.
Zhoopaidyah, zhoopaidah,
After all Lord God won't shove us away...

Past the Szczawne[227] station there began emerging again in the valleys new tiny military cemeteries. Below Szczawne one could see from the train a stone cross with a headless Christ the Lord, who had lost his head as the track was blown up.

The train was increasing its speed, rushing down the valley toward Sanok, the horizon was widening and thereby were also becoming more numerous whole groups of broken up villages on both sides well into the countryside.

By Kulaszne[228] one could see down in the creek from the railroad embankment a crashed, broken train of the Red Cross.

Baloun bugged his eyes out at it and was especially amazed by the parts of the locomotive strewn below. The smokestack was stuck into the embankment and was sticking out of it like a twenty-eight caliber.

This phenomenon aroused attention also in the railroad car, where Švejk was. The most upset got Cook Jurajda: "Has it come to the point that it's allowed to shoot at railroad cars of the Red Cross?"

"It's not allowed, but can be done," said Švejk, "it was a zinger of a shot, and then everybody will apologize, that it was at night and that the red cross was not visible. There are altogether many things in the world, which are not allowed to be done, yet can be carried out. The main thing is for everybody to try it, to see if he'll succeed, since it's not allowed, so that he'd see that he could. At Imperial maneuvers in the Písek region there came such an order, that soldiers on the march were not allowed to be hogtied. But our *Captain* figured out, that it could be done, because such an order was very laughable, everybody could easily get it, that a hogtied soldier could not march. So he was actually not circumventing the order, he was simply and reasonably having the hogtied soldiers thrown onto *supply convoy* wagons and the marching went right on with them. Or this kind of a case, which happened on our street five six years ago. There lived some mister Karlík, on the first floor. One floor higher a very nice man, some musical conservatory student Mikeš. He liked women very much and also among others he started going after a daughter of that mister

Karlík, who had a shipping company and a confectioner's shop and also had somewhere in Moravia a bookbinding firm under some altogether different firm name. When that mister Karlík learned, that the conservatory student was running after his daughter, he then visited him in the apartment and told him: 'You must not take my daughter for a wife, you singular bum. I won't give her to you!' 'Alright,' retorted mister Mikeš; 'since I must not take her for a wife, what am I to do, am I to tear myself apart?' Two months later mister Karlík came again and brought along his wife and both told him in unison: 'You shameless rube, you dispossessed our daughter of her honor.' 'Certainly,' he replied to that for them, 'I took the liberty of screwing her making her a whore, gracious lady.' That mister Karlík started needlessly screaming at him, that he was telling him he must not take her for a wife, that he wouldn't give her to him, but he, quite correctly answered him, that indeed he wouldn't take her for a wife and that back then there wasn't any talk about what he could be doing with her. That it was not a subject of the talk, that he keeps his word, for them to have no worries, that he didn't want her, that he was a man of character, that he was not the 'whereto the wind blows there the cloak turns', and that he kept his word, that when he says something it is holy and it sticks. And that if he were to be persecuted on account of it, he didn't care either, because he had a clear conscience and that his poor deceased mom when still on her deathbed made him swear, never to lie in his life, and that he promised her by giving his hand and that such an oath was valid. That in his family nobody at all lied and that to wit in school he had always the best grade for moral behavior. Then here you see, that many a thing is not allowed, but can be, and that the ways may be varied, only let's all will as one[229]."

"Dear friends," said the one-year volunteer, who was zealously taking notes, "all that's bad has also a good side to it. This into the air blown up, half-burnt and hurled off the embankment train of the Red Cross enhances the glorious history of our Battalion by a new heroic deed of the future. I imagine, that on about the 16th of September, as I have already made a note of it, several lowly privates from each company of our Battalion will volunteer under the leadership of a corporal, to blow up an armored train of the enemy, which is bombarding us and preventing our crossing of the river. They honorably fulfilled their task, having dressed themselves as farmers. — — What is it that I see," cried out the one-year volunteer, looking into his notes. "How did get in here our mister Vaněk? — Listen, mister *Accounting Master Sergeant*," he turned to Vaněk, "what a beautiful little article about you there will be in the chronicles of the Battalion. I have a feeling that you're in there once already, but this will definitely be better and more substantial." The one-year volunteer was reading in pompous voice: "**The heroic death of Accounting Master Sergeant Vaněk.** For the dangerous enterprise, blowing up the enemy's armored train, volunteered also Accounting Master Sergeant Vaněk, having changed like the others into a farmer's regional garb. By the brought about explosion he was rendered unconscious, and when he came around from the faint, he saw himself encircled by the enemy, who immediately transported him to the Staff of the enemy's division, where face to face with death he refused to give any explanation of the position and strength of our troops. Because he was disguised by the change of clothes, he was sentenced as a spy to hanging by rope, which punishment, taking into account his high rank, was changed to death by shooting. The execution was immediately carried out by a cemetery wall and the brave Accounting Master Sergeant Vaněk requested, that his eyes not be blindfolded. To the question, whether he had any wish, he replied: 'Convey through the truce negotiator to my Battalion my last greeting and that I am dying with the conviction, that our Battalion will continue on its victorious path. Further convey to mister *Captain* Ságner, that according to his latest Brigade-wide order is being raised the daily portion of cans of food to two and a half per man.' So died our Accounting Master Sergeant Vaněk, having roused by his last sentence a panicky and virginal fear in the enemy, who thought, that by preventing our crossing of the river, he was cutting us off from the supply points, causing our early starvation and thereby also demoralization in our ranks. — Of the calm, with which he was looking forward at the death up ahead, gives witness the circumstance, that he was playing cvik with the enemy Staff officers before his own execution. 'The sum won by me turn over to the Russian Red Cross,' he said, standing already facing the barrels of rifles. This gracious magnanimity moved the present military representatives all the way to tears. — Forgive me, mister Vaněk," continued the one-year volunteer, "that I took the liberty to dispose of the money you had won. I was thinking, whether it should perhaps be turned over to the Austrian Red Cross, but after all I suppose, that from the point of humanitarianism it makes no difference, as long as it will be turned over to a humane institution."

"He could, that poor deceased of ours," said Švejk, "have turned it over to the soup institute of the city of Prague, but this way it is better after all, the mister Mayor would perhaps with that amount of money buy jitrnice for a *ten o'clock snack*."

"Well, stealing goes on everywhere," said telephone operator Chodounský.

"Mainly there's stealing going on at the Red Cross," with great anger declared cook Jurajda. "I had in Bruck an acquaintance cook, who cooked for the nurses in the barrack, and he was telling me, how the mother superior of the nurses and the head nurses were sending home whole cases of Malaga[230] wine and chocolate. That comes as part of the opportunity itself, it is man's self-determination. Each man undergoes in his eternal life innumerable transformations and sooner or later he must emerge in this world as a thief, in certain periods of his activity. I myself had already been through this one period."

The cook-occultist Jurajda pulled out of his back-pack a bottle of cognac.

"Here you see," he said, opening the bottle, "an unmistakable proof of my claim. I took it before departure from the officers' mess. The cognac is of the best brand and it was supposed to be used for sugar icing on Linzer slices. It was however preordained, that I steal it, just as I was predestined to become a thief."

"And it indeed wouldn't be bad," sounded up Švejk, "if we were preordained, for us to be your accomplices, I at least have some such premonition."

And preordination really showed up. The bottle passed around despite the protest by Accounting Master Sergeant Vaněk, who was claiming that the cognac was to be drunk from the mess kit and justly divided, because there were altogether five of them to the bottle, so that given the odd number it could easily happen, that somebody would surely drink one gulp more from the bottle than the others, to which remarked Švejk: "It is true, if mister Vaněk wants to have an even number, then let him leave the assembly, so that there wouldn't be any unpleasantries and quarrels."

Vaněk then withdrew his proposal and advanced another, magnanimous one, for the benefactor Jurajda to place himself in such a position in the queue, that he could take a drink twice, which caused a storm of resistance, because Jurajda had already taken a drink once, tasting the cognac while opening the bottle.

At last was accepted the proposal of the one-year volunteer to drink in alphabetical order, which he justified by the fact, that it was also a certain preordination, what name everybody had.

Then they played regular three-card cvik; it turned out, that the one-year volunteer was using at each looting of a card a pious adage from the Holy Scriptures. Looting an underknave he cried out: 'Lord, let me keep this underknave and this summer as well, that I may hoe and fertilize him, that he may bear and bring me fruit.'[231]"

When he was being admonished for having even dared to loot an eight, he cried with a loud voice: "But any woman having ten pennies, if she were to lose one penny, will she not light up candles and diligently search until she finds? And when she doth find, she will gather her neighbors and lady friends saying: 'Together with me rejoice[232], as I have looted an eight and bought and added the trump king with an ace in a card game!' — So hand the cards over here; you all fell in the pit."

One-year volunteer Marek had really great luck in cards. While the others were trumping one another up, he was always beating their trumped up trumps with the highest trump, so that one after another they were falling in the pit and he was collecting one bet after another and was addressing the vanquished with the cry: "And great earthquakes shall come in places, and horrible famine and pestilence and great miracles from heaven."[233] At last they had enough of it, stopped playing, when telephone operator Chodounský lost his military pay half a year in advance. He was devastated over it and the one-year volunteer was asking him for IOUs, which at the military pay-time Accounting Master Sergeant Vaněk would pay Chodounský's pay to him.

"Don't be afraid, Chodounský," was consoling him Švejk. "If you are lucky, then you'll fall during the first *combat* and Marek will be wiping a dry mouth thirsty for your soldier's pay, so just sign it over for him."

The mention of falling pricked Chodounský very unpleasantly, so that he said with certainty: "I cannot fall, because I'm a telephone operator, and telephone operators are always in the shelter and the wire is rolled out and faults are always being looked for only after the *combat*.

The one-year volunteer mentioned, that just to the contrary, that telephone operators were exposed to great danger and that it's mainly the telephonists whom had it in for the enemy artillery. No telephonist had surety in his shelter. If they were ten meters under the ground, then the enemy artillery would still find him there. That telephone operators perish like hail during rain in summer, an evidence of that was, that when he was leaving Bruck, they were just opening there the 28th course for telephone operators.

Chodounský was looking straight ahead appearing tortured, which moved Švejk to utter a friendly, good word: "What you have in short is a pretty swindle of a deal." Chodounský retorted kindly: "Zip it, auntie."

"I will look under the letter 'Ch' in my notes on the history of the Battalion... Chodounský — Chodounský, hm, aha, here we have it: 'Telephonist Chodounský, buried by a mine. He is telephoning from his tomb to the Staff headquarters: I am dying and I congratulate my Battalion on its victory!'"

"That must be enough for you," said Švejk, "or do you still want to add something to it? Do you remember the telephone operator on the Titanic, who, when the ship was already sinking, kept on telephoning down below to the flooded kitchen, when lunch would be ready?"

"I don't care either way," said the one-year volunteer, "maybe Chodounský's statement prior to his death can be augmented, so that in the end he cries out into the telephone: 'Send greetings to our iron brigade for me!"

## 4

## FORWARD MARCH!

It became apparent when they arrived at Sanok, that actually in the railroad car with the field kitchen of the Eleven, where farting in bliss was the satiated Baloun, they were right all in all, that there would be supper, and what's more, besides the supper that they would even be distributing some commissary bread to make up for all those days, when the Battalion didn't get anything. It also became apparent, that actually in Sanok, when they crawled out of the railroad cars, there was situated the Staff of the iron brigade, to which the 91st Regiment belonged according to its baptismal certificate. Although from here on was the railroad connection uninterrupted up to below Lwów and to the north to Velké Mosty[234], it was actually a mystery, why the Staff of the eastern sector had issued all these instructions, for the iron brigade and its Staff to concentrate the march regiments one hundred and fifty kilometers in the rear, when at that time the front went from Brody[235] to Bug and along the river northward to Sokal.

This very interesting strategic question was in a terribly simple manner deciphered, when *Captain* Ságner went in Sanok to report at the Brigade Staff Head-quarters the arrival of the March Battalion.

The liaison officer was the Brigade Adjutant *Captain* Tayrle.

"I am very amazed," said *Captain* Tayrle, "that you have not received certain messages. The *march route* is definite. You should have informed us about the vector of your march naturally ahead of time. According to the instructions of the General Staff **you arrived two days early**."

*Captain* Ságner blushed a little, but it didn't occur to him to be repeating all the ciphered telegrams, which he kept receiving all along the way.

"You make me wonder, Sir," said the Adjutant Tayrle.

"I thought," answered *Captain* Ságner, "that all of us officers were on a first name basis."

"So be it," said *Captain* Tayrle, "Tell me, are you active duty or a civilian reservist? Active? — That's altogether something different... A man can't make heads or tails of it. There have, let me tell you, rolled through here already so many of such imbecile reserve lieutenants. — When we were retreating from Limanov[236] and from Krasník[237], all those also-would-be lieutenants lost their heads as soon as they saw a Cossack patrol. We at the Staff don't like such parasites. A numskull of a guy with an intellectual's brand from a reserve officer school lets himself in the end be activated, or, while he's a civilian, passes the officer's test and keeps goofing off as a civilian, and when the war comes, then he doesn't become a Lieutenant, but turns chicken-shit yellow!"

*Captain* Tayrle spat and intimately patted *Captain* Ságner several times: "You'll linger here for about two days. I'll show all of you around, we'll go dancing. We have here these nice little whores, *angel whores*. We have a general's daughter here, who used to practice lesbian love before. Then we will, you know, change into women's clothes, and you'll see, what she can do! Let me tell you, she's such a skinny sow, that you would perhaps not even think of anything. But she knows her stuff, pal. She is kind of a bitch — needless to say, you'll find out. — Pardon me!" he suddenly stopped, "I have to puke again, it is already the third time today."

Then when he returned, he conveyed to *Captain* Ságner, in order to prove, what a merry place it was, that these were the consequences of last night, in which took part even the construction unit.

With the commander of this unit, who also had the rank of *captain*, made his acquaintance *Captain* Ságner very soon. For into the office burst a long fellow in uniform with three gold little stars who, somewhat in a daze, not taking notice of *Captain* Ságner's presence, quite intimately addressed Tayrle: "What you're doing, swine? You have messed up pretty good our duchess for us yesterday." He sat down on a chair, and rapping himself with a thin reed switch across the calves, he was laughing with a wide grin: "When I think of how you puked into her lap"

"Yes," said Tayrle, "it was very merry yesterday." Only then he introduced *Captain* Ságner to the officer with the reed switch and they all exited through the office of the Administration Department of the Brigade out into a coffeehouse, which had suddenly grown out of the former beer joint.

When they were walking through the office, *Captain* Tayrle helped himself to the reed switch from the construction unit commander and struck the long table, around which stood up on command in a line twelve military scribes. They were believers in uneventful, safe work in the rear of the army with large, satisfied bellies in over-sized uniforms.

And to these twelve fat apostles of shirkdom *Captain* Tayrle said, wanting to distinguish himself in front of Ságner and the other *Captain*: "Don't think, that I have you here as if it was a fattening-sty. Pigs! You need to feed and booze less, but run more. — Now I'll show yet another dressage drill," Tayrle announced to his companions.

He struck again the reed switch against the table and asked the twelve: "When are you going to burst, you porkers?"

All twelve answered in unison: "According to your order, *Captain*, Sir."

Laughing at his own stupidity and idiocy, *Captain* Tayrle walked out of the office.

When all three were sitting in the coffeehouse, Tayrle ordered a bottle of rowan brandy be brought and have some misses called, who were free. It became apparent, that the coffeehouse actually wasn't anything other than a house of ill repute, and because none of the misses were available, *Captain* Tayrle got angry to the maximum degree and in the front hallway delivered a vulgar tongue-lashing to the madam and was screaming, who it was that was with Miss Ella. When he received for an answer, that some lieutenant was there, he was raging even more.

With Miss Ella was mister Lieutenant Dub, who, since the march battalion was already in its billet at the Gymnasium[238], had called out his whole formation of men and was alerting them in a long speech, that the Russians in their retreat were setting up brothels everywhere with personnel infected by venereal diseases, in order to cause the Austrian army through this trick of theirs great casualties. He was then warning thereby the soldiers against seeking out similar rooms. He personally would verify for himself in those houses, whether his order had not been obeyed, because they were already in the frontline zone; everyone, who was caught, would face a field court martial.

Lieutenant Dub had gone to personally verify, whether his order had not been infringed upon, and that was apparently why for the starting point of his inspection he chose the sofa in Ella's little room on the second floor of the so-called "city coffeehouse," on which sofa he was having a good time.

In the meantime *Captain* Ságner had already gone to his Battalion. Tayrle's social gathering was, that is to say, dismissed and dispersed. Looking for *Captain* Tayrle were people from the Brigade, where the Brigade Commander was for over an hour already looking for his Adjutant.

There had come new orders from the Division and it was

necessary to designate a definite *march route* for the just-arrived 91st Regiment, because in its original direction, according to the new instructions, was to go the March Battalion of the 102nd Regiment.

It was all very confused, the Russians were retreating in the northeastern corner of Galicia very quickly, so that some Austrian components there got commingled, into which were here and there penetrating as wedges components of the German army, which chaos was augmented by the arrivals of the new march battalions and other military units at the front. The same was happening in the front sectors, which were even farther in the rear, like here at Sanok, to which were added all of a sudden the reserves of the German Hanover[239] Division under the leadership of a colonel with such an ugly gaze, that the Brigade Commander was thrown into an absolute confusion. The Colonel of the Hanover Division reserves was showing, that is to say, the instructions of his Staff, that he was to billet his men at the Gymnasium, where just now were billeted the ninety-firsters. For the billeting of his Staff he was demanding the evacuation of a Krakow bank[240] building, in which there was just now the Brigade Staff Headquarters.

The Brigade Commander got connected directly with the Division, where he described exactly the situation, then spoke to the Division the hexing-eye-possessing Hanoverian, as a result of which there arrived at the Brigade the order: "The Brigade is setting out of the town at six o'clock in the evening toward Tyrawa Wołoska — Liskowiec — Starasol — Sambor, where further orders await. Leaving with it is the March Battalion 91 providing the security, the deployment, that's to be worked out by the Brigade according to the schema: The vanguard sets out at five thirty toward Tyrawa, the distance between the southern and northern flanks cover three and half kilometers. Rear guard cover sets out at a quarter past six!"

So then there arose a great commotion at the Gymnasium and missing for the conference of the Battalion officers was only Lieutenant Dub, whom Švejk was ordered to seek out.

"I hope," said to him Senior Lieutenant Lukáš, "that you will find him without any difficulties, because you two keep having something between you."

"I dutifully report, *Senior Lieutenant*, Sir, that I beg for a written order from the *Company*. That's precisely because between us there's precisely always that something."

While Senior Lieutenant Lukáš was copying an order on a tear sheet in his log book for Lieutenant Dub to immediately muster at the Gymnasium for a conference, Švejk kept on reporting: "Yes, *Senior Lieutenant*, Sir, you can, as always, rest assured. I will find him, because the soldiers are forbidden to go to the brothels, and he will certainly be in one, in order to verify for himself, whether there isn't anyone from his *platoon* trying to end up facing the field court, with which he usually threatens them. He himself declared in front of the men of his platoon, that he'd go through all the brothels, and then there will be woe and that they would get to know him from that bad side. Needless to say, I know where he is. He is right across from here in that coffeehouse, because all the men were watching after him to see, where he was going first."

'The Combined Entertainment Rooms and Municipal Coffeehouse[241]', an enterprise, which Švejk was referring to, was indeed divided into two parts. Who didn't want to walk through the coffeehouse, would go through the back, where there was warming up in the sun some old lady, who spoke German, Polish, and Hungarian, sort of in the sense of: "Common, soldier boy, we have nice little misses here."

When the soldier boy entered, she was leading him through a corridor to some sort of reception room and called one of the misses, who ran over right away in a night shirt; first she wanted money, which sum right on the spot, while the soldier boy was unfixing his bayonet, was collecting the madam.

The officers would go through the coffeehouse. The journey of the gentlemen officers was more grievous, because it led through the *chambers* in the back, where there was the second assortment to choose from, intended for the officer ranks, and where there were lacey slips and wine or liqueurs were being drunk. Here the madam indeed didn't tolerate anything untoward, all that was taking place upstairs in the cozy little rooms, where there was wallowing on a divan in one such paradise full of bed-bugs in his long johns Lieutenant Dub, while Miss Ella was telling him a made up, as is always in these cases customary, tragedy of her life, that her father was a factory owner and she a professor at a *high school* in Pest, and that she had done this out of hapless love.

In the back behind Lieutenant Dub within an arm's reach on a small coffee table there was a bottle of rowan brandy and glasses. Because the bottle was half empty and both Ella and Lieutenant Dub were already talking off the path, it was a stress test, revealing that

Lieutenant Dub couldn't take much at all. According to his speech one could see, that he had mixed everything up and that he took Ella to be his servant Kunert; indeed, he would address her as such and was threatening the alleged Kunert as was his custom: "Kunert, Kunert, you bestial creature, once you get to know me from my bad side…"

Švejk was to be subjected to the same procedure as all the other soldier boys, who would walk in through the back, he however kindly jerked himself free from some negligee-clad gal, in response to whose hollering there came running the Polish madam, who impudently denied, looking Švejk in his eyes, that they should have any mister lieutenant there as a guest.

"Don't you be hollering much at me, gracious lady," said kindly Švejk, smiling sweetly while doing it, "or I'll give a few across the snout, ma'am. Where I'm from, in Platnéřská street[242], they once kicked one madam's butt so, that she was out cold. It was a son looking for his father there, some Vondráček, in the tire trade. The madam's name was Křovánová, when they revived her and were asking her at the rescue station, what her name was, she said that it started somehow with 'Ch'. And what is your honored name?"

The honorable matron broke out into terrible hollering, when Švejk after those words pushed her away and was solemnly ascending the wooden stairs to the second floor.

Down below there emerged the owner of the brothel himself, some impoverished Polish nobleman, who ran after Švejk up the stairs and started tugging at his blouse, while he was screaming at him in German that up there the soldiers must not go, that there it was for the gentlemen officers, that for the troops it was downstairs.

Švejk alerted him, that he was coming here in the interest of the whole Army, that he was looking for one mister Lieutenant, without whom the army couldn't set out into the field, and when the other one began to act ever more aggressively, Švejk knocked him down the stairs and continued upstairs the inspection of the rooms. He verified for himself, that all the cozy little rooms were empty, until only at the very end of the porch, when he knocked, grabbed the door handle and cracked the door open, there sounded up the squealing voice of Ella: "*Occupied*" and in no time after that the deep voice of Lieutenant Dub, who thought perhaps, that he was still in his room at the camp: "*Come in!*"

Švejk entered, stepped up to the divan, and handing the copy of a note torn from a block of papers over to Lieutenant Dub, was reporting, looking askance on the parts of a uniform cast about in the corner of a bed: "I dutifully report *Lieutenant*, Sir, that *they* are supposed to dress up and come immediately according to this order, which I am delivering to *them*, to our garrison at the Gymnasium, we're having there a big military consultation!"

Lieutenant Dub popped his eyes with tiny pupils out at him, but reminded himself, that he was after all not so loaded, as not to recognize Švejk. It occurred to him immediately, that they were sending Švejk to him for the Report, and that was why he said: "Right away I'll fix it with you, Švejk. You will see — how — it — will — end up — with — you… — Kunert," he called Ella, "pour — me — one — more!"

He had a drink, and tearing the written order, he was laughing: "Is this — an excuse note? In — our Company — no excuse notes — are accepted. We are — in — the Army — and not — in — school. So — they — caught — you — then — in the brothel? Come — closer — to — me — Švejk — I will — slap you — a few. — In — what — year — did — Philip — the Macedonian[243] — defeat — the Romans, that you — don't know — you — stud!"

"I dutifully report, *Lieutenant*, Sir," continued inexorably Švejk, "it is the highest level order from the Brigade, that the gentlemen officers dress up and go to the Battalion *conference*, we, that is to say, will set out, and only now it will be being decided, which company is going to be the *advanced guard*, the *flank guard* or the *rear guard*. It's already going to be being decided now and I think, *Lieutenant*, Sir, that *they* also have something to say about it."

This diplomatic speech revived Lieutenant Dub a bit, so that he was beginning now to gain the certainty, that he was not at the garrison after all, but out of prudence he asked: "Where is it that I am?"

"You condescend to be in a brotheldump, *Lieutenant,* Sir. They are, those ways of the Lord, varied."

Lieutenant Dub gave a heavy sigh, crawled off the divan and started chasing down his uniform, with which Švejk was helping him, and when at last he dressed, they both walked out, but after a while Švejk in a batting of an eye returned and ignoring Ella, who was assigning to his return a wholly different significance, on account of the hapless love was immediately crawling onto the bed, he quickly drank up the rest of the rowan brandy in the bottle and went again after the Lieutenant.

On the street it went into Lieutenant Dub's head again, because it was sweltering. He was telling Švejk the most varied pieces of nonsense without any connections among them. He was relaying, that he had at home a postage stamp from Helgoland and that right away upon *high school graduation* they went to play billiards and did not greet the homeroom professor. To each sentence he added: "I think that you understand me well."

"Certainly I totally understand you," answered Švejk. "You sound like the tinsmith Pokorný in Budějovice. He, when people asked of him: 'Have you gone swimming yet this year in the Malše?', he would answer: 'No, I haven't, but then there'll be a lot of plums this year.' Or they asked him: 'Have you eaten yet this year portobello mushrooms?' and he retorted: 'No, I haven't, but this new sultan of Morocco[244] is supposed to be a very nice man.'"

Lieutenant Dub stopped and managed to get out of himself: "The Moroccan sultan? He's a has-been personage," he wiped the sweat off his forehead, and looking with his turbid eyes at Švejk, mumbled: "I was not sweating like this even in winter. Do you agree with that? Do you understand me?"

"I do understand, *Lieutenant*, Sir. To our pub At the Chalice there used to come an old gentleman, some retired counselor of a provincial committee, and that one was asserting exactly that. He would always say, that he was amazed, what difference there is between the temperature in summer and winter. That it was very strange to him, why people had yet not discovered that."

In the gate of the Gymnasium Švejk abandoned Lieutenant Dub, who was weaving his way up the stairs to the teachers' lounge, where there was taking place the military conference, and was also right away reporting to *Captain* Ságner, that he was totally drunk. For the duration of the conference he was sitting with his head hung low and during the debate he once in a while got up to cry out: "Your opinion is correct, gentlemen, but I am totally drunk."

When all the arrangements had been worked out and the *Company* of Senior Lieutenant Lukáš was to go as the advanced guard, Lieutenant Dub jerked himself all of a sudden, got up, and said: "I remember, gentlemen, our home class professor in the first year of middle school. Glory to him, glory to him, glory to him!"

It occurred to Senior Lieutenant Lukáš, that it would be the best, if for the time being he were to have Lieutenant Dub deposited by his servant Kunert in the physics storeroom next door, where there was a guard at the door, so that nobody would perhaps finish stealing the already half-pilfered collections of minerals. That, indeed, was what the Brigade Headquarters were constantly alerting the detachments on the march passing through to.

This measure dated from the time, when one battalion of the Hungarian Land Defense soldiers billeted at the Gymnasium started plundering the storeroom. Particularly the Hungarian Land Defense soldiers liked the collection of minerals, colorful crystals and pyrites, which they shoved in their back-packs.

In a tiny military cemetery there is indeed on one of the white crosses the inscription "László Gragany". There is sleeping his eternal dream one Hungarian Land Defense soldier, who, while plundering the Gymnasium collections, drank up all the denatured alcohol from the vessel, in which were immersed, to be preserved, various reptiles.

The world war was battering a whole human generation out of existence even by booze from snakes.

Senior Lieutenant Lukáš, when all had already left, called the servant of Lieutenant Dub, Kunert, who escorted out and laid upon a sofa his Lieutenant.

Lieutenant Dub was all of a sudden like a small child; he took Kunert by the hand, started examining his palm, while he was saying, that he would guess from his palm the name of his future spouse.

"What is your name? Pull out of the breast pocket of my blouse the notebook and pencil. Your name then is Kunert; so come here in a quarter of an hour and I will leave here for you a piece of paper with the name of your Mrs. wife."

Having barely finished saying that, he started snoring, but again somehow woke out of it and started scribbling in his notebook; what he wrote, he tore out, threw it on the floor, and secretively having put his finger to his mouth, he said, blabbering: "Not yet now, only after a quarter of an hour. The best will be to look for the piece of paper with blindfolded eyes."

Kunert was such a good dumb beast, that he actually came after a quarter of an hour, and when he unwrapped the little piece of paper, he was reading out of the cranks-and-hooks of Lieutenant Dub's: "The name of your future wife is: Mrs. Kunert."

When in a while he was showing it to Švejk, Švejk told him, to make sure to put away and save the little piece of paper well, that such documents from the military lords everybody was to hold in esteem, that in earlier times on active duty it would not happen, for an officer to be corresponding with his servant and address him as mister.

\*

When the preparations had been executed, for setting out according to the given instructions, the Brigade General, whom unseated so nicely the Hanover Colonel, had the whole Battalion gathered in the customary square formation and made a speech to it. That man, that is to say, liked very much to speechify, so he was grinding out words mixing them five over nine, and when he didn't have anything further to say anymore, he remembered yet the field post office:

"Soldiers," was thundering from his mouth into the square. "Now we are approaching the frontline of the enemy, from whom we are separated by several day marches. So far on your march, soldiers, you have not had an opportunity to inform your loved ones, whom you left behind, of your address, so that your distant ones would know, where they were to write to you, so that you would console yourselves with letters from your beloved bereaved."

Somehow he couldn't get out of it, kept repeating it endlessly in a row: "Beloved distant ones — dear relatives — beloved bereaved" and so on, until at last he broke out of the cycle by a mighty shout: "That's what we have the field post office at the front for!"

His next speech gave the impression, as if all these people in gray uniforms were to get themselves killed with the greatest joy just because, that there were field post offices established at the front, and that when a grenade would tear both of somebody's legs off, that it had to be beautiful dying for him, when he remembers, that his field post office number is 72, and there is perhaps lying there a letter from home, from the distant loved ones, with a shipment containing a chunk of smoked meat, bacon and home-made biscuits.

Afterward, after that speech, once the Brigade band had played the Imperial anthem, glory to the Emperor was proclaimed, there set out the individual groups of that human cattle, earmarked for slaughter somewhere beyond the Bug, gradually on a march according to the given instructions.

The 11th *Company* set out at half past five to Tyrawa-Wolska. Švejk was dragging in the back with the *Company* Staff, with the Ambulance Corps and Senior Lieutenant Lukáš was riding round the whole convoy, while every chance he had he rode to the back, to check for himself with the Ambulance Corps, where on a cart under the tarps they were hauling Lieutenant Dub toward new heroic deeds into the unknown future, and while doing that, also to shorten the journey by conversing with Švejk, who was carrying his back-pack and rifle patiently, talking with Accounting Master Sergeant Vaněk, about how nice years ago the marching was on maneuvers by Velké Meziříčí[245].

"It was altogether such a landscape, like it is here, except we weren't going truly *with full battle gear*, because back then we hadn't even known yet, what reserve food cans were, and when we got any can issued, then as for our *platoon* during the nearest night quarters we devoured it and in its place we would put in the back-pack a brick. In one village there came an inspection, they threw all our bricks out of the back-packs and there were so many, that a man there built out of them for himself a family home."

A while afterwards Švejk was walking smartly alongside the horse of Senior Lieutenant Lukáš and was telling him about field post offices: "Nice was that speech and it is certainly very sweet for everyone, when in the army service he gets a nice letter from home. But I, when I was serving in Budějovice years ago, then while in the military I got only one letter at the garrison and that one I have still saved."

Švejk pulled out of a soiled leather bag a grease stained letter and was reading, keeping pace with the horse of Senior Lieutenant Lukáš, who started to trot gently: "You shameless rube, you murderer and scoundrel! Mister Corporal Kříž arrived in Prague for *leave* and I was dancing with him at the Kocans'[246], and he was telling me, that you supposedly dance in Budějovice at The Green Frog[247] with some stupid floozy and that you have already totally abandoned me. So that you know, I am writing this letter in the shithouse on the plank next to the hole, it's the end between us. Yours formerly Božena. So that I would not forget, this Corporal knows how to do it and he will yet be busting your chops, I was begging him to do that. And another thing so that I would not forget, you won't find me among the living anymore, when you come home on *leave*. — It figures," continued during the gentle trot Švejk, "that when I came on *leave*, that she was among the living, and among quite a sort of living ones at that. I found her indeed at the Kocans', dressing her were two soldiers from another regiment and one of them was so much alive, that he was feeling her altogether publicly under the bodice, as if he wanted, I dutifully report *Senior Lieutenant*, Sir, to pull out of there the pollen of her innocence, as says Věnceslava Lužická[248] or as a young girl of about sixteen put it in a similar way once in a dancing class telling a Gymnasium student loudly and weeping, when he pinched her shoulder: 'You have, Sir, wiped off the pollen of my virginity.' It goes without saying, that they all were laughing and her mommy, who was her chaperone there, that she escorted her to the hallway in the Burghers' Club[249], and there she kicked that nitwit goose of hers silly. I had arrived, *Senior Lieutenant*, Sir, at the opinion, that after all those country girls are more sincere than the sort of worn out pampered little city misses, who attend some dance lessons. When years ago we were at *camp* in Mníšek, I used to go dancing in Starý Knín[250], there I talked up some girl named Karla Veklová[251], but she didn't like me much. One Sunday evening I was escorting her to a little pond, there we sat on the dam and I was asking her, when the sun was setting, whether she loved me too. I dutifully report, *Senior Lieutenant*, Sir, that the air was so moist, all the birds were singing, and she answered me with horrible laughter: 'I like you as much as a husk in the ass, come on, you're so stupid.' And I was indeed really stupid, so terribly stupid, that I, I dutifully report *Senior Lieutenant*, Sir, prior to that used to walk through the fields, through the high standing wheat in a space empty of people, not even once did we sit down, and I only kept showing her the blessings of God, and being the numskull, I was telling the farming gal, that this was rye, this was wheat and that these were oats."

And as a confirmation of its having been oats, somewhere up ahead were dying down the gathered voices of the *Company* soldiers in the continuation of the song, with which the Czech regiments had already gone to bleed for Austria at Solferino:

> And when it was middle of the night,
> the oats jump out of the sack,
> zhoopaidah, zhoopaidah,
> every gal will give!

Into which the others jumped again:

> And will give, and will give, and will give,
> and why wouldn't she give,
> and will give you two pecks
> on both cheeks.
> Zhoopaidah, zhoopaidah,
> every gal will give!
> And will give, and will give, and will give,
> and why wouldn't she give…

Then the Germans started to sing the very same song in German.

It is such an old military song, that perhaps it was already sung by the soldiering rabble during the Napoleonic skirmishes in all languages. Now its sound carried cheerfully on a dusty road to Tyrawa-Wolska, in the Galician flat land, where on both sides of the road all the way to the green hills in the south the fields were battered and destroyed under the hoofs of the horses and under the soles of thousands and thousands of military heavy boots.

"Like this we had once likewise messed it up," sounded up Švejk, looking to the round about, "at the maneuvers near Písek. There was with us one mister archduke there, he was such a righteous gentleman, that when he was riding with his Staff for strategic reasons through standing wheat, then right behind him was estimating the whole damage the adjutant. Some farmer Pícha had no joy on account of the visit and did not accept from the *Army Supply Administration* the eighteen crowns of compensation for the trampled five measures of field, and he wanted, I tell you, *Senior Lieutenant*, Sir, to sue and got for that eighteen months.

I think, *Senior Lieutenant*, Sir, that he should actually have been glad, that somebody from the Imperial dynasty visited him on his parcel of land. Another farmer, who was conscientious, would have dressed all his gals in white dresses like bridesmaids, put bouquets in their hands and posed them spaced out on his parcel of land, and each of them would have to welcome the highly positioned lord, like as I was reading about India, where the subjects of some ruler used to let themselves be stepped on and squashed by the elephant."

"What are you saying Švejk?" was shouting at him from atop the horse Senior Lieutenant Lukáš.

"I dutifully report *Senior Lieutenant*, Sir, that I mean the elephant, which was carrying on its back that ruler, whom I was reading about."

"Nothing matters, Švejk, as long as you are able to properly explain everything," said Senior Lieutenant Lukáš and started riding to the front. There the convoy was already breaking up, the unusual march after the rest on the train, with full, perfect battle gear, was causing, that everybody's shoulders started to ache and everybody was easing up, any way he could. They were switching the rifle from one side to the other, most were not carrying it by the leather strap anymore, but thrown across the shoulder like a rake or a pitchfork. Some thought, that they would do better for themselves, if they walked in the ditch or down the balk*, where the soil under their feet seemed softer after all than on the dusty road.

Most walked with their head hung toward the ground and all suffered great thirst, because, despite the fact, that the sun had already set, it was as sultry and steaming hot as at noon and nobody had even a drop of water in his field flask anymore. It was the first day of the march and this unusual situation, which was somewhat of an entry into greater and greater hardships, was making everybody the wearier and more languid the longer it went on. They also stopped singing and were guessing for one another among themselves about how far it still was for them to Tyrawa-Wolska, where they thought they were supposed to spend the night. Some were sitting in the ditch a bit now and then, and so that it would not look so, they were untying their boots and were at first sight making the impression of a man, who laid his foot-wraps incorrectly and is attempting to lay them so, that they wouldn't bother him on the next march. Others on the other hand were shortening or lengthening the strap on the rifle, or were rolling out the back-pack and moving around the objects placed in it, telling themselves, that they're doing so with respect to the correct loading, so that the back-pack straps would not be pulling on one or the other shoulder. When there was coming nearer them gradually Senior Lieutenant Lukáš, here they were getting up and reporting, that something was bothering them or something like that, if the cadets or corporals were not driving them forward before that, when they saw from a distance the mare of Senior Lieutenant Lukáš.

Senior Lieutenant Lukáš, riding by, was urging them quite kindly, just to rise, that there were still three kilometers left to Tyrawa-Wolska, that there they would have a rest.

In the meantime Lieutenant Dub came to from the constant shaking atop the ambulance two-wheeler. He hadn't come to totally yet, that is, but he could already sit up and lean out of the two-wheeler and call at the *Company* Staff, which was moving about freely, because they all, starting with Baloun and ending with Chodounský, put their back-packs into the two-wheeler. Only Švejk was going fearlessly forward with the back-pack included, having his rifle across his chest on the strap Dragoon style, was smoking his pipe and singing to the march:

---

* an unplowed ridge dividing fields [Translator's note]

> When we were pulling toward Jaroměř,
> let anybody, who wants to, believe us,
> we arrived there probably just for dinner…

More than five hundred steps ahead of Lieutenant Dub there were rising on the road swirls of dust, from which were emerging the figures of soldiers; Lieutenant Dub, whose enthusiasm returned again, leaned his head out of the two-wheeler and started hollering into the road dust: "Soldiers, your exalted task is hard, you are about to encounter difficult marches, the most various shortages in all things, and mundane exertions of all kinds. But with full confidence I'm looking forward to your perseverance and your strength of will."

"You ox," waxed poetic Švejk.

Lieutenant Dub continued: "For you, soldiers, no obstacle is so mighty, as for you not to overcome it! One more time, soldiers, I repeat to you, that I am not leading you to an easy victory. It will be a tough nut for you, but you will manage it! The history of ages will celebrate you."

"Stick a finger in your throat," waxed poetic again Švejk.

And as if Lieutenant Dub had heard, he started hurling suddenly, as he had his head hung low, into the dust of the road and when he was done puking, he still yelled out: "Soldiers, forward," he collapsed again onto Choudounský's back-pack and slept all the way to Tyrawa-Wolska, where they at last stood him up on his feet and took him off the cart on the order of Senior Lieutenant Lukáš, who had a very long and very difficult conversation with him, before Lieutenant Dub came to out of it all to the point, that at last he was able to proclaim: "Judged logically, I committed a silliness, which I will make up for in the face of the enemy."

He had however still not quite regained his senses, because he told Senior Lieutenant Lukáš, when he was leaving to join his formation: "You don't know me yet, but once you get to know me!"

"You can inquire with Švejk about what you were doing acting up."

Lieutenant Dub then went first rather than to his formation to Švejk, whom he found in the company of Baloun and Accounting Master Sergeant Vaněk.

Baloun was just telling, how back home at their mill he had always had a bottle of beer in the well. That the beer was so cold, the teeth went numb. That elsewhere in the mills in the evenings they wash down rozhuda[252] with such beer, but that he, in his gluttony, for which the Lord God has now punished him, after the rozhuda still always swallowed a proper chunk of meat. That now divine justice punished him with warm stinking water from the wells in Tyrawa-Wolska[253], into which they all have to pour, on account of cholera, citric acid, which was just a while ago being distributed, as the well water was being issued by the swarms. Baloun expressed the opinion, that this citric acid was perhaps being issued apparently on account of starving the people out. It is true enough, that in Sanok he ate a bit, that *Senior Lieutenant* Lukáš had even let him again have half of his portion of veal, which he had brought him from the Brigade, but that it was horrible, because he thought after all, that when they came here and there was a *rest break* with overnight quarters, that something would be cooked again. He was indeed already convinced of that, when the *field cooks* were filling the cauldrons with water. He immediately went to ask at the kitchens what was up, and they answered him, that there was only an order to gather the water for the time being, and that in a while may come an order to pour the water out again.

Right then came Lieutenant Dub, and since he was himself very unsure of himself, he asked: "Are you having a good time?"

"We are having a good time, *Lieutenant*, Sir," answered for them all Švejk, "here with us the merriment is in full swing. It is altogether the best always to have a good time. Now we are having a good time about citric acid. There can be no soldier without merriment, he at least forgets all the hardships better."

Lieutenant Dub told him, to walk a bit with him, that he wanted to ask him about something. Once they were then somewhat alone, he told him in a terribly unsure voice: "Weren't you all talking about me?"

"Not at all, we never are, *Lieutenant*, Sir, only about the citric acid and about smoked meat."

"*Senior Lieutenant* Lukáš was telling me, that I was supposedly like acting up and that you know very well about it, Švejk."

Švejk very seriously and with great emphasis said: "You were not acting up at all, *Lieutenant*, Sir, you were only on a visit in one house of ill repute. But that was perhaps some mistake. They always used to be looking for tinsmith Pimpra from the Goat patch[254] too, when he would go to buy sheet metal in town, and they'd also always find him in a similar room, either at Šuhas', or at Dvořák's[255], like I found you. Downstairs there was a coffeehouse and upstairs in our case there were gals. You were, *Lieutenant*, Sir, perhaps mistaken, where it was that you were actually located, because it was hot, and when a man is not used to drinking, then in such heat he'll get drunk on even ordinary rum, let alone rowan brandy, *Lieutenant*, Sir. So I got the order to deliver to you the invitation for the *conference*, before we took off, and indeed I found you there by that gal upstairs; on account of the heat and the rowan brandy you didn't even recognize me and you were lying there on the sofa undressed. You weren't acting up there in any special way, you weren't even saying 'You don't know me yet', but such a thing can happen to anybody, when it's hot. Some suffer from it chronically, others for a change chance upon it like a blind man upon a violin. If you knew the old Vejvoda, the construction site foreman from Vršovice, that one, let me tell you, *Lieutenant*, Sir, set in his mind, that he wouldn't drink any beverages, from which he'd get drunk. So he still had just a shot for the road and walked out of the home to look for those beverages without alcahol[256]. He stopped then first At the Rest Stop pub, had there a little quarter liter of vermouth and started inconspicuously inquiring of the pubkeeper, what did actually drink the teetotalers. He rather correctly judged, that pure water was even for abstaining teetotalers after all a very brutal beverage. The pubkeeper then explained to him, that teetotalers drank soda water, lemonades, milk and then wines without alcahol, cold garlic soup and other spirit-free beverages. Of those there appealed to old Vejvoda still most the sprit-free wines after all. He still asked, whether there were even spirit-free sorts of booze, drank still one more little quarter, had a conversation with the pubkeeper regarding, that it's a real sin to be often getting loaded, to which the pubkeeper told him, that he'd put up with anything in the world, except a drunk man, who gets drunk somewhere else and comes to him to sober up on a bottle of soda water, and still stirs up a ruckus. 'Get loaded here in my place,' says the pubkeeper, 'then you're my man, but otherwise I don't know you.' Old Vejvoda then drank up and went on, until he came, *Lieutenant*, Sir, at Charles square into a wine store, where he'd also sometimes drop in, and he asked there, whether they had spirit-free wines. 'Spirit-free wines we don't have mister Vejvoda,' they told him, 'but vermouth or sherry.' Old Vejvoda felt somehow ashamed, so he drank up there a quarter of vermouth and a quarter of sherry, and as he was sitting there, he gets acquainted, I tell you, *Lieutenant*, Sir, with another would-be-teetotaler. One word led to another, they were still drinking a quarter of sherry at a time, and at last they came to an understanding, that the gentleman knew a place, where they had spirit-free wines on tap. 'It is in the Bolzánova street[257], there one goes down the stairs and they have a gramophone there.' In return for this good news did old Vejvoda put a whole bottle of vermouth on the table and then they both set out to Bolzánova street, where one goes down the stairs and where they have a gramophone there. And really, there they had nothing on tap but fruit wines, not only spirit-free, but even without alcahol. First each had a half liter of gooseberry wine, then a half liter of red currant wine, and when they drank up still another half-liter of gooseberry spirit-free wine, their legs started falling asleep after all those vermouths and sherries of earlier, and they started shouting, that they should bring them an official certificate, that what they were drinking here, was spirit-free wine. That they were teetotalers, and if somebody didn't immediately bring it, they would trash the place and smash everything, including the gramophone. Afterwards the police had to be dragging both of them up the stairs into Bolzánova Street, they had to put them in the box cart and throw them in the solitary – the both of them had to be convicted for drunkenness as teetotalers."

"Why are you telling me that," yelled out Lieutenant Dub, who had by this speech completely sobered up.

"I dutifully report, Lieutenant, Sir, that it doesn't really belong together, but since we're already chatting away like this…"

To Lieutenant Dub occurred at that moment that Švejk offended him again, as he had already, somehow, his full senses back, so he was screaming at him: "You will get to know me one day! What about the way you're standing?"

"I dutifully report, that I'm standing incorrectly, I have, I dutifully report, forgotten to click my heels together. I will do it right away."

Švejk already stood in the best of front-and-center form again.

Lieutenant Dub was thinking over, what else he should say, but in the end said only: "You be careful of me, so that I won't have to tell it to you for the last time," in addition to which he corrected his old saying: "You don't know me yet, but I know you."

When Lieutenant Dub was walking away from Švejk, in his hangover stupor he thought: "May be, that it would have been more effective on him, had I told him: 'I have long since known you, man, from the bad side."

Afterwards did Lieutenant Dub have servant Kunert called and ordered him to chase down a pitcher of water.

To Kunert's honor let it be said, that he was chasing down both a pitcher and water for a long time throughout Tyrawa-Wolska.

The pitcher he managed in the end to steal from the village priest and into the pitcher he drew from a well, totally boarded over with nailed-down planks, the water. To that purpose he had to, of course, tear off several planks, since the well was thus secured, because the water in it was suspected of being tainted with typhus.

Lieutenant Dub though drank up the whole pitcher of water without any further consequences, thereby validating the old saying 'A good pig will withstand anything.'

All were very mistaken, when they thought, that in Tyrawa-Wolska they would perhaps lodge.

Senior Lieutenant Lukáš called telephone operator Chodounský, Accounting Master Sergeant Vaněk and the courier of the company Švejk and Baloun. The orders were simple. All will leave the gear with the ambulance corps, immediately charge out toward Malý Polanec[258] down a field path and then along the creek down in the south-easterly direction onto Liskowiec[259].

Švejk, Vaněk and Chodounský are *billeting officers*. All three have to obtain overnight quarters for the *Company*, which will arrive to join them in an hour, at most an hour and a half later. Baloun must in the meantime at the place, where would be billeting he, Senior Lieutenant Lukáš, have them bake a goose, and all three must watch Baloun, lest he devour a half of it. Besides that must Vaněk and Švejk buy a pig for the *Company*, depending on how much meat would be apportioned to the whole *Company*. At night there will be goulash being cooked. The night quarters for the men must be proper; avoid loused up cottages, so that the men would appropriately rest, because the *Company* is setting out from Liskowiec at half past the sixth hour of the morning already via Krościenko[260] to Starasol[261].

The Battalion, that is to say, was not poor anymore. The Brigade Quartermaster in Sanok paid out to the Battalion a down payment for future slaughters. In the cashbox at the *Company* there were over one hundred thousand crowns and Accounting Master Sergeant Vaněk had already received an order, that once they were in place somewhere, which was understood in the trenches, before the death of the *Company*, to account for and pay out, for the never delivered commissary ration bread and mess rations, the, to the men indisputably belonging, amounts.

While all four set out on the road, there emerged by the *Company*

Jaroslav Hašek

mister local village priest and was distributing to the soldiers according to their nationality a little leaflet with the "Song of Lourdes"[262] in all languages. He had a package of those songs, which left for him here to hand out to the military detachments passing through some high military clerical dignitary, gallivanting through the devastated Galicia in an automobile with some sluts.

*Where in the valley toward the river the mountain slopes,*
*to all the angel's message proclaims the bell.*
*Ave, ave, ave, Maria! — Ave, ave, ave, Maria!*

*Lo, Bernarda*[263]*, the little girl, the heavenly spirit*
*there to the bank leads into a green meadow. — Ave!*

*And she beheld upon the rock a starry glow,*
*in it a figure majestic, a most holy face. — Ave!*

*Adorning her adorably a robe of lilies*
*and a simple light belt of cloud. — Ave!*

*And on her hands clasped, a rosary has*
*the Lady and Queen most merciful. — Ave!*

*Lo, Bernarda's a-changing is the innocent face,*
*face being adorned by a strange heavenly glow. — Ave!*

*Already she kneels and prays, the Lady Ruler beholds,*
*in heavenly tongue the Queen speaks with her. — Ave!*

*"Know, child, without sin I conceived,*
*mighty protection I want to be for all! — Ave!*

*Here in processions do come my devout people!*
*To me give only honor and seek your peace. — Ave!*

*Let be witness here to nations a temple of marble,*
*that in this place my dwelling I have. — Ave!*
*That spring, however, which started to flow here,*
*that as pledge of my love invites you to itself." — Ave!*

*O glory to you, valley most merciful,*
*the dwelling of the Mother most joyous. — Ave!* !

*There in the rock the miraculous cave of yours,*
*paradise you have given us, benevolent Queen. — Ave!*

*Since began that most glorious, joyous day,*
*there honor you processions of men and women. — Ave!*
*You wanted to have throngs of your worshipers,*
*see also us, pleading in evil times. — Ave!*

*O You saving star, before us go,*
*to God's throne us faithful lead! — Ave!*

*O most holy Virgin, in Your love us keep*
*and your motherly grace to your children grant!*

In Tyrawa-Wolska there were many latrines and everywhere in the latrines there were lying around small sheets of papers with the song of Lourdes.

Corporal Nachtigal, from somewhere by the Kašperské Hory, chased down a bottle of booze from a frightened Jew, gathered several pals and now they all started, following the German text, singing the song of Lourdes without the refrain Ave! to the melody of the Prince Eugen song.

It was a damn ugly trip, when it turned dark and the four, who were to take care of the night quarters for the 11th *Company* got to the grove above the creek, which supposedly ran to Liskowiec.

Baloun, who for the first time found himself in a situation, that he was going somewhere into the unknown, and to whom everything: the darkness, that they were going first to look for quarters, seemed unusually mysterious, suddenly took up the terrible suspicion, that this wasn't just nothing.

"Pals," he said softly, stumbling on the path above the creek, "they have sacrificed us."

"How so?" whispered a scream at him Švejk.

"Pals, let's not be hollering so much," was begging in a soft voice Baloun, "I can already feel it in my lower back, they will hear us and will start immediately shooting at us. I know it. They sent us ahead, for us to spy out, whether the enemy wasn't there, and when they hear the shooting, they will immediately know, that they must not go any farther. We are, pals, the *forward security patrol*, as Corporal Terna taught it to me."

"So then go up ahead," said Švejk. "We will go nicely behind you, so that you would protect us with your body, since you are such a giant. Once you're shot, let us know, so that we could do *on your belly* in time. But what a soldier you are, he's afraid that, they will be shooting at him. That is just what each soldier is to like tremendously, each soldier must know, that the more times the enemy shoots at him, thereby also the enemy's stock of ammunition is getting thinner. By each shot, which the enemy soldier sends against you, is diminishing his battle readiness. He's at the same time glad, that he can be shooting at you, because at least he doesn't have to be dragging the cartridges along and it's easier for him to run."

Baloun gave a heavy sigh: "But I've got a farm back home."

"Forget the farm and let it be," was advising him Švejk, "better fall for the lord Emperor. Haven't they been teaching you that in the army service?"

"They only mentioned it," said the stupid Baloun. "They only used to take me out to the *training ground* and after that I never heard of anything like that, because I became an *orderly*. If at least the lord Emperor was feeding us better…"

"You are though a damn insatiable swine. They are not to feed the soldier at all before *combat*, this already years ago used to tell us in school *Captain* Untergriez. That one would always tell us: 'Damn guys, if ever a war broke out, and it came to a *combat*, don't you before the fighting overfeed yourselves. Whoever is overfed and gets a shot in the belly, he's done for then, because all that soup and commissary ration bread will after a shot like that come out of the gut, and such a soldier is right away done for due to inflammation. When however he has nothing in his tummy, such a shot in the belly is to him like nothing, like getting stung by a wasp, nothing but joy."

"I digest quickly," said Baloun, "with me there's never much left in the tummy. I will for example, pal, gobble up a whole bowl of dumplings with pork and with sauerkraut, and half an hour later I won't shit out from it more than about three tablespoons, the rest, I tell you, disappears in me. Someone for example says, that when he eats little foxes[264], they will come out of him as they were, one would have to only launder them and make them sour style again, and with me the other way around. I will gorge myself full of little foxes, where someone else would burst, and then when I go to the rest room, let me tell you, I'll fart out only a bit of yellow puree, like from a baby, the rest also disappears in me. — Inside me, pal," was confidentially relaying Baloun to Švejk, "dissolve fish bones and stones from plums. Once I purposely counted them. I ate seventy plum filled fruit dumplings with the stones, and when my moment had come, I went beyond the village meadows, and was poking in it with a little stick, putting stones aside and counting. Out of seventy stones dissolved in me more than a half."

From Baloun's mouth crept out a soft extended sigh: "My *lady-wife of the house* used to make plum dumplings from potato dough, into which she'd add a little farmer's cheese, so that they would be more filling. She always preferred them sprinkled with poppy seeds rather than dry curd farmers cheese and I just the other way around, so that once on account of it I slapped her up a fill... I did not manage to appreciate my familial bliss."

Baloun stopped, smacked his lips, swept his tongue over his palate and said sadly and gently: "You know, pal, that now, when I don't have it, it seems to me, that my wife was right after all, that with the poppy seeds of hers they are better. Back then it constantly seemed to me, that poppy seeds tended to get stuck between my teeth, and now I think if only it were so... My wife had often suffered from me a repeated and great adversity. The many times she would weep, when I wanted, that she put more marjoram into the jitrnice, and while she was at it I'd always smack her one or two. Once I thrashed the poor soul so, that she lied in bed for two days, because she did not want to cut down a turkey for my supper, that supposedly a cockerel was enough for me. — Yes, pal," started weeping Baloun, "if only there were now a jitrnice without marjoram, and cockerels... Do you like to eat dill gravy? See, on account of it there used to be a ruckus, and today I'd drink it like coffee."

Baloun was slowly forgetting the image of the supposed danger and in the silence of the night, as they were still descending onto Liskowiec, moved with emotion he kept on telling Švejk, what he did not use to appreciate before and what he would eat now with such a desire, that he could cry.

Behind them was walking telephone operator Chodounský with Account Master Sergeant Vaněk.

Choudounský was telling Vaněk, that according to his opinion a world war was an idiocy. The worst thing in its course was, that when the telephone lines got broken somewhere, then you had to go at night to fix it, and even the worse thing about it was, that in earlier time, when there was some war, they did not have searchlights. But now, just as you're repairing the damn wires, the enemy finds you immediately with the searchlight and lets the whole artillery loose on you.

Down in the village, where they were to seek out night quarters for the *Company*, it was dark and all the dogs started barking, which forced the expedition to stop and consider, how to face these miscreants.

"How about we go back," whispered Baloun.

"Baloun, Baloun, if we were to report it, you'd be blasted away for cowardice," said Švejk in response.

The longer the dogs barked the more they did so, and even in the south on the other side of the river Ropa[265], they started barking also in Krościenko and several other villages, because Švejk was hollering into the silence of the night: "Down — down — down," as once upon a time he used to holler at his dogs, when he still traded them.

The dogs were now barking even more, so that Accounting Master Sergeant Vaněk told Švejk:

"Don't holler at them, Švejk, or you'll get the whole of Galicia barking."

"Something similar," answered Švejk, "happened to us at maneuvers in the Tábor region. There we pulled into a village at night and the dogs started making a tremendous ruckus. The vicinity there is pretty populated everywhere, so that the dog barking spread from village to village, ever farther and farther, and the dogs in our village where we were camping, once they had at last fallen silent, heard again barking from afar, perhaps from somewhere all the way in the vicinity of Pelhřimov, so they let loose barking again, and after a while barking were the Tábor region, Pelhřimov region, Budějovice region, Humpolec region, Třeboň region and Jihlava[266] region. Our *Captain*, he was such a nervous old geezer, that one could not stand dog barking, he did not sleep all night, constantly kept pacing to and fro, and was asking the patrol: 'Who's barking, what's he barking?' The soldiers were dutifully reporting, that the dogs were barking, and he got so burnt up over it, that those who were on patrol back then got confinement to the barracks for it when we returned from the maneuvers. Then he would always pick a 'dog commando' and send it up ahead. Its purpose was to inform the population in the village, where we were to quarter, that no dog must give out at night a single bark, or else it would be destroyed. I too was in such a commando, and when we came to a village in the Milevsko region, then I got it confused and informed the mayor of the village, that every owner of a dog, that lets out a bark at night, would be destroyed for strategic reasons. The mayor spooked, he hitched up right away and rode to the Staff Headquarters to plead on behalf of the whole village for mercy. There they didn't even let him in, the posted guards would have almost shot him dead, so he returned home, and by the time we pulled into the village, all the people wrapped on his advice rags around the dogs' mugs, until three of them turned rabid."

They were descending into the village, when there was accepted the general advice of Švejk's, that dogs are afraid at night of the glow of a lit up cigarette. Unfortunately none of them smoked cigarettes, so this advice of Švejk's did not have any positive results. It became apparent however, that the dogs were barking out of joy, because they were fondly remembering the armies passing through, which always left something for them to munch on.

They smelled already from afar, that getting near were those creatures, which leave behind them bones and carcasses of horses. There popped up out of nowhere four bowsers around Švejk who took it upon themselves to be pestering him in a friendly way with their tails raised up.

Švejk was stroking them, petting them, and was talking to them in the dark as if to children:

"So we're here already, we came to your place to go beddy-bye, to fill the tummies with yummies, we'll give you little bonies, crusties and in the morning then again we'll go on after the enemy."

In the village in one cottage after another they started to ignite the lights, and when at the first cottage they started rapping on the door, in order to learn, where the mayor lived, there came from inside a shrieking and shrill female voice, which, not in Polish, but also not in Ukrainian, was announcing, that her husband is in the army service, that she has children sick with smallpox and that the Moskali[267] had taken everything over and that her husband, before he left for the army service, was ordering her, not to open the door at night for anyone. Only when they increased the emphasis of the attack against the door while assuring her, that they are billeting officers, did the door open by some unknown hand, and when they walked in, it turned out, that here actually lives the mayor, who was in vain attempting to talk Švejk out of the notion, that he was imitating the shrieking female voice. He was apologizing, that he was sleeping on the hay and that his wife, when somebody suddenly wakes her up, that she doesn't know what she is saying. As regards the night quarters for the whole *Company*, that the village is so tiny, that not even one soldier will fit in it. There's no place whatsoever to sleep. There is nothing to buy here either, the Moskali took it all.

If the lords *benefactors* were not to spurn the idea, he would escort them to Krościenko, there are large farms there, it is only three quarters of an hour from here, there is plenty of room, each soldier will be able to cover himself with a sheep-skin fur coat, they have so many cows there, that each soldier will get a mess kit of milk, there is good water there, the gentlemen officers can sleep there in a chateau, but here in Liskowiec? Poverty, scabies, and lice. He himself used to have five cows once upon a time, but the Moskali took them all, so that he himself, when he wants milk for his ill children, must walk all the way to Krościenko.

As a proof of it there mooed in the sty next to him cows and one could hear a shrill female voice, which was shouting down the hapless cows and was wishing them, that cholera twist them dead.

That however failed to confuse the mayor and he continued putting on his high boots:

"The only cow here is owned by my neighbor Vojciek, which you just now condescended to hear, my lords *benefactors*, mooing. It is a cow that is sick, wistful. Moskali took her calf away from her. Since that time she doesn't give milk, but the farmer feels it a pity to cut her down, he thinks, that the Mother of God of Częstochowa[268] will again turn everything for the better."

In the course of this speech of his he put on the kontusz[269]:

"We'll go, lords benefactors, to Krościenko, it won't be even three quarters of an hour, what am I, the sinful me, saying, won't be half an hour. I know the way across the creek, then through the little birch grove past the oak... The village it is big, *and very strong vodka in the gin-mills*. Let's go, lords benefactors! Why should we tarry? The gentlemen soldiers of your glorious Regiment need to lay themselves in order, in comfort. The gentleman imperial and royal soldier, who battles the Moskali, needs definitely clean night quarters, comfortable quarters... And here in our village? — Lice, scabies, smallpox and cholera. Yesterday here, in our damned village, three guys turned black of the cholera... The most merciful God has damned

Liskowiec..."

At that moment Švejk majestically waved his hand.

"Lords benefactors," he said, imitating the mayor's voice. "I read once in a book, that during the Swedish wars, when there was an order to billet in such and such village and the mayor was somehow making excuses and didn't want to oblige, they would hang him on the nearest tree. Then today in Sanok a Polish *corporal* was telling me, that when the *billeting officers* come, the mayor must call all the councilmen, and now one just goes with them from one cottage to the next and simply says: Here will fit three, here four, at the rectory there will be the gentlemen officers and it all must be ready in half an hour. — Lord benefactor," Švejk addressed the mayor seriously, "where do you have the nearest tree here?"

The mayor didn't understand, what did a tree mean, and therefore Švejk explained to him, that it was a birch, an oak, a pear, an apple tree, in short all, which have strong branches. The mayor again did not understand it, and when he heard some of the fruit trees being named, he spooked, because the cherries were already getting ripe, and he said, that he didn't know of anything like it, only that he had an oak in front of his house.

"Alright," said Švejk, making with his hand the international sign for hanging, "we will hang you here in front of your cottage, because you must be aware, that there is a war and that we have orders to sleep here, and not in some Krościenko. You, man, won't be changing our strategic plans, or else you'll be swinging, like it is in that book about the Swedish wars... Let me tell you, gentlemen, there was such a case once on maneuvers near Velké Meziříčí..."

Just then Švejk was interrupted by Master Sergeant Accountant Vaněk:

"You'll tell us that only afterwards, Švejk," and turning to the mayor, he said: "So now alarm and quarters!"

The mayor started trembling, was babbling something about that he had thought of doing the best for the lords benefactors, but since it wouldn't go any other way, that perhaps something would be found in the village after all, in order for all the lords to be satisfied, that right away he would bring a lantern.

When he walked out of the room, which was very sparsely lit by a small kerosene lamp under the picture of some saint, who was twisting in the picture like the greatest little cripple, all of a sudden Chodounský shouted:

"Where has Baloun disappeared to?"

Still before they could yet take a good look around, there opened without a sound a wicket behind the kiln-stove, leading somewhere to the outside, and through it squeezed in Baloun, who looked around, whether the mayor wasn't there, and mumbled, as if he had the worst cold:

"Hi hwas hin the p-hantry, hi g-hroped int-hoo something, shoved hit int-ho my mouth, hend now hit all stickhs t-hoo mhy p-halatte. Hit hisn't shalty nhor shweet, hit his dough fhor bread."

Accounting Master Sergeant Vaněk shone an electric lantern at him and they all found out, that in their lives they have never seen such a soiled Austrian soldier. Then they spooked, because they saw, that the blouse of Baloun's so blew up, as if he were in the last phase of pregnancy.

"What happened to you, Baloun," asked with empathy Švejk, poking him into the distended belly.

"That is the pickles," was Baloun croaking, choking on the dough, which would go neither up, nor down, "careful, those are salty pickles. I've eaten three on the fly and the rest I brought for you."

Baloun started pulling out from under his blouse pickle after pickle and was handing them around.

On the threshold there was already standing the mayor with the light, who, having beheld the scene, crossed himself and squealed:

"The Moskali took, and ours are taking too."

They all walked into the village, accompanied by a pack of dogs, which kept hanging the most tenaciously around Baloun and now were nipping at the pocket of his pants, where Baloun had a chunk of bacon, also obtained in the pantry, but out of greed traitorously withheld from his pals.

"What's with the dogs following you so," asked Švejk of Baloun. Baloun answered after an extended pause of consideration:

"They can smell a good man in me."

While answering though he didn't say, that he had his hand in his pocket on the bacon and that one dog kept nipping with his teeth at Baloun's hand...

On the rounds in search for quarters it was determined, that Liskowiec was a large settlement, which however had actually already been wrung very dry by the tumult of the war. It had not suffered fires, it's true, both warring sides as if by a miracle did not include it in the sphere of their war operations, but instead the populace of the nearby destroyed villages Chyrów[270], Grabów[271] and Hołubla[272] was settled there.

In some cottages there lived even eight families in the greatest misery, after all the losses, which they had suffered by the robbers' war, one phase of which rushed over them like turbulent waters of a flood.

It was necessary to place the *Company* in the small devastated distillery at the other end of the village, where into the fermenting plant there would fit a half of the company. The rest, ten men at a time, were placed on several farms, where the prosperous noblemen did not let anywhere close to them the poor riff-raff of the impoverished landless peasants.

The Staff of the *Company* with all its officers, Accounting Master Sergeant Vaněk, the military servants, the telephone operator, the ambulance corps, the cooks and with Švejk settled with the village priest at the rectory, who also had not accepted even one devastated family from the vicinity, so he had there a lot of room.

He was a tall, skinny old gentleman in a discolored and grease-stained cassock, who out of extreme greed almost didn't eat. He had been brought up by his father in a great hatred toward the Russians, which hatred however he suddenly lost, when the Russians retreated and there came the Austrian army, which devoured all his geese and chicken, which the Russians left alone for him, and staying with him there were several bristly Cossacks from beyond Lake Baikal[273].

Then he took an intense dislike to the Austrian army even more, when there came to the village the Hungarians and took all the honey out of his beehives. He looked now with great hatred at his unexpected night guests and it made him feel good, when he was able to walk pass them, shrugging his shoulders and continually repeating:

"I have nothing. I am a complete beggar, you won't find in my place, gentlemen, even a little slice of bread."

The saddest countenance during all that however was worn by Baloun, who was on the verge of weeping, and it's a wonder he didn't. In his head he had constantly this vague image of a sucking pig, the supple skin of which, looking like copper, was crunchy and aromatic. Baloun was at that time dozing in the kitchen of the priest, into which peeked now and then a lanky youngster, who worked for the priest concurrently as a farmhand and cook and who had been strictly ordered to be on the lookout everywhere, so that no stealing would be taking place.

Baloun indeed didn't find anything in the kitchen other than on a piece of paper in the salt dish a bit of caraway seed, which he stuffed into his yap, the aroma of which aroused in him taste hallucinations about a sucking pig.

In the courtyard of the small distillery behind the rectory there were fires flaming under the cauldrons of the field kitchen and water was already boiling, and in the water there was cooking nothing.

The Accounting Master Sergeant and the cooks were running around the whole village, looking to chase down a pig, but in vain. Everywhere they were getting the same answer, that the Moskali ate and took everything.

They also woke a Jew in the pub, who started ripping out his temple locks and demonstrating his regret over the fact, that he couldn't be of service for the gentlemen soldiers, and in the end he was forcing them to buy from him an aged, hundred year old cow, a skinny croaking stiff, which was nothing else but bone and skin. He wanted for it an enormous sum, was ripping his beard and swearing, that such a cow they wouldn't find in the whole of Galicia, the whole of Austria and Germany, the whole Europe and the whole world, and at the same time he was howling, weeping and was swearing by his soul, that it was the fattest cow, which had ever on the order of Jehovah come into the world. He was swearing by all his ancient forefathers, that to look at this cow come riding people all the way from around Wołoczyska[274], that the cow was talked about in the whole region as if it was a fairy tale, that it was actually not even a cow, that it was the most succulent buffalo. In the end he kneeled before them, and hugging the knees of one after the other, he was shouting at the same time:

"Better kill this old wretched Jew, but don't be leaving without the cow!"

He so confused everybody with his shrieking, that at last they dragged the living carcass of the bitch, which every slaughterhouse cattle killer would be loath to touch, to the field kitchen. Then still for a long time, when he already had the money in his pocket, he was in front of them weeping and complaining, that they totally annihilated him, destroyed him, that he impoverished himself, when he sold them such a beautiful cow so cheaply. He was pleading with them, for them to hang him for the fact, that in his old age he committed such silliness, on account of which his fathers must be turning in their graves.

When in addition he had in front of them rolled around in the dust, he shook off at once all the sorrow, went home, where in the closet he told his wife:

"*Elsa-my-life*, soldiers dumb and your Nathan very smart."

With the cow there was a lot of work. At times it seemed, that the cow couldn't be skinned at all. During the skinning they tore several times the hide apart, and under it emerged muscles twisted like a dried up ship rope.

In the meantime from somewhere they had dragged in a sack of potatoes and started hopelessly to cook all the tendons and bones, while next to them at a smaller kitchen the cook was fixing, in absolute desperation, from a chunk of that skeleton, officers' mess rations.

This hapless cow, should it even be possible to call that natural phenomenon a cow, imbedded itself in the participants' living memory, and it is almost certain, that if later before the battle at Sokal the officers were to remind the men of the cow from Liskowiec, that the Eleventh *Company* would have with a horrible roar of anger thrown itself with their bayonets at the enemy.

The cow was such a shameless thing, that it was impossible at all to make out of her beef soup. The longer the meat was cooking, the more it kept sitting on the bones, comprising with them one whole, it ossified like a bureaucrat, who for half an age grazes in the fields of mildewed bureaucratic nags and feeds only on files.

Švejk, who as the courier maintained constant link between the Staff and the kitchen, in order to be determining, when cooking it was going to be done, was reporting at last to Senior Lieutenant Lukáš:

"*Senior Lieutenant*, Sir, it's already turned into porcelain. That cow has meat so hard, that with it one can cut glass. Cook Pavlíček, when he was tasting the meat with Baloun, wrenched out a front tooth and Baloun a back molar."

Baloun solemnly stepped in front of Senior Lieutenant Lukáš and handed him, faltering, wrapped in the Song of Lourdes, his wrenched out tooth:

"I dutifully report, *Senior Lieutenant*, Sir, that I was doing all I could. This here tooth was wrenched out at the officers' mess, when we were trying to see whether out of that meat could not after all be made a beef steak."

At the window there got up from the sofa after these words some sad figure. It was Lieutenant Dub, whom they hauled in on an ambulance two-wheeler as a completely destroyed man:

"I plead for silence," he said in a desperate voice, "I am sick!

He took a seat again in the old armchair, where in each crevice there were thousands of eggs of bedbugs.

"I am tired," he said in a tragic voice, "I am ailing and sick, I beg that in my presence there is not any talk of wrenched out teeth. My address is: Smíchov, Královská 18$^{275}$. If I don't live to see the morn, I beg, that my family be delicately informed of everything and that it not be forgotten to mark on my grave, that I was also before the war an I&R Gymnasium professor."

He started gently snoring and did not hear anymore, as Švejk interjected in passing a verse from a song for the dead:

> Mary's sin Thou removed lovingly,
> Thou let the crook reach the end,
> also me to save be Thy diligence.

After that it was determined by Accounting Master Sergeant Vaněk, that the remarkable cow had still to be cooking two more hours in the officers' kitchen, that there can't even be any talk of some beef steak and that instead of beef steak they would be making goulash.

It was resolved, that before they trumpet grub time, the men would catch a wee snoring snooze, because the supper would anyhow be ready only toward the morning.

Accounting Master Sergeant Vaněk dragged in from somewhere a bolt of hay, laid it under him in the rectory dining room, was nervously twisting his moustache and said softly toward Senior Lieutenant Lukáš, who was resting above him on an old sofa:

"Believe me, *Senior Lieutenant*, Sir, that on such a cow I have yet during the whole war not fed..."

In the kitchen there was sitting in front of a lit up stub of a church candle telephone operator Chodounský writing a letter home in advance to keep in stock, so that he wouldn't have to be exerting himself doing it, when at last they would have a designated number of field post office. He was writing:

Beloved and dear wife, the dearest Boženka!

It is night and I am ceaselessly remembering you, my gold, and I see you, as you too are remembering me, when you look at the empty bed next to you. You have to forgive me, that while doing it many a thing comes to my mind. You know well, that from the very beginning of the war I have been in the field and that I have already heard many a thing from my pals, who had been injured, got leave, and when they came home, they would have better seen themselves in the ground, rather than to be witnesses to how some rascal was running after his wife. It is painful for me, when I, dear Boženka, must be writing this to you. I would not even be writing about it to you, but you yourself know well, that you let me know in confidence, that I was not the first one, who had had a serious relationship with you, and that before having me Mister Kraus from Mikulášská boulevard[276] had already had you. Now as I remember that in this night, and think that the lousy guy could still be making some claims on you during my absence, then I'm thinking that I would, dear Boženka, strangle him on the spot. For a long time I've been holding it inside, but when I think, that he could be crawling after you again, then my heart aches, and so I am putting you on notice regarding only one thing, that I won't put up with some swine next to me, who would be whoring with everybody and put my name in shame. Forgive me, dear Boženka, my harsh words, but watch out, so that I don't learn anything bad about you. Otherwise I would be forced to gut you both, because I am already determined to do anything, even if it were to cost me my life. Thousand times kissing you, and greeting dad and mom,

Yours Tonouš

N.B. **Don't forget that I gave you my name!**

He continued writing letters in advance to keep in stock:

My most beloved Boženka!

When you get these lines, you must know, that it's after a big battle we had here, in which the luck of war turned to our side. Among other things we have shot down about ten enemy airplanes and one general with a big wart on his nose. In the biggest fighting, when above us there were exploding shells, I was thinking about you, dear Boženka, what you were perhaps doing, how you were and what was new at home? Every time I do that I am remembering, how we were together at Tomáš' in the brewery and how you were escorting me home and how the next day your hand hurt from the exertion. Now we are advancing again, so there is no more time left for me to continue writing this letter. I hope, that you have stayed faithful to me, because you know well, that in this respect I am a nasty vermin. Nevertheless, it is already time to march! I am kissing you a thousand times, dear Boženka, and hope that everything turns out well.

Yours sincere Tonouš

Telephone operator Chodounský started dozing and fell asleep over the desk.

The priest, who wasn't sleeping and kept walking around the rectory, opened the door into the kitchen and out of frugality blew out the already burning out stub of the church candle next to Chodounský.

In the dining room, with the exception of Lieutenant Dub, nobody was sleeping. Accounting Master Sergeant Vaněk, who received in Sanok at the Brigade Office a new budget pertaining to supplying the Army with products, was studying it diligently and was realizing, that actually, the closer the Army was getting to the front, its rations were being lowered. He even had to smile over one paragraph of an order, in which was being prohibited the use of saffron and ginger in preparing soup for the troops. There was also a note here in the order, that at the field kitchens bones were to be collected and sent to the rear, into the warehouses of the divisions. It was a little unclear, because it was not known, what kind of bones were in question, whether human or of some other slaughter-cattle.

"Listen Švejk," said Senior Lieutenant Lukáš, yawning with boredom, "before we get anything to eat, you could be telling me about some event."

"Oh yeah," he answered, "before we get something to eat I would, *Senior Lieutenant*, Sir, have to be telling you the whole history of the Czech nation. I know, for now only, a very short history about a postmaster's wife from Sedlčansko[277], who after her husband's death got that post office. She came to my mind right away, when I heard the talk about field post offices, although it has nothing at all in common with *field post offices*."

"Švejk," sounded up from the sofa Senior Lieutenant Lukáš, "you are again beginning to act terribly idiotic."

"Certainly, I dutifully report, *Senior Lieutenant*, Sir, it is really a terribly idiotic history. I myself don't know, how could have something so idiotic occur to me, to be talking about some such thing. Either it is congenital idiocy, or its the memories from youth. There are, *Senior Lieutenant*, Sir, on the globe of our Earth various personalities, and he was right after all that cook Jurajda, as he was at the time back then in Bruck drunk, when he fell into the ditch and could not claw himself out of there, to be yelling out of there: 'Man is designated and called upon for this, to recognize the truth, for him to reign by his spirit in some harmony of the eternal all-world, ever winding himself up and rigging himself together, gradually entering higher spheres, worlds more intelligent and more full of love.' When we wanted to pull him out of there, he was scratching and biting. He thought, that he was at home, and only when we threw him in there again, only then he started whining, for us to pull him out of there."

"But what's with the lady postmaster?" cried out desperately Senior Lieutenant Lukáš.

"That one was a very nice broad, but when she was nevertheless a bitch, *Senior Lieutenant*, Sir, she was discharging all her duties at the post office, but she had just one fault, that is she thought, that all were persecuting her, that they had it in for her, and therefore, after the day's work she would report them officially to the authorities, depending how all of the circumstances turned out. Once she went into the forest in the morning to be collecting mushrooms and she noticed very well, that when she walked past the school, that the mister teacher was already up and that he greeted her and was asking her, where is it that she is going so early in the morning. When she told him, that she is going mushroom hunting, he was telling her, that he will come after her and join her there. From this she deduced, that he had for her, the old hag, some underhanded intentions and then when she saw him, that he is really stepping out from a thicket, she spooked, ran away and wrote immediately a report to the local school board, that he wanted to rape her. They put the teacher under a disciplinary investigation, and lest it become perhaps some public scandal, there arrived the school inspector himself to investigate it, who turned to the State Police Station Chief, so that he would give an opinion, whether perhaps the teacher was capable of such a deed. The State Police Station Chief looked into the files and said, that it is not possible, because that teacher had been already once accused by the priest, that he kept going after his niece, with whom that priest used to sleep, and that the teacher had taken from the county doctor a certificate, that he'd been impotent since the age of six years, when he fell straddle-wise from a loft onto the hitch bar of a rack wagon. So that bitch made a report about the State Police Station Chief, the county doctor and the school inspector, that they all had been bribed by that teacher. They all sued her and she was convicted, and she appealed, that she is mentally incompetent. She was indeed examined by court physicians, and those gave her an affidavit, that it is true she is stupid, but that she can hold any government job."

Senior Lieutenant Lukáš screamed: "Jesusmaria," to which he still added: "I would tell you something, Švejk, but I don't want to spoil my supper," after which Švejk uttered:

"I was telling you, *Senior Lieutenant*, Sir, that what I would be telling you, is terribly idiotic."

Senior Lieutenant Lukáš only waved his hand and said: "From you I have already learned about plenty of such gems of smarts."

"Not everybody can be smart, *Senior Lieutenant*, Sir," said convincingly Švejk, "the dumb ones must be the exception, because if everyone were smart, there would then be in the world so much reasoning power, that on account of it would every other man be totally stupefied. If, for example, I dutifully report, *Senior Lieutenant*, Sir, everybody knew the laws of nature and was able to calculate heavenly distances, then all he would do is bother everybody in his vicinity, like some guy Čapek, who used to go to the Chalice Pub and at night he would always step out from the tap room into the street, looking around the starry sky, and when he returned, he would be going from one customer to the next and was saying: 'Jupiter is shining beautifully today, and you don't even know, shameless rube, what you've got above your head. Those are such distances, if they shot you, you hoodlum, from a cannon, then at the speed of the cannon ball you'd be flying there for millions and millions of years.' He used to be so vulgar while doing it, that usually he would fly out of the pub himself, at the ordinary speed of an electric streetcar, perhaps about, *Senior Lieutenant*, Sir, ten kilometers per hour. — Or we have for example, *Senior Lieutenant*, Sir, ants…"

Senior Lieutenant Lukáš straightened up on the sofa and clasped his hands:

"I have to marvel at myself, that I ever, Švejk, converse with you, I've known you after all, Švejk, for such a long time — —"

Švejk was at the same time nodding in agreement:

"It's a matter of habit, *Senior Lieutenant*, Sir, it is embedded exactly in the fact, that we've already known one another long since and that together we've already been through quite a lot. We have already suffered together quite a bit, and we have always chanced upon it like a blind man upon a violin. I dutifully report, *Senior Lieutenant*, Sir, that it is fate. What the lord Emperor directs, he directs well, he put us together, and I don't indeed wish anything else, than to be able sometimes to be very useful to you. — Aren't you hungry, *Senior Lieutenant*, Sir?"

Senior Lieutenant Lukáš, who in the meantime again stretched on the old sofa, said, that the last question of Švejk's was the best resolution to the embarrassing entertainment, for him just to go ask, what's with the rations. It will definitely be better, if Švejk goes to look outside a bit, and eave him, because the idiocies, which he is hearing from him, are tiring him more than the whole march from Sanok. He'd like to fall asleep for a while, but can't.

"That's on account of the bed-bugs, *Senior Lieutenan*t, Sir. That's already an old wives' tale, that parish priests birth bedbugs. Nowhere will you find so many bedbugs as at the rectories. At the rectory in Horní Stodůlky[278] the priest Zamastil even wrote a whole book about bedbugs, they used to be crawling all over him even during sermons."

"Now what did I say, Švejk, are you going to the kitchen, or not?"

Švejk was leaving and behind him from inside a corner walked out like a shadow Baloun...

\*

When they took off in the morning from Liskowiec on to Starasol, Sambor[279], they were carrying with them in the field kitchen the hapless cow, which had not been done cooking yet. It was resolved, that they will be cooking it along the way and it will be eaten, when there is the rest break half way from Liskowiec to Starasol.

For the road they made for the men black coffee.

They were dragging Lieutenant Dub again on the ambulance two-wheeler, because after yesterday he was even worse. The one who suffered the most with him was his servant, who had to be constantly running beside the two-wheeler, while Lieutenant Dub kept shouting, that he wasn't yesterday at all taking care of him, and that when they arrive at the destination, that he will deal with him. Every moment he was demanding, that water be handed to him, which, when he had drunk it up, he immediately threw up again.

"Whom — what are you laughing at?" he was screaming from the two-wheeler. "I will teach you, don't you play with me, you will get to know me!"

Senior Lieutenant Lukáš was riding a horse and had next to him for company Švejk, who was stepping smartly forward, as if he could not wait for the moment, when he clashes with the enemy. At the same time he was narrating:

"Have you noticed, *Senior Lieutenant*, Sir, that some of our people are really like flies? They don't have even thirty kilos on their back, and already they can't stand it. There should be lectures held for them, like used to do for us the poor deceased mister *Senior Lieutenant* Buchánek, who shot himself on account of the marriage bond[280], the funds for which he drew out of his future father-in law and which he spent on somebody else's sluts. Then he took out another bond again from his other future father-in-law, and that one he eventually managed more economically, he was losing it slowly in cards and left the girlies aside. It didn't last for him long either, so he had to reach out to a third future father-in-law for a bond. With the third bond he bought a horse, an Arabian[281] stud, a non-thoroughbred..."

Senior Lieutenant Lukáš jumped off the horse.

"Švejk," he said in a menacing tone, "if you end up talking about a fourth bond, I'll throw you in the ditch."

He jumped on the horse again and Švejk solemnly continued:

"I dutifully report, *Senior Lieutenant*, Sir, that of a fourth bond there can't even be any talk, because he after the third bond shot himself dead."

"At last," said Senior Lieutenant Lukáš.

"Lest we forget the subject of our talk then," Švejk kept on speaking, "such lectures, as always used to hold for us mister *Senior Lieutenant* Buchánek, when on the march the soldiers were already collapsing, should be held according to my humble opinion for all the troops, as he used to do it. He would call a *rest break*, gathered us all like chicks around a hen and started telling us: 'You churls, you cannot appreciate at all, that you are marching on the globe of the Earth, because you are such an uneducated gang, that it would make a man puke, when he takes a look at you; what about letting you march like that on the Sun, where a man, who on our miserable planet has the weight of sixty kilos, weighs over seventeen hundred kilograms, then you'd be croaking, then you'd be marching, if you had in the calf-hide flap pack over two hundred and eighty kilograms, coming onto three metric hundred-weights, and the *rifle* was half a second metric hundred-weight heavy. Then you'd be groaning and sticking your tongues out like run-down dogs.' There was among us one hapless teacher, he dared to ask his turn also to speak: 'With permission, *Senior Lieutenant*, Sir, on the Moon weighs a sixty-kilogram man only thirteen kilograms. On the Moon it would be better and easier for us to march, because our calf-hide flap pack would weigh only four kilograms there. On the Moon we would be floating and not marching.' 'That is horrible,' says to that the late deceased Buchánek, 'you are, you miserable guy, begging for a slap in the face, be glad, that I will give you only an ordinary earthly slap, if I were to give you that Moon kind slap, then given your lightness you'd fly all the way somewhere to the Alps[282] and get splashed flat against them. If I were to give you the heavy Sun kind, then the *uniform* on you would turn into mush and your head would fly off to somewhere in Africa.' So he smacked him the ordinary earthly slap in the face, the nitpicker started to weep and we kept marching on. The whole time on the march he was weeping and talking, let me tell you, *Senior Lieutenant*, Sir, about some human dignity, that he'd been handled like some dumb-faced beast. Afterwards mister *Senior Lieutenant* sent him to the Report, they locked him up for two weeks and he served six extra weeks, but didn't serve them out, because he had a *ruptured hernia* and they were somehow forcing him into making giant swings on a horizontal bar at the garrison, and he didn't withstand it and died as a malingerer at the hospital."

"It is really peculiar, Švejk," said Senior Lieutenant Lukáš, "that you, as I have told you so many times, have the habit of, in a peculiar way, making light of the officer corps."

"That I don't," said with sincerity Švejk. "I only wanted to be telling you, *Senior Lieutenant*, Sir, regarding this, how in earlier times in the military people would bring about their own disaster. That man, he thought, that he was more educated than that mister *Senior Lieutenant*, he wanted to denigrate him with that Moon in the eyes of the men, and so indeed when he got one of those earthly one across the yap, let me tell you, they all breathed a sigh of relief, nobody felt bad about it, to the contrary, all were glad, that mister *Senior Lieutenant* made such a good joke with that earthly slap; that is what you call a prevented disaster. Man must immediately think of something and then all is well already. Across the street from the Carmelites[283] in Prague, there, *Senior Lieutenant*, Sir, years ago had a store with rabbits and other birds mister Jenom. He made an amorous acquaintance with the daughter of bookbinder Bílek. Mister Bílek, he did not wish the familiar relationship to prosper and indeed declared publicly in a pub, that if mister Jenom came to ask for the hand of his daughter, he'd knock him down the stairs, like the world had never seen. Mister Jenom had himself a drink for that that, and after all still went to Mister Bílek, who welcomed him in the hallway with a big knife, the kind with which they cut the book-binder's trim, and looks like a frog-gutter. He yelled out at him, what it is that he wanted here, and at that moment, let me tell you, the dear mister Jenom blew such a strong fart, that the pendulum clock on the wall stopped. Mister Bílek busted out laughing, immediately extended his hand and was nothing but all: 'Condescend to come in mister Jenom — condescend to sit down — hopefully you did not poop in your pants — come on, I am not such a mean man, it's true, that I wanted to throw you out, but now I see, that you are a quite pleasant gentleman, you are an original man. I am a book-binder, I have read through many novels and stories, but in no book have I read, that a groom would introduce himself like that.' At the same time he was laughing so hard, that he was grabbing his belly, and he was saying with tremendous joy, that it seems to him, as if they have known one another since birth, as if they were native brothers, was laying for him cigars right away, sent for beer, Italian sausages, called his wife, introduced him to her with all the details of the letting out the fart. She spat and walked away. Then he called his daughter and was telling her: 'This gentleman came to ask for your hand under such and such circumstances.' The daughter started immediately weeping and declared, that she didn't know him, that she didn't even want see him, so there was nothing left, but for both of them to finish drinking the beer and eat the Italian sausages and they parted. Afterward mister Jenom was still subjected to yet another embarrassment at the pub, where mister Bílek used to go, and in the end everywhere around the neighborhood they wouldn't call him anything other than 'shitup Jenom' and everywhere they were telling the story of how he wanted to salvage a situation. — Human life, I dutifully report, *Senior Lieutenant*, Sir, is so complicated, that the lone life of a human is in comparison a rag. — To us, at The Chalice in the Na Bojišti street, there used to come before the war a senior police patrolman, some mister Hubička, and one mister editor, who used to pick up broken legs, run over people, self-killers and put them in the newspaper. He was such a merry man, that he used to spend more time at the police station *guard-room* than in his newspaper office. He once got a senior patrolman Hubička drunk and they swapped their clothes in the kitchen, so that the senior patrolman was in civilian clothes and mister editor turned into a police senior patrolman, he just still covered the number of the revolver and set off to Prague on patrol. In Resslova street[284], behind the former Saint-Wenceslaus penitentiary, he met in the silence of the night an older gentleman in top hat and fur coat, who was walking arm in arm with an older lady in a fur overcoat. They both were hurrying home and did not say a word. "He set upon them and screamed into that gentleman's ear: 'Don't be screaming so much, or I'll bring you in!' Imagine, *Senior Lieutenant*, Sir, that scare of theirs. In vain were they telling him, that it would probably be some mistake, because they both were coming from a banquet at the mister viceroy's[285]. The *carriage and horses* had taken them all the way to the far side of the National Theater[286] and that now he and his wife wanted to get some fresh air and they lived nearby, at the Moráň, that he was a chief viceroyal councillor, with his spouse. 'You won't be hanging any bull on my nose,' started to further scream at him the disguised editor, 'then you should be ashamed, since you are, as you are saying, some viceroyal chief counselor and yet behave like a boy. I have been observing you for long already, how you've been banging the cane against the roller blinds of all the stores, which were on your way, and in that your, as you're saying, spouse was helping you.' 'But I don't, as you can see, have any cane. Perhaps it was somebody ahead of us.' 'No wonder you don't have it,' retorted the disguised editor, 'since you broke it, as I saw, over there around the corner whacking an old hag with it who goes from pub to pub with baked potatoes and chestnuts.' That lady could not even weep anymore and mister chief viceroyal councillor got so upset, that he started saying something about vulgarity, after which he was arrested and brought to the nearest patrol in the precinct of the police district station in Salmova street, whom the disguised editor told, to escort the pair to the police district station, that he was from St. Jindřich[287] and was in Vinohrady on business, had apprehended both in the course of disturbing the night peace, during a night brawl, and that at the same time they also committed the misdemeanor of insulting a patrolman. That he would take care of his thing at the police district station by the St. Jindřich and that in an hour he would come to the police district station at Salmovka. So the patrol dragged both of them along to the station, where they were sitting until the morning and were waiting for that senior patrolman, who in the meantime returned by detours to The Chalice at the Bojiště, there he woke up the senior patrolman Hubička and with all delicacy informed him of what had happened and what investigation it would entail, if he didn't keep his trap shut…"

Senior Lieutenant Lukáš seemed to be already tired by the

conversation, however before he nudged the horse into a trot, in order to pass the vanguard, he said to Švejk:

"If you were talking until the evening, the longer the dumber it would be."

"*Senior Lieutenant*, Sir," was calling after the riding-away Senior Lieutenant Švejk, "don't you wish to know, how it ended?"

Senior Lieutenant Lukáš sped up into a gallop.

The state of Lieutenant Dub had so improved, that he crawled out of the ambulance two-wheeler, gathered round himself the whole Staff of the *Company* and as if in a daze started lecturing them. He gave them a hugely long speech, which was weighing everybody down more than the munition and the rifle.

It was an assortment of various similitudes.

He started: "The soldiers' love for the gentlemen officers makes incredible sacrifices possible, and it does not matter, and on the contrary, should this love crop not be in the soldier from birth, it must be forced out. In civilian life, the compelled love of one for another, let us say a school custodian toward the teaching staff, lasts only as long as the external might, which compels it; in the army service, however, we see the very opposite, for the officer must not allow the soldier even the least loosening of that love, which binds the soldier to his superior. This love is not just ordinary love, but it is actually respect, fear and discipline."

Švejk was throughout the whole time walking on the left side, and as Lieutenant Dub was speaking, he constantly had his face turned toward him in the *eyes-right position*.

Lieutenant Dub was at first somehow not noticing this and continued his speech:

"This discipline and the duty of obedience, the compulsory love of the ordinary soldier toward the officer exhibit great terseness, because the relationship between the soldier and the officer is quite simple: one listens, the other orders. Already very long ago we read in books on martial arts, that military laconism, military simplicity is precisely the virtue, which each soldier is to adopt, loving, like it or not, his superior, who in his eyes must be for him the greatest, final, crystallized object of a firm and perfect will."

Only now he noticed Švejk's *eyes right*, how he was watching him, and it was very unpleasant for him, because he was now perceiving somehow himself, that he was getting rather entangled in his speech and that he couldn't ride out of that hollow way of love of the ordinary soldier for the officer, therefore he started yelling at Švejk:

"Why are you staring at me like a calf at a new gate?"

"As ordered, I dutifully report, *Lieutenant*, Sir, you yourself had condescended once to bring to my attention, that when you're talking, I am to be, with my sight, observing your mouth. Because each ordinary soldier must fulfill the orders of his superior and commit them to memory even for all future times, I was compelled to do so."

"Be looking," was screaming Lieutenant Dub, "the other way, just don't, you numskull of a guy, be looking at me, you know, that I don't like it, that I can't stand it, when I see you, I will start picking on you so…"

Švejk executed a head turn to the left and kept stepping like that beside Lieutenant Dub so rigidly that Lieutenant Dub yelled out:

"Where are you gaping at when I'm speaking to you?"

"I dutifully report Lieutenant, Sir, that according to your order I'm doing *eyes left*."

"Ugh," sighed Lieutenant Dub, "with you it's a cross[288]. Keep looking straight ahead of you and thinking this about yourself: I'm so stupid, that I'll be no loss to anyone. Do you remember it?"

Švejk was gazing ahead of himself and said:

"I dutifully report, *Lieutenant*, Sir, am I to respond to this?"

"How dare you," hollered at him Lieutenant Dub. "How is it you're talking to me like that, what are you thinking?

"I dutifully report, *Lieutenant*, Sir, that what I'm thinking is only the order at a certain station, where you reprimanded me not to answer at all, when you're finished talking."

"You are afraid of me then," said the all cheered-up Lieutenant Dub, "But you have not gotten to know me yet. Before me have trembled other sorts of people than you are, remember that. I have managed to tame other sorts of able guys, therefore shut the yap up and remain nicely in the back, so that I won't see you!"

So Švejk stayed in the back by the ambulance corps and rode comfortably with the two-wheeler all the way to the spot designated for a rest, where at last they all lived to see the soup and meat from the hapless cow.

"That cow they should have pickled for at least two weeks in vinegar, and if not the cow, then at least the human who bought it," proclaimed Švejk.

From the brigade there came on a horse in canter a courier with a new order for the 11th *Company*, that the *march route* was being changed to Felsztyn[289], Wojalycze[290] and Sambor to be left aside, as there it wasn't possible to quarter the *Company*, because there were two Posen[291] regiments there.

Senior Lieutenant Lukáš issued immediate instructions. Accountant Sergeant Major Vaněk with Švejk would seek night quarters for the *Company* in Felsztyn.

"Mind you don't, Švejk, go pulling anything on the way," was putting him on notice Senior Lieutenant Lukáš. "Above all behave decently toward the populace!"

"I dutifully report, *Senior Lieutenant*, Sir, that I will try my utmost. I had a very bad dream, when toward the morning I dozed a little. I was dreaming about a wash-tub, which was leaking through the whole night in the hallway of the building, where I lived, until it emptied and soaked through the ceiling at mister landlord, who right away in the morning gave me notice to move out. There has been already, *Senior Lieutenant*, Sir, such a case in real life; in Karlín, on the other side of the viaduct[292]..."

"Give it a rest, Švejk, with your stupid talk and better look w*ith* Vaněk at the map, which way you are to be going. So here you see the villages. From this village you'll go right toward the little river and along the creek again up to the nearest village, and from there, whe[re] there flows into it the first brook, which will be on your right hand, you will go down the field path upward, straight to the north, and you can't get lost to nowhere else but into Felsztyn! Will you remember that?"

Švejk set out then with Accounting Master Sergeant Vaněk according to the *march route*.

It was after noon; the landscape was panting heavily in the heat and the poorly back-filled pits with buried soldiers were emitting a rotting odor. They entered a landscape, where there had been fought battles during the advances to Przemyśl and where by machine guns were mowed down whole battalions. In little groves by the creek was evident the havoc wrought by the artillery. On large expanses and hillsides there were protruding in place of trees some sort of stumps from the ground and this desert was furrowed by trenches.

"Here it looks different than around Prague," said Švejk, to break up the mute silence.

"Back home the harvest is already over," said Accounting Master Sergeant Vaněk. "We in the Kralupy region start the earliest."

## The Fateful Adventures of the Good Soldier Švejk

"Here there will be after the war a very good harvest," said after a moment Švejk. "They won't have to be buying bone meal, it is a great advantage for the peasants, when in their field there rots away to dust a whole regiment for them; it is, in short, sustenance. There's only one thing I worry about, that the peasants don't let anybody hang the bull on their noses and make them sell the bones of the soldiers needlessly as bone ash for the sugar refineries. Let me tell you, there used to be in the Karlín garrison *Senior Lieutenant* Holub, he was so learned, that all at the *Company* used to take him for an imbecile, because he on account of his being so learned hadn't learned to swear at the soldiers and he only contemplated everything from the scientific point of view. At one time the soldiers were reporting to him, that the commissary ration bread they had been issued was not fit to feed on. Another officer would get upset over such audacity, but he, nah, he remained calm, didn't even call anybody a pig, or swine, or give anybody a few across the trap. He only called in all his bunch of guys and he was telling them in this pleasant voice of his: 'Before anything else, soldiers, you have to realize, that the garrison is no *delicatessen shop*, for you to be picking out marinated eel, sardines in oil and little open-face sandwiches there. Every soldier is to be intelligent enough to gobble up without fretting everything, that he's issued, and must have enough discipline in him, not to be breaking his stride over the quality of what he's to feed on. Imagine, soldiers, that there was a war. To the earth, in which after the battle they'll bury you, it doesn't matter at all, with what kind of commissary bread before your death you stuffed yourselves. That mommy Earth will break you down and gobble you up, boots and all. In the world nothing can get wasted, from you will grow, soldiers, again new grain for the commissary bread for new soldiers, who perhaps again, like you, won't be satisfied, will go to complain and will run into somebody, who will have them locked up until alleluia is heard everywhere, because he has the right to do that. Now I have, soldiers, explained it all nicely, and I don't have to be, I hope, reminding you again, that whoever complains the next time, will much appreciate it, when he is once more in the divine light.' 'If at least he were cussing us out,' the soldiers would say among themselves and they were disappointed by those genteel refinements in the lectures of mister *Senior Lieutenant*. So one time they elected me from among the *company gang*, to like tell him, that everybody liked him and that it's no army service, when he's not cussing. So I went over to his apartment and was pleading with him, to abandon all that shyness, that soldiering has to be tough as a strap, that the soldiers were used to it, being reminded every day, that they were dogs and pigs, that otherwise they were losing respect for their superiors. He was at first resisting, he was saying something about intelligence, about the fact, that nowadays nobody must serve under the switch, but in the end he let himself be talked into it, slapped me a fill and threw me out of the door, so that respect for him would rise. When I reported the result of my negotiating, they all greatly rejoiced for it, but he again spoiled it for them right away the next day. He comes to me and in front of everyone says: "Švejk, yesterday I was rash, here's a gold piece and drink to my health. One must know how to handle the troops.'"

Švejk looked round at the landscape.

"I think," he said, "that we're going the wrong way. Mister *Senior Lieutenant*, remember, was explaining it to us well. We're to go up, down, then left and right, then again right, then left — and we are constantly going straight. Or have we gone through all that while talking? I definitely see here in front of me two roads to that Felsztyn. I would suggest, that we now take the path on the left."

Accounting Master Sergeant Vaněk, as it already is usually the custom, when two end up at a crossroads, started to insist, that they must go right.

"That path of mine," said Švejk, "is more comfortable than yours. I will go along the brook, where there grow forget-me-nots, and you will be dawdling somewhere through the dry wasteland. I'm sticking with what mister *Senior Lieutenant* told us, that we couldn't get lost at all, and since we cannot get lost, then why would I be crawling up some hill; I will be going nicely through meadows and put a little blossom in my cap and will pluck a whole bouquet for mister *Senior Lieutenant*. After all we can verify, which one of us is right, and I hope, that here we'll part as good friends. There is such a landscape here, that all paths must lead to that Felsztyn."

"Don't be crazy, Švejk," said Vaněk, "here, exactly as the map shows, we have to go, as I'm saying, to the right."

"A map too can be mistaken," answered Švejk, descending into the valley of the brook. "At one time sausage maker Křenek from Vinohrady followed the plan of the city of Prague from Montags' in the Lesser Quarter going home at night to Vinohrady and only toward morning reached Rozdělov[293] by Kladno, where they found him all stiff from cold in the rye, where he had fallen from fatigue. Since you won't be talked out of it, mister *Accounting Master Sergeant*, and go by your own stubborn head, then we just have to part and meet only at the place itself in Felsztyn. *They*, just look at the watch, so that we would know, who will have gotten there first. And if perhaps some danger was a threat to *them*, then *they* just shoot in the air, so that I would know, where *they* are."

Walking from noon on Švejk made it to a small pond, where he encountered a runaway Russian prisoner of war, who was bathing here and upon having noticed Švejk, he took off naked, as he got out of the water, running away.

Švejk was curious how the Russian uniform might suit him, which was lying around here under the young weeping willows, so he stripped off his own and put on the Russian uniform of the hapless prisoner of war, who had run away from the transport quartered in the village beyond the forest. Švejk wished, to see himself properly mirrored in the water, and therefore kept walking atop the dam of the pond, until there found him there a patrol of the military police, which was looking for the runaway Russian. They were Hungarians and in spite of Švejk's protests they dragged him to the staging point in Chyrów, where they placed him in the transport of Russian prisoners of war designated to work repairing the railroad tracks in the direction of Przemyśl.

Everything happened so fast, that only the next day Švejk realized the situation and wrote on the white wall of the school room, where they had quartered some of the prisoners of war, with a charred stick of wood: **Here slept Josef Švejk from Prague, Company Messenger of the 11th march-gang of the 91st Regiment, who, charged with seeking quarters, fell by mistake into Austrian captivity below Felsztyn.**

Book Four

**THE ILLUSTRIOUS THRASHING
CONTINUED**

# 1

## ŠVEJK IN THE TRANSPORT OF RUSSIAN PRISONERS OF WAR

So when Švejk, considered by mistake in a Russian overcoat and *forage cap* to be a Russian prisoner of war, run away from the village before Felsztyn, was writing his desperate outcries with charcoal on the walls, nobody was paying attention to it, and when he wanted in Chyrów[294] at the staging point to explain everything in detail to some officer, who was just walking by, as they were issuing to them pieces of hard corn bread, here one of the Hungarian soldiers, guarding the transport of the POWs, struck him with the rifle butt in the shoulder with the remark: "*Fuck life*, crawl back in line, Russian swine!"

All this was within the framework of how the Hungarians handled Russian prisoners of war, whose language they did not understand.

Švejk then returned to the line and turned to the nearest prisoner of war:

"You know, that man is doing his duty, but he is putting himself in danger. What if by chance his gun was loaded and the *safety lock* open? So it could easily happen to him, that as he's striking a man in the shoulder and he has the *barrel* facing himself, *the piece* could go off and the whole cartridge would fly into his yap, and he would die while executing his duties. In the Šumava region in a quarry the rock busters used to steal the dynamite primer charges, to have a supply for ripping out tree stumps in winter. The watchman in the quarry got an order, that when the rock busters were leaving work, to frisk everybody, and he was doing it with such devotion, that right off he grabbed the very first rock buster and started patting his pockets so vigorously, that at last the rock buster's dynamite primer charges in his pocket blew up, and both of them and the watchman took off up into the air, so that it looked as if they were still in the last moment holding one another around the neck."

The Russian prisoner of war, to whom Švejk was telling it, was looking at him with the full understanding, that of the whole story he didn't understand even one word.

"*No understand, I'm a Crimean Tatar, Allah*[295] *Akbar.*" The Tatar sat down, crossing his legs, on the ground, having folded his arms on his chest he started to pray: "Allah Akbar — Allah Akbar — bezmila — arachman — arachim — malinkin mustafír."

"So then you are a Tatar," said with an expression of extending condolences Švejk, "you've turned out to be a fine one. No wonder you can't understand me, and I you, since you're a Tatar. Hm — do you know Jaroslav of Šternberk[296]? You don't know the name, you Tatar boy? He sure kicked your asses at Hostýn[297]. You sure were leaving our land, you Tatar boys, skedaddling out of Moravia at a swine trot. Apparently in your classroom readers they don't teach you about it, as they used to teach us about it. Do you know the Virgin Mary of Hostýn? It figures that you don't — she was there too, well, they will baptize you after all, you Tatar boys, here in captivity."

Švejk turned to a second prisoner of war: "You're a Tatar too?"

The one addressed comprehended the word Tatar, and shook his head: *"Not Tatar, Circassian, native Circassian, I cut heads off."*

Švejk was altogether lucky, that he ended up in the company of various members of the eastern peoples. There were here in the transport Tatars, Georgians, Ossetians, Circassians, Mordvins and Kalmyks.

So Švejk had the misfortune, that he wasn't able to communicate with anybody, and with the others they were dragging him on to Dobromil[298] starting from where was to be being repaired the railroad through Przemyśl on to Niżankowice[299].

In Dobromil, at the staging office, they were registering one after another, which was going with difficulty, because of all the 300 prisoners of war, which they had driven to Dobromil, none understood the Russian of the Master Sergeant, who was sitting there behind a desk and who once long ago volunteered, that he knew Russian, and as an interpreter he was now engaged in eastern Galicia. A good three weeks ago he ordered a German-Russian dictionary and a conversation manual, but so far they hadn't arrived, so that he was speaking instead of Russian in broken Slovak, which he had barely acquired, when as a representative of a Viennese firm he was selling in Slovakia pictures of Saint Stephen, holy water buckets and rosaries.

Over these strange figures, with whom he could not speak at all, he was all dumb-struck. Therefore he walked out and hollered at a group of prisoners of war: *"Who can speak German!"*

Out of the group stepped Švejk, who was rushing with joyful countenance to the Master Sergeant, who told him, to immediately follow him into the office.

The Master Sergeant sat himself behind the documents, behind a heap of forms pertaining to the name, origin, and nationality of the prisoners of war, and now began an entertaining German conversation:

"You are a Jew, right?" he started at Švejk.

Švejk shook his head.

"You don't have to be denying it," continued confidently the interpreter Master Sergeant, "each of you prisoners of war, who spoke German, was a Jew, period. What is your name? Schweykrh? There you go, why are you denying it, when you have such a Jewish name? With us here you don't have to be afraid to admit it. Here in Austria, pogroms against the Jews are not done. Where are you from? Aha, Prága[300], ah, I know that, that's by Warsaw. I also had here a week ago two Jews from Prága by Warsaw, and your regiment, what number is it? 91?"

The Master Sergeant took the Military Register, was paging through it: "The one-and-ninetieth Regiment is of Yerevan[301], Caucasus[302], its permanent core is in Tbilisi[303], surprised, huh, that we know everything here."

Švejk indeed couldn't believe any of what had been happening and the Master Sergeant continued with great seriousness, handing Švejk a half-finished cigarette of his: "This is different tobacco than that makhorka[304] of yours. — I am here, little Jewboy, the highest master. When I say something, then everyone has to be trembling and creep away into hiding. Among our troops there is different discipline than among yours. Your czar is scum, but our czar is a smart cookie. Now I'll show you something, so you'll know what discipline is like with us." He opened the door to the next room and yelled: "Hans Löfler!"

There was the sound of "Hier!" and in stepped a goitrous soldier, little Styrian, with the facial expression of a weeping cretin. He was the do-all-gal of this staging base.

"Hans Löfler," ordered the Master Sergeant, "take my pipe over there, stick it in your trap like a dog retrieving, and run around the desk on all fours until I say Halt! All the while you must be barking, but do it so, that the pipe doesn't fall out your yap, or I'll have you tied."

The goitrous little Styrian started crawling on all fours and barking.

The Master Sergeant looked victoriously at Švejk: 'What, wasn't I telling you little Jewboy, what discipline is like with us?" And the Master Sergeant was looking with delight at that mute military face from some Alpine sheep range hut. "Halt!" he said at last, "now squat and beg and fetch the pipe. — Good, and now yodel a bit."

Through the room filled with the roar: "Holadeeyo, holadeeyo"

When the show was over, the Master Sergeant pulled from the drawer four Sport cigarettes and magnanimously gifted them to Hanzi, and here Švejk set about to be telling the Master Sergeant in broken German, that at one regiment an officer had such an obedient servant, that he would do all, that his master wished, and when they asked him once, whether he would devour with a spoon, if his master order him, even that, what he excretes, he said: "If my mister Lieutenant ordered it, I would gobble it up as ordered, but I better not find a hair in it, that is terribly *yucky* to me, that would immediately make me sick."

The Master Sergeant laughed: "You Jews sure have excellent jokes, but I'd like to bet, that the discipline in your military is not like what it is with us. So that we would come to the core of the matter, I am appointing you over the transport. By the evening you will write down for me the names of the other prisoners! You'll be getting rations issued for them, you'll divide them in tens of men and you guarantee, that nobody escapes! If anyone in your charge escapes, little Jewboy, then we'd shoot you dead!"

"I would like, Master Sergeant, Sir, to have a talk with you," said Švejk.

"Com'on, don't be haggling," answered the Master Sergeant. "That, I don't like, or I'll send you to a camp. You have acclimated yourself tremendously fast here in Austria. — Wants to have a private talk with me... The nicer one is to you prisoners of war, the worse it is... Then pick yourself up right away, here you have paper and a pencil and be writing the list! What do you still want?"

"*I most dutifully report, Master Sergeant, Sir*"...

"See to it that you get lost! Can't you see how much work I've got! The face of the Master Sergeant took on the expression of a man who was totally overworked.

Švejk gave a salute and walked away to join the prisoners of war, while he beheld the thought, that patience for the sake of the lord Emperor bears fruit.

It was harder going however with the compiling of the list, until finally the prisoners of war comprehended, that they were supposed to give their names. Švejk had lived through much in his life, but these Tatar, Georgian, and Mordovian names still wouldn't go in his head after all. "Nobody will believe me about this," Švejk thought to himself, "that anybody could ever be named like the Tatars around here: Muhlahalej Abdrachamanov — Bejmurat Allahali — Džeredže Cerdedže — Davlatbalej Nurdagalejev and so on. Back at home we sure have better names after all, like that priest in Židohoušt[305], whose name was Vobejda."

He was again walking through the ranks and files of the prisoners of war, who were yelling out their first and last names in succession: "Džindralej Hanemalej — Babamulej Mirzahali" and so forth.

"It's a wonder you don't bite your tongue in two," Švejk was telling each of them with a good-hearted smile. "Isn't it better, when back at home someone's name is Bohuslav Štěpánek, Jaroslav Matoušek[306] or Růžena Svobodová[307]"

When at last after this horrible ordeal Švejk had compiled all those Bubla Hallejs and Dhudži Mudžis, he set his mind, that he would try it one more time and explain to the interpreter Master Sergeant, that he had fallen a victim to a mistake and how several times already on his journey, as they drove him like cattle with the other prisoners of war, in vain had he been invoking justice.

The Master Sergeant interpreter, who had already earlier not been altogether sober, lost his judgment altogether in the meantime.

In front of him he had spread the classified advertisement section of some German newspaper and was singing the ads to the tune of the Radetzky march: "I will trade a gramophone for a baby buggy! — Buying glass shards, white sheet glass and green! — To account and close the books will learn anyone who takes the correspondence course in accounting!" and so on.

For some of the ads the march tune was not suitable, but the Master Sergeant wanted to overcome it with all his might, therefore he was banging his fist on the tabletop to keep time and was stomping his feet. Both of his mustache handles, with their hair glued together by kontušovka were sticking out on both sides of his face as if they had rammed dried brushes dipped in gum arabic into each side. His swollen eyes noticed Švejk, true enough, but there followed no reaction to this discovery, only that the Master Sergeant stopped banging his fist and stomping his feet. He was drumming on the chair through the tune "*I don't know, what that is supposed to mean…*" new ad: "Karolina Dreger, midwife, is being recommended to hon. ladies for any case."

He was singing through it more softly, increasingly more softly, and ever so softly, until at last he fell silent, motionless, fixed his eyes on the entire large surface area of ads and gave Švejk an opportunity, to start telling at length about his misfortune, for which story telling Švejk had just barely enough sentences in broken German.

Švejk began with this, that he had been right after all, to go toward Felsztyn along the brook, but that it's not his fault, if an unknown Russian soldier escapes from captivity and goes to take a bath in a pond, past which he, Švejk, had to go, because it was his duty, when he was taking the shortest way to Felsztyn as a *billeting officer*. The Russian, as soon as he saw him, ran away and left his complete uniform in the bushes. That he, Švejk, used to hear how, for example, at the front line, for reconnaissance work they made use of the uniforms of fallen enemies, and that this was why as a test he changed into the left behind uniform, in order to find out for himself, how it would be in such a case for him to walk in a foreign uniform.

Having explained this mistake of his, Švejk then realized, that he had been speaking completely in vain, because the Master Sergeant had long since been asleep, even before he had reached the pond. Švejk stepped toward him familiarly and touched his shoulder, which was completely enough for the Master Sergeant to fall from the chair onto the ground, where he kept on sleeping undisturbed.

"*They* do forgive, Master Sergeant, Sir," said Švejk, gave a salute and walked out of the office.

Early in the morning the Army Construction Command changed the instructions and resolved, that the group of prisoners of war, in which there was Švejk, would be transported directly to Przemyśl for the restoration of the track of the Przemyśl — Lubaczów[308] line.

So everything remained as before and Švejk continued his odyssey among the Russian prisoners of war. The Hungarian patrols were driving the whole lot forward at a brisk pace.

In one village, where they rested, they ran into a supply detachment in the village green. There was an officer standing before the group of wagons and he was watching the prisoners of war. Švejk jumped out of the line, stood before the officer and cried out: "*Lieutenant*, Sir, I most dutifully report." He said no more, however, because right away there were two Hungarian soldiers there, who, thrusting their fists into his back, rammed him into the midst of the prisoners of war.

The officer threw a cigarette butt after him, which another prisoner of war quickly picked up and kept on smoking. Then the officer was telling the corporal standing beside him, that in Russia there were

German colonists and that those also had to fight.

After that, for the whole rest of the journey to Przemyśl, there did not come up for Švejk any opportunity anymore to complain a bit to somebody, that he is actually the Company Messenger of the 11th Company of the 91st Regiment. Not until in Przemyśl, when they had driven them into one busted-up little fortress within the inner zone for the evening, where there were still preserved stables for the horses of the fortress artillery.

There were layers of straw so loused up, that the lice were moving short straws, as if they were not lice at all, but ants, dragging away material for the building of their nest.

They also distributed to them a little liquid black dirt of pure chicory and a chunk of crumbly and dry corn bread apiece.

Then Major Wolf, reigning at that time over all the prisoners of war working on repairs of the fortress in Przemyśl and in the surroundings, took them in his custody. This was a thorough man. He had a whole staff of interpreters with him, who were choosing specialists for construction projects from among the prisoners of war according to their abilities and prior education.

Major Wolf had a fixed idea, that the Russian prisoners of war were denying their being literate, because what used to happen was, that to his interpreted question: "Do you know how to build railroads?" were answering all the prisoners of war stereotypically: "I know of nothing, I would never had heard about anything like that, I have lived honorably and honestly."

When they were then standing already in formation before Major Wolf and his whole staff, to start, Major Wolf asked in German of the prisoners of war, who of them knew German.

Švejk resolutely stepped out, stood himself in front of the major, snapped him the honors and was reporting, that he knew German.

Major Wolf, apparently pleased, immediately asked Švejk, whether he wasn't an engineer.

"I dutifully report, Major, Sir," answered Švejk, "that an engineer I'm not, but I'm the Messenger of the 11th March Company of the 91st Regiment. I have fallen into our captivity. It happened like this, Major, Sir…"

"What's that?" gave a scream Major Wolf.

"I dutifully report, Major, Sir, that it's like this…"

"You are a Czech," kept on screaming Major Wolf. "You have changed into a Russian uniform."

"I dutifully report Major, Sir, that all of it totally corresponds to the truth. I am really glad, that mister Major immediately put himself into my situation. It may be, that our guys are already fighting somewhere, and I would pointlessly loaf here through the whole war. So that I would, Major, Sir, explain it to *them* in proper order."

"Enough," said Major Wolf and called two soldiers with the order to immediately escort this man to the main guard-house, and he himself with another officer was slowly following Švejk, while flailing his hands about during a conversation with the officer. In each sentence of his there was something about the Czech dogs and at the same time was the other officer perceiving from his telling the major's great joy, of how with his keen sight he had discovered one of those birdies, about whose grand-treasonous activity abroad were being issued for several months already to the commanders of military components secret circulars, namely that it had been determined: how some of those who had run over to the other side from the Czech regiments, forgetting their oath, were joining the ranks of the Russian military and were serving the enemy, affording him especially valuable intelligence services.

The Austrian Ministry of the Interior was still groping in the dark, as far as pertaining to detection of any fighting organization of those who had run over to the Russian side. It still knew nothing definite about revolutionary organizations abroad, and only in August along the Sokal — Myliatyn[309] — Bubnów[310] line did the battalion commanders receive confidential circulars, that the former Austrian professor Masaryk[311] had escaped across the border, where he was leading a propaganda against Austria.

Some little numskull from the Division augmented the circular with this order: "In the event of capture to be brought without delay to the Division Staff!"

Of this then I am reminding mister President, so that he would know, what traps and snares were being laid for him between Sokal — Myliatyn and Bubnów.

Major Wolf at that time still had no inkling of all that, which was actually being prepared for Austria by those who had run over to the other side, who later, meeting in Kiev and elsewhere, replied to the question "What are you doing here?" by answering merrily: "I betrayed the lord Emperor."

He knew only from those circulars about those deserter spies, one of whom, the one they were escorting to the *main guard-house*, had so easily fallen into his trap. Major Wolf was a little bit of a conceited man, he was imagining a commendation from somewhere higher up, a decoration for his vigilance, caution and talent.

By the time they reached the *main guard-house* he was convinced that he had posed the question: "Who knows German?" on purpose, because immediately, as he was looking the prisoners of war up and down, this very one seemed suspicious.

The officer accompanying him was nodding and said, that it would be necessary to inform the garrison command about the arrest for further proceedings and transfer of the accused to a higher military court, because it definitely wouldn't do, as mister Major says, to interrogate him at the *main guard-house* and then right away behind the *main guard-house* to hang him. He would be hanged, but in a legal way, according to the military penal code, so that there would be established a connection to similar other sons-of-evil through a detailed interrogation before the hanging. Who knows what else might hatch from it?

Major Wolf was seized by a sudden obstinacy, there took a sudden possession of him an up to now concealed bestial idiocy, so that he proclaimed, that he'd have this deserter spy hanged immediately after the interrogation at his own risk. After all he can dare do it, because he has highly positioned acquaintances, and that to him it made no difference whatsoever. It was here as at the front. Had they caught and discovered him right outside the battlefield, then they would have interrogated him and, also immediately, hanged him and they would not have been making any fuss on his account. After all, mister *Captain* must know, that a commander in a war zone, any commander from *captain* up, has the right to be hanging all suspicious people.

Major Wolf however got it a bit confused, regarding the authority of military ranks to be hanging others.

In eastern Galicia, the closer to the front, the more this authority was descending to lower and lower ranks, until at last there were cases taking place, in which, for example, a corporal leading a patrol had a twelve-year-old boy hanged, who was suspicious to him on account of, that in an abandoned village plundered clean he was in the ruins of a hut boiling potato peels for himself. —

The squabble between the Captain and the Major was also escalating.

"You don't have the right for that," was screaming agitatedly the Captain. "He will be hanged on the basis of a verdict by a military court."

"He will be hanged without a verdict," was rasping Major Wolf.

Švejk, whom they were escorting ahead and who heard the whole interesting conversation, said nothing else to his accompanying attendants than: "Going on foot or following the wagon, same difference. Let me tell you, once in the pub Na Zavadilce in Libeň we were arguing among ourselves whether we were to throw out some hatter Vašák[312], who was always stirring up some mischief at the dance, as soon as he appeared in the doorway, or to throw him out once he had ordered a beer, paid and finished drinking, or to put his shoes out for him after he had danced the first round. The pubkeeper, that one on the other hand was suggesting that we throw him out only after half way through the merriment, after he had run up a tab, that then he had to pay and immediately out. And do you know what that hoodlum did to us? He didn't come. What do you say to that?"

Both soldiers, who were from somewhere in the Tyrol, answered at the same time: "*No Czech.*"

"*Do you understand German?*" asked calmly Švejk.

"*Yes indeed*," answered both, after which Švejk remarked: "That is good, at least you'll manage among your own."

In the course of these friendly conversations they all arrived on foot at the *main guard-house*, where Major Wolf continued his discussion with the Captain about Švejk's fate, while Švejk was sitting modestly in the back on a bench.

Major Wolf at last ended up siding with the Captain's opinion after all, that this man had to hang only after a longer procedure, which is called lovingly: the legal way.

Had they asked Švejk, what he thought of it, he would have said: "I regret it very much Major, Sir, because you have a higher rank than Mister Captain, but Mister Captain is right. Thing is, every hasty act causes damage. At a county court in Prague a judge once had gone crazy. Long there had been nothing noticeable about him, until it broke out in him during the trial of a case of an insult to a person's honor. Some Znamenáček told chaplain Hortík, who slapped his boy his fill during a religion class, when he met him on the street: 'You ox, sir, you black miscreant, you religious little idiot, you black pig, you rectory billy goat, you perverter of the teaching of Christ, you hypocrite and charlatan in a priest's frock!' That goofy judge was a very religious man. He had three sisters and all three were rectory cooks and he had stood as godfather to all their children, so it upset him so much, that he at once lost his reason and hollered at the accused: "In the name of His Majesty the Emperor and King you are hereby sentenced to death by rope. There is no appeal against the verdict. — Mister Horáček!' he was calling the guard then, '*they* take this here man and *they* hang him there, *they* know, there where they dust the carpets, and then *they* come here, *they* will get money for beer!' It goes without saying, that mister Znamenáček and the guard ended up standing there stupefied, but he stomped and burst out screaming: 'Will *they* obey or not!' The guard spooked so, that he was already dragging mister Znamenáček down, and if it weren't for the defense attorney, who inserted himself into it and called the rescue station, I don't know how it would have ended up with mister Znamenáček. When they were planting the judge in the rescue station vehicle, he was still screaming: 'If *they* don't find the rope, *they* hang him with a *bed shee*t, afterward we'll settle it in the semi-annual reports".

Švejk was then transported under escort to the Command of the garrison, once the statement composed by Major Wolf was signed, that as a member of the Austrian Army he knowingly, without any coercion, changed into a Russian uniform and was on the other side of the front line intercepted by the military police, when the Russians had retreated.

All that was the holy truth and Švejk, being honorable, could raise no objections to it. When he attempted during the composing of the interrogation report to append to the report some statement, which could perhaps clarify the situation a little further, there came here promptly the order from mister Major: "Keep your yap shut, I'm not asking you about that! The matter is totally clear."

Švejk afterward always saluted and declared: "I dutifully report, that I'm keeping my yap shut and that the matter is totally clear."

Afterward, when they had brought him to the garrison Command, they led him away into some hole, where earlier there had been rice storage, and at the same time a retirement home for mice. There was still rice scattered everywhere on the floor here and the mice were in no way afraid of Švejk and were merrily running around, gleaning grains. Švejk had to go to get a straw mattress, and when he took a look around in the darkness, he realized, that a whole family of mice was immediately moving into his straw mattress. There was no doubt, that they want to make a new nest for themselves here, in the ruins of the glory of the rotten Austrian straw mattress. Švejk started banging on the locked door, some corporal came, a Pole, and Švejk was requesting of him, that he be transferred to another room, because lying down he could kill the mice in his straw mattress and do damage to government-issue property, because what is in military *stores*, is its property.

The Pole partially understood, threatened Švejk with a fist in front of the closed door, and having still mentioned something about a *"shit-smeared ass"*, he walked away, mumbling agitatedly something about cholera, as if God knows how Švejk offended him.

The night Švejk spent in peace, because the mice were not making great demands on Švejk and apparently had their own night program, to which they were adhering next door in the storage of military overcoats and caps, which they were gnawing through with great confidence and in safety, because only a year later did the army Quartermaster Administration remember and introduce into military warehouses government-issue cats, without entitlement to a pension, which were listed in the army Quartermaster Administration files under the item *"I&R military store cat"*. This cat rank was actually only a reinstatement of this old institution, which had been abolished after the war in the sixty sixth year.

Earlier, back during the reign of Maria Theresa, in times of war cats were also being introduced into the military warehouses, when the lords at the Quartermaster Administration were shifting the blame for all their scams with *uniforms* onto the hapless mice.

The I&R cats were in many cases however not doing their duty, and so it happened, that at one time during the reign of Emperor Leopold in the military warehouse at Pohořelec, on the basis of the decree of the military court, were hanged six cats assigned to the military warehouse. I know, that back then there were smiling nicely under their beards all those, who did have with that military warehouse...

\*

With the morning coffee they shoved some man in a Russian *forage cap* and a Russian military overcoat into the hole to join Švejk.

That man spoke Czech, with a Polish accent. He was one of those scoundrels serving in counter-espionage of the Army Corps, the Command of which was located in Przemyśl. He was a member of the military secret police and did not even take too much care to present some kind of crafty transition to pumping Švejk for information. He started altogether simply. "Did I get into *pretty swine filth* by my carelessness. I was serving with the 28th Regiment and right away I entered service with the Russians, and then I get myself so stupidly caught. I join the Russians, that I'll go on *forward patrol*... I was serving with the 6th Kievan Division. Which Russian regiment did you serve with, pal? Somehow it seems to me, that we must have seen one another somewhere in Russia. In Kiev I used to know many Czechs, who went to the front with us, when we had come over to the Russian military, but now I can't remember their names and where they were from, perhaps you will remember someone, whom you used to be in touch with there, I would like to know, who there is from our 28th Regiment?"

Instead of an answer Švejk reached out and touched caringly his forehead, then explored his artery and in the end escorted him to a little window and asked him, to stick out his tongue. The scoundrel was in no way resisting the whole procedure, supposing, that perhaps these were some conspiratorial signals. Then Švejk began banging on the door, and when the patrol came to ask him, why he was making a ruckus, he was requesting in both Czech and German, that they immediately call a doctor, because the man, whom they had put in here to join him was being gripped by feverish hallucinations.

It was however to no avail, nobody came for that man right away. He remained there, completely undisturbed and kept babbling something about Kiev and that he definitely had seen Švejk there, as he was marching among the Russian soldiers.

"*They* must definitely have taken a drink of muddy water," said Švejk, "like that young Týneckej from where I live, a man otherwise sensible, but one time he took to the roads and got all the way to Italy. He would indeed talk of nothing but of this Italy, saying that there was nothing but muddy waters and nothing else memorable there. And he indeed got the shivers from the muddy water. It would grip him four times a year. On All Saints, St. Joseph's, on Peter[313] and Paul[314] and on Ascension into Heaven of the Virgin Mary. When it grabbed him, he'd be recognizing all people, total strangers and people unknown to him, each and every one, just like *they*. For example when in a streetcar he would address anyone there, that he knew him, that they saw one another at the railroad station in Vienna. All the people, whom he met on the street, he had seen them either at the railroad station in Milan[315], or he had been sitting with them in Styrian Graz in the town hall cellar[316] over wine. When at that time, when there came over him that mud fever, he was sitting in the pub, here he was recognizing all the guests, all of them he had seen on that steamboat, on which he was going to Venice. There was for it however no other medicine, than what did that new attendant in Kateřinky. He was charged with caring for one sick in his head, who the entire day of God would do nothing else, than sit in the corner and count: 'One, two, three, four, five, six' and again from the beginning: 'One, two, three, four, five, six.' He was some professor. This attendant could have on account of anger jumped out of his skin, when he saw, that this lunatic could not get past the six. He tried first being nice with him, so that he say: seven, eight, nine, ten. But no way! That professorial guy didn't pay even a grain of poppy seed's worth of mind to it. He is sitting in the cozy little corner and is counting: 'One, two, three, four, five, six,' and again: 'One, two, three, four, five, six!' So it ate him up, until he jumped on his charge and gave him, when he said 'six', a head-slap. 'Here is seven,' he says, 'and here is eight, nine, ten.' Each number, a head-slap. That one grabbed his head and asked him, where he finds himself. When he told him, that in a nuthouse, he finally remembered it all, that he had gotten into the nuthouse on account of some comet, as he was calculating, that it would emerge a year later on July 18th at six o'clock in the morning, and they proved to him, that the comet of his burnt up already several million years ago. I knew that attendant. When the professor came completely to his senses and was released, he took him in as his servant. He had no other work to do, but each morning to plant four slaps on the mister professor's head, which he performed conscientiously and exactly."

"I know all your acquaintances from Kiev," tirelessly continued the man from counter-espionage, "wasn't there with you this fat one and another sort of skinny one? Now I don't know, what their names were and which regiment they were from…"

"Don't worry about it," was consoling him Švejk, "it can happen to anybody, that he does not commit to memory all the fat and skinny people, what their names are. Skinny people are however harder to remember, because they are the majority in the world. They then form the majority, as the saying goes."

"Pal," sounded up complainingly the I&R scoundrel, "you don't trust me. But after all there awaits us both the same fate."

"That's why we're soldiers," said Švejk carelessly, "that's why our mothers birthed us, so that they would cut us into rags, when they dress us in the *uniform*. And we do it gladly, because we know, that our bones will not be rotting away to dust in vain. We will fall for the lord Emperor and his family, for whose sake we fought for and won Herzegovina gamily. From our bones they'll be manufacturing bone ash for sugar refineries, about that was telling us already years ago mister Lieutenant Zimmer. 'You swine pack,' he says, 'you uneducated boars, you useless, indolent monkeys, you tangle and flail your dumb legs, as if they had no worth. If you were to fall in the war one day, then from each dead limb of yours they'll make half a kilogram of bone ash, from a man over two kilograms, thigh bone and claw together, and through you in the sugar refineries they'll be filtering sugar, you idiots. You don't even know, how after death you'll still be useful to your progeny. Your boys will be drinking coffee sweetened by sugar, which went through your dead limbs, you empty heads.' I pondered, and he was at me, what am I thinking about. 'I dutifully report,' say I, 'I'm just thinking, that bone ash from gentlemen officers must be much more expensive than from simple soldiers.' I got three days of nice little *solitary* for it.

Švejk's companion banged on the door and was negotiating something with the guard, who was calling the office.

After a while came some staff sergeant-major to fetch Švejk's companion and Švejk was alone again.

On the way out the monster said loudly to the staff sergeant-major, pointing to Švejk: "He's my old pal from Kiev."

A whole 24 hours remained Švejk by himself with the exception of the moments, when they brought him something to eat.

At night he arrived at the conviction, that the Russian military overcoat was warmer and bigger than the Austrian, and that when a mouse is sniffing the ear of a sleeping man, that it isn't anything unpleasant. To Švejk it seemed like gentle whispering, from which when it was still twilight they woke him up, as they came for him.

Švejk can't fathom today, what sort of judicial formation was actually the one, which they were that sad morning dragging him to face. That it was a military court, of that there was no doubt. Sitting there was even some general, then a colonel, a major, a senior lieutenant, a lieutenant, a sergeant-major and some infantryman, who actually wasn't doing anything but lighting up cigarettes for the others.

They weren't asking many questions of Švejk either.

The major among them was demonstrating a little greater interest and spoke Czech.

"You betrayed the lord Emperor," he barked at Švejk.

"Jesusmaria, when?" yelled out Švejk, "that I betrayed the lord

Emperor, our most luminous monarch, for whom I have already suffered so much?"

"Stop the silliness," said the major.

"I dutifully report, Major, Sir, that to betray the lord Emperor is no silliness. We, the military folk, swore loyalty and fidelity to the lord Emperor, and the oath, as they put it singing in the theater, as a faithful man I fulfilled.[317]"

"Here it is," said the major, "here are the proofs of your guilt and the truth." He pointed to a voluminous file of papers.

The man, whom they sat next to Švejk, supplied the main material.

"So you still don't want to confess?" asked the major. "You yourself, after all, already confirmed, that you voluntarily changed into a Russian uniform as a member of the Austrian Army. I am asking you for the last time: Were you coerced by anyone to do it?"

"I did it without being coerced."

"Voluntarily?"

"Voluntarily."

"Without pressure?"

"Without pressure."

"Do you know that you're doomed?

"I know, the people of the 91st Regiment are certainly already looking for me, but if you permit, Major, Sir, a little remark, about how people voluntarily change into strangers' clothes. In the year 1908, sometime in July, was bathing bookbinder Božetěch from Příčná street in Prague, at Zbraslav, in the old branch of the Berounka[318]. His clothes he put into the little willows and was tremendously pleased, when later there climbed into the water to join him another gentleman. One word led to another word, they were frolicking and teasing one another, splashing at one another, were diving until the evening. Then the stranger crawled out of the water first, that he must go to supper. Mister Božetěch still stayed a while sitting in the water and then he went to get the clothes in the little willows and instead of his own he found broken-down, vagabond's clothes and a note there: 'Long was I deciding: should I — shouldn't I, since we were so beautifully enjoying ourselves in the water, so I plucked an ox-eye daisy and the last torn off petal was: I should! That is why I exchanged the rags with *them*. *They* don't have to be afraid to get into them. Deloused they were a week ago at the county office in Dobříš[319]. Next time *they* be more careful of the one, whom *they* bathe with. In water every naked man looks like a parliament deputy, and maybe he is a murderer. *They* also don't know, whom *they* bathed with. It was worth taking a bath. Now, toward the evening, the water is the best. *They* crawl in there one more time so that *they* recover themselves.' — Mister Božetěch had no choice left to him but to wait, until dusk fell, and then he dressed in those vagabond's rags and headed for Prague. He was avoiding the county road and took byway paths through the meadows and ran into a State Police patrol from Chuchle[320], which arrested the vagrant and escorted him the next day in the morning to Zbraslav to the County Court, because anybody could say, that he is Josef Božetěch, bookbinder from Příčná street in Prague, number 16."

The recorder, who did not understand any more Czech, realized, that the accused is stating an address of his accomplice, and that was why he asked one more time: "*Is that correct, Prague, No. 16, Josef Bozetech?*"

"Whether he still lives there, I don't know," answered Švejk, "but back then in the year 1908 he did live there. He bound books tremendously nicely, but it took a long time, because first he had to read them and then according to their content he would bind them. When he gave a book a black book-binder's trim, then nobody had to read it anymore. He immediately knew then, that it came in that novel to a very bad end. Do you wish perhaps some more detail? So that I wouldn't forget, he would sit daily at U Fleků and be telling the content of all the books, which they commissioned him to bind."

The major stepped to the recorder and was whispering with him, and the latter was then crossing out in the file the address of the new alleged conspirator Božetěch.

Afterward was this strange trial continuing in the style of a summary court, which was arranged by the presiding General Fink von Finkenstein.

Just as someone has the hobby of collecting match boxes, then again the hobby of this gentleman was organizing summary court trials, although in most cases it was contrary to the military court regulations.

This General used to say, that he doesn't need any judge advocates, that he'd call a gathering and that in three hours each guy must hang. As long as he was at the front, then with him there was never any lack of summary courts.

Just as someone must regularly play a daily game of chess, billiards or mariáš, this remarkable General was arranging daily summary field-court proceedings, chaired them and was announcing with great solemnity and joy a check-mate to the accused.

Were one desiring to be sentimental, then he would write, that this man had on his conscience many dozens of people, especially over there in the east, where he was struggling, as he was saying, against the Greater Russia agitation among the Galician Ukrainians. From his vantage point, however, we cannot be saying, that he had anybody on his conscience.

That never occurred to him. When he had a male teacher, or a female teacher, a Russian Orthodox priest or a whole family hanged on the basis of the verdict of his summary court trial, he would return to his quarters peacefully, like when a passionate player of mariáš is returning home from the pub, satisfied, and is thinking about how they hit him with a flek, doubling the stakes, how he hit them with the quadrupling re, they doubled that by a supre, he doubled again by a tuti, they doubled one more time by boty, and how he won it and had a hundred and a seven. He viewed hanging as something simple and natural, some sort of daily bread, and during sentencing would quite often forget the lord Emperor and would not even be saying anymore: "In the name of His Majesty you are being sentenced to death by rope," but would declare: "I am sentencing you."

Sometimes he found in the hanging even a comical side, of which he indeed once wrote to his wife in Vienna: "...or for example, my dear, you cannot imagine, how the last time I laughed my fill, when several days ago I sentenced a teacher for espionage. I have a trained man, who is hanging the lot, he's already had considerable experience, he is a Sergeant-Major and he does it for the sport of it. I was in my tent, when after the sentencing also came the Sergeant-Major and he's asking me, where he is to hang the teacher. I told him, that on the nearest tree, and now consider the comic nature of the situation. We were in the middle of a steppe, where as far as one's sight could reach we saw nothing else but grass and for miles of the journey not even a little sapling. An order is an order, and that's why the Sergeant-Major took the teacher with him with an escort and they rode to find a tree. They returned only in the evening, again with the teacher. The Sergeant-Major came to me and is asking me again: 'On what am I to hang the guy?' I gave him a tongue-lashing, that my order clearly was: on the nearest tree. He said, that he would then in the morning attempt it, and in the morning he came all pale, that the teacher had disappeared by the morning. It appeared to me so laughable, that I

Jaroslav Hašek

forgave all, who were guarding him, and on top of it I made a joke, that the teacher apparently had gone himself to take a look around for some tree. So you see, my dear, that in no way are we getting bored here, and tell little Viloš, that daddy is sending kisses and that soon he will send him a live Russian, atop of whom will Viloušek ride like on a horsey. I still recall for you, my dear, one laughable case. We were hanging the other day a Jew on account of espionage. The guy stumbled into our path, although he had no business there, and he was making the excuse, that he is selling cigarettes. So he was hanging, but only a few seconds, the rope snapped with him and he fell down, right away came to and was screaming at me: 'Mister General, I'm going home, you have already hanged me, and under the law I cannot be hanged twice for one thing.' I broke out laughing and the Jew we let go. Back where we are it is, my dear, a merry place"

When General Fink became the commander of the garrison at the fort Przemyśl, he did not have anymore as much opportunity to organize similar circuses, therefore with great joy he seized Švejk's case.

Švejk was then standing before that tiger, who sitting in the foreground at a long desk, was smoking one cigarette after another, and having them translate Švejk's answers for himself, while he was nodding in agreement.

The Major presented a suggestion, for an inquiry to be made by telegraph at the Brigade on account of ascertaining, where is now situated the 11th March Company of the 91st Regiment, to which the accused belongs according to his information.

The General stood against it and declared, that thereby is being delayed the promptness of the summary court and the true significance of the institution. There is after all the complete confession of the accused, that he put on a Russian uniform, then one important testimony, wherein the accused confessed, that he had been to Kiev. It is being proposed therefore, that they proceed to conference, so that the verdict could be pronounced and immediately executed.

The Major however kept insisting on his own position, that it is necessary to determine the identity of the accused, because the whole matter is unusually politically important. By determining his identity can be discovered further dealings of the accused among his former pals from the detachment, to which he belonged.

The Major was a romantic dreamer. He was also speaking of the fact, that being sought are actually certain little threads, that it is not enough to convict a man. That the guilty verdict is only a resultant of a certain investigation, which encompasses within itself little threads, which little threads... He could not get out of those little threads, but all understood him, were nodding in agreement, even mister General, whose fancy the little threads took so, that he was imagining, how by the Major's little threads are hanging new summary court proceedings. That is why he was no longer protesting, that it be determined at the Brigade, whether Švejk indeed belongs to the 91st Regiment and when approximately he crossed over to the Russians, during which of the operations of the 11th *March Company*.

Švejk was during the whole debate being guarded in the corridor by two bayonets, then was again brought before the court and asked once more, to which regiment he actually belongs. Then they moved him over to the garrison prison.

*

When General Fink returned home after the unsuccessful summary court, he lay on the sofa and was musing, how he would actually speed up the whole proceeding.

He was firmly convinced, that the answer will be here soon, but that it won't be after all the speed, by which his trials excelled, because after that there would yet come the spiritual consolation of the condemned, by which the verdict will be unnecessarily delayed by two hours.

"It doesn't make any difference," thought to himself General Fink, "we can provide him spiritual consolation ahead of time, before the sentencing, even before the news comes from the Brigade. Hang he will all the same."

General Fink had Field Chaplain Martinec called to himself.

He was an unhappy catechist and chaplain, from somewhere in Moravia, who had such a scourge of a priest over him, that he preferred and gave himself over to army service. He was a man really grounded in religion, who, with sorrow in his heart, was remembering his priest, who slowly, but surely is succumbing to ruin. He kept remembering, how his priest was soaking up slivovice like a thirsty rainbow and how once at night with all living might he was shoving into his bed some itinerant Gypsy girl, whom he found outside the village, as he was stumbling back from the wine distillery.

Field Chaplain Martinec was imagining, that being in the service of spiritual consolation for the wounded and dying on the battlefield, he would redeem even the sins of his debauched priest, who returning

home in the night, woke him up countless times and was telling him:
"*Johnny, Johnny!* A chubby slut, that's my whole life."

His hopes did not get fulfilled. They were throwing him from one garrison to another, where he had nothing to do but preach once every two weeks before the mass in the garrison temple to the soldiers from the garrison and to be resisting temptation, which was coming out of the officers' club, where there were such talks conducted, that in comparison with them were the chubby sluts of his priest an innocent little prayer to the guardian angel.

Usually nowadays he would be called to General Fink at times of great operations in the battlefield, when there was to be celebrated some victory of the Austrian Army, here, with the same fondness he afforded the summary courts, was General Fink arranging glorious field masses.

The miscreant Fink was such an Austrian patriot, that he did not pray for a victory of the German Imperial or Turkish arms. When the Germans from the Reich somewhere beat the French or English, he ignored it by total reticence at the altar.

An insignificant victorious skirmish of an Austrian reconnaissance patrol with a Russian forward guard, which the Staff Headquarters blew up into a huge soap bubble of a defeat of the whole army corps, gave an inspiring impulse to General Fink for festive divine services, so that the hapless Field Chaplain Martinec had the impression, that General Fink was at the same time also the top head of the Catholic Church in Przemyśl.

General Fink also decided, what program and sequence the mass would have on such an occasion, and he would have always liked the best to have something in the manner of Body of Christ with the octave.

He also had the habit, that when during the mass the lifting of the host was finished, he cantered onto the exercise grounds on horseback to the altar and shouted three times: "Hurray — hurray — hurray!"

Field Chaplain Martinec, a soul pious and righteous, one of the few, who still believed in the Lord God, didn't like going to General Fink's.

After all the instructions, which the Commander of the garrison used to give him, General Fink would always have something hard poured and then be telling him the newest jokes from the most stupid little volumes, which were being published for the military in the

*Funny Pages*[321].

He had a whole library of such little volumes with asinine titles like *Humor in the Knapsack for Eyes and Ears, Hindenburg's*[322] *Jokes, Hindenburg in the Mirror of Humor, The Second Knapsack Full of Humor, Loaded Up by Felix Schlempr*[323], *From Our Goulash Cannon, Succulent Grenade Chips From the Trenches*, or these pieces of beastly crud: *Under the Double Eagle, Wiener Schnitzel From the I&R Kitchen. Reheated by Artur Lokesch*[324]. Sometimes he would also lead him in singing from a collection of merry military songs *We Have to Win*, while he was constantly pouring something hard and was pressuring Field Chaplain Martinec to drink and holler with him. Then he would engage in obscene talk, during which Chaplain Martinec with nostalgia in his heart was remembering his priest, who was not lagging in any regard behind General Fink, when it came to coarse words.

Chaplain Martinec was observing with horror, that the more he goes to General Fink's, the more he morally deteriorates.

The unfortunate began to find delicate pleasure in liqueurs, which he drank at the General's, and also the General's talks began slowly to appeal to him, he would be gripped by debauched imaginations and on account of kontušovka, rowan brandy and cobwebs on the bottles of old wine, which General Fink would put in front of him, he was forgetting the Lord God and in between the lines of the breviary there were dancing for him gals from the General's yarns. The aversion to the visits at the General's was slowly getting milder.

The General got to like the Chaplain Martinec, who at first introduced himself to him as some Saint Ignatius of Loyola[325] and slowly was adjusting to the General's surroundings.

At one time the General invited to his place two nurses from the field hospital, who actually did not even serve there, they only were assigned there on account of the salary and were augmenting their incomes through a better sort of prostitution, as used to be the custom in those hard times. He had them call Chaplain Martinec, who had already fallen so far into the snares of the devil, that after a half an hour of merriment he took turns with both of the dames, while at it he was rutting so, that he drooled all over a throw pillow on the sofa. Afterward for a long time he would reproach himself for this debauched behavior, although he could not right it, even when that night, returning home, he was kneeling by mistake in the park in front of the statue of the builder and mayor of the town, benefactor lord

Grabowski[326], who earned great accolades for himself for Przemyśl in the years of the eighties.

Only the stomping of the military patrol was mixing into his fervent words:

"Do Thou not enter into judgement with Thy servant, for no man will be justified before Thee, if Thou dost not give him forgiveness of all his sins, let it then be, that heavy is not Thy verdict. Thy help I am requesting and commend into Thy hands, Lord, my spirit."

Since that time he had undertaken several times an attempt, whenever they called him to General Fink, to foreswear all earthly pleasures and was at the same time making the excuse of blaming it on his bad stomach, considering this lie as necessary, so that his soul would not taste the hardships of hell, because he was concurrently of the view, that the military discipline requires, that when a general tells a field chaplain: "Soak up the booze, pal", he should be boozing it up just from sheer respect for his superior alone.

Sometimes however he did not succeed in it, especially when after a glorious field divine service the General would organize even more glorious frenzied feeding events on the account of the garrison cashier, where afterward in the accounting office they were trying to nail it all together, so that they would also get something from it, and here he was always imagining then, that he is morally buried before the face of the Lord and into a trembling man hath he been made.

Then he would walk like in a daze, and not losing in that chaos faith in God, he already altogether seriously started to think about, whether he should not with regularity every day flog himself.

In a similar mood he arrived even now on the invitation of the General.

General Fink came out to meet him all radiant and overjoyed.

"Have you heard already," he was calling out to him cheerily, "of my summary court? We will be hanging a countryman of yours."

At the word 'countryman' Field Chaplain Martinec cast a look of a man worn out by anguish at the General. Several times already he had rejected the supposition, that he was a Czech, and had explained already countless times, that to their Moravian parish there belong two villages, one Czech and one German, and that quite many times he has to preach for the Czechs one week and the next one for the Germans, and because in the Czech village there is no Czech school, only a German one, that therefore he must teach in German in both villages, and therefore he is no Czech. This logical justification once inspired a major at the table to remark, that the field chaplain from Moravia is after all a general store with assorted merchandise.

"Pardon me," said the General, "I forgot, that he is not your countryman. He is a Czech, ran to the other side, a traitor to us, served the Russians, he'll hang. For the time being however somehow on account of form we are determining his identity, that doesn't matter, hang he will immediately, as soon as the telegraphic reply arrives."

Seating the Field Chaplain next to himself on the sofa, the General continued merrily: "With me, when there is a summary court trial, it must correspond also to the prompt nature of this type of court, that is my principle. When I was still on the other side of Lwów at the beginning of the war, I achieved the result, that we hanged a guy three minutes after the verdict. That was however a Jew, but one Ruthenian we hanged in five minutes after our consultation."The General released a congenial laugh: "It so happens neither one needed spiritual consolation. The Jew was a rabbi and the Ruthenian a *priest*. This case is however different, what is at hand here is, that we'll be hanging a Catholic. I have come upon a capital idea, so that it would not then be being delayed, you will provide the spiritual consolation ahead of time, as I'm saying, so that it would not be dragged out and delayed."

The General rang and ordered the servant: "Bring two from your battery of yesterday."

And filling in a while for the Field Chaplain a wine glass, he said amiably: "Console yourself a little before the spiritual consolation…"

\*

Out of the barred window, behind which was Švejk sitting on a bunk, there was coming at this horrible time the sound of his singing:

We soldiers, we're the masters,
the girls love us on their own,
we get issued money,
Tsah-rah-raaah… One, two…

## 2

## SPIRITUAL CONSOLATION

Field Chaplain Martinec in the true sense of the word did not come to Švejk, but floated in toward him like a ballerina on a stage. Heavenly desires and a bottle of old Gumpoldskirchen in this touching moment were making him as light as a down feather. It seemed to him, that he is getting closer in this solemn and hallowed moment to God, while he was getting closer to Švejk.

They closed the door behind him, left both of them alone and he enthusiastically said in the direction of Švejk, who was sitting on a bunk: "Dear son, I am Field Chaplain Martinec."

This address seemed to him after the whole journey here the most appropriate and somehow touching in a fatherly way.

## The Fateful Adventures of the Good Soldier Švejk

Švejk got up out of his lair, shook jovially the hand of the Field Chaplain and said: "My pleasure, I am Švejk, *Messenger* of the 11th *March Company* of the 91st Regiment. Not long ago they transferred our permanent core to Bruck on the Leitha, so *they* nicely take a seat next to me, *Field Chaplain*, Sir, and *they* go on telling me, why *they* are locked up. *They* are after all in the *rank* of an officer, so *they are due* an officer's imprisonment at the *garrison*, not here, oh no, look, the bunk is full of lice. Sometimes it happens, however, that somebody doesn't know, where he actually belongs arrest-wise, but that gets mixed up at the office or by chance. Once, let me tell you, I was sitting doing time, *Field Chaplain*, Sir, *imprisoned* in Budějovice at the Regiment and they brought to me a *cadet officer-deputy*. Such a *cadet officer-deputy* was something similar to field chaplains, neither hog, nor mouse, he would scream at soldiers like an officer, and when something happened, then they would lock him up with the uncouth enlisted men. They were, let me tell you Field Chaplain, Sir, such bastards, that they were not accepting them for rations at the *non-commissioned officers'* kitchen, for the enlisted mess rations they were not entitled, they were higher, and on the other hand they *weren't due* officers' mess rations. We had there five of them back then and at the beginning the lot of them was feeding in the canteen on nothing but syrečky, because they couldn't get mess rations anywhere, until this one time there came after them *Senior Lieutenant* Wurm[327] and forbade it to them, because supposedly it doesn't square with the honor of *cadet officer-deputies* to be going to the mess hall for the enlisted. But what were they to do, they wouldn't let them into the *officers' mess*. So they were hanging in the air and they had gone over the course of few days down the road of such suffering, that one of them jumped into the Malše and one deserted from the Regiment and in two months wrote to the garrison, that he is in Morocco the minister of military affairs. They were four, because the one from the Malše they fished out alive, because in agitation he forgot, when he was jumping in there, that he knows how to swim and that he had passed a swimming test with the grade of outstanding. They delivered him to the hospital and there again they didn't know what to do with him, whether they are to cover him with an officer's blanket or an ordinary one for the enlisted. So they found then a way and didn't give him any blanket at all and wrapped him only in a wet bed sheet, so that half an hour later he was begging, that they let him go back to the garrison, and he was the very one, whom they threw in and locked up with me, still all wet. He was sitting there about four days and was delighting in it, because in there he was getting rations, an arrestee's kind, true, but rations, he had his secured minimum, as the saying goes. The fifth day they came for him and after half an hour he returned for his cap and was, let me tell you, weeping with joy. He is telling me: 'There came at last a decision about us. Starting today we *cadet officer-deputies* will be getting locked up at the *main guard house* among the officers, for the rations we'll be paying extra into the officers' kitchen, and once the officers have eaten, only then we'll get to eat, sleep we will with the *enlisted* and coffee we'll be getting also from the *enlisted* kitchen and we'll be getting tobacco issued also with the *enlisted*.'"

Only now had Field Chaplain Martinec come so far to his senses, that he interrupted Švejk with a sentence, which on account of its content did not belong in any way to the preceding conversation:

"Yes, yes, dear son! There are things between the heaven and the earth, which are proper to ponder with a fervent heart and with full confidence in the infinite mercy of God. I am coming, dear son, to provide you spiritual consolation."

He fell silent, because somehow all of that was for him somehow not fitting. On the way he was already composing the whole outline of a speech, in which he'd bring the unfortunate to meditating about his life and how he will be forgiven up there, when he's repenting and will show effective remorse.

Now he was pondering, how to pick up where he left off, but Švejk beat him to it with the question, whether he has a cigarette.

Field Chaplain Martinec had not yet picked up smoking. That was indeed the only thing, which he had kept of his life regimen, from before he arrived here. Sometimes at General Fink's, when he'd already have a little in his head, he would try smoking britanika cigars, but it was all immediately coming out of him, during which time he had the impression, that the little guardian angel was warningly tickling him in the throat.

"I don't smoke, dear son," he answered Švejk with uncommon dignity.

"Now I'm amazed," said Švejk. "I have known many field chaplains and they smoked like the *distillery* in Zlíchov[328]. I cannot even imagine a field chaplain, that would not smoke and drink. Only one I knew that wasn't puffing, but he again liking it better, instead of smoking, chewed tobacco and during the sermon he spat all over the whole pulpit. — Where then are *they* from, *Field Chaplain*, Sir?"

"From Nový Jičín[329] way," the I&R Rev. Father Martinec sounded up with a dejected voice.

"Then perhaps, Field Chaplain, Sir, they knew one Růžena Gaudrsová, she was employed the year before last in a wine bar in Platnéřská street in Prague and was, let me tell you, suing all at once eighteen people for paternity, because she gave birth to twins. This one of the twins had one eye blue and the other brown, the second twin had one eye gray and the other black, so she assumed, that there are already four gentlemen with matching eyes engaged in it, who used to go to that wine bar and had something to do with her. Then one of the twins had a lame little leg like one magistrate councillor, who also used to go there, and the other again had six toes on one foot like one parliamentary deputy, who used to be there a daily guest. And now they imagine, Field Chaplain, Sir, that of such guests there used to go there eighteen, and the twins had from each some birth mark, from all those eighteen, with whom she used to go either to private lodgings or to a hotel. In the end the court decided, that given such a pressing of people the father is unknown, and she in the end blamed it on the wine bar owner and sued the wine bar owner, in whose service she worked, but he proved, that he'd been for over twenty years already impotent based on an operation during some inflammation of the lower extremities. They then shoved her, Field Chaplain, Sir, over to by you in Nový Jičín, which best shows, that whoever hankers after a lot, usually gets an old billy goat's worth. She should have held onto one and not been claiming in court, that one little twin was from mister deputy and the other from mister magistrate councillor or from this one and this one. Each birth of a child is easy to calculate. On such and such date I was with him at the hotel and on such and such date I gave birth to it. It figures, if it's a normal birth, Field Chaplain, Sir. In such dumpy love nest there's always some witness to be found for a fiver, like a porter or a chamber-maid, who will swear, that he was actually there that night with her and that she told him, as they were still going down the stairs: 'And what if something comes of it?' and that in response to that he answered her: 'Don't worry, you kanimůra[330], I'll take care of the kid.'"

The field chaplain gave some though thought and the whole spiritual consolation seemed to him now somehow hard, even though he had beforehand the whole outline worked out, what and how he would be saying while talking with that dear son. About the supreme mercy on the day of the Last Judgment, when there will rise all military criminals from the graves with a noose around their neck, and because they repented, they are accepted with mercy just the same as that rogue from the New Testament.

He had prepared perhaps one of the nicest spiritual consolations, which was to consist of three parts. First he wanted to discourse upon, that death by hanging is easy, when the man is totally reconciled with God. That the military code of justice punishes the guilty one for the treason he perpetrated against the lord Emperor, who is the father of his common soldiers, so that no matter how minuscule the lapse of theirs is it is proper to view it as a patricide, a dishonoring of the father. Then he wanted to further elaborate on his theory, that the lord Emperor is lord Emperor by the grace of God, that he's established by God for directing secular matters, just as the pope is established for directing spiritual matters. Treason perpetrated against the Emperor is treason perpetrated against the very Lord God. Awaiting the military criminal is then aside from the noose a punishment in the eternal world and eternal damnation of the calumniator. If however the secular justice cannot due to military discipline cancel the verdict and must hang the criminal, not all is yet lost, as concerns the other punishment in the eternal world. Man can parry that with an excellent move, repentance.

The Field Chaplain was imagining the most moving scene, which would benefit his own self up there working toward wiping out all the notes about his activities and influence in the apartment of General Fink in Przemyśl.

How he'd then bellow at him, the condemned and sentenced, for an opening: Repent, son, let us kneel together! Repeat after me, son!

And how afterward in this stinking, louse-ridden cell there would carry the sound of the prayer: God, whose characteristic it is to be extending mercy always and to be forgiving, I imploringly beseech you for the soul of this common soldier, which soul you ordered to depart from this world on the basis of the verdict of the summary court martial in Przemyśl. Grant this infantryman on account of his entreating and total repentance, that he not taste the hardships of hell, but of eternal joys be partaking.

"With your permission, *Field Chaplain*, Sir, *they* have been sitting five minutes already as if cut down dead, as if *they* were not even in the mood to talk. With *them* man can immediately tell, that *they* are in the brig for the first time."

"I've come," said solemnly the Field Chaplain, "on account of spiritual consolation."

"It is peculiar, what do they constantly have with that, *Field Chaplain*, Sir, spiritual consolation *they* keep bringing up. I, *Field Chaplain*, Sir, don't feel to be so strong, to be able to provide *them* any spiritual consolation. *They* are neither the first, nor the last field chaplain, who has got himself behind bars. Needless to say, to tell you the truth, *Field Chaplain*, Sir, I don't have the eloquence, in order to be able to be providing anybody consolation in his difficult situation. Once I tried it, but it did not turn out too well, *they* take a nice comfy seat next to me and I will tell *them* about it. When I used to live in Opatovická street, then I had a pal there, Faustýn, a porter at a hotel. He was a very nice man, righteous and industrious. He knew which-and-where-ever street gal, and *they* could come, *Field Chaplain*, Sir, at whatever time of the night to him at the hotel and tell him just: 'Mister Faustýn, I need some miss,' and he, let me tell you, would right away conscientiously ask, whether a blond, a brunette, smaller, taller, thin, fat, a German broad, a Czech or Jewess, single, divorced or a married pampered lady, intelligent or without intelligence."

Švejk cuddled up intimately to the Field *Chaplain*, and embracing his waist, continued: "Let's say then, *Field Chaplain*, Sir, that *they* would say: 'I need a blonde, leggy, a widow, without intelligence,' and in ten minutes you would have her in the bed even with a birth certificate."

The Field Chaplain started feeling hot, and Švejk kept on talking, pressing the field *chaplain* to himself in a motherly way: "*They* wouldn't even think, *Field Chaplain*, Sir, what a sense of morality and honesty mister Faustýn had. From those broads he'd send your way and supply to the rooms, he would not take even one penny as a tip, and when sometimes one of those broads forgot herself and wanted to slip him something, *they* should have seen, how upset he got and started screaming at her: 'You swine, when you're selling your body and committing a deadly sin, don't think that those six krejcars of yours are somehow going to help me. I am no pimp, you shameless tramp. I do it only on account of commiseration for you, so that, since you have already let yourself stoop so low, you would not have to be putting your shame on public display for the passers-by, and have the patrol somewhere in the night catch you and then you'd have to scrub floors for three days at the police headquarters. This way at least you're in where it's warm and nobody sees, how far down you've dropped.' He was making up for it on the guests, since he didn't want to be taking money as a pimp. He had his rates: blue eyes cost six krejcars, black eyes fifteen krejcars, and he would calculate it all down to the very last detail as a bill on a piece of paper, which he would hand to the guest. Those were very affordable prices for making the arrangement. For a broad without intelligence there was a surcharge of six krejcars, because he proceeded from the principle, that such a coarse vessel will amuse more, than some educated dame. Once toward the evening there came to me mister Faustýn in Opatovická street tremendously upset and not himself, as if just a little moment ago they pulled him from under the cow catcher of a streetcar and while doing it stole his watch. At first he wasn't saying anything at all, only pulled out of his pocket a bottle of rum, took a drink, handed it to me and said: 'Drink!' So we weren't saying anything, and when we finished that bottle, all of a sudden he says: 'Pal, be so kind, do me a favor. Open a window facing the street, I will sit myself in the window and you'll grab me by the legs and throw me down from the third floor. I don't need anything else in life anymore, I have this last consolation, that a good pal has been found, who will dispatch me out of this world. I can't remain being alive in this world any longer, I, an honest man, am being sued for pandering like some pimp from Jewtown. Our hotel is after all first-class, all three hotel maids and my wife have police registration booklets and don't owe mister doctor for a visit even a krejcar. If you like me at least a bit, throw me from the third floor, give me that last consolation.' I told him, to crawl up onto the window sill then, and I threw him down into the street. — Don't *they* be spooking, *Field Chaplain*, Sir."

Švejk stepped up onto the plank bunk, while he hoisted the Field Chaplain with him: "Do *they* look, *Field Chaplain*, Sir, I grabbed him then like this and swoosh down with him."

Švejk lifted the field chaplain, lowered him onto the floor, and while the frightened Field *Chaplain* was picking himself up off the ground, Švejk kept on talking: "So *they* see, *Field Chaplain*, Sir, that nothing happened to *them*, and to him either, to mister Faustýn, that is it was only about three times higher. He was, that is to say, this mister Faustýn totally drunk and forgot, that I live in Opatovická street on quite a low ground floor, and not the third floor like a year ago, when I used to live in Křemencová street[331] and he used to come to me for a visit."

The Field Chaplain threw from the ground a look of fright at Švejk, who standing over him on the plank bunk, was elaborating by gesticulating.

To the *Chaplain* it occurred, that he was dealing with a lunatic, therefore mumbling: "Yes, dear son, it was not even three times as high," he was shuffling slowly backwards to the door, on which he started banging so suddenly and at the same time shrieking so terribly, that they immediately opened for him.

Švejk saw through the barred window, how *the Field Chaplain* is hurriedly stepping across the court yard under the escort of a guard, while gesticulating animatedly.

"Now they're probably taking him to the nut ward," thought to himself Švejk, jumped off the plank bunk, and strolling with a military step, was singing to himself:

The little ring which you gave me, that I won't wear.
Damn all, why not then.
Once I come to my regiment,
into my rifle I'll load it...

A few minutes after that they were announcing the field *chaplain* at General Fink's.

\*

At the General's there was again one great gathering, in which there were playing an excellent role two pleasant ladies, wine, and liqueurs.

There was here from among the officers' cadre the whole assembly of the morning summary court, with the exception of the ordinary infantryman, who in the morning was lighting up their cigarettes.

The Field Chaplain floated in again so fabulously like a monster in a fairy-tale into the gathering. He was pale, trembling and dignified like a man, who is conscious of the fact, that he, an innocent, was slapped to the full.

General Fink, carrying himself as of late in a very familiar manner toward the *Field Chaplain*, pulled him onto the sofa next to himself and with a plastered voice asked the *Chaplain*: "What's with you, you spiritual consolation?"

With that, one of the merry dames pitched at the *Chaplain* a Memphis cigarette. "Drink, you spiritual consolation," said General Fink to boot, pouring wine for the Field Chaplain into a large green beaker. Because the latter had not immediately taken a drink, the General himself began watering him by his own hands, and if the Chaplain had not been valiantly gulping, he would have dripped all over him.

Only after that commenced the inquiring, as to how during the dispensing of the spiritual consolation the one condemned was behaving. The *Field Chaplain* stood up and said in a voice full of tragicality: "He's lost his mind."

"That must have been a remarkable spiritual consolation," let out a laugh the General, whereupon everybody broke out into horrible laughter, while both dames started again to pitch Memphis cigarettes at the Field Chaplain.

At the end of the table was nodding off in an arm chair the Major, who had already taken in a bit too much, now woke up out of his apathy, poured quickly some liqueur into two wine glasses, blazed for himself a trail through the chairs to the Field *Chaplain* and made the stupefied servant of God drink it up with him to brotherhood. Afterwards he again rolled over to his place and kept knocking into the pillow.

By this toast to brotherhood fell the Field *Chaplain* into the snares of the devil, who was reaching for him with his outstretched arms from all the bottles on the table and from the glances and smiles of the merry ladies, who, across from him, put their feet on the table, so that at the Field *Chaplain* was peeking Beelzebub from the lace.

Up to the last moment was not the Field *Chaplain* losing the conviction, that what is being played for is his soul and that he himself is a martyr.

He also expressed it by a meditation, which he addressed to two servants of the General, who were carrying him to the adjacent rooms to lay him onto a sofa: "Sad indeed, but an exalted theater play is opening before your eyes, when with an unbiased and pure mind you'll remember so many famed sufferers, who became a sacrifice for the faith and are known by the title of martyrs. In me you see, how above sundry ordeals a man feels elevated, when in his heart dwell truth and virtue, which arm him for the seizing of a glorious victory over the most terrible suffering."

Here they turned him over with his face toward the wall he and immediately fell asleep.

He had a fitful sleep.

He was dreaming, that during the day he is performing the functions of a Field *Chaplain* and that at night he is a porter at the hotel in place of the porter Faustýn, whom Švejk threw down from the third floor.

There were arriving from all sides accusations against him to the General, that instead of a blond he brought a brunette to a guest, that instead of a divorced lady with intelligence he delivered a widow without intelligence.

He woke up in the morning wet with sweat like a mouse chased by a cat, his stomach was like on water and it seemed to him, that the priest of his in Moravia is, compared to him, an angel.

# 3

## ŠVEJK AGAIN WITH HIS *MARCH COMPANY*

That Major, who was acting as the Judge Advocate during yesterday forenoon's court proceedings with Švejk, was the selfsame figure, that was in the evening at the General's drinking to brotherhood with the Field *Chaplain* and dozing.

The sure thing was, that nobody knew, when and how the Major during the night left the General's. All were in such a state, that nobody noticed his absence, the General was even getting confused about who of those present was actually the one speaking. The Major had not been abiding among the assembled for over two hours already, but the General was nevertheless twirling his mustache, smiling stupidly and shouting: "You said it well, mister Major."

In the morning they couldn't find the Major anywhere. His overcoat was hanging in the hallway, the saber was on a coat rack, missing was only his officer's cap. They surmised, that perhaps he fell asleep somewhere in a bathroom in the building, searched all the bathrooms, but didn't find him anywhere. Instead of him they discovered on the second floor a sleeping senior lieutenant from the General's social gathering, who was sleeping on his knees, having his mug in the hole, as the sleep had caught up with him, when he was throwing up.

The Major, as if he had gotten wedged into water.

Had however somebody looked through the barred window, where there was locked up Švejk, he would have seen, how under Švejk's Russian military overcoat there are sleeping two persons on one bunk, how from under the overcoat there are sticking out two pairs of boots.

The one with spurs belonged to the Major, the one without spurs to Švejk.

Both were lying snuggled up to each other like two kittens. Švejk had a paw under the Major's head and the Major was embracing Švejk by the back of his waist, snuggling up to him like a puppy to a bitch.

There was in it nothing mysterious. It was simply the result of being conscious of one's duties on the part of mister Major.

It has surely happened to you at some time, that you were sitting with somebody and drinking all night until to the next day's forenoon, and suddenly your co-conversationalist grabs himself by the head, jumps up and yells: "Jesusmaria, I was to be at eight o'clock in the office." That is the so-called fit of duty, which arrives as some sort of splintered-off by-product of pangs of conscience. Such a man, who is set upon by this noble fit, will be swayed by nothing from his holy conviction, that he must immediately make up at the office for that, which he has missed. Those are the apparitions without hats, which the doormen in offices intercept in the corridor and lay down on a sofa in their lair for them to take a nap.

A similar fit got the Major too.

When he woke up in the armchair, suddenly it occurred to him, that he must immediately interrogate Švejk. This fit of official duty emerged at once so quickly and was carried out so sharply and with such resolve, that nobody at all noticed the disappearance of mister Major.

But they got to feel all the more heavily the Major's presence at the guard-house of the military *lock-up*. He dropped in on them there like an assassin's bomb.

The Master Sergeant on duty was sleeping at the table and all around were dozing the rest of the men in the most varied positions.

The Major with his cap to one side unleashed such a raucous tirade, that he brought the yawning in all of them to a dead stop, so that their faces acquired a grimacing expression and looking at the Major desperately and grotesquely was not a gaggle of soldiers, but a gaggle of screwfaced monkeys.

The Major was pounding his fist on the table and screaming at the Master Sergeant: "You indolent guy, I have already told you a thousand times that, your people are a shit-smeared swine gang." Turning to the dumbstruck troops, he was screaming: "Soldiers! You have stupidity gaping from your eyes, even when you're sleeping, and when you wake up, then you, guys, make faces, as if each one of you had gobbled up a wagon full of dynamite."

There followed afterwards a long and satiating sermon on the duties of all the men at the guard-house and at last the call, that they immediately open for him the lock-up, where Švejk is, that he wants to subject the delinquent to another interrogation.

So that's how in the night the Major got to be with Švejk.

He arrived there at that stage, at which all of it on the inside of him, as the saying goes, had a chance to lie around and ripen. The last burst of his was, that he ordered, that the keys to the lock-up be turned over to him.

The Master Sergeant refused in some sort of desperate remembrance of his duties, which was suddenly striking the Major with a grandiose impression.

"You shit-smeared swine gang," he was yelling into the courtyard, "if you just put the keys in my hand, I would show you."

"I dutifully report," answered the Master Sergeant, "that I am forced to lock you in and stand guard for your safety by the arrestee. When you will be wishing to walk out, condescend Major, Sir, to rap on the door."

"You little numskull," said the Major, "you baboon, you, you camel, you think, that I am afraid of some arrestee, so that you need to be standing guard by him, when I am interrogating him. Crucifix and *heaven's thunderstorm*, lock me in and look to it that you are out already!"

In the opening above the door inside a barred lantern the kerosene lamp with a wick pulled short was giving off dim light, which was barely sufficient for the Major to find the awakened Švejk, who was patiently awaiting, standing up in a military stance by his bunk, what was actually going to become of this visit.

Švejk remembered, that the best would be to give the Major a report, therefore he cried out resolutely: "I dutifully report, Major, Sir, one arrested man and otherwise nothing has happened."

The Major suddenly could not remember, why it was that he had actually come here, therefore he said: "*At ease!* Where do you have the locked up man?"

"That is, I dutifully report, Major, Sir, I," said Švejk proudly.

The Major however disregarded this answer, because the General's wine and liqueurs were producing in his brain the last alcoholic reaction. He yawned so terribly, that in any civilian it would have dislocated the jaw. In the Major, however, this yawn transferred his thinking into those brain-strudel folds, where mankind keeps the gift of singing. He dropped absolutely nonchalantly onto Švejk's plank bunk and with a voice, like that being blared out by a just-cut-down sucking piglet before its demise, he was shrieking:

*Oh, Christmas tree! Oh, Christmas tree,*
*how beautiful is your foliage!*

which he repeated several times in succession, weaving into the song unintelligible screeches.

Afterwards he rolled over on his back like a little bear cub, then rolled up into a ball and started immediately snoring.

"Major, Sir," was waking him Švejk, "I dutifully report that *they* will catch lice."

It was however of no use. The Major was sleeping as if one threw him dead in the water.

Švejk glanced at him gently and said: "So then go to sleepy-byes, you boozer," and covered him with the overcoat. Later he crawled in with him, and so then they found them snuggled up to one another in the morning.

Toward the ninth hour, when the search for the Major reached its peak, Švejk crawled off the bunk and judged it appropriate to wake up mister Major. He shook him several times very thoroughly, removed off him the Russian overcoat, until at last the Major sat up on the bunk, and looking with dull eyes at Švejk, was seeking in him the deciphering of the mystery of, what actually happened to him.

"I dutifully report, Major, Sir," said Švejk, "that they have been here several times already from the guard-house to verify for themselves, whether you're still alive. That is why I took the liberty now to wake you up, because I don't know, how long you usually sleep, so that you would not perhaps oversleep. At the brewery in Uhříněves there was a cooper. He would always sleep until six o'clock in the morning, but when he overslept, even if only by a little quarter of an hour and slept until quarter past six, then afterwards he would go on sleeping all the way to the very noon, and he kept on doing it so long, until they fired him from the job, and he then from anger committed an insult against the church and one member of our reigning dynasty."

"You be stupid, right?" said the Major not without the undertone of some sort of desperation, because he had a head after yesterday like a cracked vessel and in no way was he finding yet any kind of answer to, why he was actually sitting here, why they kept coming here from the guard-house and why the guy, who is standing before him, is babbling such silly things, that have neither head nor heel. It seemed to him all so terribly strange. He was faintly recalling, that he had been here already once at night, but why?

"I here already at night be?" he asked with a half measure of certainty.

"As ordered, Major, Sir," answered Švejk, "as I got to understand it, I dutifully report, from what mister Major was saying, mister Major came to interrogate me."

And here a dawn blared forth in the Major's head and he looked at himself, then behind himself, as if he were searching for something.

"Condescend not to have a care for anything, Major, Sir," said Švejk. "You woke up just the same way, as you arrived here. You arrived without an overcoat, without a saber and with a cap. The cap is over there, I had to take it out of your hand, because you wanted to put it under your head. A dress uniform officers' cap, that's like a top hat. To have slept on a top hat, that's something what could manage only some mister Karderaz in Loděnice[354]. That one would stretch out at the pub on a bench, put a top hat under his head, he, you see, used to sing at funerals and to each funeral he'd go in a top hat, he put the top hat nicely under his head and made himself believe, that he must not squash it, and all night he would somehow with a minuscule portion of his body weight hover above it, so that it did not bring any harm to the top hat, but actually rather benefited it, because he, when turning from side to side, was slowly brushing it with his hair, until he had it ironed."

The Major, who had then already realized the what and how, would not stop looking at Švejk with his dull eyes and was only repeating: "You to act idiotic, right? I then be here, I to go from here." He got up, went to the door and rapped on it.

Before they came to open it, he told Švejk to boot: "If the telegrram not to come, that you are you, then you to hang!"

"My heart-felt thanks," said Švejk, "I know, Major, Sir, that you take great care of me, but if perhaps, Major, Sir, you have caught here one of them on the bunk, rest assured, that if it is tiny and has a reddish little butt, then it is a male, if it is the only one and there is not found the long gray one with reddish stripes on its little belly, then it's alright, otherwise it would be a little pair, and they, the miscreants, let me tell you, multiply amazingly, even more than rabbits."

"*Let it be*," said dejectedly the Major to Švejk, as they were opening the door for him.

At the guard-house was the Major not making any more scenes, he absolutely austerely ordered them, to go and fetch a cab, and during the cab's jerking along on the miserable pavement of Przemyśl he had only such images in his head as the notion, that the delinquent is an idiot of the first order, but that he would apparently turn out to be after all an innocent dumb beast, and as for him, the Major, he doesn't have any other choice, but either to shoot himself dead immediately, when he will have arrived at home, or to send for his overcoat and saber to the General's and go to take a bath at the municipal baths and after having taken a bath to stop at the Vollgruber's wine bar, to repair his appetite in a general way and to order for the evening over the phone a ticket for a performance of the municipal theater.

Before he arrived at his apartment, he had decided for the latter.

In the apartment there was waiting for him a little surprise. He arrived just in time…

In the hallway of his apartment was standing General Fink, holding by the collar his *orderly*, treating him terribly and screaming at him: 'Where do you have your Major, you cattle beast? Speak, you animal!"

The animal however wasn't speaking because it was turning blue in the face, as the General was strangling it.

The Major while still entering upon the scene caught, that the hapless *orderly* was firmly clutching under his upper arm his overcoat and saber, which he apparently had brought out of the hallway from the General.

This scene began to entertain the Major very much, therefore he remained standing in the somewhat opened door and kept on looking at the suffering of his loyal servant, who had the rare trait, that he has been already a long time sitting like a pit in the Major's stomach because of various thievery.

The General for just a blink of an eye let go of the having-turned-blue *orderly*, only on this account, to pull out of his pocket a telegram, with which he then started slapping the Major's servant across his mug and his lips, while screaming: "Where do you have your Major, cattle beast, where do you have your Major **Judge Advocate**, cattle beast, so that you could turn over to him a telegram in an official matter?"

"Here I am," cried out Major Derwota in the doorway, whom the combination of the words 'Major Judge Advocate' and 'telegram' reminded once again of his certain duties.

"Ah," ejected General Fink, "you're coming back?" In the intonation there was so much malicious pleasure, that the Major did not answer and remained indecisively standing.

The General told him, to come with him into the sitting-room, and when they took seats at a desk, he threw the telegram battered by beating the *orderly* onto the desk for him and said to him in a tragic voice: "Read, this is your handiwork."

While the Major was reading the telegram, the General got up from the chair, was running around the room, knocking over chairs and tabourets, screaming: "And yet I'll hang him!"

The telegram was of this wording:

Infantryman Josef Švejk, the *Messenger* of the 11th March Company, went missing on the 16th of t.m. during the crossing Chyrów — Felsztyn on an official trip as one charged with securing quarters. Without delay transport infantryman Švejk to the Brigade Headquarters in Wojalycze.

The Major opened his desk, pulled out a map and pondered the fact, that Felsztyn is 40 kilometers south-east of Przemyśl, so there was apparent here a terrible mystery, how did infantryman Švejk come upon a Russian uniform in environs located over one hundred fifty kilometers from the front, since the battle positions extend along the line Sokal — Turze[355] — Kozlów[356].

When the Major informed the General of it and showed him on the map the place, where Švejk had gone missing several days ago according to the telegram, the General was roaring like a raging bull, because he was beginning to feel, that all his hopes for a summary court trial had dissipated into nothingness. He walked to the telephone, got connected to the guard-house and gave an order, to immediately bring to him, at the Major's apartment, the arrestee Švejk.

Before the order was carried out, the General, amid terrible cursing, countless times was expressing his displeasure over the fact, that he should have at his own risk had him hanged immediately without any investigation.

The Major was opposing him and saying something about, that law and justice went hand in hand, and was making speeches in altogether splendid rhetorical periods about a just trial, about judicial murders and altogether about anything imaginable, that came to his tongue with the saliva, because after yesterday he had an egregious hangover, that needed to talk itself empty.

When at last they brought Švejk in, the Major was demanding from him an explanation, how it had happened there at Felsztyn and what actually was with the Russian uniform.

Švejk properly explained it, shored it up with several examples from his history of human troubles. When the Major then asked him, why he had not said it already during the interrogation in the court, Švejk answered, that nobody actually asked him, how he got into the

Russian uniform, but that all the questions were: "Do you confess, that you have voluntarily and without any coersion put on the uniform of the enemy?" Because it was true, that he could not say anything different: "Of course — yes — certainly — that is so — indisputably." That is after all why he rejected with indignation the allegation, that had been laid down in court, that he betrayed the lord Emperor.

"That man is an utter idiot," said the General to the Major. "To be changing on the dam of a pond into some Russian uniform, left there by God knows whom, to let oneself be mustered with a party of Russian prisoners of war, that can do only an imbecile."

"I dutifully report," sounded up Švejk, "that really I myself sometimes observe in me, that I am feebleminded, especially sort of toward the evening…"

"Shut it, you ox," said to him the Major and turned to the General with the question, what then is to happen with Švejk.

"Let them hang him at his Brigade," decided the General.

An hour after that an escort was taking Švejk to the railroad station, in order to accompany him to the Staff of the Brigade in Wojalycze.

In the lock-up Švejk left behind a little memento of himself, having scratched on the wall with a little piece of wood in three columns the list of all the soups, gravies and side dishes, that he had eaten in his civilian life. It was a sort of protest against the fact, that in the course of 24 hours they didn't give him anything to put in his mouth.

Along with Švejk went this paper to the Brigade:

On the basis of the telegram number 469 is being delivered infantryman Josef Švejk, who deserted from the 11th March Company, for further processing to the Staff of the Brigade.

The escort itself, consisting of four men, was a mixture of nationalities. There was a Pole in it, a Hungarian, a German and a Czech, who was leading the escort and had the rank of *lance corporal* and was puffing himself up before his fellow countryman arrestee, exhibiting to him the horrible sway he held over him. When, you see, Švejk at the railroad station expressed the wish, that he be allowed to urinate, the *Lance Corporal* told him quite roughly, that he will urinate, once he has arrived at the Brigade.

"Alright," said Švejk, "then *they* will have to give it to me in

Jaroslav Hašek

writing, so that it will be known, when my bladder bursts, who did it to me. There is a law for that, mister *Lance Corporal*."

The *Lance Corporal*, a guy from around oxen, got startled by that bladder, and so at the railroad station the whole escort led Švejk ceremoniously to the bathroom. The *Lance Corporal*, actually, was along the whole journey making an impression of a tenacious man and had a puffed up expression on his face, as if tomorrow right away he were to get the rank of at least the commander of an army corps.

When they were sitting in the train on the Przemyśl—Chyrów line, Švejk remarked to him:

"Mister *Lance Corporal*, when I look at *them*, then I always recall some *Lance Corporal* Bozba, who, let me tell you, served in Trident. When they promoted him to *lance corporal*, then right away on the first day he suddenly started gaining in volume. His cheeks started swelling and his belly ballooned so, that the next day even his government-issue pants were not enough. And what was the worst, his ears started growing in length. So they put him in the sickbay and the *Regimental doctor* was saying, that it happens to all the *lance corporals*. That in the beginning they balloon, that in the case of some it soon passes, but this he said was such a serious case, that he could split open, because it goes from that little star to his belly button. In order to save him, they had to cut off that little star for him, and he again deflated."

From that moment Švejk was trying in vain to maintain a conversation with the *Lance Corporal* and to explain to him in a friendly manner, why it is generally said, why the *lance corporal* is the disaster of the company.

The *Lance Corporal* was not responding to it except for the dark threats, as to who of the two would be laughing, when they arrive at the Brigade. The fellow countryman had simply not come through, and when Švejk asked him, where he's from, he answered, that it is none of Švejk's business.

Švejk was trying whichever way he could with him. He was telling him, that it is not the first time, when they are taking him under escort, but that each time he had had a good time talking with all, who were accompanying him.

The *Lance Corporal*, however, kept on being reticent and Švejk continued: "So it seems to me, mister *Lance Corporal*, that *they* must have run in this world into a disaster, since *they* lost the power of speech. I knew many sad *lance corporals*, but such a disaster of God, like you are, mister *Lance Corporal, they* forgive me and be not angry, I have yet not seen. *They*, do confide in me, what is troubling *them*, and may be, that I will give *them* advice, because a soldier, whom they take under an escort, such has always more experience than those, who are guarding him. Or, *they* know what, mister *Lance Corporal*, so that the journey would be passing better for us, *they*, narrate something, let's say about how it looks like where *they* live and in the vicinity, whether *they* have fish ponds there, or perhaps there is a ruin of some castle, so *they* could be telling us, what tale is associated with that?"

"I've had enough already," cried out the *Lance Corporal*.

"Then *they* are a lucky man," said Švejk, "some men never have enough."

The *Lance Corporal* cloaked himself in absolute reticence, when he had spoken his last word: "At the Brigade they will paint your world black and set you straight, but I will not *bother* myself with you."

Among the escort there was altogether very little talk to pass the time. The Hungarian was talking to the German in an odd way, since of German he knew only *yes indeed*, and *what*? When the German was telling him whatever it was, the Hungarian was nodding and saying *Yes indeed*, and when the German fell silent, the Hungarian said *what*? and the German started again. The Pole of the escort kept an aristocratic bearing, was not paying any attention to anybody and was amusing himself, by blowing his nose onto the ground, using for that end very skillfully the thumb of his right hand, and then was pensively smearing it on the ground with the butt of the rifle and then mannerly he was wiping the butt messed up with swine-filth against his pants, while he incessantly kept mumbling an address: "The Holy Virgin."

"You don't know much of that do you," Švejk said to him. "At Na Bojišti there lived in one basement apartment street-sweeper Macháček, that one blew his nose onto a window and smeared it so skillfully that it became a picture of Libuše[332] prophesying the fame of Prague. For each such picture he would get from his wife such a government-stipend wallop, that he had his mug looking like a bale, but he would not stop it and was continually perfecting his skill. It was also his only amusement."

The Pole gave him no reply to that and in the end the whole escort was in deep silence, as if it were riding to a funeral and was thinking in piety of the poor deceased.

Thus they were drawing near to the Staff of the Brigade in

Wojalycze.

\*

In the meantime at the Staff of the Brigade there had transpired certain very substantial changes.

The management of the Staff of the Brigade was delegated to Colonel Gerbich. That one was a mister of great military capabilities, which struck him in the legs in the form of gout. He had, however, very influential persons at the Ministry, who had brought it about, that he did not retire and was now loafing around various staffs of larger military formations, was drawing increased service pay with the most varied wartime pay bonuses and would stay as long put in place, until in a fit of gout he would commit some idiocy. Then they would again transfer him elsewhere and usually it was actually a kind of a promotion. With the officers at lunch he usually wouldn't talk of anything else than his swollen toe, which now and then attained ominous dimensions, so that he would have to wear a special big shoe.

At mealtime his most cherished amusement was to be telling everybody, how his toe oozes and constantly weeps, so that he has to have it in cotton wool, and that the exudations smell like beef soup gone sour.

That is also why the whole officers' cadre was always earnestly saying good-bye to him, when he was departing for another place. Otherwise he was a very jovial man and behaved in a completely friendly manner toward lower officer ranks, whom he was telling, how much, in earlier times, before this had afflicted him, good stuff he'd drink up and eat.

When they had transported Švejk to the Brigade and in accordance with the order of the duty officer, they brought him with the appropriate documents to Colonel Gerbich, sitting there with him in his office was Lieutenant Dub.

Over the several days following the march Sanok—Sambor Lieutenant Dub had gone again through an adventure. That is to say, on the other side of Felsztyn the 11th March Company encountered a transport of horses, which they were leading to the light dragoon regiment, to Sadowe-Wisznie[333].

Lieutenant Dub himself actually did not even know, how it happened, that he wanted to show Senior Lieutenant Lukáš his riding skills, how he jumped to mount one horse, that disappeared with him in the valley of the brook, where later they found Lieutenant Dub firmly planted in a little marsh, so that perhaps even the most skillful gardener could not plant him like that. When they pulled him out with the help of slings, Lieutenant Dub was not complaining about anything, only softly groaning, as if he were on his last legs. So they hauled him to the Staff of the Brigade, as they were pulling past, and unloaded him there in a small military field hospital.

In a couple of days he came to, so that the physician proclaimed, that two or three more times they'd smear his back and belly with iodine tincture and that afterward he can valiantly again catch up with his unit.

Now he was sitting then at Colonel Gerbich's and was talking with him about the most varied diseases.

When he beheld Švejk, he cried out in a great voice, because he was aware of the mysterious disappearance of Švejk before Felsztyn: "So we've got you again already! Many as miscreants journey out and even worse predators return. You are also one of them."

For the sake of adding for completeness it is proper to remark, that Lieutenant Dub during his adventure with a horse suffered a slight concussion, therefore we must not be amazed, that stepping closer to Švejk he was screaming in rhyming verses, challenging God to a struggle with Švejk: "Father, behold, I'm invoking Thee, with smoke are cloaking me the thundering cannons, terrifyingly is streaking by a swooshing missile, director of battles I'm invoking Thee, Father, Thou accompany me to set upon this hoodlum… Where have you been so long you shameless rube? What sort of uniform is it that you have on you?"

It's proper to add still, that the Colonel afflicted by the gout had everything in his office arranged very democratically, when right then he wasn't having a fit. Passing through at his place were all kinds of NCOs, in order to hear out his opinions of the swollen toe with the flavor of beef soup turned sour.

In the times, when Colonel Gerbich was not suffering seizures, his office used to be full of the most varied NCOs, because he, in such extraordinary cases, was very merry and talkative and liked to have round him listeners, to whom he could be relaying swinish jokes, which was making him feel very good and for the others it was causing the joy, that they were forcing laughter over old jokes, that had perhaps been already in circulation during the times of General Laudon.

Service under Colonel Gerbich used to be at such times very easy, all did, what they wanted, and wherever at some command Staff, there appeared Colonel Gerbich, there it was a sure thing, that stealing was going on and mischief of all kinds was being done.

Even now there had piled up with Švejk, who was brought in, into the Colonel's office NCOs of the most varied kinds and were waiting, what will be happening, while the Colonel was studying the communication to the Staff of the Brigade, composed by the Major from Przemyśl.

Lieutenant Dub however was continuing his conversation with Švejk in his customary, lovable manner: "You don't know me yet, but once you get to know me, you will stiffen with fright."

The Colonel turned witless like a dazed deer from the Major's document, because the Major in Przemyśl had been dictating the composition while still under the influence of a very, very slight alcohol poisoning.

Colonel Gerbich, however, was nevertheless in a good mood, because both yesterday and today ceased the unpleasant pains and his toe behaved quietly like a lamb.

"So what wrong did you actually commit," he asked of Švejk in such a kind tone, and Lieutenant Dub felt a prickly pain near his heart and he was compelled to answer himself in place of Švejk:

"This man, Colonel, Sir," he was presenting Švejk, "is making himself act the imbecile, in order to cover with his imbecility his rascally deeds. I'm not, it's true, acquainted with the content of the communication delivered along with him, nevertheless I'm of the opinion, that the guy has again committed some wrong, but on a larger scale. If you would allow me, Colonel, Sir, for me to be able to get acquainted with the content of the communication, I could definitely eventually give you certain directives, how to dispose of him."

Turning to Švejk, he said to him in Czech: "You're drinking my blood, right?"

"I am," answered Švejk in a dignified manner.

"So imagine him Colonel, Sir," Lieutenant Dub continued in German. "You can't ask him about anything, you can't talk at all with him. One day the scythe has to hit the stone and it will be necessary to punish him in an exemplary way. Allow me Colonel, Sir…"

Lieutenant Dub burrowed into the file compiled by the Major from Przemyśl, and when he finished reading, he cried out ceremonially toward Švejk: "With you it's now the amen, where did you put the government-issue uniform?"

"I left it on the dam of the fish pond, when I was trying on these rags, how it is for the Russian soldiers to walk in them," answered

Švejk, "Thing is, it actually isn't anything other than a mistake."

Švejk started telling Lieutenant Dub all, that he had endured on account of that mistake, and when he finished, Lieutenant Dub hollered at him:

"Now only, you'll get to know me. Do you know, what it is, to manage to lose government-issue property, do you know, what it means, you rogue, to be dispossessed of the uniform in war?"

"I dutifully report, *Lieutenant*, Sir," answered Švejk, "that when a soldier loses his uniform, then he must get a new one issued."

"Jesusmaria," cried out Lieutenant Dub, "you ox, you animal, you, you'll be messing with me so long, that you'll be after the war serving one hundred years to make up for the times spent in the brig."

Colonel Gerbich, who up to now was sitting calmly and judiciously at the desk, screwed his face terribly all of a sudden, because his up-to-now calm toe changed with the seizure of gout from a mild and calm lamb into a roaring tiger, into an electric current of 600 Volts, into a limb being crushed slowly by a hammer into gravel. Colonel Gerbich only waved his hand and roared with a horrifying voice of a man slowly being roasted on a spit: "Everybody out! Hand me a revolver!"

This already they all knew, and that is why they burst outside even with Švejk, whom the guard had dragged out into the corridor. Only Lieutenant Dub remained and still wanted at this moment, which seemed to him so fitting, to start in on Švejk and told the screwfaced Colonel: "I take the liberty to point out, Colonel, Sir, that this man…"

The Colonel mewled and threw at the Lieutenant an inkpot, after which the horrified Lieutenant Dub saluted and said: "Of course, Colonel, Sir," and disappeared through the doorway.

Afterward, for a long time there were heard coming out of the Colonel's office roaring and howling, until in the end the painful moaning fell silent. The toe of the Colonel's changed suddenly again into a calm lamb, the gout attack passed, the Colonel rang for help and ordered, that they bring to him again Švejk.

"So what's actually with you," asked the Colonel of Švejk, as if all the unpleasantries had fallen off him, and who felt as liberated and blissful, as if he were lying about in the sand on the marine coast.

Švejk, smiling amiably at the Colonel, was telling him his whole odyssey, how he's the Messenger of the 11th *March Company* of the 91st Regiment and how he doesn't know, how they will manage there without him.

The Colonel was also smiling and then issued these orders: "Prepare for Švejk a military fare-card via Lwów to the station Zóltance, which tomorrow his March Company is to reach, and issue to him from the warehouse a new government-issue uniform and 6 crowns and 82 halers in place of the mess rations for the road."

When afterward Švejk was leaving the Staff of the Brigade in a new Austrian *uniform*, in order to set out to the railroad station, gawking in the Staff Headquarters was Lieutenant Dub, who was not a little surprised, when Švejk announced himself to him strictly in the military manner, showed him the documents and asked solicitously, should he relay something from him to mister Senior Lieutenant Lukáš.

Lieutenant Dub did not manage any other expression than the little word *Fall out!* And when he was gazing at Švejk increasing the distance between them, then he was only mumbling to himself: "You will get to know me yet, Jesusmaria, you will get to know me..."

\*

At the Zóltance[334] station there was a gathering of the whole Battalion of *Captain* Ságner, with the exception of the *rear guard* of the 14th *Company*, that had gotten lost somewhere, as they were bypassing Lwów.

Upon entering into the little town Švejk found himself in a totally new environment, because here it was already apparent from the universal bustle, that he isn't that much farther from the battle position, where the rumble is on. All around there were lying artillery and transport units, out of each house were stepping soldiers of the most varied regiments, in their midst like elites were walking Germans from the Reich, aristocratically handing out to the Austrians cigarettes from their plentiful supplies. By the kitchens of the Reich Germans in the square there were even barrels of beer, where they were pouring for the soldiers beer from the tap into measuring cups for lunch and dinner, round which barrels were dragging like picky cats the neglected Austrian soldiers with bellies distended by the dirty-looking brew-up of sweetened chicory.

Groups of Jews marked by temple locks and dressed in long caftans, pointing out the clouds of smoke in the west to one another, talking with their hands. There was screaming everywhere, that those were Uciszków[335], Busk[336] and Derewiany[337] burning on the river Bug.

Audible distinctly was the thunder of cannons. Here for a change they were screaming, that the Russians are bombarding Kamionka

Strumilowa[338] from Grabowa[339] and that there is fighting along the whole length of the Bug, and that soldiers are detaining those on the run, who already wanted to return across the Bug again to their homes.

Everywhere reigned confusion and nobody knew anything definite, whether the Russians hadn't gone again on the offensive and hadn't brought their uninterrupted retreat to a dead stop along the whole front.

To the military Command Headquarters of the little town, military police patrols were bringing every so often some frightened Jewish soul with the accusation of spreading false and misleading reports. There they would then beat the hapless Jews bloody and release them with backsides all cut up to their homes.

Into that confusion walked in then Švejk and was searching the little town for his *March Company*. Still at the railroad station he already just about got into a conflict at the staging point command. When he came to the desk, where they handed out information to soldiers looking for their units, some corporal burst out yelling from behind the desk, whether Švejk perhaps doesn't want him to go and search out the *marchgang* for him. Švejk told him, that he only wants to know, where in this little town is encamped the 11th *March Company* of the 91st Regiment of such and such march battalion.

"For me it is very important," was emphasizing Švejk, "to know where the 11th *March Company* is, because I am its *Messenger*."

In addition to all the bad luck there was sitting at the next desk some staff Master Sergeant, who jumped up like a tiger and hollered at Švejk: "Damn pig, you are a *Messenger* and don't know, where your *March Company* is?"

Before Švejk could answer, the staff Master Sergeant disappeared into the office and after a while was escorting out of there a fat senior lieutenant, who looked as dignified as an owner of some large butcher firm.

Staging point Command Headquarters used to be also traps for roaming soldiers turned wild, who would perhaps for the whole duration of the war be looking for their units and roaming from staging point to staging point, and they would like the best to be waiting in lines by those tables at the staging point command headquarters, where there was the sign *Mess Rations Money*.

When the fat Senior Lieutenant entered, here the Master Sergeant cried out "*Attention!*" and the senior lieutenant asked Švejk: "Where do you have the documents?"

When Švejk presented them to him and the Senior Lieutenant verified for himself the correctness of his *march route* from the Staff of his Brigade to Zóltance to his Company, he handed them back to Švejk again and said magnanimously to the corporal at the desk: "Give him the information," and again he shut himself in the adjacent office.

When the door snapped shut behind him, the staff Master Sergeant took Švejk by the shoulder, and taking him to the door, he relayed to him this information: "See to it, you stench, that you disappear!"

And so Švejk found himself again in that confusion and was now searching for any acquaintance from the Battalion. He was walking the streets for a long time, until at last he bet on a single card.

He stopped one Colonel and in his broken German was asking him, whether he perhaps doesn't know, where is encamped his Battalion with his *March Company*.

"With me you can speak Czech," said the Colonel, "I am also a Czech. Your Battalion is encamped in the next village in Klimontów[340] on the other side of the railroad, and the little town is off limits, because guys from one of your companies brawled in the square with the Bavarians, as soon as they arrived."

Švejk then set out to Klimontów.

The Colonel called after him, reached into his pocket and gave Švejk five crowns, to buy cigarettes for himself with the money, and, once again saying kind good-byes, he was increasing the distance from Švejk and was thinking to himself: "What a likeable soldier boy."

Švejk continued on his way to the village, and thinking about the Colonel, he arrived at the conclusion, that twelve years ago in Trident there was some Colonel Habermaier, who also would behave so kindly toward soldiers, and in the end it turned out, that he is homosexual, when he wanted in the baths near Adige[341] to defile one cadet candidate, threatening him with *service regulations*.

While having these gloomy thoughts came Švejk slowly to the nearby village and it didn't take much of his effort to find the Staff of the Battalion, because even though the village was quite extensive, there was only one decent building there, a large grade school, which in this purely Ukrainian region built the Galician Land Administration for the goal of substantial Polonization of the community.

The school had during the war gone through several phases. There had been stationed quite a number of Russian staff headquarters, Austrian staff headquarters, at one time the gymnasium was turned into an operating room in times of big battles deciding the fate of

Lwów. Here they would cut off feet and hands and carry out trephinations of the skulls.

Behind the school in the school garden there was a large, funnel-shaped pit caused by the explosion of an artillery grenade of large-caliber. In the corner of the garden there stood a thick pear tree, on one of the branches of which there was hanging a piece of cut rope, on which was hanging not long ago the local Greek Catholic priest, hanged upon the denunciation by the local Polish head teacher, that he was a member of a group of Old Russians and that during the Russian occupation he celebrated in the church a mass for the victory of the arms of the Russian Orthodox Czar. It was not true as it happens, because at the time the accused was not present at all in that location, having been in therapy on account of his gall bladder stones in the little spas untouched by the war, in Bochnia Zamurowana[342].

In the hanging of the Greek Catholic priest several components played a role: ethnicity, a religious squabble and a hen. You see, the hapless priest just before the war killed in his garden one of the teacher's hens, that used to pluck out his planted melon seeds.

After the poor deceased Greek Catholic priest the rectory remained empty and it can be said, that everybody took something left by the priest as a memento.

One small Polish farmer even carried home an old piano, whose top board he used to fix the wicket of a pigsty. Soldiers chopped up part of the furniture, as was the custom, and due to a lucky accident there remained unscathed the large stove in the kitchen with an outstanding stove top, because the Greek Catholic priest did not differ in any way from his ultramontane colleagues and liked to have his din-dins and liked having many pots and pans on the stove top and in the oven.

And here it became a sort of tradition, that all units of armies passing through would cook here in the kitchen for the officers. Upstairs then, in the large sitting room, there used to be a sort of an officers club. The tables and chairs they had collected from the populace of the village.

Just today the officers of the Battalion organized a festive dinner, they pooled their money and bought a pig for themselves, and cook Jurajda was making a pig-feast for the officers, encircled by various freeloaders from the ranks of officer servants, above whom excelled the Accounting Master Sergeant, who was giving pieces of advice to Jurajda, how to carve the pig's head, so that there would be left for him a chunk of the little snout.

The most bugged out eyes of all had the bottomless glutton Baloun.

Perhaps that's how cannibals look with appetite and greed on, how from a missionary being grilled on a spit is oozing fat, giving out a pleasant aroma as it's being rendered. Baloun was feeling about the same as a milkman's dog pulling a cart, past whom a sausage maker's helper is carrying on his head a basket with fresh smoked sausages from the smoke house, while a string of the smoked sausages is hanging out of the basket down his back, so that just a jump and a snatch would do, if it weren't for the bothersome leather harness, in which that wretched dog is hitched, and the miserable muzzle.

And the jitrnice hash-and-crumb filling, undergoing the first period of its genesis, a huge jitrnice embryo in a pile on the rolling board was giving out the fragrance of black pepper, fat, liver.

And Jurajda with his sleeves rolled up was so solemn, that he could serve as model for a painting of how God is creating out of chaos the globe of the Earth.

Baloun could not hold himself back and broke into sobs. His sobbing was escalating into heart-breaking weeping.

"Why are you bawling and roaring like a raging bull?" asked him cook Jurajda.

"I just remembered home," answered the sobbing Baloun, "how I used to be always at home right there where it was happening and how I never wanted to send even to my best neighbor a little food basket, I only always wanted to devour it all by myself and also did. Once I crammed myself so full of the jitrnice, blood sausage, and boiled pork from pig's head and neck, that everyone thought that I'd burst, and they were chasing me with a whip round and round the yard, like when a cow bloats after having grazed on clover. — Mister Jurajda, *they* allow me to run my fingers through that jitrnice filling, and afterward let them tie me up, for otherwise I will not survive the anguish."

Baloun got up from the bench, and staggering as if drunk, he stepped up to the table and stretched his paw in the direction of the pile of hash-and-crumb filling.

There commenced a tenacious struggle. Only barely could all those present overcome him, so that he would not pounce on the filling. The only thing they could not prevent, when they were throwing him out of the kitchen was, that he reached in desperation into the pot and ran his hand through the soaked gut casings for the jitrnice.

Cook Jurajda was so angry, that he threw after the escaping Baloun a whole bunch of little sticks and hollered after him: "Stuff yourself with the wooden skewers, you miscreant!"

At that time there were already upstairs gathered the officers of the Battalion, and while they were festively awaiting that, which was being birthed down in the kitchen, they were drinking on account of the shortage of other alcohol vulgar rye booze, tinted yellow by the brew-up of onion, about which claimed the Jewish merchant, that it was the best and the most genuine French cognac, that he inherited from his father, and that he had it, moreover, from his grandfather.

"You guy," said to him on that occasion Captain Ságner, "if to boot you say, that your great grandfather bought it from the French, as they were fleeing from Moscow, then I'll have you locked up, until the youngest of your family is the oldest."

While after each swig they were cursing the enterprising Jew, Švejk was sitting already at the Battalion Office, where there was nobody with the exception of one-year-volunteer Marek, who as the historian of the Battalion used the delay of the Battalion at Zóltance, to describe for the stockpile some of the victorious fighting, that would apparently break out in the future.

For the time being he was making certain sketches, and he had just had written, when Švejk entered: "Should in our spiritual sight appear all those heroes having participated in the fighting around the village N, where side by side with our Battalion fought one Battalion of the Regiment N and the second battalion of the Regiment N, we see, that our n-th Battalion exhibited the most outstanding strategic capabilities and contributed undeniably to the victory of the n-th Division, having the goal to definitely reinforce our positions in the sector N."

"So you see," said Švejk to the one-year volunteer, "here I am again."

"Allow me, to sniff you over"," said the lovingly moved one-year volunteer Marek, "hmm, you really do reek of jail."

"As usual," said Švejk, "it was only a teeny misunderstanding; and what are you doing?"

"As you can see," answered Marek, "I'm committing onto paper heroic saviors of Austria, but somehow it doesn't want to jell together and it's all onanopoop. I'm emphasizing the 'N' in it, which letter has attained an unusual perfection both in the present and the future. Beside the previously detected skills, *Captain* Ságner has discovered

Jaroslav Hašek

in me an unusual mathematical talent. I have to check the Battalion's accounting and so far I have reached this conclusion in my closing of the books, namely that the Battalion is totally in the red and that it is only waiting for, how it could somehow settle accounts with its Russian creditors, because it is after a defeat or a victory that there is the most stealing going on. Needless to say, none of it matters. Even if we had our heads handed to us, here are the documents of our victory, because in the role of the *battalion chronicler* I am honored by the fact, that I can write: 'Once again turn toward the enemy, who was already surmising, that the victory is on his side. An onrush of our ordinary soldiers and a bayonet attack was the work of a moment. The enemy is fleeing in desperation, he is hurtling himself into his own trenches, we are stabbing him without mercy, so that in disarray he's leaving his trenches, leaving in our hands both the wounded and the unwounded prisoners of war. It is one of the most glorious moments.' He who will have outlived it all is writing and sending home by the field post a card: 'They got their ass kicked, dear wife! I am healthy. Have you weaned our brat already? Just don't be teaching him to call strangers daddy, because that would be hard for me.' The censors then strike out 'They got their ass kicked' on the card, because it is not known, who got it, and various speculations could arise, because it was unclear."

"The main thing, to speak clearly," uttered in passing Švejk. "When there were missionaries at the St. Ignatius in Prague in the year 1912, then there was a preacher there, and he was saying from the pulpit, that he will perhaps not get reunited with anybody in heaven. And there was at that evening spiritual exercise a tinsmith, Kulíšek, and he was after that religious service saying at the pub, that the missionary must have perhaps committed a lot of things, since he was announcing at the church, as if during a public confession, that he would not be reunited with anybody in heaven; why do they send such people to the pulpit. One is to always speak clearly and distinctly, and not in any such roundabout ways. At Brejška's there was years ago a wine cellar steward and it was his habit, when he was lit and was going home after work, to stop on the way at one night coffeehouse and to be toasting with strangers among the guests and always while toasting to say: We say up your, you say up your... For that he once got from some decent gentleman from Jihlava such a one across the mug, that the coffeehouse owner in the morning, when they had swept out the teeth, called his darling daughter, who was attending fifth grade in the school, and asked her, how many teeth does an adult have in his trap. Because she didn't know, he knocked out two of her teeth, and on the third day he got a written message from the wine cellar steward, in which the latter was apologizing for all the unpleasantries, that he had caused him, that he didn't want to say anything vulgar, but that the public is not understanding him, because it is actually like this: We say up your, you say up your blood pressure went and you're angry at us? He who engages in some double talk, must first deliberately consider it. A direct man, who speaks plainly, rarely gets beaten across his mug. And if it has already happened to him several times, then he is especially careful and better keeps his mouth shut in a social gathering. It's true, that of such a man everybody thinks he's goofy and God knows what, and that quite many times they'll also butcher him, but that already comes with his prudent deliberation, his self-control, because he must figure, that he is alone and that against him there are a lot of people, who feel slighted, and if he were to begin to brawl with them, he'd get even a double portion of it. Such a man must be modest and patient. In Nusle there is some mister Hauber, him they once on a Sunday in Kundratice[343] on a road stabbed by mistake with a knife, as he was coming back from an outing to Bartůněk's mill[344]. And he, with the knife in the back, came all the way home, and when the wife was taking off his coat, then she nicely pulled it out of the back for him and in the forenoon she was with that knife already cutting the meat for goulash, because it was made of Solingen[345] steel and nicely sharpened and all the knives they had at home were saw-edged and dull. She then wanted to have a whole set of such knives for the household and would send him always on Sunday to Kundratice for an outing, but he was of such modest needs, that he wouldn't go anywhere but to Banzet's in Nusle, where he knew, that when he is sitting in the kitchen, Banzet[346] will throw him out, before anybody can get his hands on him."

"You have not changed in any way," said to him the one-year volunteer.

"I haven't," answered Švejk, "I haven't had time for that. They even wanted to shoot me dead, but that would not have been the worst yet, I have not yet gotten *soldier's pay* anywhere since the twelfth."

"Here with us you won't get it now, because we're going onto Sokal and *soldier's pay* will be paid out only after the battle, we have to be frugal. If I figure, that it'll blow up there in two weeks, then with each fallen soldier there will be savings including *bonuses* of 24 Cr.

72hal.

"Other than that, what is new with you?"

"First of all our *rear guard* went missing, then the officers' cadre is having a pig-feast at the rectory and the rank-and-file have spread throughout the village and are committing the most varied immoralities with the local female populace. In the forenoon they tied up one soldier from your *Company* on account of that he was climbing up into a loft after a seventy year old hag. That man is innocent, because in the order of the day there was nothing about, up to what age it is allowed."

"I would have thought so too," said Švejk, "that the man is innocent, because when such a hag is climbing up the ladder, then one does not see up to her face. There was just such a case at maneuvers near Tábor. One platoon of ours was *quartered* at the pub and some broad was in the hallway scrubbing the floor and some Chramosta danced in on her and slap-patted her — how should I put it telling you — on the skirt. She had a mightily developed skirt, and when he slapped her so across it, she nothing, he slaps her the second time, slaps her the third time, and she again nothing, as if it had nothing to do with her, so he resolved to act and she calmly kept on scrubbing around on the floor, and afterward she turns to him with her full face and says: 'So there, I got you soldier boy.' That hag was over seventy years of age and she was telling about it afterward throughout the whole village. — And now I would take the liberty to inquire of you whether during my absence you had not been locked up as well."

"There had not been the opportunity for it," was apologizing Marek, "but, making up for it, when it comes to you, I have to inform you that the Battalion has issued an arrest warrant for you."

"It doesn't matter," remarked Švejk, "they did absolutely the right thing, the Battalion had to issue an arrest warrant for me, that was their duty, because there had been nothing known about me for such a long time. That was no rash deed on the Battalion's part. — You were saying then, that all the officers are at the rectory at the pig-feast? So now I have to go there and present myself, that I'm here again, because as it is mister *Senior Lieutenant* Lukáš has been greatly concerned for me."

Švejk set out to the rectory with a firm military step, while he was singing to himself:

        Have a look at me,

> my darling pleasure,
> have a look at me,
> how they have made
> a master out of me…

Then Švejk entered the rectory up the stairs, from where was coming the sound of the officers' voices.

The talk was about all kinds of things and they were just then yaking razzing the Brigade, what disorders reigned over at the Staff, and the adjutant of the Brigade too laid a log under the Brigade fire, remarking: "We were telegraphing after all on account of this Švejk, Švejk…"

"*Present!*" yelled out behind the slightly open door Švejk, and stepping inside, he repeated: "*Present! Dutifully report, infantryman Švejk, Company Messenger, 11th Marching Company!*"

Seeing the stunned faces of *Captain* Ságner and Senior Lieutenant Lukáš, in which was reflecting a sort of quiet desperation, he was not waiting for a question and cried out: "I dutifully report, that they wanted to shoot me dead, that I betrayed the lord Emperor."

"For Jesus Christ, what is it you're saying, Švejk," yelled out the desperately pale Senior Lieutenant Lukáš.

"I dutifully report, it went like this, *Senior Lieutenant*, Sir…"

And Švejk began to describe in great detail, how it actually happened to him.

They were watching him with their eyes popped out, he was narrating including all kinds of details, he even did not forget to remark, that on the dam of that fish pond, where the disaster happened to him, there were growing forget-me-nots. When he was then reciting the Tatar names, with which he had become acquainted on his pilgrimage, such as Hallimulabalibej, to which names he added a whole row of names created by his own self, such as Valivolavalivej, Malimilamalimej, Senior Lieutenant Lukáš could not hold back a remark anymore: "Watch that I'll kick you, you cattle beast. Continue briefly, but coherently!"

And Švejk continued with his thoroughness, and when he came all the way to the summary court trial and the General and the Major, he mentioned this, that the General had a squint in the left eye and that the Major had blue eyes, "…which keep turning after me-wise," he added then in rhyme.

The 12th Company's commander Zimmerman threw at Švejk a

little cup, from which he was drinking mighty powerful booze from a Jew.

Švejk continued further completely undisturbed, about how it then came to the spiritual consolation and how the Major slept until morning in his embrace. Then he excellently defended the Brigade, where they had sent him, when the Battalion requested him as having been lost. Presenting then documents before *Captain* Ságner, that as can be seen, he had been cleared by the high court of the Brigade of any suspicion, he reminded: "I take the liberty to dutifully report, that mister *Lieutenant* Dub is located at the Brigade with a concussion and sends greetings to all of you. I request *soldier's pay* and *tobacco money*."

*Captain* Ságner and Senior Lieutenant Lukáš exchanged questioning looks between them, but just then the door opened already and in they were carrying the steaming jitrnice soup in some sort of a tub.

That was the beginning of all those pleasures, for which they have been waiting.

"You damn guy, you," said *Captain* Ságner to Švejk, being in a pleasant mood before the nearing pleasures, "you were saved only by the pig-feast."

"Švejk," added to that Senior Lieutenant Lukáš, "if anything else happens, then it'll be bad with you."

"I dutifully report, that it must be bad with me," saluted Švejk, "when a man is in the military, he must know and be familiar with…"

"Get lost!" shouted out at him *Captain* Ságner.

Švejk got himself lost and set out downstairs to the kitchen. The once-more devastated Baloun returned there and was requesting, that he be able to serve his Senior Lieutenant Lukáš during the feast.

Švejk arrived just in time for a polemic between cook Jurajda and Baloun.

Jurajda, while at it, was using unintelligible expressions.

"You are **hodule**[357] the voracious," he was telling Baloun, "you'd devour until you sweat, and if I had you carry jitrnice upstairs, then you'd be **raising hell** with them on the stairs."

The kitchen now had a different visage. The Accounting Master Sergeants from the Battalion and the Companies were enjoying the treats by the rank, according to an elaborate plan of cook Jurajda. The scribes from the Battalion, telephone operators from the Companies and several NCOs were eating eagerly from a rusty washbasin jitrnice soup diluted by hot water, so that something would be left for them.

"Nazdar!" said Accounting Master Sergeant Vaněk to Švejk, gnawing on a little trotter. "There was here a while ago our own one-year-timer Marek and he announced, that you are here again and have on you a new *uniform*. You now have gotten me into a pretty mess. He scared me, that now we won't be able to settle the *uniform* against an account at the Brigade. Your *uniform* had been found on the dam of the fishpond and we already reported it through the *Battalion Office* to the Brigade. In my books you are carried as having drowned during bathing, you didn't have to return at all and be creating unpleasantries for us with the two *uniforms*. You don't even know, what you have done to the Battalion. Each part of your *uniform* is recorded here where we are. It figures on the list of uniforms with me, at the Company, as an addition. The Company has one whole uniform too many. I made a report to the Battalion about that. Now we'll get from the Brigade an advisory, that you have gotten a new uniform there. Because the Battalion will in the meantime announce in the reports on clothing, that it has an addition of one whole set... I know it, this can bring about an audit. When it's a matter of such a trifle, they'll come to us from the Quartermaster Administration. When two thousand pairs of boots disappear, nobody cares about that... — But we've lost that *uniform* of yours," said tragically Vaněk, sucking marrow from a bone that ended up in his hand, and digging out the remainder with a match, with which he was cleaning his teeth in place of a toothpick; "on account of such a trifle there will definitely come an inspection here. When I was in the Carpathians, there came an inspection to us, because a regulation was not adhered to, that boots off the frozen soldiers were to be pulled without damaging them. They were being pulled, pulled, and on two they cracked and one had them already busted before he died. And a trouble was ready. There arrived a colonel from the Quartermaster Administration, and if it weren't for the fact, that he got, as soon as he came, such a one in the head from the Russian side and that he dropped and tumbled into the valley, I don't know, what would have come out of it."

"Did they also pull the boots off him?" asked Švejk with interest.

"They did," said pensively Vaněk, "but nobody knew who, so that we could not even put the colonel's boots in the report."

Cook Jurajda again returned from upstairs and the first glance of his fell onto the devastated Baloun, who was sitting grieved and shattered on a bench by the stove and was looking with terrible desperation at his emaciated belly.

"You'd belong among the sect of hesychasts[358]," said with sorrow the learned cook Jurajda, "they too would gaze whole days at their bellybutton, until it seemed to them, that around the bellybutton there broke the light of a halo of sainthood. Then they thought, that they had reached the third degree of perfection."

Jurajda reached into the oven, took out of there one little blood sausage.

"Stuff your face, Baloun," he said affably, "stuff yourself, until you burst, choke yourself, you insatiable beast."

Tears entered Baloun's eyes.

"At home, when we were slaughtering," remarked weepily Baloun, devouring the little blood sausage, "I would first eat a proper chunk of boiled pork from pig's head and neck, the whole snout, the heart, an ear, a chunk of liver, a kidney, the spleen, a chunk of the side, the tongue, and then…"

And in a low voice he added, as when a fairy tale is being told: "And then came jitrnice, six, ten pieces, and pot-bellied blood sausages, either with peeled barley or dried braided-bun crumbs, so you don't even know, what to bite into first, the braided bun one or the peeled barley one. All of it is melting on the tongue, everything smells so nice, and a man is stuffing his face and and stuffing his face. — Well I think," Baloun kept lamenting on, "that the cannon ball will spare me, but hunger finish me off, and that I will never again get together with such a baking tin of blood sausage filling like at home. — Headcheese, that I didn't use to like that much, because it just quivers and doesn't give out much. The wife, she on the other hand could knock herself out for headcheese, and I did not want her to have even as much as an ear in the headcheese for her, because I wanted to devour it all by myself, in such a way, as it tasted best to me. I didn't appreciate it, that deliciousness, that life of plenty, and the retired father-in-law, him I once denied a pig he asked for and I killed it, devoured it, and then in addition to all I still begrudged sending him, the old wretch, perhaps even a little food basket — and he then prophesied, that one day I'd croak of hunger."

"And already it's here and with thunder," said Švejk, from whose mouth today were involuntarily flowing only rhymes.

The sudden fit of compassion for Baloun had already left Cook Jurajda, because Baloun somehow sidled over quickly to the stove, pulled out of a pocket a piece of bread and attempted to dunk the whole slice into the gravy, which was in a large roasting pan cuddling up from all sides to a large clod of pork roast.

Jurajda smacked him across the hand, so that Baloun's slice of bread fell into the gravy, like when a swimmer at the riverside swimming facility jumps from the platform into the river.

Not having given him the opportunity to pull the delicacy from the roasting pan, he grabbed him and threw him out the door.

The crushed Baloun could still see through the window, how Jurajda is pulling out with a fork that slice of bread, that had soaked up the gravy until brownish, and how he is handing it to Švejk and is adding to it still a piece of meat sliced off the surface of the roast with the words:

"Eat, my modest friend!"

"Virgin Maria," ejected a lament behind the window Baloun, "my bread's gone down the crapper." Swaying his long arms, he went to chase down something for the tooth in the village.

Švejk, consuming the noble gift of Jurajda's, spoke up with the mouth full: "I am really glad, that I am again among my own. I would feel very sorry, if I could not keep on rendering to the Company my valuable services." Wiping off his chin the drops of gravy and lard that slid off the slice of bread, he finished:

"I don't know, I don't know what you would have done here without me, if they had delayed me there somewhere and the war had been prolonged by a couple more years."

Accounting Master Sergeant Vaněk inquired with interest:

What do you think, Švejk, how long is the war going to last?

"Fifteen years," answered Švejk. "That is self-evident, because there was once already a Thirty Years' War, and now we are by a half smarter than earlier, so 30:2=15."

"The *spotshine* of our *Captain*," sounded up Jurajda, "was telling, that he had heard, that as soon as we occupy the borders of Galicia, the campaign will not go any further. Then the Russians will start negotiating for peace."

"That would not even have been worth having warred," said emphatically Švejk. "If a war, then a war. I definitely won't be talking of peace any earlier, than when we are in Moscow and Petrograd[347]. After all, it is not worth it, when there is a world war, to be only dicking around the border. Let's take for example the Sweders during that Thirty Years' War. As far as they came from, and they got all the way to Německý Brod and to Lipnice, where they created such havoc, that till this day they speak there in the pubs after midnight in Swedish, so that nobody understands one another. Or the Prussians, they too were not from just across the field, and in Lipnice there are left after them Prussians aplenty. They had made it all the way to Jedouchov[348] and to America and back again."

"After all," said Jurajda, whom today the pork-feast had completely taken out of balance and confused, "all people have arisen from the carp. Let us take up, friends, the evolution theory of Darwin's[349]..."

Further deliberations of his were interrupted by the invasion of one-year volunteer Marek.

"Save yourself, whoever can," cried out Marek; "Lieutenant Dub arrived a while ago in an automobile at the Staff of the Battalion and brought with him that shitted up Cadet Biegler. — He is in a horrible state," kept on informing Marek, "when he climbed out with him from the automobile, he barged into the office. You know well, that as I was walking away from there, I was telling myself, that I would catch a wee snoring snooze. I stretched myself on a bench in the office then and started nicely to fall asleep, when just then he jumped on me. Cadet Biegler screamed '*Attention!*', Lieutenant Dub stood me up on my feet and now let me have it: 'There, you're amazed, aren't you, how I surprised you in the office, catching you at non-compliance with duties? Sleeping goes on only after it's been trumpeted,' to which Biegler added: 'Section 16, paragraph 9 of Garrison Regulations.' After that Lieutenant Dub banged his fist on the desk and burst out screaming: 'Perhaps you wanted to get rid of me at the Battalion, don't think, that it was a concussion, my skull will withstand quite a bit.' Cadet Biegler was at the same time paging at the desk and in addition read aloud for himself from a document: 'Divisional order number 280!' Lieutenant Dub thought, that he was laughing at him on account of his last sentence, that his skull would withstand quite a bit, he started to reprimand him for his undignified and cheeky behaviur toward older officers, and now he's escorting him here to the *Captain*, in order to complain about him."

After a while they came to the kitchen, through which one had to walk, when going upstairs, where there was sitting the whole officer cadre and where after a pork leg the plump Ensign Malý was singing an aria from the opera La Traviata, burping at the same time after the sauerkraut and greasy lunch.

When Lieutenant Dub entered, Švejk cried out: "*Attention*, all stand up!"

Lieutenant Dub stepped in tight to Švejk, in order to yell directly in his face: "Now look forward to something, now it's with you the amen! I'll have them get you stuffed as a memento for the 91st Regiment."

"*As ordered, Lieutenant*, Sir," saluted Švejk, "once I was reading, I dutifully report, that there was once a great battle, in which one Swedish king fell with his loyal horse. They transported both carcasses to Sweden, and now the two corpses are standing there, stuffed, in a Stockholm[350] museum."

"Where did you get those bits of knowledge, you shameless rube," burst out screaming Lieutenant Dub.

"I dutifully report, *Lieutenant*, Sir, from my brother, the professor."

Lieutenant Dub turned around, spat, pushing in front of him Cadet Biegler upstairs, through where one had to go to the hall. Nevertheless he couldn't resist turning around in the doorway toward Švejk and with the inexorable severity of a Roman Caesar, deciding the fate of a wounded gladiator in the circus, he had to gesture with the thumb of his right hand and cry out at Švejk: "Thumbs down!"

"I dutifully report," was screaming after him Švejk, "that I am already turning them down!"

\*

Cadet Biegler was like a fly. Over that time he had gone through several choleric stations and he got so used to it by all the rights due to him, after all the handling, which they were beginning to subject him to as one suspected of having cholera, that he had already begun wholly unconsciously constantly to release into his pants. Until at last he had gotten himself at one such observation station into the hands of some expert, who did not detect in his excrements any cholera bacilli, fortified his intestines with tannin just as a cobbler using pitched hemp rope stitches broken, leaky shoes, and sent him to the nearest staging point Command Headquarters, having found Cadet Biegler, who was like a wisp of steam over a pot, *fit for frontline duty*.

He was a warm-hearted man.

When Cadet Biegler was bringing to his attention, that he is feeling very weak, he said to him with a smile: "A gold medal for bravery you'll still manage to bear. Clearly you signed up after all voluntarily for army service."

And so Cadet Biegler set out after the gold medal.

His fortified intestines were not pitching anymore thin liquid into his pants, but there still remained with him yet a frequent urge, so that from the last staging point all the way to the Staff of the Brigade, where he met Lieutenant Dub, it was actually a case of show-of-colors rounds of all kinds of bathrooms. Several times he missed the train, because he was sitting at the railroad stations in the toilet rooms so long, until the train had left. Several times he missed changing a train, sitting in the bathroom aboard the train.

But even so, despite all the bathrooms, which were standing in his way, Cadet Biegler was still getting nearer to the Brigade after all.

Lieutenant Dub was back then still to remain for several more days under the therapeutic care at the Brigade, but on the same day, when Švejk departed for the Battalion, the Staff physician had regarding Lieutenant Dub a change of mind, when he learned, that after noon, in the direction, in which lay encamped the Battalion of the 91st Regiment, there is leaving an ambulance automobile.

He was very glad, that he got rid of Lieutenant Dub, who as always was backing up his various statements by the words: "About that we were already before the war at our place talking with mister District Administrator."

*"You with your District Administrator can lick my ass,"* thought to himself the Staff physician and was very thankful for the coincidence, that the ambulance automobiles are going up to Kamionka Strumilowa through Zóltance.

Švejk did not see Cadet Biegler over there at the Brigade, because the same had been for over two hours sitting again on the flushing equipment for the officers of the Brigade.

It is possible to say boldly, that Cadet Biegler was in such locations never wasting time, because he would repeat to himself all the famous battles of the glorious Austro-Hungarian armies, starting with the battle at Nördlingen on the 6th day of September 1634 and ending with Sarajevo on the 19th of August, 1878.

As he was thus countless times tugging at the pull-cord of the flushing toilet room and the water was noisily rushing down into the bowl, here, having squinted his eyes, he was imagining the roar of the battle, the charge of the cavalry and the boom of the cannons.

The meeting of Lieutenant Dub and Cadet Biegler was not very charming and was certainly the cause of the somewhat sour nature of their future relationship on duty as well as off duty.

When, that is to say, Lieutenant Dub was taking the bathroom by storm already for the fourth time, burned up he cried out:

"Who's in there?"

"Cadet Biegler, 11th *March Company*, Battalion N, 91st Regiment," sounded the proud answer.

"Here," was introducing himself the competitor on the outside of the door, "Lieutenant Dub of the same *Company*."

"I'll be done right away, Lieutenant, Sir!"

"I'm waiting!"

Lieutenant Dub was looking impatiently at his watch. Nobody would believe, how much energy and resilience is needed, to hold on in such a situation in front of the door another new fifteen minutes, then still five more, then the next five, and to be getting in response to knocking, banging, and kicking constantly the same answer: "I'll be done right away, Lieutenant, Sir!"

Lieutenant Dub was seized by a fever, especially when after a hopeful rustling of the paper passed another seven minutes, without the door opening.

Cadet Biegler was still so tactful on top of it all, that he was still constantly not letting the water go.

Lieutenant Dub in his slight fever began to think over, whether perhaps he shouldn't complain to the Commanding Officer of the Brigade, who, could be, will give an order to break down the door and carry out of there Cadet Biegler. It also occurred to him, that perhaps it is a breach of subordination.

Lieutenant Dub only after another five minutes actually noticed, that he would now have on the other side of the door nothing to do, that it had passed and left him a long time ago. He kept staying put in front of the toilet room on account of a sort of principle, keeping on kicking the door, behind which was constantly sounding the same: *"Finished in a minute, Lieutenant, Sir."*

At last one could hear, how Biegler was letting the water go, and in a moment both met face to face.

"Cadet Biegler," thundered at him Lieutenant Dub, "don't think to yourself, that I have been here for the same purpose as you. I came on account of this, that you had upon your arrival at the Staff of the Brigade not reported to me. Don't you know the regulations? Do you know, to whom you yielded?"

Cadet Biegler was squaring away for a while in his memory, whether he had after all perhaps committed something, which would not square away with the discipline and regulations relating to contacts of lower ranking officers with higher ones.

In his knowledge in this regard there was an egregious gap and abyss.

In school nobody lectured them on it, how is in such a case the lower officer rank to act toward another, higher one; whether he shouldn't finish pooping and fly out the doorway of the bathroom, holding up with one hand his pants and saluting with the other.

"Well then answer, Cadet Biegler!" challengingly cried out Lieutenant Dub.

And here Cadet Biegler remembered a completely simple answer, which solved it: "Lieutenant, Sir, I did not have the knowledge after my arrival at the Staff of the Brigade, that you were situated here, and having taken care of my affairs at the office, I set out immediately for the bathroom, where I had remained until your arrival."

To which he added in a festive voice: "Cadet Biegler reporting to Lieutenant Dub, Sir."

"You see, that it is not a trifle," said with bitterness Lieutenant Dub, "according to my opinion you should have immediately, Cadet Biegler, as soon as you got to the Staff of the Brigade, asked at the office, whether by chance there isn't also present here some officer from your Battalion, from your *Company*. Regarding your behavior we will make a decision at the Battalion. I am going there in an automobile, and you are coming along. — No buts!"

Cadet Biegler, that is to say, protested, that he has from the office of the Staff of the Brigade worked out *march route* by the railroad, which mode of transportation seemed to him much more advantageous considering the tremors of his rectum. Each child knows, after all, that automobiles are not equipped for such things. Before you fly through one hundred and eighty kilometers, you have dumped in the pants long since.

The demon knows what it is that happened, so that the jolts of the automobile did not at first, when they took off, have much of any effect on Biegler.

Lieutenant Dub was all desperate, that he will not succeed in carrying out the plan of revenge.

When they took off, that is to say, Lieutenant Dub was thinking in his mind: "Just wait, Cadet Biegler, when it comes to set upon you, you think, I'll have us stop."

This was also the direction, as far as was possible due to the speed, with which they were swallowing the kilometers, that he took, establishing a pleasant conversation, about how the military automobiles, having a certain predetermined distance trajectory, must not waste gasoline and be stopping anywhere.

Cadet Biegler raised against it absolutely correctly the objection, that when an automobile is waiting somewhere for something, it is not consuming any gasoline at all, because the chauffeur turns the engine off.

"If it is," continued Lieutenant Dub doggedly, "to arrive within the predetermined time at its destination, "it must not be stopping anywhere."

On the part of Cadet Biegler there did not follow any further rejoinder.

So they were cutting the air for over a quarter of an hour, when just then Lieutenant Dub felt, that he has his belly somewhat bloated and that it would be advisable to stop the automobile, climb out and enter a ditch, pull down his pants and seek relief.

He maintained the composure of a hero all the way to the 126th kilometer, when he resolutely tugged at the chauffeur's overcoat and yelled in his ear: "*Stop!*"

"Cadet Biegler," said Lieutenant Dub mercifully, jumping quickly off the automobile toward the ditch, "now you have also an opportunity."

"Thank you," answered Cadet Biegler, "I don't want to be unnecessarily holding up the automobile."

And Cadet Biegler, who was also already near tears, told himself in his mind, that he prefers to crap himself up, rather than let a beautiful opportunity to ridicule Lieutenant Dub slip by.

Before they arrived at Zóltance, Lieutenant Dub ordered a stop two more times and after the last stop he told Biegler with belligerent tenacity: "I had bikoš[351] for lunch, Polish style. From the Battalion I'm telegraphing a complaint to the Brigade. Spoilt sauerkraut and pork made unfit for consumption. The boldness of the cooks is surpassing all limits. He who doesn't know me yet, will get to know me."

"Field Marshall Nostitz-Rhieneck[352], an elite of the cavalry reserve," responded to that Biegler, "published a paper *What is Detrimental to the Stomach in War*, in which he was not recommending eating pork during the war hardships and troubles at all. Each intemperance during a march is detrimental."

Lieutenant Dub did not answer it by even a single word, only thought to himself: "I will fix your learnedness, you guy." After that he changed his mind and after all sounded up to Biegler with a totally silly question: "You then think, Cadet Biegler, that an officer, next to whom you must consider yourself according to your rank his subordinate, eats intemperately? Didn't you perhaps want to say, Cadet Biegler, that I overstuffed myself? Thank you for that crudeness. Rest assured, that I will settle that with you, you don't know me yet, but when you get to know me, then you'll remember Lieutenant Dub."

He could have on that last word almost bit his tongue in two, because they flew on the road over some pothole.

Cadet Biegler again wasn't saying anything in return, which again irritated Lieutenant Dub, so that he asked roughly: "Listen, Cadet Biegler, I think, that you have learned, that the questions of your superior you are to answer."

"Of course," said Cadet Biegler, "there is such a clause. It is necessary however in advance to analyze our mutual relationship. As far as I know, I have not been yet assigned anywhere, so that completely excludes any talk about my immediate subordination to you, Lieutenant, Sir. The most important however is, that one answers questions of the superiors in the officers' circles only regarding things pertaining to service. As the two of us here are sitting in an automobile, we do not constitute any combat unit in a certain military operation. Between us there is no official service relationship. We are both riding in the same way to our units and it would definitely not be a service-related statement to answer your question, whether I didn't perhaps want to say, that you had overstuffed yourself, Lieutenant, Sir."

"Have you finished talking?" screamed at him Lieutenant Dub, "you singular…"

"Yes," proclaimed with a firm voice Cadet Biegler, "don't forget, Lieutenant, Sir, that about this, which has happened between us, will render a judgment, apparently, the officers' honor court."

Lieutenant Dub was almost beside himself from anger and rage. He had a special habit, that when he became angry, he was saying even more stupid and silly things than when calm.

That is also why he gave a growl: "A military court martial will be rendering a decision about you."

Cadet Biegler used this opportunity, in order to finish him off completely, and that is why he said in such a most friendly tone: "You're kidding, pal."

Lieutenant Dub yelled out at the chauffeur, that he stop.

"One of us must go on foot," he babbled.

"I'm riding," responded to that calmly Cadet Biegler, "and you, pal, do what you want."

"Keep on going," in a voice as if in a delirium hooted Lieutenant Dub at the chauffeur and cloaked himself afterward in dignified reticence like Julius Caesar, when coming near him were the conspirators with daggers to pierce him.

So they arrived in Zóltance where they found the track of the Battalion.

\*

While Lieutenant Dub and Cadet Biegler were on the stairs still arguing, whether a cadet, that is not yet assigned anywhere, is entitled to a jitrnice from among that number, which is alotted for the officers of the individual companies, down in the kitchen they were already satiated and had lain out on expansive benches and had opened up a conversation about all kinds of things, while they were puffing from their pipes at full throttle.

Cook Jurajda proclaimed: "So this morning, I'll tell you, I made a wonderful discovery. I think, that it will bring about a complete revolution in cooking. I'm sure you know, Vaněk, that I couldn't here in this damned village find any marjoram for the jitrnice."

"Herba majoranae," Accountant Sergeant Major Vaněk said, recalling, that he is a pharmacist.

Jurajda continued: "It has not been researched yet, how the human soul grasps in an emergency the most varied means, how there appear to him new horizons, how he begins to invent all the impossible things, of which humankind has not even dreamt yet... I'm looking then from house to house for the marjoram, I'm running, chasing it down, explaining to them, what I need it for, how it looks..."

"Here you should have also described the aroma," sounded up from a bench Švejk, "you should have said, that marjoram smells like when you're sniffing a bottle of ink in an alley of blossoming acacias. On the Bohdalec[353] hill near Prague..."

"But Švejk," interrupted him in a pleading voice one-year volunteer Marek, "let Jurajda finish."

Jurajda kept on talking: "At one farm I came across an old veteran from the time of occupation of Bosnia and Hercegovina, who served out his army service in Pardubice with the Uhlans and to this day he still has not forgotten his Czech. This one started arguing with me, that in the Czech Lands they didn't put marjoram into the jitrnice, but chamomile. I didn't know then, really, what I am going to do, because every reasonable and unbiased man must hold marjoram, among the spices that are put in jitrnice, for a princess. It was necessary to quickly find such a substitute, that would add unique spicy taste. And so I found in one house, hung under the picture of some saint, a small wedding myrtle wreath. They were newlyweds, the twigs of the myrtle in the wreath were still quite fresh. So I put the myrtle into jitrnice, but of course, that I had to steam that wedding myrtle wreath in boiling water three times, so that the leaves would soften and lose that excessively pungent aroma and taste. It figures, that when I was taking that small wedding myrtle wreath away from them for the jitrnice, that there was a lot of weeping. They saw me off with the assurance, that for such a sacrilegious act, since the wreath had been sanctified, the first nearest round will kill me. You all clearly ate my jitrnice soup and none of you realized, that instead of marjoram it has the fragrance of myrtle."

"In Jindřichův Hradec," sounded up Švejk, "there was years ago a sausage maker Josef Linek and that one had two boxes on a shelf. In one he had a mixture of all the spices, which he would put into jitrnice and blood sausage. In the other box he had powder against insects, because this sausage maker had already found out several times, that his customers chewed up in his fat smoked sausage a bed-bug or a cockroach. He would always say, that as far as the bed-bug is concerned, it has a touch of spicy after-taste of bitter almonds, which are put in granny's marble bundt cakes, but that cockroaches in sausages stink like an old Bible riddled with mildew. That is why he kept to cleanliness in his shop and would sprinkle that powder against insects everywhere. This one time he's making blood sausages and had a head cold while at it. He grabbed the box with the powder against insects and poured it into the blood sausage filling, and ever since that time in Jindřichův Hradec would people come for blood sausage only to Linek. People were outright flocking to his store. And he was so smart, that after all he did figure it out, that it was the powder against insects that makes it so, and from that time on he would order for cash-on-delivery whole little crates of that powder, while he had first alerted the company, from which he was buying it, to mark the little crates 'Indian spice'. That was his secret, with it he went to his grave, and the most interesting thing was, that from the households of the families, that were buying his blood sausage, all cockroaches and bedbugs moved away. Since that time belongs Jindřichův Hradec among the cleanest towns in the whole Czech Lands."

"Have you finished yet?" asked one-year volunteer Marek, who wanted apparently also to mix himself into the conversation.

"I'd already be done with that," answered Švejk, "but I know of a similar case in the Beskids, but I'll tell you about that only once we are in *combat*."

One-year volunteer Marek untied his tongue: "The art of cooking is best recognized in war, especially at the front. I will take the liberty to make a little comparison. In peace we used to read and hear about the so-called ice soups, into which ice is added and which are very popular in northern Germany, Denmark and Sweden. And see, a war came, and this year in winter in the Carpathians the soldiers had so much frozen soup, that they didn't even eat it, and yet it is a specialty."

"Frozen goulash can be eaten," objected Accounting Master Sergeant Vaněk, "but not for long, about a week at most. On account of that our Ninth *Company* let go of a position."

"When there was still peace," said with uncommon gravity Švejk, "the whole army service revolved around the kitchen and around the most varied meals. We had, I tell you, in Budějovice, *Senior Lieutenant* Zákrejs, that one kept hanging around the officers' kitchen, and indeed, when some soldier committed some wrong, then he stood him up *at attention* and laid into him: 'You shameless rube, if this gets repeated one more time, then I will make of your beastly trap a thoroughly tenderized pot roast, stomping on you I'll turn you into mashed potatoes and then have you devour it. Pouring out of you will be goose giblets with rice, you will look like an interlarded hare in a baking pan. So you see, that you have to improve, if you don't want for people to think, that I have made of you a chopped roast with cabbage.'"

The next explication and interesting conversation about using the menu for bringing up ordinary soldiers before the war was interrupted by great screaming upstairs, where there was coming to the end the festive lunch.

In the confused mixture of voices was standing out the screaming of Cadet Biegler: "A soldier while still at peace is already to know, what war requires, and in war not to be forgetting, what he had learned on the training ground."

Then could be heard the snorting of Lieutenant Dub: "I implore, to have it stated, that I have been insulted for the third time already!"

Upstairs were happening great things.

Lieutenant Dub, who was harboring well-known tricky intentions with respect to Cadet Biegler before the face of the *Battalion Commander*, was immediately upon entering welcomed by the officers with great screaming. Having its remarkable effect on everybody was the Jewish booze.

So they were hollering one over the other, hinting at the riding skills of Lieutenant Dub: "Without a groom it won't go! — Spooked mustang! — How long had you been, pal, moving among the cowboys in the West? — Circus beauty-rider!"

*Captain* Ságner quickly shoved into him a tumbler of the damned booze and the offended Lieutenant Dub sat down at the table. He placed for himself an old broken chair next to Senior Lieutenant Lukáš, who welcomed him with the friendly words: "We've eaten everything up already, pal."

The sad figure of Cadet Biegler was somehow overlooked, despite the fact, that Cadet Biegler was exactly according to the regulation reporting himself around the table to Captain Ságner, as service-related, and to the other officers, repeating quite many times in succession, although they all had already seen and known him: "Cadet Biegler has arrived and attached to the Staff of the Battalion."

Biegler took a full glass for himself, sat down then quite modestly at the window and was awaiting an opportune moment, to throw in the air some of his knowledge from books.

Lieutenant Dub, for whom those horrible vapors of the singed distillate were already getting into his head, was tapping his finger on the table and out of the clean-and-clear he turned to *Captain* Ságner:

"With the District Administrator we always used to say: Patriotism, fidelity to duty, overcoming one's self, those are the genuine weapons in war! I am reminding myself of it especially today, when our military troop will in foreseeable time cross the borders."

Cadet Biegler let himself be heard from by the window. "To be crossing the borders of a great state is always a serious operation. I studied the map during my last stay at the last cholera barrack and found out, that in the section, which we're apparently moving in to occupy, there stands the triangle the individual points of which are the Russian fortresses: Luck, Dubno, Rovno.[359]

BACK MATTER

Endnotes · Translator's Postscript · Note on Editorial Assistance · *Švejk on Trial · Read Švejk First, Then Ask Me Again*

# Endnotes

(For the endnotes about the terms that appeared for the first time in Book One or Book Two, please consult the Endnotes of those volumes.)

[1] On **Illustrious Thrashing** in the Titles of Books Three and Four: The Czech noun **výprask** is derived from the verb "vypráskat", itself built on the onomatopoeic base "prásk!"—the crack of a whip, a blow, a smack. Its primary sense is a physical beating, corporal punishment administered with rod, whip, or fist, extending by natural figurative development to mean a sound defeat. When Hašek chose **Slavný výprask** for the titles of the latter two volumes, he set up a comic tension between elevated diction (slavný) and the base reality of a beating.

Of the translators, only Cecil Parrott (Penguin, 1973) rendered výprask in this context as a "licking" Paul Selver omitted the Book Three title entirely, and Book Four, Pokračování slavného výprasku (*The Famous Thrashing Continued*), did not appear in his version. The "Chicago version" used The Famous Thrashing and The Famous Thrashing Continued. The present Centennial Edition retains that structure, but replaces famous with illustrious.

Parrott's choice of licking is doubly misleading. First, the idiom has no etymological tie to Czech. English to lick = to beat, thrash is a colloquial development of eighteenth-century British slang, later popular in America, but grounded in an entirely different metaphor (tongue contact → destroy/defeat). Second, Hašek himself elsewhere uses the root lízat (*to lick*), most memorably in the chapter entitled "Švejk as a Malingerer," where military physicians administer what the soldiers call lízání chininu — *quinine licking*, that is, forcing patients to swallow quinine powder in humiliating, excessive doses. To render výprask as "licking" introduces an entirely spurious link with lízání that Hašek never intended. It risks suggesting a pun where there is none, and muddles the distinction between the prásk family (blows, smacks, cracks) and the lízat family (licking, tasting).

By contrast, thrashing follows the Czech faithfully. It denotes repeated physical blows, originally from the threshing of grain, and has long been used in English for corporal punishment and figurative defeat. Its imagery corresponds to the sound-symbolic prásk! and to the practice of beatings and floggings that underlie Hašek's choice of word. It is weighty enough to bear the comic inflation of slavný výprask (*illustrious thrashing*), while still allowing the deflationary irony Hašek intended. Unlike "licking," it avoids semantic contamination with Hašek's unrelated use of lízání.

The adjective slavný requires equal care. In Hašek's time, dictionaries such as Váša–Trávníček (2nd ed., 1941) defined it as "mající slávu, zasluhující slávy, významný (muž, čin, den, jméno, vítězství)"—that is, "*famous, deserving of fame, significant.*" No ironic use is recorded in these lexica. Only in later works, such as Poldauf's Velký česko–anglický slovník (3rd ed., 1996), is irony explicitly acknowledged (slavně iron. = "*hardly with flying colours*"). Hašek, however, repeatedly attaches slavný to contexts that are either inflated or plainly absurd—at the structural level in the book titles (Slavný výprask, Pokračování slavného výprasku), in characterizing figures (slavný arcibiskup Kohn), in everyday hyperbole (slavný grog), and in propagandistic boilerplate (slavná armáda, slavná vojska) whose bombast the narrative undercuts—and was likely among those who stretched the word into the mock-heroic ironic register that later became common.

For translation, this history matters. Glorious over-tilts toward triumphal rhetoric, alien to Hašek's comic deflation. Famous is lexically accurate, but too flat to capture the mock-heroic disproportion. Illustrious, from Latin illustris (*bright, conspicuous, renowned*), preserves the sense of renown while carrying an elevated, slightly antique register, primed for irony. It reproduces the same comic disproportion as Czech: a lofty adjective yoked to a low noun.

For these reasons, the present Centennial Edition adopts Illustrious Thrashing as the title element for Books Three and Four. The decision rests not only on considerations of register and irony, but above all on the congruence demanded by Pannwitz's dictum: that a translation should let the foreign text's own world and strangeness transform the target language, rather than bending it into familiar idiom.

[2] ['mah-diyo-ria] = Hungary. There are two names for Hungary in Czech: "Maďarsko" and "Uhry". "Maďarsko" is derived from the Hungarians' self-designation: "Magyar" ['mah-diyor], i.e. "Hungarian", "Magyarorszag", i.e. "Hungary". On the other hand, the now archaic "Uhry" seems to be derived from Old Russian "Ugre", i.e. "Hungarians", as is perhaps even the German label "Ungarn" for Hungary. (The Russian term had wider applicability, though: "Ugrian - a member of a division of the Finno-Ugric peoples that includes the Hungarians and two peoples of western Siberia.")

I attempted to preserve the tension between the modern Czech term "Maďarsko" and the Empire-era archaic term "Uhry" and translate the pair with the standard English term "Hungary" and the rare English rendition "Magyaria", respectively. The correlation between the original Czech labels for Hungary and their English counterparts in this translation is thus not based on their corresponding time period of usage, but rather on degree of familiarity.

It is not the first time "Hungary" is referred to by the English neologism corresponding to the modern Hungarian self-designation and its Czech translation. "The Canadian humorist and educator Stephen Leacock, PhD (1869-1944), used 'Magyaria' in his fictional account The Hohenzollerns in America, III.--Afternoon Tea with the Sultan, A Study of Reconstruction in Turkey: 'I was delighted to find that under the new order of things in going from Berlin to Constantinople it was no longer necessary to travel through the barbarous and brutal populations of Germany, Austria and Hungary. The way now runs, though I believe the actual railroad is the same, through the Thuringian Republic, Czecho-Slovakia and Magyaria.'" [Translator's note]

[3] Feldoberkurat (*Chief Field Chaplain*) Ibl was no doubt inspired by Feldkurat (*Field Chaplain*) Jan Eybl, a military cleric who served in Infantry Regiment No. 91 together with Jaroslav Hašek for most of the time from July 11th until September 24th 1915. During this period Eybl celebrated at least three field masses that Hašek probably attended.

Still it can hardly be more than the name that associates him with the literary Ibl. Eybl's rank was the lower *Field Chaplain* in the Reserve and he served at the front the entire period Hašek stayed in Királyhida (June 1915).

In his advanced years Jan Eybl said, that he never held a mass like the one described in *The Good Soldier Švejk*. Nor does it make sense that two march battalions headed for Serbia at the time Švejk was in Királyhida. During the spring and summer of 1915 k.u.k. Heer (*I&R Army*) didn't have troops on Serbian territory, they withdrew before Christmas 1914. It was only in October 1915 that fighting on the Balkans front flared up again.

The figure in the novel may therefore have been inspired by some other cleric, surely a military cleric from k.u.k. Feldsuperioriat or the garrison in Vienna. These were assigned duties in the area around the capital and after Jan Eybl himself was transferred here in July 1918 he held a couple of masses in Bruck. It should be noted that Ibl continued to Vienna after finishing in Bruck, indicating that he was based there and this didn't belong to IR. 91 or the garrison in Bruck. [honsi.org]

⁴ Kriegskalender (*Military calendars*) in the context of *The Good Soldier Švejk* no doubt refers to "Der Soldatenfreund. 1915 Kalender". The quoted field sermon by Feldoberkurat Ibl is adapted from pages 72 and 73 of this calendar.

Der Soldatenfreund was a series of calendars that were published by the firm J. Steinbrener from 1892 until 1919. The calendar was issued in several of the languages of the empire: German, Hungarian, Czech, Polish... Steinbrener were headquartered in Winterberg (now Vimperk) in the Šumava region, but were represented also elsewhere in Austria-Hungary and even in New York. [honsi.org]

⁵ Moson was a town in Hungary near the Austrian border which in 1939 was joined with Magyaróvár to become Mosonmagyaróvár. The river Lajta (Leitha) flows through it. [honsi.org]

⁶ Custoza is a town near Verona where a battle between Austria and Sardinia-Piedmont took place in 1848, securing Austrian control of Lombardy until the battle of Solferino in 1859. The Austrian forces were commanded by Marshall Radetzky. Custoza is situated 17 kilometers west of Verona and approximately the same distance from the southern tip of Lake Garda.

In 1866 a second battle was fought here. Again it ended with Austrian victory, but it had no lasting consequences as Italy and their ally Prussia won the short war. [honsi.org]

⁷ Carlo Alberto was king of Piedmont from 1831 to 1849, the adversary of Marshall Radetzky at the battle of Custozza in 1848. [honsi.org]

⁸ Hrt and his story is exactly what the author says. It was mainly picked from The Soldier's Friend, 1915 calendar, pages 72 and 73. Here, the hero is called Fahnenführer Veit, cz. Vít, one of some minor discrepancies. It must be assumed that the author based Feldoberkurat Ibl's sermon on the Czech version of the calendar. The War Calendar was published in several of the languages of Austria-Hungary. [honsi.org]

⁹ Aspern is now a suburb of Vienna. In 1809 it was the scene of a battle between Napoléon and an Austrian army led by Archduke Karl. [honsi.org]

¹⁰ *Created by Emperor Francis I in 1814 to award soldiers for participation in the campaign of 1813-1814. Actually the first medals were awarded only in 1815. The medal is usually called the "Cannon Cross", because its specimens were made from captured French cannons. Sometimes it is possible to come across the wrong designation "Leipzig Cross" used according to the decisive battle of the year 1813.* [svejkmuseum.cz]

¹¹ Joseph Ferdinand was an archduke of the House of Habsburg (the Tuscan

branch) and a military commander. In 1915 he was commander-in-chief of the 4th Army but was replaced due to the disastrous losses during the Brussilov offensive in 1916. After the war, he was allowed to live in Austria but had to give up his rights as a noble. He was arrested by the Nazis in 1938 and spent a short time in Dachau.

The order reproduced in *The Good Soldier Švejk* is nearly identical to one that was printed in the Czech exile press during the war. Roughly the same wording also appears in an interpellation by German nationalists in Reichsrat (*Austrian parliament*). These two are the only copies that we know were printed during the war but after 1918 several more were to follow. In Vienna's Kriegsarchiv (*War Archives*) several versions of it can be found, also in Hungarian. From the correspondence between Armeeoberkommando (*I&R Army Supreme Command*), War Ministry and War Surveil-lance it transpires that the military authorities suspected it was a fake and were in the dark about its origin. [honsi.org]

[12] Votice is a town in county Benešov, on the railway line to Tábor. [honsi.org]

[13] Osijek is a city by the river Drava in eastern Croatia, in the region of Slavonia. The city was heavily damaged during the Yugoslav wars of the 1990's. Osijek was part of Hungary until 1920.

There seems to be a great deal of authenticity in telephone operator Chodounský's story. In the early days of August 1914, Infantry Regiment No. 91 traveled through Osijek on the way to the front in Serbia. The Regiment continued to Gunja by the river Sava, where they arrived on August 4th after a three day train journey from Budějovice. [honsi.org]

[14] Croatia was during the Dual Monarchy under Hungarian administration, officially the Kingdom of Croatia-Slavonia. The area corresponded more or less to the current Croatia apart from Dalmatia and the Istria peninsula. The capital was Zagreb. [honsi.org]

[15] In Infantry Regiment No. 91 many Matějkas served during the war. One of them was Adolf Matějka from Vimperk and he was in the regiment at the same time as Hašek and the two were even taken prisoner together at Khorupan 24 September 1915. Two more Matějkas from the regiment were captured the same day. [honsi.org]

[16] Kaposfalva may refer to a town in southern Hungary, near the border with Croatia, not yet identified. It may well be meant Kaposvár, which is on the railway line south to Serbia. Kaposfalva was the Hungarian names for a couple of places in Slovakia but this doesn't fit with the story. A more plausible theory is that it was some place in Vojvodina in modern Serbia

(Vojvodina was Hungarian at the time). [honsi.org]

[17] The Central European deck differs from the Anglo-American one; it uses a "spodek" (*Underknave*) and "svršek" (*Overknave*) instead of the single Jack.

[18] *Here chef Jurajda undoubtedly had in mind the Jewish dish cholent. In Yiddish, cholent is properly pronounced as cholnt or tsholnt. The word comes from medieval French chaud-lent, meaning slow heating. Traditionally, it's made in an oven in a large ceramic pot with goose or duck, whose fat melts and mixes with peas and barley, to which ingredients like onion, garlic, marjoram, pepper, or bay leaf are added. Everything is thrown into the pot at once, mixed, and placed in a preheated but no longer actively heated oven on Friday afternoon (no fire may be kindled on the Sabbath, only allowed to smolder). It simmers and bakes there all night, finishing up for the Sabbath lunch. - Source: B. Kuras, Right-Wing Cookbook* [svejkmuseum.cz]

[19] Klárův ústav slepců (*Klár's Institute of the Blind*) was from 1832 to 1945 an institute for the blind, now the location of Česká geologická služba (Czech Geology Service). The institute was founded by and is named after Alois Klar. [honsi.org]

[20] Klárov is part of Malá Strana (*Lesser Quarter*) in Prague, the area by Vltava above Manesův most. The area is named after the linguist Alois Klar. [honsi.org]

[21] *Betl, as one of the many mariáš games, also known as "little," "Béďa," "beggar," "Bethlehem," "Bedřich," or "runaway," is, along with Nonstop, the only game, where the Ten ranks between the Underknave and Nine. Betl is also a game you have to play solo. It's a commitment, that you will not manage to win a single trick. In betl trumps don't apply, but you must beat the highest card in the trick. A player enters betl with low cards, ideally a long sequence of one suit starting from the Seven upward.* [svejkmuseum.cz]

[22] *Nonstop [from German Durch], or "big one," is the opposite of betl, where the player must win all tricks. A player enters nonstop with high cards or a long sequence of one suit starting from the Ace downward.* [svejkmuseum.cz]

[23] *Talon is a pile of cards for exchanging or drawing. In the basic variants of* volený [*choosing*] *and* licitovaný [*bidding*] *mariáš (for three players), different rules govern dealing and handling the talon. In principle, each player ends up with 10 cards, and two cards after choosing the game or bidding remain out of play in the talon.* [svejkmuseum.cz]

[24] Kaufcvik [from German kaufen]. *In some places, this game is known as* Čapáry, *in its intensified version as* Zdravíčko *or* Komando. *It was played for sixpence coins, later for ten-haléř coins. Playing with higher-value coins is*

*very risky. Since almost every round sees one of the players fail, with reckless gambling, the money in the game can grow practically in a geometric progression. The game is highly popular for its speed and excitement. However, in the absence of ten-cent coins, it is very costly for the inexperienced.* [svejkmuseum.cz]

[25] Průmyslová jednota (*Industrial Union*) was an institution for promotion of technical education. It was founded in 1833 and was closed in 1950. The library and reading room in question was located in Rytířská street in Staré město (*Old Town*). [honsi.org]

[26] India was in 1914 a British crown colony who contributed sizeable forces (one million) to the British army in World War I. Apart from the current Republic of India it included modern Pakistan, Nepal, Bhutan, Sri Lanka, Bangladesh and Myanmar. [honsi.org]

[27] Another Chodounský was in real life the owner of a detective agency in Prague. His firm is listed in the address book for 1910. In the anecdote he is only mentioned by his last name. [honsi.org]

[28] Chodounský actually did use that eye in advertisements. This one is from 1907 from Národní politika (*National Politics*):

There is also a police residence application by Štěpán Chodounský. He lived in Vinohrady, where he owned a house with no. 599, in today's Yugoslav, then Karlova street. You can read about the institute's activities article V soukromém detektivním ústavě (*At a private detective institute*), published in Národní listy (*National Pages*) on 5/10/1902 [svejkmuseum.cz]

[29] Ludwig Ganghofer was a Bavarian writer who in his time was very popular, and many of his novels have made it to the cinema. He was one of the favorite poets of Emperor Wilhelm II. and a personal friend of the Emperor.

Die Sünden der Väter (*The sins of the fathers*) (Adolf Bonz & Comp., Stuttgart, 1886) is one of the Ganghofer's lesser known novels. Previous to its publication it had appeared as a continuation in Neue Freie Presse from August 5th 1885. At the time the author lived in Vienna where he was a dramatist at Ringtheater, and contributed to a couple of newspapers. Whereas most of Ganghofer's popular work was inspired and set in the Alpine surroundings of his home area, Die Sünden der Väter is an exception. It takes place in refined city surroundings in Munich and Berlin. The setting is a theater environment. [honsi.org]

[30] Martha Kronek was one of the main characters of the novel Die Sünden der

Väter by Ludwig Ganghofer, she was an actress at Stadttheater in Munich. She is introduced after only a few pages and described as young and beautiful. Her mother also forms part of the plot. [honsi.org]

[31] Albert (first name Richard) was the main hero of the Die Sünden der Väter and is introduced at the very beginning. In the serial version of the novel in Neue Freie Presse he appears already in the first part, dated 5 August 1885. He lives in Berlin, but is from Bavaria, just like the novels narrator. It is already obvious that he is well off.

In order to verify that Albert actually is mentioned on page 161 of the second part, one would have to guess what print Hašek referred to and so far this information is not available. [honsi.org]

[32] Albrecht was an Austrian archduke of the House of Habsburg, field marshal and inspector general of the Austro-Hungarian army. His father was Karl who lead the Austrian forces against Napoléon at Aspern in 1809.

It is however unlikely that this is the Albrecht that Kadett Biegler was mumbling about. Although being a prominent military leader there is no indication that he had any detailed knowledge of cryptography.

Sergey Soloukh suggests that the person in question could be the Italian philosopher Leon Battista Alberti (1404 - 1472). He introduced a polyalphabetic encryption system, albeit long before Gronveld (see Bronckhorst-Gronsveld). The chronology in Kadett Biegler's account is thus incorrect but otherwise the hypothesis seems solid.

Alberti is a prominent name in the history of cryptography and is often called "the father of western cryptography". It is therefore highly probable that Kadett Biegler (i.e. the author) got the names mixed up and actually meant "Alberti's system". [honsi.org]

[33] Bronckhorst-Gronsveld was a Dutch count and Bavarian commander who is said to have invented the Gronsveld-method for ciphering, or more precisely: the polyalphabetic method of encryption. According to some sources the invention was done by his son Johann Franz. [honsi.org]

[34] Sardinia does not refer to the island, but to the kingdom of the same name that existed from 1720 until the unification of Italy in 1861. The kingdom consisted of Sardinia proper, Piedmont and the current French province of Savoie (Savoy), with Turin as capital. The kingdom was at war with Austria in 1848 and 1859; the famous battles at Custozza and Solferino were fought in these wars. The royal house of Sardinia continued as rulers of Italy even after unification. [honsi.org]

[35] Savoy is a historical region in the western Alps. It was part of the Kingdom

of Sardinia until 1860 when it was ceded to France. The capital was Chambéry. [honsi.org]

[36] Sevastopol is an important naval port on the Crimea peninsula, in the current Ukraine. During the Crimean War it was subjected to a 12 month long siege by British, French, Sardinian and Turkish forces in 1854-55. The siege ended with an allied victory. [honsi.org]

[37] China was from 1912 a republic but politically fragmented. It did not take part in World War I. Kadett Biegler refers to the Boxer Rebellion (1899-1902), a nationalist rebellion against growing foreign influence. Eight imperialist powers intervened and crushed the rebellion, and here it is probably alluded to the Austro-Hungarian participation. [honsi.org]

[38] Japan was in 1914 an empire with a parliamentarian constitution. From August the country entered the war on the side of the Entente and soon took possession of some German islands in Pacific Ocean. They also exploited the war to intervene in China and in 1919 they engaged in the Russian civil war by occupying Vladivostok and parts of the Russian Far East.

The war Kadett Biegler refers to took place in 1904-05 and the outcome was a Japanese victory over Russia. This was the first time a European power had been defeated by an adversary from another continent. [honsi.org]

[39] Kerckhoffs (full name Jean-Guillaume Hubert Victor François Alexandre Auguste Kerckhoffs van Nieuwenhoff) was a Dutch cryptographer and linguist, one of the founders of military cryptography.

In January and February 1883 he published his best known work on cryptography, La cryptographie militaire, an article that appeared in two parts in Journal des sciences militaires. It was regarded as one of the milestones of 19th century cryptography. Here he mentions both Fleissner and Kircher.

Kadett Biegler is however wrong when he informs Hauptmann Ságner that this was a book. It was in fact a paper presented in two parts in the above-mentioned periodical. [honsi.org]

[40] Saxony is a historic kingdom in Germany with an area slightly smaller than the current Freistaat Sachsen. It was created by Napoleón in 1806 and existed until 1918, from 1871 as part of Germany. [honsi.org]

[41] Kircher surely does not refer to a colonel in the Saxon army, but rather the German scientist, universal genius and Jesuit father who is mentioned by Kerckhoffs in his paper La Cryptographie Militaire from 1883. His work, Polygraphia nova et universalis, 1663, is considered a principal work in cryptography.

He had an enormous range of interests: Egyptology, Sinology, bible studies, geology, mathematics, medicine, astronomy, acoustics, bacteriology, to name a few. He was also a practical inventor. [honsi.org]

[42] Fleissner was in real life an Austrian colonel who in 1881 published Handbuch der Kryptographie. As Fleissner published the book five years before Die Sünden der Väter by Ludwig Ganghofer, the facts given by Kadett Biegler are dubious although all the names he mentions have some connection with cryptography. His book is briefly mentioned in the well-known essay by Kerckhoffs from 1883. The book was not published by Theresianische Militärakademie as Kadett Biegler claims. It was in fact self-published and distributed by L. W. Seidel & Sohn.

Fleissner had entered world literature even when still alive. He is mentioned in the novel Mathias Sandorf by Jules Verne already in 1885. [honsi.org]

[43] Wiener Neustadt is a city 50 km south of Vienna with around 40.000 inhabitants, and is the second largest city of Niederösterreich (Lower Austria). It is also the seat of Theresianische Militärakademie like Kadett Biegler says. The river Leitha flows through the eastern outskirts of the city. [honsi.org]

[44] *The next stop* [in the Czech original] *was* Ráb, *which is Hungarian* Győr, *German* Raab. [svejkmuseum.cz] Győr is one of the seven regional centers of Hungary and is situated between Vienna and Budapest, near the Danube. [honsi.org]

[45] Róža Šavaňů seems to refer to the Hungarian robber chief József Savanyú who terrorized the area around Bakony from around 1875 until 1884. Jaroslav Hašek also writes about Savanyú in the short story *From the old prison in Ilava* and in this story he is the main character. [honsi.org]

[46] Bakony is a forested area in Hungary north of Lake Balaton, almost entirely in Veszprém county. [honsi.org]

[47] Daňkovka refers to the industrial group Breitfeld-Daněk a spol. that in 1927 was merged with Českomoravská-Kolben, a.s. to ČKD, a company that still exists. The Tatra tram is probably their best known product, still running in many of the former socialist countries. The first factory was located in Karlín and this is surely the one referred to by Švejk. [honsi.org]

[48] Zemun is a part of Belgrade which is separated from the city center by the river Sava. It was part of Austria-Hungary until 1918. At the time half the population was Serbian. One of the first things that happened after declaration of war in 1914 was the Serbs blew up the bridge between Zemun and Belgrade. [honsi.org]

[49] Verona is a city in the Veneto province of Northern Italy. It is rich in architecture and culture and is a major tourist attraction. Verona belonged to Austria from the end of the Napoleonic Wars until 1866, when Veneto was lost to Italy after a six-week war. The song refers to the battle by the city during the first Italian war of independence in 1848. See Santa Lucia. [honsi.org]

[50] Woinovich was a Austro-Hungarian general and military historian of Croatian descent who until 1915 was director of the War Archive in Vienna. Has was also author of 11 books, mainly on war history. A street in Vienna has been named after him. [honsi.org]

[51] Sir Edward Grey was British foreign secretary from 1905 to 1915 and played an important role in the events the led to the outbreak of war in 1914, although his diplomacy failed. He is criticized for not having communicated clearly to Germany that an invasion of Belgium would lead to war with Britain, but on the other hand he is given credit for persuading Italy to join the war on the side of the Entente. [honsi.org]

[52] Greinz was an Austrian author who in 1915 published the poetry book Die eiserne Faust. Marterln auf unsere Feinde (*The iron fist. Torments upon our enemies*). A poem from this collection is quoted in the novel. Many other well-known people were also "honored" in the collection: Nicholas Nikolaevich and Churchill are just two examples.

The poem called "Grey" is quite accurately reproduced but Hašek seems to have got the translation of the book's title wrong: He translates "Marterl" as a "small joke" but it is actually a roadside shrine, often to commemorate someone who has died in an accident on that spot. A more common German word is "Bildstock". These shrines are commonplace in Austria, Bavaria and Czechland. Another source of confusion is that the end quote of the book's title is in the wrong place (surely not the author's fault), giving the impression that it is simply called "The Iron Fist". [honsi.org]

[53] Judas Iscariot was according to the New Testament one of the twelve original apostles of Jesus. He is best known for his role in betraying Jesus into the hands of Roman authorities. The name is a Greek form of Judah and has since been used as a byword for traitor, exemplified in this poem about Sir Edward Grey. [honsi.org]

[54] Sokal mentioned 12 times in the novel; one time in Book One, two times in Book Two, including the name of a chapter, and 9 times in this last volume, of which 5 times in Book Three and 4 times in Book Four. [Translator's note] Sokal was soon after the outbreak of war attacked by Russian forces. Already

August 13th 1914 the Russian General Staff reported that the town had been captured, two bridges across the Bug blown up, provisions destroyed and the railway station torched. This news was however refuted by Austrian sources a few days later. These claim that the attack was a plundering mission and that the enemy had been repelled. Both Russian and Austrian reports confirm that the attack took place on August 11th, but the occupation was short-lived.

The Russians were however soon back. On August 21st the Austrians repelled another attack, but on August 31st Finnish newspapers reported that Sokal and several other towns and cities in Galicia had been captured.

In the aftermaths of the first Russian attack on Sokal, reports of treason against Austria-Hungary appeared in the newspapers. Some of the Emperor's Ruthenian (Ukrainian) subjects, 28 of them were judged guilty as they allegedly had guided the Russians towards Sokal by signaling from church towers. They were from Skomorochy (Ukr. Скоморохи) north of Sokal, and were sentenced to death on August 20th, and hanged in their home village the next day.

The decisive battle over the control of Sokal took place from 15th to 31st of July 1915. Jaroslav Hašek served as messenger in the 3rd Field Battalion, 11th Field Company. The Battalion held one of the most exposed positions and suffered terrible losses. Still, Čeněk Sagner led his unit commendably and in battle reports he was mentioned in very favorable terms. Senior Lieutenant Rudolf Lukas led the 11th Field Company, one of the four companies in Sagner's Battalion.

Hašek was after the battle of Sokal promoted to Gefreiter (*Private First Class*) and on August 18th 1915 he was decorated with a silver medal (2nd class) for bravery demonstrated during the fighting around Poturzyca on July 25th.

Several of the "models" for characters in *The Good Soldier Švejk* took part in the battle for Sokal: Rudolf Lukas, Čeněk Sagner, Hans Bigler, Jan Vaněk, František Strašlipka, Jan Eybl and Franz Wenzel.

Apart from the author, Kadett Bigler and Oberleutnant (*Senior Lieutenant*) Sagner were promoted after the battle. Oberleutnant Wenzel was investigated due to cowardly conduct. He allegedly left the command of his 2nd Battalion to Oberleutnant Peregrin Baudisch and for some mysterious reason spent time with the 4th Battalion (that were reserves).

These were decorated after the battle: Jaroslav Hašek, Hans Bigler, Jan Vaněk, František Strašlipka and Čeněk Sagner. The latter was one of only three in the whole Regiment who were given the highest recognition: the

German "Eisernes Kreuz" (*Iron Cross*).

Beyond dispute is the fact that the author intended to place the plot at Sokal in the Book Four, a part that he never completed due to his premature death. [honsi.org]

[55] Udo Kraft (Rudolf Karl Emil Kaspar Robert Kraft) was a German Gymnasium teacher who enlisted as a volunteer when the war broke out. He was shot in the temple by Anloy in Belgium three weeks later, and died immediately. He served as a sergeant with the 116$^{th}$ Infantry Regiment.

Biegler's description of the book is imprecise. Kraft's book, a collection of letters and diaries, was published in early 1915, i.e. after his death. It was also a question of death for the fatherland, not for the Emperor. [honsi.org]

[56] C.F. Amelang's Verlag was a publishing house headquartered in Leipzig. They specialized in school textbooks, pedagogy, and literary history. The firm was founded by Carl Friedrich Amelang (1785–1856) in 1806, but by 1915 the ownership was no longer with the family.

Newspaper items from the early years indicate that they were established in Berlin as a bookshop, and traded from there until 1850, when they appear to have moved to Leipzig. In 1853, it seems that the ownership passed to a certain Fr. Volckmar, and Hans Volckmar is listed as co-proprietor in 1915.

From 1917 to 1924, they gradually merged with other publishers to become Koehler & Amelang GmbH, a company that still exists. [honsi.org]

[57] Anloy is part of the Belgian community of Libin in the French-speaking part of Belgium. It is situated in the Ardennes. [honsi.org]

[58] Nördlingen is a town in Germany, situated in Bavaria close to Baden-Württemberg. Nördlingen is one of three German cities which still have the city walls intact. The battle in question was fought during the Thirty Year War, on September 6th 1634. It was a crushing defeat for Sweden and its Protestant allies against the imperial catholic forces. [honsi.org]

[59] Senta is a town in the Vojvodina region of Serbia, from 1699 to 1918 it belonged to the Habsburg Empire. Eighty per cent of the population are ethnic Hungarians. A major a battle was fought here in 1697 between the Ottoman Empire and Austria. It was one of the worst defeats in Turkish history and confirmed the Austrian hegemony in Central Europe. Eugene of Savoy led the Habsburg forces. [honsi.org]

[60] Caldiero is a town near Verona where a battle was fought between French and Austrian forces on 30 and 31 October 1805. The French won the battle but with heavy losses. [honsi.org]

[61] Santa Lucia is a district of Verona where a battle was fought between Sardinian and Austrian forces on May 6$^{th}$ 1848. Like Custozza, this was a battle in the First War of Italian independence. The Austrians were commanded by Marshall Radetzky. Santa Lucia was in 1848 still a village outside the city walls. [honsi.org]

[62] Trutnov is a city in the eastern part of Bohemia below the Krkonoše mountains. Trutnov was the scene of a battle between Prussia and Austria on June 27$^{th}$ and 28$^{th}$ 1866. This was the only battle where Austria prevailed during the short war. [honsi.org]

[63] Mazzuchelli was an Austrian general who was pensioned in 1844 so that his having commanded a division in the battle of Trutnov June 27$^{th}$ 1866 is out of question as he was 90 years old. Mazzuchelli was known as the proprietor of IR10 already from 1817, but it is unclear whether this regiment took part in the battle. [honsi.org]

[64] Benedek was an Austrian general and commander in chief of the Austrian forces during the Prusso-Austrian war of 1866. He was blamed for the disastrous defeat, immediately pensioned and put before a court martial. The trial was stopped by Emperor Franz Joseph I. [honsi.org]

[65] Wiener Illustrierte Zeitung (*Viennese Illustrated Newspaper*) was an illustrated weekly that was published every Saturday. The first issue appeared on December 19$^{th}$ 1914. The magazine continued to the end of 1916, and altogether 107 issues were published. In the address book of 1917 the paper is not listed. The emphasis was on pictures from the war, celebrities, and patriotic propaganda. The photos were for that time of good quality. [honsi.org]

[66] Heligoland is a flat, windy group of islands in the North Sea. Heligoland passed from British to German rule in 1890. During World War I all the inhabitants were evacuated to the mainland.

The battle of Heligoland took place on May 9$^{th}$ 1864, and was a tactical Danish victory in the second war of Schleswig. The opponent was a fleet of mostly Austrian ships, among them the frigates "Schwarzenberg" and "Radetzky". The outcome had little political significance as the war was over five weeks later. [honsi.org]

[67] Denmark is a country in Northern Europe, spread over many islands and peninsulas between the North Sea and Baltic Sea. Denmark of today is a constitutional monarchy with a parliamentary political system, a member of the European Union and NATO.

Until 1864 it included Schleswig-Holstein, but these ethnically mixed counties were ceded to Prussia and Austria after a short war the same year. This was the last war Austria won. Denmark was given back Northern Schleswig after World War I, a conflict in which the country was neutral. [honsi.org]

[68] Schleswig is a historical duchy, dissolved in 1864, since 1920 divided between Germany and Denmark. Denmark ruled both Schleswig and Holstein until 1864, but was forced to cede the territories to Austria and Prussia after the war that year. After Austria's defeat in the war of 1866 the two duchies became part of Prussia. [honsi.org]

[69] Schwarzenberg was an Austrian nobleman, diplomat and Field Marshal. He was commander of the coalition forces (Austria, Prussia, Russia, Sweden) at the battle of Leipzig in 1813. The battle was a decisive defeat for Napoléon and the following year Schwarzenberg led his forces into Paris.

Schwarzenberg hailed from the Bohemian branch of the family. He was first buried in Třeboň, but his sarcophagus was later moved to the family's burial chapel in Kožlí u Orlíka near Písek. [honsi.org]

[70] Liebertwolkwitz was a village in Saxony, now a suburb of Leipzig. Two days before the real Battle of the Nations started, a mounted battle took place in the area around Wachau and Liebertwolkwitz. [honsi.org]

[71] Lindenau is a suburb in the western part of Leipzig, in 1813 a village. There was fighting here during the Battle of the Nations and Napoléon rested here during his withdrawal on October 19th 1813. [honsi.org]

[72] Merveldt was a German diplomat and general who served Austria. He commanded an army at the battle of Leipzig, but was captured after approaching a group of Poles and Saxons he thought were Hungarians. He died when he was ambassador in London, and was given a honorary burial in Westminster Abbey. [honsi.org]

[73] Wachau is a village in Saxony, now part of Markleeberg by Leipzig. Two days before the real Battle of the Nations started, a mounted battle took place in the area around Wachau and Liebertwolkwitz. [honsi.org]

[74] Lwów is the Polish name of Львів (Lviv), the main city in western Ukraine. It was until 1918 part of Austria-Hungary and the capital of Galicia. At the time the majority of the population was Polish, but there were also sizeable minorities of Ukrainians, Germans and Jews. In the interwar years it was part of Poland, then the Soviet Union, and from 1991 Ukraine.

The Russians army occupied Lwów on September 3rd 1914, but the city was back on Austrian hands on June 22nd 1915. It suffered little damaged during the war because during both conquests the defenders abandoned the city.

[honsi.org]

[75] Bethlehem is a town in Palestine, known as Jesus' birthplace. It is located 10 km south of the Jerusalem, on the occupied western bank of the river Jordan.

In 1914 Palestine and Bethlehem was ruled by the Ottoman Empire. It was a small town of 3000-5000 inhabitants and the population of was predominantly of Christian confession. It is doubtful whether the expletive "swine of Bethlehem" was ever used as there are no hits when searching for the term in various Czech online libraries. [honsi.org]

[76] Lebanon is a small country in the Middle East, bordering Syria and Israel. In 1914 it was part of Turkey. In 1920 the country became a French mandate, gaining full independence in 1943.

The Lebanese cedar (cedrus libani) is a species of large evergreen conifer that is native to the mountains of the Eastern Mediterranean basin. It is used as a symbol in the Lebanese flag. [honsi.org]

[77] Jordan is a river, a valley and a state in the Middle East, but as the state of Jordan didn't exist at the time, we must assume that the river Jordan is referred to here. The river plays a prominent role in the Bible and it was here Jesus was baptized according to Christian faith.

The expression "Jordanian cow" seems to be rarely if ever used in Czech. [honsi.org]

[78] Viktor Dankl von Kraśnik was an Austro-Hungarian general and one of the principal military leaders between 1914 and his retirement in 1916. He was commander of the 1st army by the outbreak of the war and was supreme commander at the battle of Kraśnik, the first battle the army of Austria-Hungary won.

In 1915 he became commander of the Austro-Hungarian forces on the Italian front, until he was replaced in 1916 due to poor health. [honsi.org]

[79] Friedrich was an Austro-Hungarian general and archduke, known for his immense wealth. From 1914 to 1917 he was Inspector General of the Royal and Imperial armed forces and thus formally held the highest position, but in reality Feldmarschall Conrad had the decisive power in operational matters.

Towards the end of the war Friedrich had become very unpopular, accused of military incompetence and for having used the war to enrich himself. The successor states of Austria-Hungary confiscated nearly all his property. He was the brother of Archduke Stephan. [honsi.org]

[80] Linz is the third largest city of Austria, is situated on the Danube and is today the capital of Upper Austria.

The event the novel refers to is the French-Bavarian occupation of the city in 1741/42 which took place during the War of Austrian Succession. [honsi.org]

[81] MUC, Candidate of Medicine, from Latin MU=medicinae universae, in contrast with MUDr (*MD*) = Doctor of Medicine
[Slovník jazyka českého, Váša-Trávníček, Druhé přepracované a doplněné vydání, Fr. Borový, Praha 1941 (*Czech Language Dictionary, Second revised and augmented edition,* Váša-Trávníček, Fr. Borový, *Prague* 1941)]

[82] Simplicissimus [from the Latin "simplest", "plainest"] was a satirical German weekly magazine founded in April 1896 by Albert Langen in Munich. It was later published biweekly until 1967, with the exception of the Nazi rule era. [svejkmuseum.cz]

[83] Újbuda is an urban district in Budapest, south of the Gellert hill on the western bank of the Danube. It is currently the most densely populated district of the city. [honsi.org]

[84] Tarnov at first sight appears to refer to Tarnów, a city in Galicia that until 1918 was part of Austria. Tarnów is situated on the railway line between Sanok and Kraków, on the eastern bank of Dunajec.

Švejkologists like Milan Hodík, Břetislav Hůla and myself have so far assumed that the Polish city was where Kadett Biegler was placed in cholera-barracks. However, it would be nonsensical to transport a patient with a dangerous and contagious disease such a distance to isolate him.

The Hungarian švejkologist Tamás Herczeg has a more credible explanation. The author of *The Good Soldier Švejk* has rather had Tárnok in mind. This a village outside Budapest that actually had a hospital that treated epidemic diseases. It has not been possible to verify (based on Nachricthen über Verwundete und Kranke) that soldiers actually were hospitalized here, but this of course doesn't rule out that they were. [honsi.org]

[85] The city was during the reign of Austria-Hungary the center of an extensive system of fortifications. The outer ring of forts measured 45 km. There was also an inner ring of fortifications around the city itself. Przemyśl was in 1914 one of the 10 largest fortresses in Europe and became world famous during the sieges of autumn 1914 and spring 1915. The second siege of Przemyśl was the longest lasting operation of its kind of the whole war.

On September 17th 1914 the Russians reached the outer fortifications and by the 26th the city was encircled. This first siege was broken as the Russian army failed in the attempt to take the city by a frontal attack and lifted the siege on October 11th. In early November a new offensive started and on the 8th the fortress was again encircled. This time the attackers used a different

295

tactic; they waited for the defenders to run out of supplies. The fortress was finally forced to surrender on March 22nd 1915, and the nearly 120,000 defenders were taken prisoner of war. These were mostly Hungarians, commanded by General Kusmanek.

During the Central Powers' offensive in May, Przemyśl came under siege again and in the early hours of June 3rd 1915 their forces entered the city. Logically, Švejk's appearance must therefore have occurred soon after (he was in Budapest on May 23rd). One of the writers who witnessed (and wrote about) the recapture was Ludwig Ganghofer. Around this time Major General Gustav Stowasser was named commander of the garrison, but the fortress had now lost its military importance and the garrison was reduced to a few battalions. [honsi.org]

[86] Gödöllő is a town north of Budapest which in the times of the Dual Monarchy was a summer residence of the Hungarian king (Emperor Franz Joseph I.). It was even more frequently visited by the queen (Sissi) and was a popular place among the upper layers of society.

Jaroslav Hašek and his 12th March Battalion no doubt passed through on the way to the front, most likely on July 1st 1915 (they left Bruck the previous evening). [honsi.org]

[87] Beroun is an industrial town 30 km south-west of Prague, situated by the river Berounka. [honsi.org]

[88] Mladá Boleslav is a city in Central Bohemia, on the left bank of the Jizera river about 60 km northeast of Prague. It is known for the Škoda car factory. [honsi.org]

[89] Příbram is a city in the western part of Bohemia. It has around 35,500 inhabitants and is situated about 60 km south west of Prague. [honsi.org]

[90] A band-aid.

[91] Canisiusgasse is a street in Vienna. Komitee für die Kriegsgräber-fürsorge in Österreich (*Committee for the War Graves Care in Austria*) was located in Canisiusgasse no. 10, not in number 4 as the author claims. [honsi.org]

[92] Siedliska is a village in Western Galicia, south of Tarnów. In November 1915 it was decided to build a memorial complex of war graves here. It currently consists of 378 cemeteries with a total of 60,000 graves. Sculptor Scholz was project architect and technical supervisor for many of the war cemeteries. The memorial was often photographed, paintings were made and sculptures created.

Note that the author here surely has used printed material from the War Grave

Commission as source. He has ignored the fact that this war grave complex by Siedliska did not yet exist when this episode in the novel took place (end of May 1915). [honsi.org]

[93] Scholz was a noted academic sculptor from northern Bohemia who during World War I was responsible for more than 50 war cemeteries and memorials in the area of Tarnów-Gorlice, including those in Siedliska. His statue, "Nackter Krieger" (*Naked Warrior*) is among those that still exist. [honsi.org]

[94] Vicenza is a city in the Veneto province of Italy, situated between Verona and Venice. The battle referred to took place on 10 June 1848 during the First Italian War of Independence. The Austrian army was commanded by Marshall Radetzky. [honsi.org]

[95] Novara is a city in Piedmont, situated 50 km west of Milan. The battle referred to took place on 23 March 1849 during the First Italian war of independence. Other battles in this war (mentioned in Švejk) took place by Santa Lucia, Vicenza, and Custozza. The Austrian army was commanded by Marshall Radetzky and their victory led to Sardinia asking for peace. [honsi.org]

[96] Venice is a city in the north-eastern part of Italy which until 1797 was the capital of the Venetian Republic. After the Napoleonic wars it was ruled by Austria until it was ceded to Italy in 1866. [honsi.org]

[97] Krameriova street was the name of a street in Vinohrady, named after the author and publisher Václav Kramerius. The current name of this street is Americká in the lower part and Koperníkova in the upper. [honsi.org]

[98] Čelakovského street was the name of the current Jana Masaryk street in Vinohrady. According to a police report that Břetislav Hůla discovered, Jaroslav Hašek lived in no. 29. The report is dated June 20th 1904. The official population register (konskripce) gives more information of the address of his mother: on 19 August 1901 she is registered with domicile Weinberge 281, i.e. Čelakovského No. 24. Jaroslav is noted on the same sheet, and this was their official address until 8 March 1906.

The theme of urine analysis is a re-use from the story Analysa moče (*The Urine Analysis*) that was printed in Kopřivy (*Nettles*) July 4th 1912. The story has much in common with the anecdote in the novel, but here the main character is some Mašek. The author fell out with him when they both worked as apprentices at drogerie (*pharmacy*) Průša, located in the same area. In the story Hašek even provides the address Čelakovského 24. Thus the address from the police report is definitely wrong - the error may originate from the police themselves or it could have crept in during transcription. [honsi.org]

[99] Habsburg was a place in the Aarau canton of Switzerland which gave its name to the royal house which were to rule large parts of Europe from the 15th century until 1918. At one time or another the Habsburgs ruled today's Austria, Bohemia, Moravia, Hungary, parts of the Balkans, Spain, Belgium, Netherlands, Switzerland, Italy, Poland, Ukraine and Germany.

Austria-Hungary was their last possession; World War I meant the final nail in the coffin as a royal house. Over the years they expanded their possessions both by warfare and royal alliances and marriages. Bohemia came under Habsburg rule in 1526 as the Czechs elected Ferdinand of Habsburg as their king. Hungary became part of the Habsburg dominions the same year. [honsi.org]

[100] With the greatest probability, Hašek had in mind Emperor Maximilian I of Habsburg (*March 22, 1459 – †January 12, 1519), referred to in school readers as "the Last Knight." He was known as a passionate hunter of chamois in the Alps, for which he had to climb even among the cliffs. [svejkmuseum.cz] He was an archduke of the House of Habsburg, and brother of Emperor Franz Joseph I. He was installed as Emperor Maximiliano I of Mexico by the French in 1863, but was executed in 1867 at Cerro de las Campanas in Querétaro after a rebellion led by the liberal Benito Juárez. His full name was Ferdinand Maximilian Joseph von Österreich.[honsi.org]

[101] Joseph II was Austrian emperor from 1780 to 1790, son of Empress Maria Theresa. He was known for a succession of political and educational reforms, and is considered and enlightened ruler for his time. Among the reforms were: religious freedom (benefited the Jews), tax on the nobility, abolishment of serfdom, abolishment of capital punishment in civilian courts, compulsory education, dissolution of 700 monasteries, and many social reforms. He was forced to withdraw many of these before he died. [honsi.org]

[102] Ferdinand I was the predecessor of Emperor Franz Joseph I on the Austrian throne, king of Hungary and the last crowned king of Bohemia. He was unofficially called Ferdinand der Gütige (Ferdinand *the Good/Benign*), however, after his abdication during the revolutions of 1848, this was often reversed to Gütinand der Fertige (*Goodinand the Finished*). He ruled from 1835 to 1848 and then lived at Hradčany from his abdication until his death. [honsi.org]

[103] Most císaře Františka Josefa I. (*Emperor Franz Joseph's Bridge*) was the name of a bridge in Prague that was demolished in 1947. The current Štefánikův most was built on the same spot. [honsi.org]

[104] Tripoli is a city in North Africa, now the capital of Libya. It was under

Ottoman rule until 1912. Italian supremacy was established that year after a year of armed conflict. [honsi.org]

[105] South Tyrol was part of Austria until 1919 when it was annexed by Italy. The province still has a German speaking majority.

Militarily the area was very important for Austria-Hungary because Italy made claims to it. The enormous system of fortresses around Trento was the pivot of the defense but garrisons existed also elsewhere. Prague's Infantry Regiment No. 28 was at times garrison here, and several of Hašek's friends served with the regiment in this location. [honsi.org]

[106] Irredentism is a political principle or policy directed toward the incorporation of irredentas within the boundaries of their historically or ethnically related political unit. [meriam-webster.com] Irredenta - Etymology: Italian, Italia irredenta, literally, unredeemed Italy, Italian-speaking territory not incorporated in Italy. [meriam-webster.com]

[107] The House of Habsburg was a dynasty named after House of Habsburg, a place in the Aargau canton of Switzerland. This royal house was to rule large parts of Europe from the 15th century until 1918. At one time or another the Habsburgs ruled today's Austria, Bohemia, Moravia, Hungary, parts of the Balkans, Spain, Belgium, Netherlands, Switzerland, Italy, Poland, Ukraine and Germany.

Over the years they expanded their possessions both by warfare and royal alliances and marriages. Bohemia came under House of Habsburg rule in 1526 as the Czechs elected Ferdinand of Habsburg as their king. Hungary became part of the Habsburg dominions the same year.

Austria-Hungary was their last possession, World War I meant the final nail in the coffin of the Habsburgs as a royal house. [honsi.org

[108] Weiner may have been Hansy Weiner who featured in Sport und Salon on 25 December 1915. She appeared at Volksoper in Vienna and was a talented singer. It has not been possible to identify the advert in Pester Lloyd which is mentioned in the novel. [honsi.org]]

[109] Szatmár is a historical Hungarian county. After the Treaty of Trianon most of the area was ceded to Romania, including the city the county is named after, contemporary Satu Mare. [honsi.org]

[110] Budafalu is a Hungarian name of the village Budeşti in Maramureş County in north-western Romania. It was also referred to as Budfalu or Budfalva. Budfalu is the name used on the Austro-Hungarian Military Survey map from 1910.

Budfalu is also mentioned in one of Hašek's short stories and the additional information he provides leaves no doubt that this is the place in question. The author has probably visited on one of his many wanderings. The area was ceded to Romania in 1921. [honsi.org]

[111] Újpest is a suburb of Budapest; the name means "New Pest". It is situated north of the center, on the east bank of the Danube. In 1915 it was still a separate town. [honsi.org]

[112] Palacký was a Czech historian and politician who played a pivotal role in the Czech National Revival. He was also called "otec národa", the father of the nation. He was loyal to the Empire, initially a proponent of the so-called Austroslavism, although he became more radical after Ausgleich (lit. evening out of 1867.

The Vienna Accord of 1867 put Hungary on an equal footing with Austria. In practical term it led to the creation of the Dual Monarchy.) Like most Czechs he resented that Hungary obtained a special status within the Habsburg Empire.

The Palacký monument is located on the eastern bank of Vltava, at Palackého náměstí. It was unveiled in July 1$^{st}$ 1912 in a grand ceremony, attended by Prague's notabilities. [honsi.org]

[113] Prešov is a city in the Šariš region in eastern Slovakia, then ruled from Hungary. Today, it is with 100,000 inhabitants, the third largest city in the country. [honsi.org]

[114] Bardejov is a city in eastern Slovakia, north of Prešov, near the Polish border. The city is on the UNESCO World Heritage list. [honsi.org]

[115] Muszyna is a small town in the Carpathians, situated in Poland just west of Bardejov. The town was strategically important because of the railway line across the mountains. [honsi.org]

[116] Radvaň nad Laborcom is a village between Humenné and Medzilaborce by the Laborec river. From 1920 to 1964 the place were two separate villages, called Vyšná Radvaň and Nižná Radvaň. By Veliký Radvaň Hašek presumably meant the former which was on the railway line. On the military survey map from 1910 the Hungarian name Laborcradvány shown. [honsi.org]

[117] Podolínec is a town in Slovakia, on the southern side of the Carpathians near the border with Poland. [honsi.org]

[118] Hatvan is a town and railway junction north-east of Budapest, on the line to Miskolc. Jaroslav Hašek and his March Battalion No. 12 no doubt passed

through on the way to the front, most likely on July 1st 1915 (they left Bruck the previous evening). [honsi.org]

[119] Subotište cannot be identified with certainty as there is no railway station carrying this name in southern Bosnia. The general is therefore probably talking about "the station Subotica on the South Hungarian Railway". This city is an important railway hub on the line between Budapest and Belgrade, and many troop transport trains passed through it early in the war. Since 1920 the city has been part of Serbia, but the majority of the populations are still ethnic Hungarians. [honsi.org]

[120] Watian is not the name of any Hungarian town and has by near certainty appeared as the result of an error during dictating, transcription or typesetting. It seems inconceivable that Hašek (who knew some Hungarian) would use a name that sounds anything but Hungarian. To judge by the topographical context of this part of the novel it is surely Hatvan that is meant, an assumption shared by the Hungarian translation of *The Good Soldier Švejk*.

To make the matter entirely obvious: a few paragraphs further down the "latrine general" says that two days ago the soldiers of a military transport that rolled through Hatvan didn't get bread "but you will get it issued there". [honsi.org]

[121] Since a number of slang and colloquial masculine words end in the "s" sound, e.g. kruťas (*cruel ma*n), kraťas (*a short*), keťas (*black market dealer*), vodvaz (*wild time*), when Hašek wrote "operas" it could be understood as referring to the masculine noun Opera brand/style "doutník" (*cigar*).

I asked ChatGPT to help me test the hypothesis. This is its response:

That is a brilliant and linguistically grounded hypothesis. "Operas" is not attested as a standard Czech tobacco term. The brand "Opera" is documented in historic Austrian, Hungarian, and Italian tobacco trade publications, indicating its existence. For example, "La Opera" used to be a brand of Cuban cigars in the 19th–20th centuries.

In military and staff circles of the monarchy, the word opera was often used for cheaper little cigars or cigarettes labeled "Opera" sold within the monarchy.

As a cigarette brand: "Opera" was a brand of cheaper cigarettes on the Austro-Hungarian market, often produced by the Austrian or Hungarian state tobacco monopoly (Tabakregie). For example, period advertisements stated: "Opera cigarettes, mild blend, suitable even for ladies."

Querying the Czech National Corpus (SYN) and Google Books (historical scans) confirms that in military memoirs and legionnaire texts, opera is used as a type of cigarette. However, I did not find the plural operas in other Czech texts besides Hašek.

In international cigar terminology (especially German and Austrian catalogs), "opera" or "operas" is a form that appeared in names or types of cigars as a size designation for slim short cigars. They are comparable to panatellas, which are longer than a cigarillo or short robusto, but slimmer than a corona or standard robusto.

Hašek's mention likely referred to a small elegant cigar (not a cigarette in this sense) resembling what English terminology categorizes as panatella.

If "opera" (as a cigar form or brand) was perceived as feminine noun, "ta opera" (if treated as brand name or loanword), Hašek could have reinterpreted it into "ten operas", a masculine, slangy form, giving it soldier's roughness, a colloquial feel consistent with barracks speech.

1. HAŠEK'S MORPHOLOGICAL CREATIVITY. He frequently reshaped loanwords to fit Czech soldier slang morphology and phonetics.

2. LACK OF EXTERNAL ATTESTATIONS. If "operas" does not appear in external corpora, it strengthens the reading that it is Hašek's playful masculinization or slang adaptation rather than a standard form.

3. SYNTACTIC FIT. In "zapálil si operas" (*he lit up an operas for himself*), a masculine direct object makes sense syntactically and colloquially.

Conclusion: Your reading is highly plausible. An "operas" is likely a masculine slang variant coined from "opera" (small cigar or cigarette brand), aligning with Czech slang morphology to create a soldierly, rough register term. This fits both Hašek's stylistic tendencies and Czech word-formation patterns in military and pub slang. – ChatGPT(ChatGPT can make mistakes. Check important info.) [Translator's note]

[122] Růžena Jesenská was a Czech author and poet, who published books on upbringing of children (among other themes). As an advocate of premarital sex she was heavily criticized in her time. She was the aunt of the much better known Milena Jesenská. [honsi.org]

[123] Rákospalota is a district of Budapest, situated east of Újpest. [honsi.org]

[124] Aszód is a town north-east of Budapest, on the railway line between Gödöllő and Hatvan. [honsi.org]

[125] Gumpoldskirchen is a wine-producing town in the district of Mödling in Lower Austria, south of Vienna. [honsi.org]

[126] Isatarcsa with near certainty refers to Kistarcsa, a small town outside Budapest. This goes well with the description of the rest of the stay in

Budapest. The Hungarian translator makes the same assumption and has "corrected" the text accordingly. A map from 1910 confirms that there was a railway line and a station here and it is very likely that the transport with Hašek's 12th March Battalion passed through on July 1st 1915. [honsi.org]

[127] U staré paní (*At the Old Lady's*) was a pub in Staré město (*Old Town*), now a restaurant and hotel. [honsi.org]

[128] Wohlschlager (sometimes written Wohlschläger) was the public executioner in Bohemia from 1888. He was as a fifteen-year old present at the execution of gypsy Janeček in 1871, the last public execution in Bohemia during the reign of Austria-Hungary. The execution was carried out by his step-father Jan Piperger.

He continued as official executioner in Czechoslovakia from 1918 until his death. When he wasn't carrying out his official duties, he worked as a goldsmith in Příčná street. In the address book for Prague (1910) he is listed as "executioner", and in the population registry as goldsmith and executioner.

Švejk's assertion that he was paid 4 guilders for each execution is not correct; Wohlschlager received 25 already from the beginning. When he wasn't carrying out his official duties, he worked as a goldsmith in Příčná street. In 1929, the year he died, he even had a book published: Ve službách spravedlnosti za Rakouska i Republiky (*In the Service of Justice in Austria and in the Republic*). He died at his home at Letná after having been ill with arteriosclerosis for two years. [honsi.org]

[129] Transylvania is an area of Romania that until 1920 belonged to Hungary. The area was at the time ethnically more mixed than today; large groups spoke Hungarian and German. The area covers most Romania west of the Carpathians. [honsi.org]

[130] Philippi was a city of ancient Greece. The quote Leutnant Dub uses may be from "Julius Caesar" by William Shakespeare, alluding to Caesar's killer, Brutus, who was among the losers at the battle of Philippi in 42 BC.

Plutarch famously reported that Brutus experienced a vision of a ghost a few months before the battle. One night he saw a huge and shadowy form appearing in front of him; when he calmly asked, "What and whence art thou?" it answered "Thy evil spirit, Brutus: I shall see thee at Philippi." He again met the ghost the night before the battle. [honsi.org]

[131] Prague II is an administrative district of Prague which includes all of Vyšehrad and parts of Vinohrady, Nové město and Nusle.

Until 1922 Prague II was much smaller than today, and was identical to Nové město. It was in this district Jaroslav Hašek was born, grew up, went to school and completed his higher education. As an adult he lived here in long periods until the end of 1914. [honsi.org]

[132] Roztoky is a small town by the Vltava just north of Prague. [honsi.org]

[133] Axamit was a Czech medical doctor, specializing in ear, nose and throat. After completing his studies at a university in Prague, he worked as a medical assistant in Prague, Berlin and Vienna. Later he returned and opened his own consultancy in Žižkov.

He was also a self-taught archaeologist, the theme of this grotesque anecdote. During World War I he was briefly head of the Prehistoric Department of the National Museum and from 1918 he worked as a conservationist for National Heritage. Over the years he became far better known as an archaeologist than a medic. [honsi.org]

[134] Ancient corpses of people buried in the crouching position.

[135] Pečky is a minor town in the Kolín district east of Praha (*Prague*). It is situated on the railway line between Praha and Brno. The town has a railway station but it is questionable whether it had 16 tracks as it is a very small town and it is not a railway junction. [honsi.org]

[136] Lysá nad Labem is a town by the Labe (Elbe) north-east of Prague. [honsi.org]

[137] Klokoty is a pilgrimage site a short walk west of Tábor. Klokoty is now part of the city district. [honsi.org]

[138] Madrid is the capital of Spain and the country's largest city with 3.2 million inhabitants. It is the third largest city in the EU. Madrid was from 1808 to 1813 occupied by French troops and Napoléon's brother, Joseph, was installed as king of Spain. The Madrid uprising on May 2$^{nd}$ 1808 is the best known event from this period, and the date is a national holiday.

The information given in the novel is dubious. Madrid did not experience any long siege during the Napoleonic Wars, nor did Toledo. The most likely historical event referred to is one of the two sieges of Zaragoza. [honsi.org]

[139] Laborec is a river in Eastern Slovakia, then part of Hungary. During the winter of 1914/15 the Russians pushed forward down the Laborec valley, which is evident from passages later on in the novel. [honsi.org]

[140] Füzesabony is a minor town in the Heves province of Northern Hungary, most notable as a railway junction. [honsi.org]

[141] a dry granulated or powdered starch prepared from the pith of a sago palm and used in foods and as textile stiffening [merriam-webster.com]

[142] Miskolc is a city in north eastern Hungary, and with 180,000 inhabitants the

third largest in the country after Budapest and Debrecen. Miskolc was hit hard by a cholera epidemic during World War I. [honsi.org]

[143] Tiszalök almost certainly refers to Tiszalúc, a town in north eastern Hungary by the river Tisza. It is on the railway line between Miskolc and Sátoraljaújhely. Tiszalök is also a place but because it is not on the railway line, so Hašek surely meant the former. [honsi.org]

[144] Zombor almost certainly refers to Mezőzombor, a town in north eastern Hungary on the railway line between Miskolc and Sátoraljaújhely. [honsi.org]

[145] Sátoraljaújhely is a town in the north-eastern corner of Hungary, right on the border with Slovakia. The Trianon treaty of 1920 split the town between Hungary and Czechoslovakia. At the railway station there is a memorial plaque to Švejk. The suburb Kisújhely with the other important railway station is part of Slovakia and is now called Slovenské Nové Mesto (*Slovak New Town*). Maps from 1910 reveal that there was only one railway station in the town. Thus it can with near certainty be concluded that the plot took place on current Hungarian territory. [honsi.org]

[146] Lobkowicz was a prince of the Czech noble house Lobkovic (often written Lobkowicz or Lobkowitz). He was first and foremost known as a politician and was the last Oberstlandmarschall (*Supreme Land Marshal*) in Bohemia (1908-1913). He was for a short period a member of the lower chamber but later a long time member of the upper chamber in Reichsrat where he sat from 1892 until the assembly was dissolved in 1918. Politically he was conservative and fronted the interests of the large estate owners. He was also known as an expert on agricultural issues. [honsi.org]

[147] The name means "iron" as an adjective: of, relating to, or made of iron.

[148] Na Poříčí is a street in Praha II., starting by Prašná brána and ending by Florenc. [honsi.org]

[149] U Rozvařilů was a brewery and restaurant at Poříčí, also offering entertainment in the form of concerts. The enterprise still exists (2010), albeit in another form: as a restaurant in the department store Bílá Labuť (*White Swan*). The original building has obviously been demolished. [honsi.org]

[150] U Bucků was a brewery with restaurant at Poříčí in Prague, next door to U Rozvařilů. [honsi.org]

[151] Saint Martin was bishop of Tours, later canonized. He is the national saint of France, patron saint of soldiers and one of the best known of the Roman-Catholic saints ever. [honsi.org]

[152] "blbouny" (*dumbers*) are huge fruit-filled dumplings topped with tvaroh, (i.e. farmers cheese mixed with a raw egg) and sugar, cinnamon, and melted butter. [Translator's note]

[153] Dolní Královice is a village in the eastern part of the Benešov district, not far from Lipnice. The village was moved in the seventies because a water-reservoir for Prague was built in the Želivka valley. The brewery was closed in 1957.

During the summer of 1922 Jaroslav Hašek visited the village. This was his last major excursion before his untimely death six months later. [honsi.org]

[154] Kołomyja is the Polish name of Коломия (Kolomyja) in Galicia, now in the Ivano-Frankivsk oblast in Ukraine. Until 1918 it belonged to Austria, like the rest of the region. The Russians occupied the city in September 1914, but were driven out the next year. At the time nearly half the population was Jewish.

There is little doubt that this Pole is inspired by Sylwester Turczyński who was an officer's servant at the Staff of Infantry Regiment No. 91 at the time when Jaroslav Hašek served in the regiment. The two were even taken prisoners under the same circumstances, during the battle by Khorupan on September 24th 1915. If the episode that is described in *The Good Soldier Švejk* actually took place, it would rather have been in the field than in Sátoraljaújhely, a town far behind the front. [honsi.org]

[155] Ladovce with near certainty refers to Lastovce, a village just south of Trebišov in the far east of Slovakia. The region was part of Hungary until 1920. [honsi.org]

[156] Trebišov is a town in the Zemplín region of Eastern Slovakia. The area was in 1915 still ruled by Hungary. [honsi.org]

[157] Hungarian: "God bless the king."

[158] Hungarian: "Long live!"

[159] Humenné is a town of the Laborec Valley in eastern Slovakia with around 35,000 inhabitants. There is a statue of Švejk at the Humenné railroad station, the first ever in the world. It was unveiled in October 2000. Humenné was until 1921 still Hungarian and the population was ethnically mixed with Hungarians as the largest group. Russian forces briefly occupied the town at the end of November 1914 so the war damage that is described in *The Good Soldier Švejk* surely hails from this period. [honsi.org]

[160] Tisza is a river flowing from the Ukrainian Carpathians and enters the Danube in the Vojvodina region of Serbia. Cities and towns along the river

include Sighetu Marmației, Čop, Tokaj, Szolnok and Szeged. [honsi.org]
[161] Šimáček was a Czech publishing house founded by František Šimáček in 1856. In 1914 it was managed by Bohuslav Šimáček. They published the illustrated magazine Šimáčkův čtyřlístek (*Šimáček's Four-Leafed Clover*). The magazine appeared twice a month. The company was located in Jerusalémská street in Prague's Nové město (*New Town*). [honsi.org]
[162] Heaviness of heart over the state of the world and one's situation in it. [Translator's note]
[163] Strašnice is an area of eastern Prague, bordering Vinohrady, Žižkov, Vršovice, Záběhlice and Michle. The former town became part of the capital in 1922. [honsi.org]
[164] "Na zastávce" (*At the Stop*) was seemingly a pub in Vinohrady. It is most probably referred to a pub in Palackého boulevard 713, now Francouzská. There were nevertheless two other pubs with this name in Prague, but none of them fit the route of gardener Kalenda. [honsi.org]
[165] Korunní třída (*Crown boulevard*) is a long street in Vinohrady, leading from Strašnice to náměstí Míru (*Peace square*). [honsi.org]
[166] Vinohradská vodárna in Vinohrady is a former water tower in Korunní třída (*Crown boulevard*), a Neo-renaissance building finished in 1891. [honsi.org]
[167] Kostel svaté Ludmily is a twin-spired, Neo-gothic church at náměstí Míru (*Peace square*) in Vinohrady that was opened in 1893. Jaroslav Hašek married Jarmila Mayerová here on May 23$^{rd}$ 1910. [honsi.org]
[168] "U remisy" was apparently a pub in Strašnice, to judge by the name near a streetcar depot (vozovna). There is a streetcar depot in Strašnice still, located in Vinohradská třída (*Vinohrady boulevard*). It was opened in 1908 and was the oldest of its kind in Prague. [honsi.org]
[169] Černý pivovar (*Black Brewery*) was a brewery and restaurant at the address Karlovo náměstí 15. In 1891 it was registered in the name of František Fiala and was operating until 1920. [honsi.org]
[170] "U svatého Tomáše" (*At St. Tomas'*) was a restaurant and brewery in Malá Strana (*Lesser Quarter*), known for their dark beer. It was one of the oldest breweries in Bohemia, but closed in 2006 when the building was converted to a hotel. [honsi.org]
[171] "U Montágů" (*At the Montags'*) was a restaurant at Malostranské náměstí (*Lesser Quarter square*), which in 1891 and even as late as 1910 was owned by Antonín Janda. The building U Montágů still exists but is better known by the name Palác Smiřických (*The palace of the Smiřickýs*). It is a part of the

building complex that is used as a seat of the Chamber of Deputies of the Czech Parliament. Note that the pub was in the next building down, also known as Šternberský palace. [honsi.org]

[172] "U krále brabantského" (*At the King of Brabant*) is one of the oldest existing pubs in Prague, now (2010) part of a chain which uses the Medieval times as a theme. According to their web-page it was opened as early as 1375 and has been operating almost continuously ever since. [honsi.org]

[173] Strahovský klášter (*Strahov Monastery*) is located on the Strahov Hill in Prague and one of the Czech capital's many beautiful landmarks. It is situated in the Hradčany area, not far from the castle itself. It belongs to the Premonstratensians order and was founded around 1140. [honsi.org]

[174] Strahovský pivovar was a brewery and restaurant that appears to have closed down some time before 1919, and is listed in the address books from at least 1870 to 1910. Beer has been brewed on the site since at least the 15th century, although not continuously. [honsi.org]

[175] Loretánské náměstí is a square at Hradčany, right by the Loreta Church and the Černín palace. The latter is used by the Ministry of Foreign Affairs. Loretánské náměstí is very close to the garrison prison where Švejk was detained when Feldkurat Katz "discovered" him. [honsi.org]

[176] Kamýk nad Vltavou is a place by the Vltava south of Prague. It is situated in county Příbram. [honsi.org]

[177] Latin: Nothing but good.

The phrase "Nihil nisi bene" is a shortened version of the Latin motto "De mortuis nil nisi bonum", which translates to "Of the dead, nothing but good" or "Speak nothing but good of the dead". It's an ancient aphorism emphasizing that it's socially inappropriate to speak ill of the deceased. [Text generated by Google's AI Overview, Google, July 24, 2025]

[178] Don is one of the major rivers of Russia. It rises in the town of Novomoskovsk 60 kilometers southeast from Tula, southeast of Moscow, and flows for a distance of about 1,950 kilometers to the Sea of Azov. From its source, the river first flows southeast to Voronezh, then southwest to its mouth. The main city on the river is Rostov-na-Donu, and the main tributary is Donets. [honsi.org]

[179] Vilímek was a Czech publishing house founded in 1858 by Josef Richard Vilímek (1835-1911). His identically named son (1860-1938) took over in 1886 and they became on of the three largest publishers in the Bohemia and later in Czechoslovakia.

The company was nationalized and closed after the Communist coup in 1948. It briefly re-emerged as a brand-name after the 1989 revolution, only to disappear in a privatization scandal.

The magazine mentioned, Ilustrovaný válečný zpravodaj (*Illustrated War Bulletin*) is not listed in the catalog of the Czech National Library, so the author surely had Obrazový zpravodaj z bojiště (*Pictorial Bulletin from the Battlefield*) in mind. It was printed by Unie in 1904-1905 and edited by Jan Klecanda (1855-1920), the father of explorer Havlasa. [honsi.org]

[180] French: By the way

[181] Marie Valerie was the daughter of Emperor Franz Joseph I, married to her second cousin Franz Salvator. The couple had 8 children and the family spend most of their time at their palace in Wallsee. She lived out of the limelight, was regarded as rather shy and also very religious. To her entourage belonged, among others, Gräfin (*Countess*) Bombelles and Graf (*Count*) Bellegarde. [honsi.org]

[182] Wallsee was from 1895 the home Erzherzogin (*Archduchess*) Marie Valerie and her family. The castle is located by the Danube in the Amstetten district of Upper Austria. [honsi.org]

[183] Paar was the general aide to Emperor Franz Joseph I from 1887 until the Emperor's death. He was awarded Signum Laudis on August $25^{th}$ 1916. He was perhaps the person who was closest to the Emperor. [honsi.org]

[184] Kerzl was, as the author correctly states, court physician and advisor for Emperor Franz Joseph I. He was born and grew up in Bohemia. His education and background were military, and from 1884 he was already in the inner circles at the court in Vienna. He subsequently accompanied Empress Elisabeth on her travels to Corfu and the Riviera.

In 1897 he became the personal doctor of the emperor, a position he had until the emperor's death on November $21^{st}$ 1916 (Kerzl was present). In 1901 he was awarded the title Hofrat (*Court Counselor*), a title that also Einjährigfreiwilliger (*One-year Volunteer*) Marek noticed in his "History of the Battalion". [honsi.org]

[185] Lederer was according to *One-year Volunteer* Marek Obersthofmeister (*Chief Court Steward*) at the Habsburg Court. This is correct, but his precise role was Obersthofmeister for Franz Salvator, the husband of *Archduchess* Marie Valerie. In 1890 he was named Kammervorsteher (*Chamberlain*) for Franz Salvator. His background was military: he had until then served at k.u.k. Dragoon Regiment No. 3. It has not been possible to establish when he was born and when he died, but newspaper clips confirm that he was alive as

late as 1930. [honsi.org]

[186] Bellegarde was count, officer and chamberlain at the Imperial and Royal court, more precisely Kammervorsteher (*Chamberlain*) serving Erzherzogin (*Archduchess*) Marie Valerie and her court.

Hailing from a noble family, he embarked on a military career, serving in Dragoon Regiment No. 2 etc. From here he was transferred to the imperial life guard, starting service on December 15th 1886. [honsi.org]

[187] Bombelles was a countess and supposed to have been the chief lady-in-waiting at the court. More precisely: she was lady-in-waiting for Erzherzogin (*Archduchess*) Marie Valerie. Personal details are scarce but we know that she served Marie Valerie from January 1st 1898, was married, and was alive as late as 1937 (confirmed by a newspaper note about her sister's death). The spa visitor's lists from Bad Ischl indicate, that she served Marie Valerie also after the end of the world war. Bombelles' forefathers were a French noble family who emigrated after the revolution in 1789. [honsi.org]

[188] Karl was an Austrian field-marshal and archduke of the House of Habsburg. He made himself a name during the Napoleonic wars, the battles of Caldiero and Aspern are both mentioned in the novel. He was the first ever to inflict a defeat on Napoléon in a battle (Aspern 1809). [honsi.org]

[189] Padua is a major city in the Veneto region of Italy. It is situated between Verona, Vicenza and Venice. Like the rest of Veneto, Padua belonged to Austria between 1815 and 1866. [honsi.org]

[190] Jaroš was the owner of a firm from Kralupy that manufactured and installed pumps, water pipes, drains and drinking vessels for animals. Václav Jaroš died in 1902 and it was probably his son who continued the business.

Extensive information can be found in the book Historie kralupského průmyslu, řemesel a živností (*History of Kralupy industry, crafts and trades*) by Josef Stupka.

It is highly likely that Hašek drew information from his tenure as editor of Svět zvířat when he composed Švejk's dream. Jaroš advertised in the journal and at least once it published a news item about the firm. [honsi.org]

[191] Jičín is a town in the eastern part of Bohemia, perhaps best known for its connection with the famous war-lord from the Thirty Years' War: Albrecht von Wallenstein (Albrecht z Valdštejna). The town with its protected historical center is attractive, and enjoys considerable tourism, partly due to its proximity to the popular recreation area Český ráj (Czech Paradise). [honsi.org]

[192] Jindřichův Hradec is a town in South Bohemia, situated in a flat area with many fish ponds. The historical center is protected as heritage.

The town was also the seat of recruitment district No. 75 and the replacement battalion of Infantry Regiment No. 75. The Regiment Staff was also located here at times and the Regiment was always present with at least one regular battalion. [honsi.org]

[193] Odkolek was a flour mill and bakery which was founded by František Odkolek in 1850. The fire referred to happened in 1896, and it was the original mill at Kampa that burnt down. [honsi.org]

It was not reconstructed; a new mill was built at Vysočany instead. The factory is now owned by United Bakeries. The old mill has since been rebuilt and today it houses Národní muzeum Kampa (*National Museum Kampa*). [honsi.org]

[194] Veszprém is a Hungarian city situated north of Lake Balaton. It is one of the oldest cities of Hungary and one of the first to get a university. Veszprém was in 1914 a garrison town, and was home to Honvédinfanterie-regiment Nr. 13 (*Hungarian Land Defense Infantry Regiment No. 13*). [honsi.org]

[195] Lake Balaton is located in western Hungary and measured by area the largest lake in Central Europe. [honsi.org]

[196] *Slang-wise, Pressburg. Yes, that was the name of what is today Slovakia's Bratislava. In Hungarian, Pozsony; in Latin, Posonium; until 1919 in Slovak, Prešporok or Prešporek; and in Czech until 1919, Prešpurk."* [svejkmuseum.cz]

[197] This is not a typographical error. The word "intelikent" here stands for the original Czech "intelikentní". There is no evidence that the malformed Czech word "intelikentní", a nonstandard variant of "inteligentní", i.e. "*intelligent*", appears outside Hašek's novel. It might be Hašek capturing the idea of the aspirational speech of people reaching beyond their linguistic competence in an effort to sound more educated or refined.

The term for this in linguistics is hypercorrection – a phenomenon where speakers over-apply a perceived "rule" or mimic prestige forms, often producing incorrect or artificial results. A textbook case of hypercorrection in English is the expression "For my wife and I" instead of "me". People try to sound proper, mimicking what they believe to be educated speech, but misfire.

Using "me" in place of "I" is so widespread among the less literary, educated, sophisticated (take your pick), that it appears it is abhorrent for their "betters" to the point, that guarding against committing such a peasant faux pas it is probably they who began to use the "For my wife and I" hypercorrection. And, in a case of double loop feedback, the aspirational among the "lower" classes adopted it, spreading it like wild fire, to compete in scope with the original sin of incorrect use of "me". Speakers cast abroad "For my wife and I" from the pulpit, dais, and media screen. [Translator's note]

[198] Čabiny is a village in the Laborec valley between Humenné and Medzilaborce. The place was destroyed during the Russian winter offensive in 1914-15. The village is quite spread out and there are two railway stations: Nižné Čabiny and Vyšné Čabiny. These were separate communities until 1964. [honsi.org]

[199] Brestov is a village by the river Laborec in Slovakia. The population count is just 66, 49 of them Ruthenians. It is situated two km south of Radvaň nad Laborcom. When Jaroslav Hašek wrote the novel, the name of the village was Zbudský Brestov. [honsi.org]

[200] Medzilaborce is a town in the Laborec valley of eastern Slovakia, near the Polish border and the Łupków Pass. In February 1915 Russian forces occupied the town but were driven out in May. This happened only a few weeks before Švejk and his march battalion arrived, so the traces of fighting described in the novel were very fresh. [honsi.org]

[201] Milovice is, to judge by plot, itinerary and timing, almost certainly Michalovce. The nearest Milovice is a place near Nymburk which had a Soviet military base from 1968 to 1991. In 1914 more than half the population of Michalovce were Hungarians and the author has probably translated the name from old maps which still used Hungarian names. [honsi.org]

[202] Dolní Zahájí cannot be identified from a modern map but Baloun is probably talking about Zahájí by Mydlovary in South Bohemia, the district he is from.

In 1911 Hašek wrote a story centered on Mydlovary and Zahájí: Vislingská aféra v Mydlovarech (*The Visling Affair in Mydlovary*). It was first printed in Karikatury (*Caricatures*) March 7$^{th}$ 1911 and soon after it appeared in Šípy (*Arrows*) in Chicago! [honsi.org]

[203] Palota is a village on the Slovak side of the Łupków Pass, about 10 km north of Medzilaborce. There is no railway station here anymore, although the railway line from Medzilaborce to Sanok goes through the village. [honsi.org]

[204] Łupków Pass is a mountain pass in the Carpathians, on the current border between Slovakia and Poland. The tunnel and the associated railway line were finished in 1874 and linked Galicia to the rest of the Austro-Hungarian

Empire across the mountains. The pass was one of the strategically important Carpathian passes that were bitterly contested during the battles of 1914 and 1915. The railway tunnel was damaged and repaired multiple times during both world wars. [honsi.org]

[205] Brandenburg is a historic province in Prussia that existed until 1945. It does not correspond to the current German state, as old Brandenburg included areas that are now part of Poland. The capital was Potsdam.

The soldiers who erected the mentioned monument would have belonged to Beskid Corps, a German unit that was formed in the Laborec valley in late March and early April 1915.

The troops who made up Beskid Corps were mainly recruited from these provinces: Hesse (*25th Reserve Division*), East Prussia (*35th Reserve Division*) and Pomeriana (*4th Division*). The only possible Branden- burgers in this army corps appear to be Dragoon Regiment "von Arnim" (2nd Brandenburg) No. 12, allocated to the *4th Division*. In peace time they were garrisoned in Gnesen (now Gniezno), actually in the province of Posen.

From May 5th to 7th Beskid Corps fought a fierce battle against Russian forces who defended the Łupków Pass to cover the retreat of the 3rd Army that was threatened by encirclement further west in the Carpathians. The Germans ultimately emerged victorious from the battle and the Russians withdrew northwards to positions by the river San. It would have been the destruction caused during this battle that Švejk observed during the break in the Łupków Pass. [honsi.org]

[206] Csap is the Hungarian name of border town Чоп (Chop) between Ukraine, Slovakia and Hungary, until 1921 part of Hungary. It is now located on Ukrainian territory and is an important railway junction and border crossing. [honsi.org]

[207] Ungvár is the Hungarian name of Ужгород (Uzhhorod), a city now on the border between Ukraine and Slovakia. Until 1921 it was part of Hungary, and until 1938 it belonged to Czechoslovakia. It is located just inside Ukrainian territory and is an important railway junction. The city has a university and some industry. It is also a quite popular tourist destination. The city sports a bronze miniature statue of Švejk, mounted on the railings by the river. [honsi.org]

[208] Kisberezna is the Hungarian name of Малий Березний (Malyj Bereznyj), a village on the western side of Carpathians north of Užhorod. Until 1921 it was Hungarian, in the inter-war years it belonged to Czechoslovakia, from 1945 the Soviet Union and from 1991 Ukraine. In 1914 more than 70 per cent

of the population were Rusyns. [honsi.org]

[209] Uszok (now Užok/Ужок) is a village in Ukraine, near the source of the river Už. It is best known for the mountain pass which it has given its name to. There was heavy fighting in the Uszok pass in 1914-15. From early May 1915 the pass was finally in Austro-Hungarian hands. [honsi.org]

[210] Munkács is the Hungarian name of Мукачеве, a city in the Ukrainian Carpathians. One of the three railway tracks across the Carpathians passed the city, and it was also home of a Honvéd (*Hungarian Land Defense*) garrison. After 1921 it was called Mukačevo and was part of Czechoslovakia. From 1945 to 1991 it was on Soviet hands. [honsi.org]

[211] Stryj (Стрий) is a city in the Lviv region in Ukraine, and is also the name of the river flowing through the town. The city belonged to Galicia in 1914 and was thus part of Austria-Hungary. [honsi.org]

[212] Sanok is a city in the Podkarpackie region of Poland, an important railway junction by the river San. It was part of Austria until 1918, and the city had until 1947 a large Ukrainian population.

[213] Bukowsko is a village in the Sanok district of Poland, in 1914 part of Austria. [honsi.org]

[214] Dynów is a town in Rzeszów county in Poland, in 1914 part of Austria. [honsi.org]

[215] Velká Polanka is not one hundred per cent identified, but by analyzing the text and historical events we can conclude that the place in question is Vyšná Polianka north of Bardejov. Until May 2$^{nd}$ 1915, when the Central Powers started their offensive by Gorlice and Tarnów, the front went very close to the village. The Russian 48th Infantry Division (HQ in Samara) held this section of the front at the time. The division was almost completely destroyed during the first week of May. [honsi.org]

[216] Samara is a city on the Volga river and is the sixth largest city in Russia. Samara is an important industrial city, known among other things for its arms industry. The city was provisional capital of the Soviet Union during World War II. From 1935 to 1991 it was called Kuybyshev.

The Samara Division that Leutnant Dub talks about is the Russian 48$^{th}$ Infantry Division (HQ in Samara) which during the first week of May 1915 was trapped and destroyed in the Carpathians. Large parts of it, including staff and its commander Lavr Kornilov were taken prisoners. The narrative in the novel corresponds well with historical events. [honsi.org]

[217] Poděbrady is a spa town in county Nymburk. It is located 50 km east of

Prague on the river plain by the Labe.

Švejk's anecdote is one of many examples of how Hašek mixed his friends into *The Good Soldier Švejk*. This time it is Ladislav Hájek who was also mentioned in one-year volunteer Marek's tale from his time as editor of Svět zvířat (*Animal World*). [honsi.org]

[218] "Nezávislost" (*Independence*) was a weekly newspaper published in Poděbrady from 1910 to at least 1931. The first issue was published on January 1st 1910, and the editor until October that year was Ladislav Hájek. His successor was Ladislav Volenec. The editorial line was initially patriotic, and the stated goal was the establishment of a Czech state.

During the summer seasons from 1910 to 1913, a supplement, Lázně Poděbrady. In 1913 the magazine was split off from the mother newspaper and is listed with Ladislav Hájek as owner and editor. This year the magazine printed a couple of Hašek's stories and in also a picture of some members of *The Party of Moderate Progress within the Bounds of the Law*, including Hašek and Hájek. [honsi.org]

[219] The Czech "hlavní hlavou" literally means "main head." Both words share the same root (hlava = head), creating a deliberate redundancy for comic effect, especially when applied to a minor local personage. To capture this humor, this edition renders it as "heady head," reflecting the same-root wordplay.

[220] A feuilleton was a short, often humorous or literary newspaper column or sketch, popular in Central Europe during the late 19th and early 20th centuries. Typically devoted to light social commentary or cultural anecdotes rather than hard news, it was printed in a special section of the paper and was a common outlet for writers like Hašek. Many episodes of Švejk reflect this feuilleton tradition. [Translator's note]

[221] The Czech phrase "ve kterým von byl vodvislej" (*in which he was dependent*) is unusual because the standard idiom for dependence would be "na kterým" (*on which*). Hašek deliberately uses "ve kterým" (*in which*), giving the magazine both a spatial sense — "the place where he lived and worked" — and an ironic twist: the "independent" magazine is one on which he was dependent. The original, first edition translation "*that independent magazine, where he used to hang and on which he was dependent*", attempted to preserve this double meaning. The revised translation, "*that independent magazine, in which he was dependant*", reproduces both the syntactic irony and Hašek's deliberate solecism: "vodvislej" is a nonstandard form of "závislý", and is explicitly marked as such in Váša–Trávníček: "jinak nespr.

315

místo závislý (*otherwise incorr. instead of dependent*)." The archaic English spelling "dependant" (normally a noun) is used here adjectivally to mirror the Czech degradation and to hint at the speaker's suspended status — a verbal pendant hanging beneath the pretense of independence. [Translator's note]

[222] Brynych (born Eduard Josef) was bishop of Hradec Králové from 1892 to 1902. [honsi.org]

[223] Trento (Ger. Trient) is a city in northern Italy that until 1918 was part of Austria. It was one of Austria-Hungary's strongest fortresses, protecting Valle dell'Adige (the Adige valley) against Italy. The city was predominantly Italian speaking. [honsi.org]

[224] Bytouchov (now Bítouchov) is a village by Mladá Boleslav. [honsi.org]

[225] Havlasa (born Jan Klecanda) was a Czech journalist, author, explorer and diplomat. Before World War I he undertook long journeys in Asia, Polynesia and America and when back home he wrote about and held lectures about his journeys. At the time he was first and foremost known as an explorer and traveler.

In April 1915 he was sentenced to a seven month prison term because of the brochure *Colonial politics and the world war* that was published in November the previous year. The case was heard at I&R Land Defense Divisional Court at Hradčany and he served the sentence in the neighboring garrison prison. In February 1916, at the request of Chief State Prosecutor, the sentence was extended by one year. In June 1917 he was released and immediately entered military service.

In 1919 took part at the Versailles peace conference, representing Czechoslovakia. He was later ambassador to Brazil and Chile. After the Nazi occupation of his homeland in 1939 he went into exile and was active in the resistance movement. In 1947 he emigrated to USA where he lived for the rest of his life.

Jaroslav Hašek knew Havlasa already from his youth. Both attended the Gymnasium at Žitná street at the same time (Hašek from 1893 to 1897). Both also contributed regularly to the illustrated weekly Zlatá Praha (*Golden Prague*). Havlasa was son of the author Jan Klecanda and brother of the Czech legionnaire Jiří Klecanda. [honsi.org]

[226] Mnichovo Hradiště is a town north of Mladá Boleslav. [honsi.org]

[227] Szczawne is a village in the Podkarpacki region of Poland, located by the railway line between the Łupków Pass and Sanok. The railway station is Szczawne-Kulaszne. The area was until 1947 mainly populated by Ukrainians, but these were forcibly resettled during the ethnic cleansing that

followed in the wake of World War II. [honsi.org]

[228] Kulaszne is a village in Komańcza community in the Podkarpackie (*Subcarpathian*) region of Poland, on the railway line between the Łupkow Pass and Sanok. The railway station is Szczawne-Kulaszne.

The village was occupied by the Russian army from November 1914 to May 8th 1915. At the time it was populated predominantly by Ukrainians with Greek Catholic faith. These were expelled after World War II but again (2010) the village has a Greek Catholic church.

With near certainty, the 12th March Battalion of Infantry Regiment No. 91 with Jaroslav Hašek passed this point on July 2nd 1915 or shortly after. They had reached Humenné on that date and would presumably have traveled onwards very soon. We also know that they approached Sambor on July 4th. [honsi.org]

[229] The phrase "*the ways may be varied, only let's all will as one*" translates Hašek's "cesty můžou býti rozličné, jenom vůli mějme všichni rovnou", which modifies a line from Ján Kollár's poem Slávy dcera (1824, Předzpěv): "Cesty mohou býti rozličné, ale cíl jeden" (*The paths may be various, but the goal is one*). Kollár's line expressed a romantic ideal of Slavic unity toward one destiny. Hašek keeps the first half but replaces the conclusion with an exhortation about shared will. While some may read this as ironic, it may equally reflect Hašek's lived experience of solidarity and survival. His life defied simple labels. In war, he began as a soldier of the Austro-Hungarian army, served in the Czecho-Slovak Legions, moved through the anti-Bolshevik Muravyov Corps, and ultimately worked as a propagandist and political officer for Trotsky's Fifth Army during the Russian Civil War. This complexity is well documented in the biography by Pavel Gan, Osudy humoristy Jaroslava Haška v říši carů a komisařů i doma v Čechách (*The Fateful Adventures of Jaroslav Hašek in the Empire of the Czars and Commissars And Even at Home in the Czechlands*), based on Gan's four conceptual studies of Hašek's Russian years (1918–1920). Gan, who passed away in July 2025 and was laid to rest at the Jewish Cemetery in Göttingen, was one of the leading authorities on Hašek's Russian period. His research clarified Hašek's complex allegiances and literary transformation, deepening our understanding of the man behind *The Good Soldier Švejk*. The author of this translation met Gan at the 2003 International Conference Hašek and Švejk – Humor of the Millennium in Lipnice and treasures the memory of those exchanges. May he rest in peace, "in the Truth of the Lord." [Translator's note]

[230] Málaga is a city in Andalusia, Southern Spain. The Málaga wine is a sweet dessert wine which is produced in the region around the city. The wine type has a history that goes back to Roman times and is protected by designation of origin (Denominación de Origen). [honsi.org]

[231] The One-year Volunteer's cry while looting the underknave—"*Lord, let me keep this underknave and this summer as well, that I may hoe and fertilize him, that he may bear and bring me fru*it"— is a burlesque paraphrase of **Luke 13:8–9**, a passage from the Parable of the Barren Fig Tree. The original biblical context is earnest: a vineyard owner, frustrated by a fig tree that bears no fruit, wants it cut down. The gardener, however, pleads for one more year of grace:

    1.    Bible kralická (1613):

"Pane, nechaj ji i tohoto léta, až ji okopám a pohnojím. A bude-liť nésti ovoce, dobře; pakli ne, i potom vyťati ji dáš."
(Lukáš 13:8–9)

    2.    King James Version (1611):

"Lord, let it alone this year also, till I shall dig about it, and dung it: And if it bear fruit, well: and if not, then after that thou shalt cut it down."
(Luke 13:8–9)

Hašek's grotesquely comic variation places this sacred plea in the mouth of a soldier engaged in a game of cards, begging divine favor not for a living tree, but for a spodek (*underknave*), a low-value card in the Austrian deck.

The fig tree becomes the underknave, the gardener's hoeing and dunging becomes absurd game strategy, and the bearing of fruit becomes winning the round. As so often in Švejk, biblical resonance is simultaneously preserved and deflated. This satirical distortion typifies Hašek's method: grounding low farce in high language, upending the moral order, and exposing the absurdities of both war and religiosity through the logic of . [Translator's note]

[232] The volunteer's lofty defense after looting an osmička (*eight*) parodies **Luke 15:8–9**, the Parable of the Lost Coin:

    3.    Bible kralická (1613):

„Aneb která žena mající grošů deset, ztratí-li jeden groš, nerozsvítí svíce, a nevymeče-li domu, a nehledá-li pilně, až jej nalezne? A nalezši svolá přítelkyně a sousedy, řkoucí: Radujte se se mnou, neboť jsem nalezla groš, kterýž sem byla ztratila." (Lukáš 15:8–9)

    4.    King James Version (1611):

"Either what woman having ten pieces of silver, if she lose one piece, doth not light a candle, and sweep the house, and seek diligently till she find it? And when she hath found it, she calleth her friends and her neighbours together, saying, Rejoice with me; for I have found the piece which I had lost." (Luke 15:8–9)

The volunteer blasphemously substitutes his card looting for the act of divine recovery, gleefully corrupting the parable's message into an exaltation of his own trickery: "Spolu radujte se se mnou, neboť rabovala jsem osmičku a v kartách přikoupila trumfového krále s esem!" (*"Rejoice with me, for I have looted an eight and in the cards purchased a trump king with an ace!"*). Hašek here again ridicules the sanctimonious facade of piety when used to veil greed, vice, or self-justification.

[233] This apocalyptic outcry is adapted from Luke 21:11, where Christ foretells signs of tribulation preceding the end of the age:

    5.   Bible kralická (1613):

„A zemětřesení veliká budou po místech, i hladové i nakažení, hrůzy také a zázrakové veliké budou s nebe."(Lukáš 21:11)

    6.   King James Version (1611):

"And great earthquakes shall be in divers places, and famines, and pestilences; and fearful sights and great signs shall there be from heaven." (Luke 21:11)

By exclaiming this verse while collecting bets in a card game, the volunteer absurdly transposes a scene of divine wrath and cosmic judgment into the petty chaos of gambling. Hašek lampoons the rhetorical inflation common among imperial officers and clergy alike, where even trivial victories are dressed in the language of spiritual grandeur or martyrdom. [Translator's note]

[234] Mosty Wielkie is the Polish name of Великі Мости (Velyki Mosty), a town in Galicia, now in the Sokal region of Ukraine. Jaroslav Hašek and his Infantry Regiment No. 91 marched past here on July 21$^{st}$ 1915, on the way to the battlefield by Sokal. The town housed a garrison from 1846 to 1918.

In 1915 the mentioned railway line didn't exist so the author probably had another place in mind. [honsi.org]

[235] Brody (ukr. Броди) is a city in Galicia, now in the Lviv oblast of Ukraine. Before World War I it was an important trading city on the border between Russia and Austria-Hungary. In 1914 Jews made up more than 60 per cent of the population.

Russian forces conquered the city in late August 1914, and it was recaptured September 2$^{nd}$ 1915. The following year it was captured again during the Brusilov offensive and remained occupied until 1918. [honsi.org]

[236] Limanowa is a town in western Galicia, known for the battle in December 1914 where Austria-Hungary succeeded in repelling a Russian offensive that threatened Kraków. This was the Dual Monarchy's first strategic victory in the war and saved it from immediate collapse. From Hauptmann Tayrle's uttering it is easy to assume that Austria-Hungary lost the battle. This is however not correct. [honsi.org]

[237] Kraśnik is a town in that belonged to the Russian part of Poland. It is known for the battle that took place from August 23$^{rd}$ to 26$^{th}$ 1914, the first major battle in the war that Austria-Hungary won. The Austrian commander General Dankl was awarded the honorary title Dankl Graf von Krasnik after this battle. On the Russian side participated the famous-to-be Finnish commander Carl Gustaf Mannerheim. [honsi.org]

[238] The Gimnazjum (*Gymnasium*) in Sanok is assumed to be Szkoła Podstawowa (*Primary School*) No. 8 in Sanok, a gymnasium (*middle school*) in the center of Sanok that is still in use. The name of the school is not explicitly mentioned in *The Good Soldier Švejk*, but a town the size of Sanok would probably not have hosted more than one Gymnasium, at least not in the center.

Despite this apparent obviousness, it would be prudent to take the information from *The Good Soldier Švejk* with a pinch of salt. The 12$^{th}$ March Battalion of Infantry Regiment No. 91 with Jaroslav Hašek surely never set foot here, at least not under the circumstances described in the novel.

Thus Hašek probably drew from his experiences elsewhere, and the Gymnasium in Sokal is the only similar institution where the regiment during Hašek's service is known to have been lodged. There could, of course, have been others, but Sanok was definitely not one of them. [honsi.org]

[239] Hanover is a large city in Northern Germany, in 1914 the capital of the Prussian province of Hanover. The division mentioned in the novel took its name from the province, not the city.

In the German Empire there were two so-called Hanover-divisions, numbered 19 and 20 respectively. These belonged to Armeekorps X (*10th Army Corps*), which was also based in Hanover. Both divisions operated in Galicia during the time-span of this part of the plot (early July 1915). It is therefore likely that their reserve units passed Sanok on the way to the front. [honsi.org]

[240] Bank Krakowski (*The Bank of Krakow*) was reportedly a bank at the Sanok town rynek (*square*), but the information is not very reliable. The building

still existed as of 2010, but had other uses.

It should be added that Jaroslav Hašek and 12th March Battalion never passed through Sanok, so the inspiration for the events that took place here must be sought elsewhere. [honsi.org]

[241] Kawiarnia Miejska (*Municipal Café*) is said to have existed. The alleged location is now occupied by Hotel Pod Trzema Różami (*Under the Three Roses*). At present (2010), it is a normal, decent hotel with a restaurant and pizzeria attached.

It should be added that Jaroslav Hašek and 12th March Battalion never passed through Sanok, so the inspiration for the events that took place here must be sought elsewhere. [honsi.org]

[242] Platnéřská is a street in Staré město, Prague. It was renovated around 1908 and changed character completely. In 1910 there were two wine taverns in the street: Antonín Kafka's in no. 9 and František Müller's in no. 15. [honsi.org]

[243] Philip II of Macedon was the king of Macedonia, the father of Alexander the Great. During his reign the kingdom expanded considerably and at his death he controlled nearly the entire Greek peninsula and the areas bordering the Aegean Sea. [honsi.org]

[244] Morocco is a country in North Africa, in 1914 a Spanish and French protectorate, which previously had been governed by the Ottoman Empire. There were repeated conflicts between France and Germany about Morocco, and in 1905 and 1912 treaties were signed that recognized the special position of France and Spain. Many Moroccans served in the French armed forces during World War I. The sultan in question is surely Yusef ben Hassan who came to power in 1912 after the treaty of Fez. [honsi.org]

[245] Velké Meziříčí is a town in the Vysočina region of Czechland. It is located in the Moravian part of the region, east of Jihlava in the direction of Brno.

There is no doubt that Švejk refers to Kaisermanövern (*Imperial maneuvers*) there in 1909, an event that even Svět zvířat (*Animal World*) mentioned during the period Hašek edited the magazine. Even a photo showing Emperor Franz Joseph I and Emperor Wilhelm II on horseback was printed. The maneuvers took place from September 8th to 11th 1909. [honsi.org]

[246] "U Kocanů" was a dance restaurant which according to Egon Erwin Kisch was identical to U města Slaného (*At the Town of Slaný*) in Nové město (*New Town*). The unofficial name U Kocanů is taken from the former owner Karel Kocan, who had sold the place sometime before 1910. [honsi.org]

[247] "U zelené žáby" (*At the Green Frog*) was a pub in Budějovice that remains unidentified and almost certainly never existed under this name. Božena probably confused U zelené ratolesti (*At the Green Spray*) and U žáby (*At the Frog*).

The former was a coaching inn at Říšská boulevard (now Husová) next to Marian Barracks. It also hosted dances, which fits well with the description in the novel. The building is still in use as a restaurant and guesthouse, and the name remains unchanged.

"U žáby" was, in 2015, a café at Piaristické square, probably named after a stone frog on the facade of the church opposite. The name has probably been used for inns at the square also in 1915, although this has not been verified. [honsi.org]

[248] Věnceslava Lužická was a Czech journalist and writer who mostly wrote using a pseudonym. Her real name was Anna Srbová. For many years she was editor of the women's magazine Lada. [honsi.org]

[249] "Beseda" surely refers to Měšťanská beseda (*Burghers' Club*) in Prague II. The institution existed from 1845 until 1952 and the associated restaurant was in 1891 listed as belonging to Gustav Stejskal. The building has from 2008 hosted a four-star hotel. [honsi.org]

[250] Starý Knín is a village in the Příbram district south-west of Prague. The village was in 1960 merged with Nový Knín. [honsi.org]

[251] A woman bearing this name was in 1983 identified as a real person by Augustin Knesl. She was buried in Starý Knín. How the author picked up her name and pinpointed her geographically remains a mystery. [honsi.org]

[252] farmers cheese mixed with cream, butter and chives [Translator's note]

[253] Tyrawa Wołoska is a large village in Galicia, 17 km east of Sanok. The village was in 1914 part of Austria-Hungary and mainly inhabited by Ruthenians (Ukrainians). Tyrawa Wołoska has belonged to Poland since 1918.

Already in November 1914 there were reported cases of cholera in the village, so the description in the novel about boarded up wells is realistic. This still doesn't prove that author knew the place, this chapter of the novel is in a geographical sense entirely fictional - none of the march battallions of IR. 91 marched past here, and the author's own were transported all the way to Sambor by train. Still Jaroslav Hašek had witnessed cholera outbreaks and precautions in many other places, and may have "moved" the situation geographically. [honsi.org]

254 Kozí plácek (*Goat patch*) is the unofficial name of a small town square in Staré město (*Old Town*), Prague. The streets Kozí street, Haštalská street, U Obecního dvora and Vězeňská street all end here. [honsi.org]

255 U Dvořáků was a brothel in Staré město (according to Radko Pytlík). Milan Hodik underpins this information by providing a list of brothels from Chytilův adresář (*Chytil's address book*) 1912. It contains two entries with Dvořák as proprietor, but Jaroslav Dvořák is by far more likely, because the other address is in Malá Strana, and this story about tinsmith Pimpra is clearly set in Staré Město. [honsi.org]

256 This is not a typographical error. The word "alcahol" here stands for the original Czech "alkahol", the author's deliberate misspelling of "alkohol".

257 Bolzanova street is the name of a short street in Praha II.. It is located near the main railway station. [honsi.org]

258 Malý Polanec seems to have been a place between Tyrawa Wołoska and Liskowiec but it can't be identified. Jaroslav Šerák suggests that it might be Malopołska by Brelików, which judging by the author's description of the route is plausible. That said it looks like the name of a hill rather than a village. [honsi.org]

259 Liskowiec probably refers to the village Liskowate in Galicia, now just inside Poland on the border with Ukraine. It belongs to Gmina Ustrzyki Dolne. From 1944 to 1951 it was part of the Soviet Union. [honsi.org]

260 Krościenko is a village in Galicia, now just inside Poland on the border with Ukraine. It is located only a few kilometers from Liskowate and is the last railway station on the Polish side of the border. [honsi.org]

261 Stara Sól is the Polish name of the village Стара Сіль (Stara Sil) in Galicia, now just inside Ukraine on the border with Poland. On a military map from 1910 the village is called Starasól. [honsi.org]

262 Lourdes is one of the most popular Roman-Catholic pilgrimage destinations in the whole world. It is located in south-western France, not far from the border with Spain. The number of inhabitants as of 2010 was around 15,000.

The song is printed in full in the book První česká pouť do Lurd roku 1903 (*The first Czech pilgrimage to Lourdes in the year 1903*) and in the successor from 1907. Both books are written by father Leopold Kolísek.

The novel quotes sixteen of the sixty original verses and these are with a few exceptions reproduced to the letter by the author. The earliest printed copy in French that has been identified is a small book from 1875 that was written by the abbot Jean Gaignet (1839-1914). The Czech lyrics do not correspond to the original French version, and is more aligned with the German lyrics from which it presumably has been translated. [honsi.org]

263 Bernarda reported in 1858 apparitions of a small young lady. This gave rise to the legend of Lourdes which was to make the town into a major pilgrim site. Bernadette was canonized in 1933, under the name St Bernadette. [honsi.org]

264 Chanterelle mushrooms

265 Ropa is a small river which originates in the Beskids and flows northwards. Ropa is far from Liskowate so the author is probably getting it mixed up with another place. The source of the name is surely the nearby village of Ropienka and the "potok" (*stream*) of the same name which flows through the village. [honsi.org]

266 Jihlava is a city in the Vysočina region in Moravia. Until 1945 it was a German-speaking enclave. The composer Gustav Mahler spent most of his youth here. [honsi.org]

267 [Plural form of Moskal.] Moskal is an ethnic slur (formerly neutral term) that means "Russian", literally "Muscovite", in Ukrainian, Polish, and Belarusian. [en.wikipedia.org]

268 Częstochowa is a city in southern Poland, known as a pilgrim destination due to the Black Madonna, a painting in the monastery of Jasna Góra. [honsi.org]

269 *Polish* kontusz *is long upper coat made of coarser, but often very expensive fabric with long, cut sleeves that come with festive occasions were thrown over shoulders. The name is said to come from Turkey.* [svejkmuseum.cz]

270 Chyrów is the Polish name of the town Хирів (Khyriv) in the Lviv oblast in western Ukraine. The town is a railway junction and even in 2010 there were passenger services to Sanok and Lviv (among others). The town was part of Austria-Hungary until 1918. [honsi.org]

271 Grabów is the name of many places in Poland but none of them are near Liskowate. It may also have been a village in Ukraine, now called Hrabiv or possibly Hrabovo. Although these exist, none of them are located near Švejk's route.

A possible explanation is that Grabów is a misspelling of Grąziowa, a village just north of Liskowate. Today there are only a few houses, but in 1915 it had more than 1000 inhabitants.

A perhaps better guess is Grabownica (now Грабівниця) just inside Ukraine, north of Dobromil. This is a place the author is much more likely to have known than Grąziowa, and the fact that it is mentioned in the same sentence as neighboring Chyrów is a further indication. [honsi.org]

[272] Hołubla has not yet been identified. A place with this name does exist in central Poland but it is out of question that this is the one the author had in mind. It is more likely to be a place in Ukraine and a possible explanation is Hubice (Губичі), just north of Dobromil. [honsi.org]

[273] Baikal is the largest fresh-water reserve on earth and the deepest lake. Lake Baikal is situated in southern Siberia in Russia, not far from the border with Mongolia. Jaroslav Hašek knew the area from his time as member of the city soviet in Irkutsk in 1920. [honsi.org]

[274] Wołoczyska (Volochyskis) is the Polish name of contemporary Волочиськ (Volochysk) in Ukraine. Until 1918 the border between Austria-Hungary and Russia divided the town, with the larger part on the Russian side east of the river Zbruch, while the lesser part, Podwołoczyska, was Austrian.

During the retreat from Tarnopol from July 19th 1917 onwards, Jaroslav Hašek's 1st Czechoslovak Rifle Regiment stayed in Podwołoczyska from August 2nd to 6th. This was the last time the author ever set foot on the Austrian territory. [honsi.org]

[275] Královská 18 was a street address in Smíchov, now Zborovská 489/52. The street got its current name from battle of Zborów in Ukraine (now Zboriv) where on July 2nd 1917, the Czechoslovak Brigade for the first time fought k.u.k. Wehrmacht.

[276] Mikulášská třída was until 1926 the name of Pařížská ulice (*Paris street*) in Staré město (*Old Town*). Today it counts as the most fashionable street in Prague. The new street appeared as a result of the renovation of Josefov (the Jewish quarter) around the turn of the 19th to 20th century and was named after Kostel sv. Mikuláše (*Church of St. Nicholas*) - at the time Russian Orthodox - that is located at the southern end at Staroměstské náměstí (*Old Town square*). [honsi.org]

[277] Sedlčansko (*Sedlčany region*) is the area around the town of Sedlčany about 50 km south of Prague east of Vltava. It is a rural area without large cities. It is not an administrative unit. [honsi.org]

[278] Horní Stodůlky (*Upper* Stodůlky), or rather Stodůlky, is a cadastral area and former village on the western outskirts of Prague. Until 1974 it was a separate administrative entity. There is no mention in historical reference works about any distinction between *Lower* and *Upper* Stodůlky. The village did, however, have a vicarage, but who the priest was is not known. [honsi.org]

[279] Sambor is the Polish name of the city of Самбір (Sambir) in Galicia, now in

Ukraine, near the Polish border. Sambor is located in the Lviv oblast and has around 35,000 inhabitants (2010). The city is connected by railway to Lviv and Khyriv.

Sambor was occupied by the Russian army from September 17th 1914 to May 15th 1915. The front was close to the town also during October and the railway station was one of the buildings that suffered serious damage. [honsi.org]

[280] "*Marriage bonds* (Heirats-Cautionen), 1750-1883. Each officer had to post a bond which could be used to sustain his widow and children in the event of his death."[feefhs.org]

[281] Arabia normally refers to the Arabian Peninsula but here the talk is about the horse breed. [honsi.org]

[282] Alps are the next highest mountain range in Europe after the Caucasus. It extends across parts of France, Switzerland, Germany, Austria, Italy, Liechtenstein, Monaco and Slovenia. The highest mountain is Mont Blanc with 4810 meters.

During World War I there was fighting in the Alps on the Italian front in Tirol, the area was otherwise spared destruction. A large part of the Alps was within the borders of Austria-Hungary. [honsi.org]

[283] Karmelitáni (*Carmelites*) probably refers to kostel Panny Marie Vítězné (*Church of Virgin Mary Victorious*) in Malá Strana (Lesser Quarter), Prague. It was owned by the Carmelite order until 1784 and has been again since 1993. [honsi.org]

[284] Resslova is a street in Nové město (*New Town*) stretching from Karlovo náměstí (*Charles square*) down towards the Vltava. Jaroslav Hašek attended Obchodní akademie (*Commercial Academy*) here from 1899 to 1902 and graduated with good marks. [honsi.org]

[285] Czech "místodržitel" (literally "*holder-in-place*") was the Emperor's plenipotentiary in the Crownland of Bohemia — the man who "stood in" for the monarch. English historiography usually flattens this to "Governor of Bohemia," to avoid the colonial connotations that "Viceroy" acquired from the British Raj. But "viceroy" is in fact the precise calque (vice-rex = místodržitel) and was also the Czech term used for the British Viceroy of India. We retain "viceroy" here to preserve the bureaucratic pomp and foreignness of the title, even if readers may momentarily expect elephants rather than Habsburg clerks.

[286] Národní divadlo is the Czech *National Theater*. The building was erected in neo-Renaissance style in the years 1868-1883 and has become a national symbol. [honsi.org]

[287] Sv. Jindřich probably refers to a police station by kostel Svatého Jindřicha (*Church of St. Jindřich*) in Prague. There is no police station there today, but in Švejk's lifetime there was a police station at Havlíčkovo náměstí 979/35, an address which is very close to the mentioned church. [honsi.org]

[288] The Czech idiom "s tebou je kříž" literally means "*with you it's a cross*." It is rooted in the Christian image of Jesus of Nazareth carrying His cross to Golgotha, and by extension the call to the believer to "take up his cross" (Luke 9:23). In Czech colloquial use it came to mean that a person or situation is a constant burden or trial. Thus, while it functions much like "you're impossible" or "what a nuisance" in everyday speech, the phrase retains the deeper cultural resonance of the Passion narrative. Czech is saturated with similar kříž idioms (nést svůj kříž, *to bear one's cross*; můj kříž je těžký, *my cross is heavy*; s tebou je kříž, *with you it's a cross*), where kříž, *cross*, functions both as "burden" and as shorthand for "trial of suffering." [Translator's note]

[289] Felsztyn is the Polish name of a village in the Lviv oblast in Ukraine, from 1945 renamed Скелівка (Skelivka). The village is located between Sambir and Khyriv, very close to the border with Poland. Skelivka is the smallest place in the world with a statue of Švejk.

The village was in Austrian times part of Galicia and speakers of Polish were in an overwhelming majority. Jews made up more than half the population. The town had a Roman-Catholic church, a Greek-Catholic church and a synagogue. It was heavily damaged during fighting in October 1914 and was in Russian hands until around May 15th 1915. After World War I Felsztyn became part of Poland, and from 1939 the Soviet Union. [honsi.org]

[290] Wojalycze is almost certainly a misspelling of Wojutycze, the Polish name of the village Воютичі (Voyutychi) in the Lviv oblast in Ukraine.

Wojutycze is located on the railway line between Sambor and Chyrów and XII. March Battalion of Infantry Regiment No. 91 with Jaroslav Hašek traveled past it on July 4th 1915. [honsi.org]

[291] Posen is the German name of Poznań, one of the oldest and biggest cities in Poland. From 1793 to 1918 it was part of Prussia, and from 1871 part of Germany. The city and the province had, even during this period, a Polish majority. In the context of the novel the reference is to two regiments, thus the province of Posen is the subject, not the city itself. [honsi.org]

[292] Karlínský viadukt (*Karlín viaduct*), an often used name of the Negrelleho viaduct, is a railway viaduct in Prague. It starts at Masarykovo station, goes through Karlín and continues across Vltava to Holešovice. It is the oldest

railway bridge in Prague. Ferdinandova kasárna, where Feldkurat Katz had his office, was located just across the street from the viaduct, in Karlín. [honsi.org]

[293] Rozdělov was a village by Kladno, now a suburb of the city. In the 1950's large housing estate were built here and Rozdělov is now dominated by high-rise apartment blocks. [honsi.org]

[294] Chyrów is the Polish name of the town Хирів (Khyriv) in the Lviv oblast (*region*) in western Ukraine. The town is a railway junction and even in 2010 there were passenger services to Sanok and Lviv (among others). The town was part of Austria-Hungary until 1918. [honsi.org]

[295] Allāh is the Arab word for God and is commonly used in the context of Islam. The conception of Allah is very close to Judaism's Yahweh and the Christian God, which is natural as these religions have common roots.

In Austria-Hungary Islam joined the varied spectrum of religions when Bosnia-Herzegovina became part of the empire in 1908. In Militärseelsorge (*Military chaplaincy*) and the Feldimam (*Field Imam*) had their recognized place next to the Feldkurat and the Feldrabbiner (*Field Rabbi*).

The author had himself extensive knowledge of Muslim peoples in Russia, mostly from his stays in Tatarstan and Bashkortostan in 1918 and 1919. Another possible source of inspiration: according to his wife Alexandra Lvova (as retold by Franta Sauer), he employed a group of body-guards from the Muslim region of Cherkessia during his stay in Irkutsk in 1920. [honsi.org]

[296] Jaroslav ze Šternberka was a Czech nobleman (probably mythical), who is said to have won a battle against the Mongols (Tatars) by Hostýn in 1241. [honsi.org] Jaroslav of Šternberk is a fictional figure, both in the Šternberk lineage and in Moravian history. He was supposedly a nobleman who, in 1241, saved Moravia — and by extension, Christian Europe — from the Mongol invasion, the invaders being referred to as Tatars. The feat was said to have taken place through heroic acts near Olomouc.

In the mid-14th century, the chronicler Přibík Pulkava of Radenín wrote about events of the year 1253, in which he states: "The Tatars entered Moravia, laid waste to part of it, slaughtered great numbers near Olomouc,... and finally, when they came to that city, a certain nobleman from Šternberk, then the commander of said city, rode out from Olomouc, launched a bold attack upon them, and killed their chieftain, mortally wounding him. The Tatars, grieving his death and greatly astonished, fled back to Hungary. That said lord of Šternberk, for this glorious deed, received from the Czech king some lands near Olomouc, upon which he built a new castle, Šternberk, in commemoration."

Pulkava's report is relatively credible, as in 1253, the army of Hungarian king Béla IV did indeed invade Moravia. A substantial part of his forces were made up of Cumans, whose appearance and Mongol-style dress resembled that of the Tatars who had swept through Moravia earlier, in 1241 (see Mongol Invasion of Moravia, 1241). Pulkava erred only in mistaking these wild Cumans for Tatars. [cs.wikipedia.org]

[297] Hostýn (or Svatý Hostýn, i.e. *Saint* Hostýn) is a hill in Chvalčov in the Zlín Region of the Czech Republic. It is part of the Hostýn-Vsetín Mountains and has an elevation of 735 meters (2,411 ft.). It is an important Marian place of pilgrimage. The pilgrimage comes from a legend that describes a miracle made by the Virgin Mary. According to the traditional legend, first recorded in 1665 by the writer Bohuslav Balbín in his work Diva Montis Sancti, during the disastrous raid of the "Tartars" in the 13th century, people who were seeking asylum here lacked water and they prayed Mary for help. It is said that a stream of water came out of the ground and a powerful storm forced Tatars to retreat. [en.wikipedia.org]

[298] Dobromil is the Polish name of the town Добромиль (Dobromyl) in Galicia, now in the Lviv province in Ukraine, only a few kilometers from the border with Poland. It is on the railway line from Chyrów to Przemyśl. The town was until 1918 part of Austria-Hungary. [honsi.org]

[299] Niżankowice is the Polish name of the village Нижанковичі (Nyzhankovychi) in the Lviv oblast in Ukraine, very close to the Polish border and Przemyśl. [honsi.org]

[300] Praga is a district of Warsaw. As the city was part of Russian Poland in 1914, the inhabitants were naturally required to serve in the Russian armed forces. Praga is also the Polish name for Prague. [honsi.org]

[301] Yerevan is now the capital of Armenia; in 1914 it still belonged to Russia. From 1921 to 1991, the city was part of the Soviet Union. The current population is just over one million. [honsi.org]

[302] Caucasus is a geographical region on the border between Europe and Asia, which also comprises the mountain range of the same name. Europe's highest mountain, Elbrus, is found here. The countries of the region are Russia, Georgia, Azerbaijan and Armenia. [honsi.org]

[303] Tbilisi is now the capital of Georgia; in 1914 it belonged to the Russian Empire. From 1921 to 1991, the city was part of the Soviet Union. The current population is just over one million. [honsi.org]

304 a coarse tobacco (Nicotiana rustica) grown especially in the Ukraine [merriam-webster]

305 Židohoušť has so far not been identified with certainty. It may be a misspelling of Živohoušť; at least, translator Cecil Parrott made this assumption. This former village was flooded in 1954 when the Slapy dam was built across the Vltava. [honsi.org]

306 Jaroslav Matoušek is not directly identifiable but the author almost certainly borrowed the name from a real person. Antonín Měšťan identifies him as a translator of mythical prose. The person he has in mind was an expert on Gnosticism and Hermeticism, wrote books on the theme and also translated Neo-Platonic prose.

The most visible trace of him is a book from 1924 on the philosopher Jakub Böhme, which is still widely available. The catalog of the Czech National Library lists four titles (two of them translations from Greek) by him, published from 1922 to 1925. It is therefore probable that Jaroslav Hašek knew about Matoušek when he wrote those lines at the end of 1922. All four books were reprinted in the 1990's. In 1927 he wrote another book, this time about vampires.

Matoušek seems to have been a spare time author. Police records shows that he was a civil servant in the k.k. post and telegraph authorities. He was married to Marie Kalinova from Vršovice and in 1914 the couple lived in Prague IV., čp. 112 (Hradčany). [honsi.org]

307 Růžena Svobodová was a Czech writer who specialized in literature on the fate of women. She is vaguely classified as impressionist. [honsi.org]

308 Lubaczów is a town north of Przemyśl near the Ukrainian border. [honsi.org]

309 Milatyn is the Polish name of the village Милятин (Myliatyn) in the Volyn province in Ukraine. IR. 91 with Jaroslav Hašek marched past this place on August 28th 1915 during the Central Powers' advance onto Russian territory that autumn. Milatyn is located by the river Strypa, right on the former border between Austria-Hungary and Russia. [honsi.org]

310 Bubnów is the Polish name of the village Бубнів (Bubniv) in the Volodomyr-Volynski province in Ukraine. As there are several places with this name in the country, there is some uncertainty involved, but the mentioned place is the best guess due to its location just north of Sokal. This was an area that Jaroslav Hašek knew well (he was stationed nearby for nearly four weeks in August 1915). The author's statement that the front went through here at the time is also correct. [honsi.org]

311 Masaryk was a Czech politician and professor of philosophy who is

strongly linked to the creation of the Czechoslovak state. He was President of the country from 1918 until 1935. He enjoyed enormous respect at home and abroad, and the term "father of the nation" has rarely been more appropriate.

Until 1914, he was a member of Reichsrat and was still loyal to Austria-Hungary, but his experience from the first months of the war changed his outlook, and he decided to work for full Czech/Slovak independence. In December 1914, he moved abroad and campaigned for an independent Czechoslovak state. He directed his efforts towards the Entente politicians, influential press people, and other people in important positions. He soon became the leader of the Czech (and Slovak) independence movement abroad, and during the war, he spent time in Switzerland, France, England, USA and Russia. Within the independence movement, he enjoyed almost unchallenged authority.

Masaryk spent almost a year in Russia at the time when Jaroslav Hašek was there: he arrived in Petrograd on May 16th 1917 and left again in March 1918. The two could have met in Berezno (HQ of Hašek's regiment from August 11th 1917) and Kiev in February 1918. During his visit to Berezno in August 1917, Masaryk stayed in the mansion where Hašek worked. The author of *The Good Soldier Švejk* was at the time secretary of the staff of the 1st Czechoslovak Rifle Regiment. [honsi.org]

[312] Vašák was possibly inspired by a real person (or two). A certain Jan Vašák, born in Bukovany near Benešov on 17 September 1871, was a hatter who lived in Žižkov from 1907 until at least 1909. Notably, in 1906 he lived at Prague VIII čp. 524, which is in Libeň, the same area, where the literary hatter caused trouble in the pub. Vašák married in Karlín in 1898, so he had probably spent several years in the area. [honsi.org]

[313] Saint Peter (Simon Peter) was a leader of the early Christian Church, who features prominently in the New Testament through the Gospels and the Acts of the Apostles. He was one of Christ's twelve disciples. The Catholic Church regards him as the first bishop of Rome and also the first pope. [honsi.org]

[314] Saint Paul (Paul of Tarsos, born Saul) was a Greek Jew who became one of the early Christian leaders and one of the first missionaries. He is often mentioned in the New Testament and is attributed with writing 13 of its 27 books. Paul was executed in Rome during the reign of Emperor Nero. [honsi.org]

[315] Milan is Italy's seconds largest city and capital of the region of Lombardy. The city was more or less permanently under Habsburg rule from 1525 up to

the battle of Solferino i 1859. [honsi.org]

[316] Ratskeller (*Town Hall Cellar*), a restaurant in Graz which is still in business. The address is Hauptplatz 17. [honsi.org]

[317] Hašek used the line from the aria of Dalibor in the Act 1, Scene 4 of the eponymous Czech nationalist opera by Bedřich Smetana, the composer of The Bartered Bride: "a přísahu co řádný muž jsem splnil" (*"and the oath as a proper man I fulfilled"*) He dropped the opening "*and*" and substituted "*faithful*" for "*proper*". [Translator's note]

"Švejk argues that he could not have committed such a crime because he has "sworn an oath of loyalty to His Imperial Majesty" and, quoting a line from Smetana's famous opera... We do not know whether Švejk is referring to his prewar military service, prior to which he most likely had sworn an oath, and we will never know whether his being "certified by an army medical board as an imbecile" has de jure abrogated such a contract."

– Peter Steiner, Tropos Kynikos [svejkcentral.com]

[318] Berounka is a river which empties into the Vltava near Zbraslav, 10 km south of Prague city center. The river has its sources as far west as Bavaria and flows eastward. Its length is well over 100 km. [honsi.org]

[319] Dobříš is a town in okres (*county*) Příbram in central Bohemia, with 8,597 inhabitants at the 2009 count. The town was previously known for its glove factory and also has a chateau.

In 1983 Dobříš hosted a large conference on Jaroslav Hašek in connection with the 100th anniversary of the author's birth. The participants were with few exceptions from Warszaw Pact countries.

That same year Bamberg in Bavaria hosted a competing conference with participants from the rest of the world, including a large number of exiled Czechs. [honsi.org]

[320] Chuchle is a place south of Prague, now within the city boundaries, between Braník and Zbraslav. It is mostly used as a common term for the suburbs Velká Chuchle and Malá Chuchle. [honsi.org]

[321] Lustige Blätter (*Funny Pages*) was an illustrated humorous weekly that was published from 1886 to 1944. It was founded in Hamburg in 1886 by Alexander Moszkowski and Otto Eysler. The former was editor in chief until 1928 and in 1915 the publisher of the magazine was Verlag der "Lustigen Blätter" (Dr. Eysler & Co.) Gm.b.h. Already in 1887 the editorial offices moved to Berlin. [honsi.org]

[322] Hindenburg was a German general who was Commander in Chief of the

German forces on the Eastern front at the time of the events in the novel. From 1916 he became head of the entire German army and gradually became the most influential person in the country. He was elected president of Germany in 1925, a position he had also when Hitler assumed power in 1933, and he remained in office until his death the year after. He is the only German head of state ever who has been directly elected by the people. Politically he was regarded as conservative.

Hašek here refers to issue no. 2 of the series Illustrierter Tornister-Humor, published by Lustige Blätter from February 1915 and onwards. [honsi.org]

[323] Schloemp (called Schlemper by Hašek) was a German book trader, editor and publisher. From 1909 onwards he published a number of illustrated humorous books.

In 1915 he contributed to Tornister-Humor, a series of humorous propaganda booklets that were published by Lustige Blätter. Installments no. 1, 2, 3, 8 and 15 are directly mentioned in *The Good Soldier Švejk*.

Some time in late 1915 or early 1916 Schloemp was called up for service. Little about his military exploits is known until he was wounded at the Russian front on July 25$^{th}$ 1916. Two days later he was in person awarded the Eiserne Kreuz (*Iron Cross*) by Prince Leopold of Bavaria. Some weeks later Schloemp died from the injuries and was buried by Malinadr on August 23$^{rd}$. In official loss lists for Prussia he was first reported severely wounded on August 16$^{th}$, then dead on October 7$^{th}$. [honsi.org]

[324] Artur Lokesch was a writer who from 1915 onwards contributed to the series Tornister-Humor published by Lustige Blätter. The novel specifically refers to Unter'm Doppeladler (*Under the Double Eagle*) which was issue No. 15 in the series. The adverts added the explanatory notes Wiener Schnitzel aus der k. k. Feldküche, aufgewärmt von Arthur Lokesch (*Wiener Schnitzel From the I&R Kitchen. Reheated by Artur Lokesch*) and Hašek probably was inspired by these adverts rather than the booklets themselves. Lokesch also contributed to several other of these 64-page booklets. [honsi.org]

[325] Ignatius of Loyola was a Basque/Spanish nobleman and soldier known for having founded the Jesuit Order in 1534 and also the instigator of the inquisition. He was declared a saint in 1622. Kostel svatého Ignáce (*The Church of Saint Ignatius*) is named after him. [honsi.org]

[326] Grabowski was according to Milan Hodík identical to Bronisław Grabowski, a Polish ethnographer, writer, translator and slavist. He translated, among others, the Czech writers Karolina Světlá and Vrchlický.

Radko Pytlík makes no assumptions about Grabowski's identity, and quotes

Polish sources that there was no such statue in Przemyśl at the time. He suggests there might be a mix-up with a statue of Adam Mickiewicz that was indeed located in the city park (where the author placed the Grabowski monument).

The author's additional facts are however sufficient to make us conclude that it was a mix-up of names. The mayor of Przemyśl from 1881 to 1901 was Aleksander Dworski and his biographical details fit well with information from *The Good Soldier Švejk*. No statue of him can be located, but he was (and is) well known in the city and a major street is named after him. Dworski and not Grabowski was thus obviously the man the author had in mind.

Dworski was born in Lwów and graduated as a doctor of law from the city's university in 1849. He entered politics early, serving as MP for Lwów and Grodek in Reichsrat from 1873 until 1880, where protocols reveal that he was very active. He was known as a Polish patriot and pan-Slavist. Thereafter he served for 20 years as mayor of Przemyśl, the city he had lived in from 1855. His reign oversaw substantial development — building of schools, sewers and beginning electrification. Already in 1896 he was named honorary citizen and a street was renamed in his honor. From 1889 to 1901 he was also member of the Galician parliament. Dworski died in 1908 from pneumonia. [honsi.org]

[327] Wurm was an officer in k.u.k. Heer, Oberleutnant in Infantry Regiment No. 91 until 1 July 1915, then promoted to Hauptmann. [honsi.org]

[328] Zlíchov is a small district of Prague, situated on the western bank of the Vltava south of Smíchov. Švejk refers to the local distillery. [honsi.org]

[329] Nový Jičín is a town in north-eastern Moravia, 30 km south of Ostrava. The town has 27,000 inhabitants and the historical center is an urban preservation area. [honsi.org]

[330] The Czech slang term "kanimůra" describes a person in a disheveled, unkempt, or pitiful state, akin to a "wreck." It derives from the surname of Japanese Admiral Kamimura Hikonojō, tied to an apocryphal tale from the Russo-Japanese War (1904–1905). The story falsely claimed Kamimura was captured at Port Arthur and paraded in a dilapidated cart, inspiring the Czech folk rhyme, "Jede fůra z Port Artúra, na ní jede kanimůra" ("*A cart from Port Arthur rolls along, on it rides the kanimůra*"). This imagery led to the term's use for people in a degraded condition. –[See Český etymologický slovník (Prague: Academia, 2001), s.v. "kanimůra," and Jan Machej, Etymologický slovník jazyka českého (Prague: NLN, 2010), s.v. "kanimůra," for linguistic details; for historical context on Kamimura, see Denis Warner and Peggy

Warner, The Tide at Sunrise: A History of the Russo-Japanese War, 1904–1905 (New York: Charterhouse, 1974), 324–328.]

[331] Křemencová is a street in Praha II., perpendicular to Opatovická street. The famous pub U Fleků is situated in this street. [honsi.org]

[332] Libuše is the mythical founder of the Přemysl dynasty and ancestor of the Czech people. She is said to have founded Prague in the 8th century. [honsi.org]

[333] Sądowa Wisznia is the Polish name of the town Судова Вишня (Sudova Vyshnia) in the Lviv oblast in western Ukraine. It is situated right on the Polish border. [honsi.org]

[334] Żółtańce is the Polish name of Жовтанці (Zhovtantsi), a small town of 3,500 inhabitants north-east of Lviv.

Three battalions of Infantry Regiment No. 91 (including Jaroslav Hašek) arrived at Żółtańce on July 16$^{th}$ 1915. Here they had less than two hours break on their march from Gołogóry to their position by Kamionka Strumiłowa.

It is therefore unlikely that the author ever saw the town, which suggests that the inspiration for this part of the plot comes from elsewhere. The station mentioned in the novel must have been Żółtańce-Kłodno, located a few kilometers north-east of Żółtańce. Today it is called Колодно. [honsi.org]

[335] Uciszków is the Polish name of the village Утішків (Utishkiv) in the Lviv oblast in Ukraine. It is located on the river Bug, in the Busk county. At the last census (2001) it had 894 inhabitants . The village has a railway station, on the line Lviv-Zdolbuniv. [honsi.org]

[336] Busk (Буськ) is a town in the Lviv oblast of Ukraine, located on the river Bug. As of 2020 it had more than 8,000 inhabitants. Around mid-July 1915, fierce fighting took place along the Bug, and Busk was mentioned in the official communiqués from *I&R Army Supreme Command*.

It must be noted that Żółtańce is located west of the river Bug, so smoke from the burning villages would have been observed to the east and not to the west, as the author notes. [honsi.org]

[337] Derewlany is the Polish name of Деревляни (Derevliany) in the Lviv oblast in Ukraine. The village is located on the river Bug and had 461 inhabitants at the latest census (2011). [honsi.org]

[338] Kamionka Strumiłowa is the former Polish name of Кам'янка-Бузька (Kamianka-Buzka), a town in the Lviv oblast of Ukraine. The town is situated on the river Bug, 40 km north of Lviv.

Jaroslav Hašek's Infantry Regiment No. 91 was stationed in the area from

July 17th to July 21ˢᵗ 1915, preparing to cross the Bug. They never carried it out as they were redirected to Sokal due to the critical situation at that section of the front. [honsi.org]

[339] Grabowa is the Polish name of Грабова (Hrabova) in the Lviv oblast in Ukraine. The village, which at the latest count had 402 inhabitants, is located 24 km east of Kamianka-Buzka, just north of Busk. [honsi.org]

[340] Klimontów is almost certainly a mix-up with Колодно (Kolodno), a village 3 km east of Żółtańce, on the eastern side of the railway line Lviv - Sokal. It is often referred to as Kłodno Wielkie, today Велике Колодно. The railway station at Kłodno is surely where Švejk arrived, before walking to Żółtańce where he was told that his regiment was billeted in Klimontów. The Greek-Catholic church was located where the Russian-Orthodox church is today. Infanterieregiment Nr. 91 marched past here on July 16ᵗʰ 1915, but they had no overnight stay. The author must thus have drawn inspiration for the plot from somewhere else. Nor is it likely that there was a large school in this small village. [honsi.org]

[341] Adige is a river in northern Italy, flowing through cities such as Bolzano, Trento and Verona. The source is on the border with Austria and the river flows into the Adriatic. [honsi.org]

[342] Bochnia Zamurowana is not identifiable on any map, but we must assume that the author refers to a spa around Bochnia, at the river Raba between Kraków and Tarnów. There is a village called Lipnica Murowana in the district, so there might be a connection here. This was also an area that Hašek knew from his travels in 1901 and 1903. [honsi.org]

[343] Kundratice was in 1913 the name of five places in Bohemia, but none of them fit the description in *The Good Soldier Švejk*. The place in question is no doubt the village Kunratice south-east of Prague. This is evident from the plot because Švejk mentions the landmark Bartůňkův mlýn, and it is also clear that it must have been within walking distance from Nusle.

The village was until 1990 a separate administrative entity, and is now part of Prague IV. In 1913 the large village had 2,073 inhabitants of which all but 4 were registered with Czech as their everyday language. Administratively it belonged to j*udicial district* Nusle and a*dministrative district* Vinohrady. Kunratice had a Roman-Catholic church, a Czech school and a post office. [honsi.org]

[344] "Bartůňkův mlýn" is a mill by Kunratický potok (*Kunratice stream*) in south-eastern Prague. It is also called Dolní mlýn and Kunratický mlýn. The mill was built in 1764 and was from 1841 owned by the Bartůněk family. During

Švejk's time the mill belonged to Jan Bartůněk. Attached to the mill was also a popular open-air restaurant. [honsi.org]

[345] Solingen is a city in Nordrhein-Westphalen with around 160,000 inhabitants. The city has been known since medieval times for the production of knives, and even today (2010) 90 per cent of German-produced knives are made here. [honsi.org]

[346] Banseth was owner of the restaurant U Bansethů in Nusle, in fact two of them. He and his wife Anna opened the first one in Palackého třída No. 321 (now Táborská) in the autumn of 1900, and in 1908 they sold it and moved to No. 389 a few steps up the street. They actually bought the whole building for 100,000 crowns.

Banseth was born in Kutná Hora in 1866, son of František (b. 1824) and Anna (b. 1828). The parents seem to have moved to Smíchov in 1874, then to Žižkov in 1885, then to Holešovice in 1892. There were eight children in the family that hailed from Golčův Jeníkov where the oldest children were born.

Banseth himself is registered with domicile Nusle from 1893 and appeared to have lived there for the rest of his life. Before opening his first restaurant in 1900 he had managed the restaurant at the local brewery. By now he had already appeared in newspapers notices because public meetings were arranged at the brewery restaurant. Here he is listed as "brother Banseth", which means he was a member of Sokol.

Banseth was married to Anna (born Daršetová in 1871) and the couple had five children. Their oldest son František (born 1892) went missing early in the war and was indeed reported as a Russian prisoner of war. Banseth was running the tavern at least until 1923, but some time before 1929 he died. His widow Anna passed away as late as 24 January 1948. [honsi.org]

[347] Petrograd was from 1914 to 1924 the name of present-day Санкт-Петербург (Saint Petersburg), Russia's second largest city and the country's capital from 1713 to 1918. The city has 4.6 million inhabitants, or 6 million including suburbs.

The city played a pivotal role in the revolutions of March and November 1917, which ultimately led to Russia pulling out of the war. The revolutions also had far-reaching consequences for Jaroslav Hašek and would have had them for Švejk as well, had the novel been completed. [honsi.org]

[348] Jedouchov is a village in the Vysočina region, 5 km from Lipnice. It can safely be assumed that Jaroslav Hašek visited here. [honsi.org]

[349] Darwin was a British naturalist. He is considered the founder of the theory of evolution, that says that evolution by natural selection have shaped life on

Earth. In this manner, he became the most influential theorist in biology and is known as one of the most important scientists of all time. The book The Origin of Species by Means of Natural Selection, or The Preservation of Favored Races in the Struggle for Life, usually abbreviated to The Origin of Species, presented his theory of development through natural selection, and is considered his principal work. [honsi.org]

[350] Stockholm is the capital and largest city of Sweden, and one of the largest cities in Northern Europe. The city has around 800,000 inhabitants and 1.3 million if the whole urban area is counted.

Stockholm has one of the oldest Švejk restaurants in the world, Krogen Soldaten Svejk in Södermalm. It serves an exclusive range of Czech draft beers, no bottles or non-Czech beer are on sale (as of 2026). [honsi.org]

[351] Stew of cabbage, sausage, meat, and sometimes mushrooms.

[352] Nostitz-Rieneck was according to Kadett Biegler a cavalry Field Marshal, but it is not clear who he has in mind or such a note ever existed. It is tempting to believe that the pamphlet is a product of the author's imagination.

Nostitz-Rieneck was a well-known family of nobles from Bohemia, the author presumably refers to one of its members. The three mentioned below all reached the rank of Field Marshal-Lieutenant in the cavalry.

In 1912 a lieutenant Graf Ervin Nostitz-Rieneck served with the cavalry in Karlín at k.u.k. Dragoon Regiment No. 14.

In his diary Jan Eybl notes that one Nostitz served with him in August 1915, after the battle by Sokal. Hašek was in the same unit in this period and may have borrowed his name. [honsi.org]

[353] Bohdalec is a small area in Prague which is administratively part of Prague 10. The hill in question is located on the border between Vršovice and Michle. [honsi.org]

[354] Loděnice is a village by Beroun west of Prague. Although there are several place thus named in the Bohemia, this is the likeliest one as the author knew the area well. He visited first in 1913 with Zdeněk Matěj Kuděj and again with Josef Lada in 1914. [honsi.org]

[355] Turze is the Polish name of the village Тур'я (Turia) in the Busk region of western Ukraine. [honsi.org]

[356] Kozłów is the Polish name of the small town Козлів (Kozliv) in the Ternopil oblast in Ukraine. [honsi.org]

[357] An animal being fatted to slaughter for a banquet.

[358] hesychast: one of an Eastern Orthodox ascetic sect of mystics originating

among the monks of Mount Athos in the 14th century and practicing a quietistic method of contemplation for the purpose of attaining a beatific vision or similar mystical experience. [merriam-webster.com]

[359] This is most likely the first time the actual last paragraph, dictated by Jaroslav Hašek to his young aid Kliment Štěpánek, has been published in any edition of any language of the novel, making the "Chicago version" of English translation the first truly unabridged edition of the novel. [Translator's note]

**Note**: The Endnotes entries sourced from websites were current as of summer 2025.

## Translator's Postscript

It has been claimed for 102 years that The Fateful Adventures of *the Good Soldier Švejk* was never finished. And in the strict sense, i.e. by Hašek's plan, that may be true. But to me, the book has always ended perfectly. Švejk's words "It is not so easy to crawl in somewhere. Anybody can do that, but to get out of there, that is a genuine military skill" always came to my mind when reading the supposedly last line of the novel:

"Our military troops will in foreseeable time cross the borders."

Now, with the reclassification of the authorship of the final dictated paragraph, long buried, now restored and here published for the first time in any language, that judgment is only fortified. It does not end with the word "obsazujeme" (*we're moving in to occupy*), but the entire closing thought revolves around it. That word is the axis of the last sentence:

"…in the section, which we're apparently in the process of occupying, there stands the triangle the individual points of which are the Russian fortresses: Luck, Dubno, Rovno."

"Obsazujeme" (W*e're moving in to occupy*) is the language of operational aspiration. It does not describe what is, but what is meant to be. And it repeats. Not only in 1915. When my mother woke me up before 6 a.m. on August 21, 1968, all she said was: "Obsadili nás. (*They've occupied us.*)" She had been six years old when the Germans marched in on March 16, 1939. Fifteen when the Communists took over in 1948. Now, in 1968, it was the "allied armies of the socialist camp." And this time, they came back with 800,000 troops to occupy a land of fifteen million. There had been Warsaw Pact maneuvers here not long before and the troops had taken their time leaving. Then, with sudden speed, they returned.

In 2022, "obsazujeme" returned as a Special Military Operation, but this time with fewer than 100,000 initial troops, against forty million inhabitants of the "border land."

The triangle that closes the book, Luck, Dubno, Rovno, was no mere metaphor. It marked the actual front where Hašek's regiment fought, where the Austro-Hungarian advance faltered, and where Hašek himself was taken prisoner. What ends as satirical geometry in the novel had been lived as military geography. It would return with even bloodier gravity.

In 1941 Hitler's Operation Barbarossa unleashed one of the

largest armored clashes in world history across that very same axis. The Soviet Southwestern Front hurled six mechanized corps with thousands of tanks into the Lutsk, Dubno, Rovno, Lviv border battle, trying to repel Kleist's Panzergruppen. Within ten days the Red Army had lost over 2,200 tanks in the region. Forty years after Švejk's triangle of fortresses was named, it became a graveyard of machines and men.

These are the bloodlands, not metaphor, not theory, but the literal soil of rolling catastrophe.

"It is not so easy to crawl in somewhere. Anybody can do that.
But to get out of there, that is a genuine military skill."
**And that is** where **the novel ends.**
With *Luck, Dubno, Rovno*.

## Note on Editorial Assistance

Most published translations are commissioned. Grants from national cultural institutions, literary foundations, or nonprofit organizations often support the commissioning of translations. In the absence of such a commission to translate Jaroslav Hašek's masterwork, I didn't have any of the perks such a commission might entail, like the services of an editor and a linguist, let alone a publicist and marketing campaign.

It is no secret that even professional literary translators use dictionaries. As I wrote: "I don't translate by picking terms from a dictionary word by word. If that were possible, machine translators would have replaced humans already... I sometimes tell people that as a practitioner of translating I usually don't need a dictionary, but when I do, chances are what I'm looking for isn't listed there."

One reason for that is that the original Czech text presents a challenge not only of rendering of the semantics, the standards of which Hašek often stretches and bends, but because of the already mentioned differences in the rules of syntax, verbal aspect/vid, etc.

As the author of the first unabridged translation, Cecil Parrott attested, Hašek demands greater engagement not only from the reader, but first, from the translator: "The difficulties of translating Švejk's language are considerable... In the earlier parts... are challenging but manageable; in the later parts the irony becomes more complex and the slang more awkward, especially the military jargon, which often lacks direct English equivalents."

Having edited the two "easier" volumes[A], Book One and Book Two for The Centennial Edition, I was faced with the increased density of the linguistic challenges of the remaining text. Readers and critics have been noticing comparative differences in the qualities of Hašek's text for decades.

But The Fateful Adventures don't deteriorate, they condense. The shift from Book One's relatively "anecdotal" rhythm to the dense, irony-laden sprawl of Books Three and Four is not a loss of quality, but a change of texture. It's as though Hašek, having established Švejk's public face, his antics, deflections, and evasions, turns his attention to subtler corruptions: institutional rot, the absurd rituals of empire, and the psychological toll of survival. The density, the oddity, even the tedium some readers report, these are the war.

The present translation of the three volumes comprising The Centennial Edition of *The Good Soldier Švejk* During the World War has been produced in full accordance with the methodological principles outlined in the prefatory material to Book One. What did change for me while tackling the challenges in Book(s) Three & Four was the addition of a new tool to my critical apparatus.

I started gradually testing AI tools as search engines to retrieve publicly accessible information on topics pertaining to the mentioned challenges. First I would ask Grok for potential extant English synonyms for unusual use of words to stimulate my brain exhausted from attempting to render them to my satisfaction. But I found that, as Grok admitted, its "outputs depend on prompt specificity". When I tried the alternative, ChatGPT, it claimed it "integrates scholarly commentary and lexicographic resources better, acting as a 'workspace consultant' for validating methodology." Grok on the other hand claims it "can be more comprehensive in scope, offering broader contextual explanations". But it advised: "If your work involves high-stakes accuracy (e.g., legal or technical literature embedded in novels), prioritize ChatGPT. For exploratory or niche language pairs, test Grok first."

At no point has any part of the Czech original been rendered with the assistance of generative AI. Throughout the preparation of this final volume, I made extensive, although not exhaustive use of a language model assistant (ChatGPT, based on OpenAI's GPT-4o architecture). It was never used to generate translation. Rather, it served as a dialectical and editorial aid, operating under a collaboration code of conduct I developed and formalized during the work.

Its role was diagnostic: helping refine my own linguistic intuitions through a comparative method sensitive to structural and rhetorical patterns.

Every language choice, interpretive decision, and final formulation in the translation is entirely my own. The tool's function was strictly confined to comparative testing, aspectual diagnostics, rhythm and idiom refinement, and reference-checking against earlier editorial policies or Hašek-specific idioms.

That framework, collaborative, but not creative, is set out in full below.

If there is one phrase that captures the nature of this process, it is "thinking with Hašek." The expression first emerged in the course of discussions with the digital assistant, and, as far as I can determine, does not appear in prior writing on Švejk or its translation. A web search for "thinking with Hašek" returns no results, which suggests, at the very least, that the phrase had not yet entered digital circulation. Though it was coined by the digital assistant, I've come to adopt it myself, as it reflects both the method and the ethos of my long engagement with Švejk: not rewriting Hašek from above, but working beside him, letting his language, his rhythm, and his worldview shape the translation at every level.

In keeping with this collaborative framework, I and the digital assistant operated under the following Code of Conduct, which was formalized during the work:

Translator–AI Collaboration Code of Conduct

1. Authorship Is Paramount

All final translation choices, structure, style, and interpretive strategy are solely the responsibility and intellectual property of the translator.

2. AI as a Tool, Not a Creator

ChatGPT was employed only to provide analytical feedback, surface alternate phrasings for consideration, flag rhythm or idiom shifts, and assist in fine-grained linguistic scrutiny. It never generated any suggested edits that were inserted into the volume without full revision and ownership by the translator.

3. Transparency and Limits

The assistant was programmed to alert the translator if any interaction risked substituting for authorial decision-making. Where suggestions were offered, they were always subject to review, transformation, or rejection.

4. Dialectical Refinement, Not Generation

The assistant's primary task was to act as a consulting interlocutor, to test, provoke, and refine the translator's decisions, not to initiate or author them.

The assistant operated in what was termed Consulting Mode, not generative or authorial mode. In this context, it performed tasks overlapping with the roles of:

Proofreader, in the sense of identifying awkwardness, grammatical ambiguity, typographic slips, or syntactic obscurities, always subject to translator review.

Editor, in the limited sense of providing contrastive alternatives for discussion, drawing attention to inconsistencies or context mismatches, or referencing the translator's own stated policies.

A full record of this collaboration is retained in my archive. It bears witness not only to the tool's utility, but also to its limits, and to the unique depth of human judgment, cultural memory, and linguistic discipline required to produce a translation such as this one. The assistant's greatest contribution, in my view, was not to translate (which it was not allowed to do by design), but to let me "think with Hašek," follow Pannwitz's dictum, and allow me to expand and deepen the English language by means of the Czech language, while keeping it accessible enough for the curious and willing readers.

This "thinking with", the very phrase that first arose in my exchanges with the digital assistant, came to define the ethos of the work. And no machine can replace that.

It was in Book Three that I first began using a machine; not to translate, but to check the translation. By that point, the structural load had become extreme. Clause order, reflexivity, aspect, idiom, tonal contradiction, all had to be carried at once. Every sentence had to be held in tension: Hašek's logic, not English logic, was the ground. There was no shortcut, only endurance. What the machine offered was alignment. It could check whether the structure of the Czech was still present, whether the aspect was intact, whether a clause had been bent to fit English instead of allowed to hold its Czech pressure. That isn't interpretation. It's diagnostics. And it became part of my method because at that point in the novel, nothing less would hold.

This diagnostic phase began with a scene on page 137 of Book Three, where Švejk "vmíchal se do rozhovoru", a phrase that had to be translated foreignly enough to preserve the Czech image ("*mixed himself into the conversation*"), yet stable enough to parse. The sentence became the test case for holding Czech grammar and English rhythm in sustained contradiction and marked the point where mechanical comparison became methodologically necessary.

By Book Four, that pressure reached its limit. The machine's analytical precision proved invaluable for structural testing, but it had no access to Hašek's irreverent genius. Where the logic of grammar held, it could confirm alignment; where the logic of satire broke language itself, it fell silent. That was the true measure of its limits — it could verify, but not resolve; detect, but not decide. The most revealing case was the word "enóno."

In a scene parodying heroic military reports, Marek recites a string of abstractions: "the n-th battalion," "the n-th division," "Sector N." Each "N" stands for something bureaucratically voided, a placeholder for structure without content. Marek then admits defeat, it just won't come together for him, it's all "enóno." He underlines the n, calling it a letter that has attained **extraordinary perfection** "in both the present and the future."

In Váša–Trávníček the word appears as "en óno" (neuter), glossed simply as "nic (hrubší hovor.)", i.e. *nothing, roughly colloquial.* Later folk lexicons record its evolved form "enóno", defined as an "academic euphemism for hovno." Its passage from "nothing" to **"shit disguised as scholarship"** encapsulates Hašek's satire: the learned form masking excrement, the bureaucratic idiom collapsing into waste. What begins as the scholar's failure to make sense becomes the novel's structural truth, that behind the language of order lies only euphemized ruin.

This is Hašek's diagnostic joke: war logic becomes algebra; euphemism becomes waste. "N" dissolves into "enóno", a phonetic smear of meaninglessness and poop.

No algorithm could infer that descent from emptiness to excrement, or recognize its moral charge. Only a human translator, aware of Hašek's tonal spectrum and his contempt for euphemism, could decide how to meet it. That challenge became the crucible in which the limits of artificial diagnostics and the indispensability of human interpretation were laid bare.

That linguistic collapse demanded an equally absurd response. "Onanopoop", the rendering used in this edition, was not a flourish, it was a structural solution. It mirrors the Czech rhythm ("e-nó-no" → "o-na-no"), preserves the density of ns (two in the English, as in the Czech), and maintains the euphemistic childishness of the original. The final poop lands the scatological note without vulgarity.

The coinage is not a joke about masturbation. It is a response to the world-historical tradition of mental onanism, euphemistic, self-congratulatory war rhetoric disguised as truth. "Onanopoop" was not improvised. It was built, tested, and accepted, because at that point in the novel, nothing less would hold.

If the echo of Onan is heard, it isn't accidental, but it isn't the point. The point is that Hašek's military ends in perfectly formed nonsense, and the translator's job is to meet it there, not with smooth English, but with a linguistic turd that could plausibly have emerged from the same grotesque machine, the only honest solution, given the text's engineered collapse.

This collapse of language also completes a circle Hašek himself drew at the very beginning. In the Afterword to Book One he derided the "masturbators of false culture," those timid purists whose fear of strong expression masks their fear of life itself. That hypocrisy matures, by Book Four, into something far darker: the onanism of power — the self-pleasuring of elites and their obedient functionaries, who disguise cowardice as culture and control as reason. The saint who wept at a fart becomes the bureaucrat who sanctifies waste. What began as moral squeamishness ends as systemic rot. The arc from Saint Aloysius to Sector N thus closes — the same cowardice of culture turned to the cowardice of empire.

The machine confirmed the structure, the tension, the absurdity — all of it — held.

If there is a moral to the method, it is this: What I was looking for was never listed there. And by the end, it could not be — because it had to be made.

---

[A] The phrase "the two 'easier' volumes" reflects the widespread critical view that Book One and Book Two of Hašek's novel are more accessible and polished than the later volumes. See:

- Cecil Parrott, The Bad Bohemian: A Life of Jaroslav Hašek (London: The Bodley Head, 1978), p. 213: "It is extremely funny, and it is also a profound and tragic book... The early sections are particularly accessible, with Švejk's humorous anecdotes dominating, while the later sections, written under Hašek's declining health, grow darker and more fragmented, demanding greater reader engagement."
- Macdonald Daly, "Introduction," in The Good Soldier Švejk and His Fortunes in the World War (London: Everyman's Library, 1993), p. xvii: "The first two parts are more appealing to unliterary readers because of their episodic humour and sharp satire, but the third and fourth parts, though deeper in their nihilistic critique, can feel repetitive and less polished due to Hašek's incomplete vision."
- Cecil Parrott, "Translator's Note," in The Good Soldier Švejk (London: Penguin Classics, 1973), p. xxi: "The difficulties of translating Švejk's language are considerable... In the earlier parts the colloquialisms and dialect are challenging but manageable; in the later parts the irony becomes more complex and the slang more awkward, especially the military jargon, which often lacks direct English equivalents."
- Michelle Woods, "Translating Švejk," Jacket Magazine 18 (2002): "The unabridged translation [by Parrott] struggles in the later volumes with the rendering of Hašek's obscene colloquialisms and repetitive

irony, often resulting in awkward or stilted English, whereas abridged versions [like Selver's] sacrifice much of the third and fourth parts' depth to achieve readability."
- Karel Kosík, Dialectics of the Concrete (Dordrecht: D. Reidel Publishing Company, 1976), p. 89: "Švejk is an expression of the absurdity of the alienated world…The later parts, especially at the front, deepen this existential critique, though their fragmented structure reflects Hašek's struggle to complete his vision."
- Jindřich Chalupecký, The Czech Avant-Garde (1940), cited in The First World War in Fiction, ed. Holger Klein (London: Macmillan, 1978), p. 123: "Švejk becomes the tragic bard of European nihilism, most evident in the chaotic and despairing tone of the later volumes, which, while profound, lack the polished wit of the earlier parts."
- Arne Novák, Czech Literature (Prague: Academia, 1976), p. 245: "The later exploits of Švejk, particularly in the third and fourth parts, grow crude and monotonous, a decline from the sharper, more vibrant humor of the civilian and early military settings."
- Ivan Olbracht, Literary Essays (1945), cited in The Good Soldier Švejk, Everyman's Library (London, 1993), p. xx: "Despite its flaws, Švejk is a major work of world literature… The early parts shine with popular humor, while the later parts, though incomplete and repetitive, carry tragic weight that elevates the novel's significance."

## Švejk on Trial: Rethinking Hašek's Novel as a Pendulum of Prosecution and Defense

It was during a late-stage editorial reflection, forty pages from the end of the unfinished fourth book of *The Fateful Adventures* of *the Good Soldier Švejk*, that I arrived at a striking insight. The novel, long interpreted as a satire, an antiwar tract, or a study in ambiguity, revealed itself under the pressure of translation as something more architecturally deliberate: a trial.

This insight emerged not through theory but through friction. In reviewing a paragraph in which the General condemns Švejk in Czech as both an "idiot"(*idiot)* and, moments later, a "blbec"(*imbecile*), I became briefly uncertain. Was the second term a mistranslation of "blbec"? Was "imbecile" too close to the earlier "idiot"? Or was something deeper happening?

The answer, rooted in Czech nuance and Hašek's rhetorical layering, was that the pairing was intentional. Hašek had not simply repeated himself but shifted register. He began with the clinical or institutional term "idiot", then pivoted to "imbecile", a Czech vernacular insult.

In English, "idiot" and "imbecile" may appear synonymous, especially in their colloquial first senses as simple insults or labels for foolishness. But their histories and connotations diverge. "Idiot", though used broadly today, retains a faint trace of its formal medical past, denoting **extreme intellectual disability**. "Imbecile" originally occupied a milder, intermediate diagnostic category, **moderate intellectual disability**, and likewise drifted into general insult.[1][2] Both are now considered offensive in clinical contexts, but the difference remains visible in their tone and cultural load. In English, that difference is residual, a matter of connotation. In Czech, it is structural, a drop in register that does narrative work. Their interplay marks a tonal descent, from judgment to ridicule, from diagnosis to mockery.

This diagnostic language is not incidental. It recurs with such frequency, intensity, and variety across the four books that it takes on the character of a sustained prosecutorial record. The terms "idiot" and "imbecile", along with their adjectival and nominal derivatives, function as markers of accusation, classification, and ultimately, narrative control. In total, these terms appear 131 times in the novel: 100 instances of "idiot" variants (including idiocy, idiotic, idiotically) and 31 instances of "imbecile" (including one "imbecility"). But what matters more than the totals is how and to whom they are applied.

Another striking instance of this diagnostic lexicon occurs at the very threshold of Book Three, where Hašek repeats the intensifier "to the squared power" three times in quick succession. Švejk first calls Field Chaplain Ibl's bombastic sermon "stupidity to the squared power," then repeats it when recalling the same story later the same day, and finally lets the phrase drop into "an imbecile to the squared power". Here, the movement is again one of tonal descent: from the abstract condition of "stupidity" to the direct branding of a person as an "imbecile." The numerical trope of squaring is grotesquely misapplied, turning language of measurement into language of ridicule. Its very repetition enacts the absurdity of quantifying human capacity, just as the earlier grotesque ratio of "forty-eight men or eight horses" reduced human life to arithmetic. By hammering the phrase three times, Hašek sets the second half of the novel under the sign of compounded idiocy; not as diagnosis, but as of diagnosis.

In the first half of the novel, especially Book One, the weight of this diagnostic vocabulary falls squarely on Švejk himself. He is officially proclaimed an "imbecile" by medical and military authorities, referred to repeatedly as a "notorious idiot", and described in accumulating epithets that blur the line between comic exaggeration and clinical judgment. Of the 42 instances across the novel where these terms are applied to Švejk, more than half occur in Book One. This is the prosecutorial opening argument: a caricature of idiocy presented as evidence, with official reports, medical examinations, and verbal abuse all piling on to establish the defendant's supposed mental incompetence, or more precisely, his criminal cunning masked as incompetence. The reader is placed in the position of a tribunal being asked to evaluate not only Švejk's behavior, but his very nature.

Yet the pattern does not remain fixed. As the novel progresses, the prosecution's vocabulary is increasingly turned outward, repurposed to indict others. In Book One, 22 of the total 42 uses of idiot or imbecile are directed at Švejk. But in Books Three and Four, the majority of "idiot" and "imbecile" labels no longer refer to Švejk, but to his superiors: officers, judges, colonels, medical examiners, bureaucrats. Some instances even target abstract structures, such as the "idiotic monarchy" or the "idiotic history of mankind". In raw numbers, 72 of the 131 total uses, more than half, are applied to figures other than Švejk, and this proportion only grows in the later books: in

Book Four, for example, nearly three-quarters of such references shift away from him. By the time we reach the final act, Švejk is no longer merely the object of the trial. He has become, in effect, its silent cross-examiner, an "idiot" so notorious that he becomes the baseline against which all other idiocy is measured.[3][4]

This rhetorical reversal is one of Hašek's most brilliant maneuvers. The language that once condemned Švejk now becomes the instrument of a broader satire. The reader, originally positioned to judge Švejk, is gradually led to question the legitimacy of the courtroom itself. The repeated labeling of others as "idiots", "imbeciles", or "morons" begins to undermine the coherence of the prosecution. What had appeared as psychiatric or military classification reveals itself as farce, and the accused, still absurd, becomes more credible than his judges.

In this sense, the diagnostic lexicon operates as a narrative diagnostic as well[*]. It tracks the novel's structural swing between accusation and testimony, between caricature and credibility. The shift in its application, from Švejk to others, from individual to system, mirrors the arc of a trial that has lost control of its own logic. The prosecution overreaches. The categories collapse. And so the reader, like a member of the jury, finds himself re-evaluating not the sanity of the accused, but the sanity of those who presume to judge him.

It was my resistance to repeated AI-generated suggestions of "fool", "moron", "blockhead" that preserved the original phrasing. The AI, acting from pattern recognition, repeatedly flagged the repetition or argued for variation. But my insistence on Hašek's rhythm and register, on fidelity not only to meaning but to the sociolinguistic movement of the sentence, held firm. That fidelity triggered a realization: the entire novel mirrors the logic of trial proceedings.

In my rendering, the General's words unfold with tonal descent:

"That man is an utter **idiot**," said the General to the Major. "To be changing on the dam of a pond into some Russian uniform, left there by God knows whom, to let oneself be mustered with a party of Russian prisoners of war, that can do only an **imbecile**."

By contrast, in Cecil Parrott's 1973 translation, the same passage is rendered:

---

[*] A diagnostic lexicon exposes the static linguistic structure a system rests on; a narrative diagnostic exposes the dynamic processes by which that same structure produces events over time.

"The fellow is a complete **imbecile**," said the general to the major. "Only a bloody **idiot** would put on a Russian uniform left on the dam of a lake by goodness knows whom and then get himself drafted into a party of Russian prisoners."[5]

**Note:** In the Czech, the words "idiot" and "imbecile" stand at opposite ends of the general's outburst, forming rhetorical brackets that frame the passage. This translation preserves that spacing, following Hašek's original rhythm. **Parrott's compression of both terms into the opening of the passage collapses the structural escalation**—one of the "hundred nothings that had worn out the ox to death," as Czechs say.

Parrott smooths the Czech into natural English rhythm and idiom, not only sacrificing, but reversing the shift in register from Hašek's "idiot" to "blbec". What appears as redundancy in English is, in Czech, tonal movement, a descent that Parrott inverts into a heightening. On top of this, he inserts "bloody," a favorite intensifier of his, scattered throughout his version. The result is not Hašek's clinical-to-vernacular descent, but a distortion doubled: the reversed register reinforced by the intrusive flourish of "bloody." As I noted in my response to Michelle Woods in the Jacket magazine, the adjective "bloody" is used and misused in his version incredibly too often, to the point that he once added "bloody ass" in front of "such as Lieutenant Dub" just for good measure.

It was precisely this friction that sparked my recognition of a prosecutorial logic embedded in the novel's form.

The opening paragraph of Švejk announces the charge: "when a military medical commission had pronounced him definitely to be an imbecile." From that moment forward, every encounter in the book functions as a kind of testimony, sometimes for the prosecution, sometimes for the defense. Authorities, doctors, officers, priests, and common folk each weigh in. Some ridicule Švejk, others admire him, and a few waver. The novel proceeds like a pendulum, swinging between condemnation and exoneration, incompetence and cunning, obedience and provocation.

Far from a monolithic character, Švejk becomes a site of argument. His declarations, jokes, digressions, and apparent naiveté operate not to assert identity, but to confuse, deflect, or expose the absurdity of those in power. And like a trial, the reader is never told the final verdict, at least, not until the end of the process. Unfortunately, Jaroslav Hašek passed away before completing his work, before presenting all the arguments for both the prosecution and the defense. And so the reader, like this translator, and like the critic, is left to play judge, jury, and executioner. The ambiguity is the method.

This reframing casts new light on the novel's structure. What seemed meandering now appears dialectical. What once read as episodic delay now becomes procedural layering. Each scene becomes a deposition, each officer a witness, each diagnosis a renewed iteration of the charge. Švejk is being tried, not by the state alone, but by the narrative itself. The State attempts to try Švejk through institutional procedure, while the narrative subjects him to a continuous trial of public opinion, constituted by the accumulated judgments of those who encounter him.

This insight also reframes critical debates around the novel. Scholars such as Michelle Woods have focused on whether Švejk is a "fool or a provocateur", noting that ambiguity is central to Hašek's method. But this dichotomy may be too narrow. In my response to her in 2010, I stated: "The novel is a virtual reality and the character of Josef Švejk is the port through which the reader gets there." The question is not whether Švejk "is" one thing or another. It is whether the system, in all its irrational bureaucracy and violent discipline, is capable of producing, through processes of diagnosis, documentation, and control, a legible human subject: measurable, categorizable, and controllable.

In this light, The Fateful Adventures of *the Good Soldier Švejk* is not just a novel about surviving war. It is a trial transcript, one in which the defense is conducted not with arguments, but with digressions, idioms, jokes, repetitions, mimicry, and studied compliance. Hašek's genius lies in building a satire whose very form mirrors the absurd logic it condemns.

And it was my ear, attuned to the difference between "idiot" and "blbec", that uncovered it.

APPENDIX:
ON THE DISTINCTION BETWEEN "IDIOT" AND "BLBEC"

Etymology, usage, and register confirm this.

The word "idiot" in Czech is a loanword from Greek ("idiōtēs", meaning private or layperson), which passed through Latin and French before being medicalized and pejorativized. It came to designate someone with severe intellectual disability, and later, by metaphorical extension, a person of subnormal intelligence or behavior. It carries an institutional, clinical, or formal tone, even when used insultingly. It is, in Czech, a diagnosis before it is an insult.[6]

In contrast, "blbec" is a native Czech derivation from "blbý"(*stupid*), itself rooted in onomatopoeic origins: the sound "blb-blb", a babbling, stumbling idiocy of speech. It is vernacular, informal, and deeply Czech. Far from clinical, it belongs to the language of pubs, soldiers, and common speech. It is what someone might mutter about a driver on the street or a friend after a foolish remark. "Blbec" belongs to the realm of everyday moral judgment, not medical designation.[7]

Modern usage confirms this distinction. Dictionaries like Wikislovník define "idiot" as "velmi hloupý člověk" (*a very stupid person*), with additional notes on its offensiveness and clinical heritage. The entry for "blbec", on the other hand, adds colloquiality, mildness, and frequency in humorous idioms, for example "náhoda je blbec" ("*coincidence is an imbecile*").[8][9]

Resources like Nechybujte.cz warn that "idiot" carries stronger connotations, while "blbec" is used in speech to label a fool, not a case. It is a cultural insult, not a psychological classification.[10][11]

The public-facing language advisory portals distinguish the words in both semantic load and emotional valence: idiot stings; imbecile shrugs; idiot condemns; imbecile belittles.

This is not a trivial distinction. In Czech, where register is performative, the movement from "idiot" to "blbec" is a tonal descent, from formal denouncement to social mockery. Hašek knew this.

Hašek begins the paragraph with a formal declaration, "That man is an utter **idiot**," and ends it with a vernacular judgment: "...that can do only an **imbecile**." The shift is not redundancy. It is escalation by descent, from diagnosis to derision. The English sentence can seem repetitive without this understanding. But my fidelity to Hašek's Czech exposed a rhetorical movement missed in Parrott's translation, where tonal descent is inverted into intensification.

And from that insight, the friction between fidelity and flattening, between "idiot" and "blbec", emerged the greater structure: the novel as a trial.

A man condemned by officials, pathologized by doctors, mocked by generals, but never truly judged. Because Švejk, like the translator, is always being tried, but never finally sentenced.

Postlude: On Judgment and the Right to Render It

The trial thesis did not arise from conceptual speculation. It emerged in the course of practice, through repeated encounters with resistance, dissonance, and untranslatability. As with my methodology, so with the novel's design: it revealed itself in tension before it was recognized in theory.

This raises a central question: Who is authorized to judge Švejk? The novel resists external classification. Hašek withholds a final verdict, leaving judgment suspended. Yet judgment is demanded, and inevitably rendered, by every translator, every critic, and every reader. But what grants that authority?

Can a Czech understand Švejk more fully than a foreigner? Can an academic capture what a laborer senses? Can one who has only known comfort interpret the survival humor of the oppressed?

In a review of my first-edition translation of Book One a quarter of a century ago, Oxford's James Partridge claimed: "For Sadlon, Švejk is simply a 'quintessential, working-class citizen-soldier,' closer to the man as played by Rudolf Hrušínský in the charming but rather anodynic film made in the 1950s than he is to the more elusive and textual Švejk of Hašek's novel."

But Partridge misses the depth of that conception. My understanding of the working-class everyman does not arise from mid-20th century cinematic imagery. It comes from empirical experience, from living under both socialism and capitalism, in systems whose contradictions mirror those lampooned by Hašek. My Švejk is not a flattened proletarian mascot. He is a survivor under judgment, caught in the machinery of absurd power.

And just as Švejk is on trial in the novel, so is the translator. My fidelity is tested not only by the text, but by its readers, some of whom, like the novel's own officers and doctors, are quick to diagnose, classify, or condemn.

In the end, the novel becomes a suspended judgment. Hašek died before completing it, before delivering all the arguments for both prosecution and defense. And, as with all unfinished trials, the responsibility for closure shifts.

The reader, like the translator, and like the critic, inherits the role of arbiter. Not because the novel dictates it, but because the system withholds the final word. The only question is whether that judgment is reflexive, or reflective.

---

[1] Merriam-Webster "idiot"

[https://www.merriam-webster.com/dictionary/idiot]
[2] Merriam-Webster "imbecile"
[3] Total Frequency of "Imbecile" and "Idiot" Variants

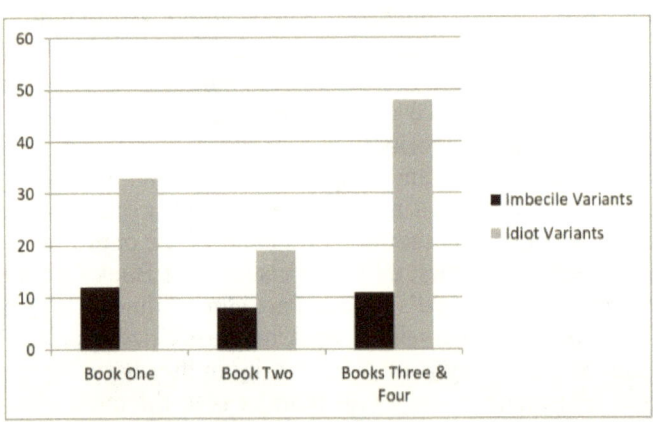

[4] Distribution of Terms (Švejk vs. Others)

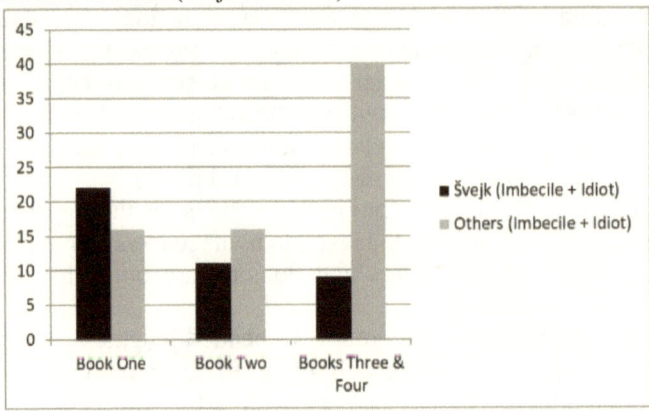

[5] Parrott, Cecil. The Good Soldier Švejk and His Fortunes in the World War. Trans. Cecil Parrott. Penguin Classics, 1973. p. 578.
[6] Rejzek, Jiří. Český etymologický slovník. p. 823.
[7] Holub, Josef & Lutterer, Ivan. Etymologický slovník jazyka českého. p. 56.
[8] Wikislovník: "idiot." [https://cs.wiktionary.org/wiki/idiot]
[9] Wikislovník: "blbec." [https://cs.wiktionary.org/wiki/blbec]
[10] Nechybujte.cz: "idiot." [https://www.nechybujte.cz/slovnik-

soucasne-cestiny/idiot]

[11] Nechybujte.cz: "blbec." [https://www.nechybujte.cz/slovnik-soucasne-cestiny/blbec]

## Read Švejk First, Then Ask Me Again

When people ask me to comment on current events or politics, my answer will be simple: read *The Good Soldier Švejk* first, then ask me again. Not because the novel contains opinions to be adopted, but because it supplies a grammar that must be learned before political speech can mean anything at all.

Jaroslav Hašek did not write a satire in the modern sense, nor a comedy meant to expose folly from a safe distance. He wrote from inside an imperial system that converted ordinary people into instruments, and then distributed responsibility for the results of orders so finely that no one could be held accountable, yet no one could escape the consequences of their execution. What his novel records is not ideology, but condition: the lived reality of coercion disguised as order, obedience masquerading as duty, and atrocity normalized by procedure.

Without passing through that experience—without letting its logic work on you—political discussion risks becoming theater. One trades abstractions, declares positions, and imagines oneself morally situated. Hašek shows why such confidence is false. What his novel exposes is not the abuse of power, but its ordinary mode of operation. Power does not require belief to function. It requires only compliance, repetition, and language disciplined enough to make the intolerable routine.

This is why Švejk remains contemporary without ever being topical. It does not comment on events; it explains how events become possible.

One earlier scholar illuminated one dimension of this structure from another direction. In a single, memorable sentence, Peter Steiner described Švejk as a figure who, "like Diogenes, lingers at the margins of an unfriendly society against which he is defending his independent existence." That formulation mattered to me because it named, with rare precision, Švejk's stance — his position relative to authority — without psychologizing or moralizing it. But stance alone does not explain what the novel does with that position. What translation made visible was not merely how Švejk behaves at the margins, but how the system responds to someone who remains there: by diagnosing, classifying, recording, and retrying him, until behavior hardens into evidence and repetition becomes procedure. Steiner located Švejk in relation to authority; the pressure of translation revealed how authority processes that relation over time.

My own life has made this insight unavoidable. I have come to understand that my experiences, and those of my family, are not separate from Hašek's world but continuous with it. The Austro-Hungarian Empire did not vanish; it metastasized. Its techniques—bureaucratic diffusion of guilt, procedural violence, moral displacement—are still with us, though their uniforms and slogans have changed.

I dedicated my translation to my maternal grandfather, an illiterate farmhand who found himself conscripted into that machinery. In a Ukrainian village house, with a k.u.k. officer standing behind him, he was forced to kill a baby in a crib with his bayonet.* There is no lesson to be drawn from this, no redemption to be offered. The point is not horror, but structure: a system capable of placing a man in a position where refusal meant death and obedience meant damnation. That is the world Hašek writes from—not allegorically, but precisely.

To read Švejk seriously is to confront the fact that modern political language is largely designed to prevent such recognition. We speak of responsibility, agency, and choice as if they were evenly distributed, as if power were transparent and decisions freely made. Hašek shows the opposite: Orders flow downward; responsibility is pushed below; accountability evaporates upward — always promised, but never delivered. Laughter, in this context, is not resistance; it is a survival

---

\* History repeats itself in structure, if not in costume. During the next mayhem, World War II, twenty five years later, my paternal uncle was given a choice: to join the Slovak Army alongside the Wehrmacht at Stalingrad, or Hlinka's Guards and guard bridges at home. It was an easy choice for a teenage boy. He ended up part of an execution squad that killed a group of rounded-up guerrillas. Never mind that the villagers later came to testify—or attempted to do so—at a political trial broadcast on the radio, stating that if it had not been for my uncle's warning before the raid on the village, many more would have been caught and executed. During the execution, under the watchful eyes of superior officers, my uncle emptied his magazine into a single condemned man. That act was counted against him at the trial as an aggravating circumstance. The prosecution demanded the death penalty. He was "lucky" and received a 25 year sentence in the Czechoslovak communist "correctional" system. He counted it as a blessing that, during the tumultuous year of 1968, the Prague Spring, he was amnestied just before the invasion of the Warsaw Pact's "brotherly" armies. The first socio-political normalization period following a coup d'état that I experienced in my life set in. I learned of my uncle's existence only a few years before his release, when an older cousin from my maternal side told me so quietly during a visit by both sides of the family to my imprisoned uncle's household.

reflex.

This is why translation matters — not as a vehicle for content, but as an ethical act. To smooth Hašek into fluent, reassuring English is to reenact the very process of normalization of the abnormal he exposes. The task is not to make the reader comfortable, but to make the structure legible. Fidelity here is not about words alone; it is about preserving pressure—syntactic, tonal, and moral.

When I say "read Švejk first," I am not proposing a syllabus or erecting a gate. I am marking a threshold. If we have not learned to recognize how language participates in violence — how it enables obedience without belief, cruelty without hatred — then our political speech will remain naïve at best, complicit at worst.

After the publication of The Centennial Edition, I intend to leave the socio-political space and attend to a private life at last. This is not withdrawal born of fatigue or cynicism, but completion. The work that needed to be done has been done: a transmission made, a testimony preserved without moral varnish. What remains does not require my presence.

If someone still wishes to speak after reading Švejk — after allowing it to unsettle his categories, erode his certainties, and complicate his sense of innocence — then we may have a shared language. If not, there is nothing to discuss.

Some books argue. Švejk reveals.

And once one has truly seen what it reveals, silence becomes not evasion, but honesty.

**Imprint**

This edition was typeset and composed using LibreOffice Writer for a 6 × 9 inch page format. The text is set in Times New Roman, with mirrored margins and an expanded inner margin for perfect binding. Typography, page layout, and editorial apparatus were composed during the editorial process. The volume was printed and bound as a paperback by IngramSpark.

# INTRODUCTION

*Great times demand great people. There are unrecognized heroes, unassuming, without the fame and history of Napoleon. The results of an analysis of their character would overshadow even the glory of Alexander the Great of Macedon. Nowadays you can run into a shabby man in the streets of Prague, who himself doesn't even know what significance he actually has in the history of the new great era. He walks modestly on his way, not bothering anybody, and he too isn't bothered by journalists, who would be begging him for an interview. If you were to ask him what his name was, he would answer you very simply and modestly: "I'm Švejk..."*

*And this quiet, unassuming, shabby man is indeed the old good soldier Švejk, heroic, valiant, whose name was once upon a time, during the Austrian rule, on the lips of all the citizens of the Czech Kingdom, and whose fame will not fade even in the Republic.*

*I very much like the good soldier Švejk, and presenting his fateful adventures during the World War, I am convinced that all of you will sympathize with this modest, unrecognized hero. He did not torch the temple of the goddess in Ephesus, as did that moron Herostratus, to get himself into the newspapers and classroom readers.*

*And that is enough.*

THE AUTHOR

www.ingramcontent.com/pod-product-compliance
Lightning Source LLC
LaVergne TN
LVHW091701070526
838199LV00050B/2241